"I am one of you," Danaus said gently, dousing my anger in an instant. "I want no claim to the human race if this is what they are to become."

A surprised smile tweaked the corners of my mouth as I wrapped my arms around his waist, pulling him close. The time when mankind discovered the existence of nightwalkers and lycanthopes was drawing uncomfortably close, and deep down I had always wondered which side Danaus would fall on when the time came . . .

Praise for JOCELYNN DRAKE's DARK DAYS

"An intoxicating mix of jet-setting action and sparkling turns of phrase. . . . Filled both with action and satisfying characters. I wanted to slowly savor it, but I reached the end far too soon, left hungry and impatient for the next adventure."

Kim Harrison

"Darkly suspenseful and blessedly surprising . . . with prose as silky and enticing as her protagonist."

Vicki Pettersson

By Jocelynn Drake

The Dark Days Novels

NIGHTWALKER
DAYHUNTER
DAWNBREAKER
PRAY FOR DAWN
WAIT FOR DUSK
BURN THE NIGHT

JOCELYNN DRAKE

burn the night

THE FINAL DARK DAYS NOVEL

HARPER Voyager

An Imprint of HarperCollins Publishers

This is a work of fiction. Names, characters, places, and incidents are products of the author's imagination or are used fictitiously and are not to be construed as real. Any resemblance to actual events, locales, organizations, or persons, living or dead, is entirely coincidental.

HARPER Voyager

An Imprint of HarperCollins*Publishers*
10 East 53rd Street
New York, New York 10022-5299

Copyright © 2011 by Jocelynn Drake
Cover art by Don Sipley
ISBN 978-0-06-185182-7
www.harpervoyagerbooks.com

First Harper Voyager digest printing: July 2011
First Harper Voyager mass market printing: July 2011

Harper Voyager and ⟩ is a trademark of HCP LLC.

Printed in the U.S.A.

10 9 8 7 6 5 4 3 2

To Gage Miller and Chad Marshall
Thanks for pointing my life in a positive direction.

Acknowledgments

Each book proves to be its own special challenge, no matter how much you think you've learned from the previous books. As a result, I would like to give a special thanks to my friend Robert for giving me a quick lesson on sparring to help improve Mira and Danaus's combat skills. In addition, I would like to thank my amazing editor Diana Gill for pushing me to be a stronger writer. I would also like to thank my wonderful agent Jennifer Schober for constantly checking on me to make sure that I was happy, healthy, and somewhat sane.

burn the night

ONE

The clang of clashing swords echoed through the woods. Gritting my teeth, I dodged one blow and swung my short sword at her throat, aiming to remove her head. Rain pelted us in large, heavy drops, blurring vision and soaking clothes. I had called down the rain, but was holding back on the lightning, knowing I would finally need it when they tried to overwhelm me. The torrential downpour I had created wasn't succeeding in slowing down my opponents as much as I'd hoped. Only the one light clan naturi seemed bothered by the weather, while the four earth clan members stalked me like a pack of wolves looking for a weakness in their prey.

As I fought my onetime brethren, I could easily hear Cynnia's voice ringing in my head, when I would have liked to walk away from this battle and return to her side.

Please, Nyx, I need him.

The moment Cynnia spoke those words, I knew I was in trouble. Rowe had become a nightmarish creature among our kind, the first in all of memory to ever be banished. Yet, I also understood my young sister's thinking. Rowe was a powerful naturi, a force to be reckoned with. He would make a powerful ally if we could win him over to our side, which was looking thin and sickly in comparison to those that had gathered to Aurora's skirts.

After traveling for more than a month, word finally leaked into my camp that a group of earth naturi had gotten their hands on Rowe and were dragging him toward Aurora's domain in the western part of the United States. I could only guess that their plan was to throw a weakened Rowe at Aurora's feet so she could deliver his death, rather than allow his continued banishment. He was too much of a threat to leave alive.

Sparing a glance out of the corner of my eye, I found that Rowe still lay on his side not far from the fire they had tried to start before my arrival. His arms were bound behind his back and his clothes appeared to be torn and muddy. Whatever their grand scheme was, Rowe was not going to see his wife-queen willingly. He was being dragged before her.

When I had got within feet of the camp, they did not hesitate to attack, while the light clan member hung back and vainly attempted to maintain the fire they had been building. Blocking blows and sliding out of harm's way with a practiced ease, I managed to edge closer to the camp while avoiding my opponents.

"I've come for Rowe," I announced, not looking at my fallen compatriot. "I have need of him. Please hand him over."

"Aurora desires his presence as well," the light clan member smirked as the others circled me. It was the smirk that caused me to recall that this was Claudia, one of Aurora's longtime assistants and loyal followers. Now, she was reduced to errand runner, as there were too few that Aurora felt she could count on. Paranoia and mistrust had sunk its fangs deep into the queen over the past several years.

My grip tightened on my sword, but my gaze never wavered from Claudia. "What does she want with him? He's been banished."

I could feel a gathering of energy beneath my feet. One of the earth naturi had edged closer. Someone was about to make their move and I needed to be ready. However, I preferred to know what Aurora was up to before I started killing my adversaries.

"She's willing to forgive him if he can hand her the Fire Starter."

"I doubt that." Forgiveness was not something my sister understood or even believed in. While I wasn't too fond of Rowe, I was willing to let him live *if* he assisted Cynnia in her endeavors.

"Hand him over to me and no one will get hurt," I commanded. The muscles throughout my body tensed as I readied for the attack.

"You're just one pathetic warrior without a nation to protect. We outnumber you now, Nyx, and our queen has ordered your death. It's you who should run," Claudia mocked.

Pressing my lips into a firm line, I swung my left hand to grab the small crossbow at my side. As my arm swung up with the weapon, the bolt shot out and embedded itself deep within Claudia's throat, causing her to stumble backward, gasping in horror and pain. She was the obvious leader of the group, and now would be unable to shout orders while I decimated her comrades. The crossbow was hooked back on a strap at my side before she finally hit the ground.

My sword whipped through the air, slicing one earth naturi across the chest. It was little more than a flesh wound, but the blood saturating his shirt was enough to give some of the clan second thoughts about continuing the fight. Another earth naturi with more common sense and clarity awoke the trees around us. A large limb reached down to grab me, but

I ducked out of the way, sliding in the mud and leaves. I grabbed a sleeping branch and swung up so I was looking down on the little camp. Darkness had thickened in the area, giving me an edge. I had spent too many centuries working exclusively at night, making my night vision sharper, keener than that of my brethren.

The tree shuddered once, trying to shake me loose. My balance held as I reloaded the crossbow and wounded two more naturi. I wouldn't kill my own kind unless they backed me into a corner and left me with no other choice. For now, I would be content to grab Rowe and run.

With the five naturi writhing on the ground with their injuries, I jumped down from the tree and walked across the small camp to where Rowe lay, completely oblivious to the fight that had just occurred over his possession. Unfortunately, being with me wasn't going to be much more advantageous for him than going to Aurora. Our lovely queen would be happy to have his head if he failed to hand over Mira. And I would be happy to remove his head if he made a single false move toward Cynnia. He was surrounded by would-be enemies, but weren't we all these days?

Kneeling beside Rowe, I cut the leather thong binding his wrists behind his back. That wasn't enough to keep him bound by a long shot. He should have been able to break free, barely trying. I could only guess that they were also keeping him drugged in an effort to keep him docile. With a frown, I sheathed my short sword.

Scooping Rowe up, I cradled him awkwardly in my arms before dropping him on one shoulder to carry him out of the clearing. His weight was easy enough to manage. It was just his size, with his broad shoulders and long legs, that made it difficult.

"You belong together, Nyx!" came a rough, garbled voice. Claudia's throat had healed enough so she could now shout at me. "Two outcasts destined to be slaughtered by Aurora! We'll come after you. You're not free."

"I'm counting on it, Claudia," I said as I disappeared into the night.

My footsteps were silent on the rain soaked ground, sinking into the soft earth. As I reached a clearing in the woods, I tilted my head back and let the rain hammer against my cheeks, eyes, and forehead, washing away the blood that had splashed over me in the brief fight. Claudia and her group had not been prepared for me. In fact, they were not even strong enough to take down Rowe. Someone else had accomplished that task and then handed Rowe over for delivery.

With a sigh, I summoned up my powers and touched the clouds that were still unloading their wealth of rain on the earth. It took only a slight shove to reduce the rain to a mist and then nothing at all. With Rowe in my arms, I leaned forward and braced my legs as a pair of black wings grew from my back, tearing through a shirt specially made to mend itself each time the wings disappeared.

My muscles stretched and relaxed for the first time since I'd come upon Claudia and her group. I fully extended my wings, shaking them out, ensuring that each feather was in its proper place. They flapped twice on my back, stretching stiff muscles. The wind naturi were meant to fly, and fly as often as possible.

Tightening my grip on the sleeping Rowe, the earth seemed to cringe beneath my feet as I took a few running steps forward. The wind gusted at the same time, lifting us both into the air with practiced ease. It was rare for me to carry such a heavy load, but I had done it before.

Overhead, the thick clouds began to part and the nearly full moon broke through, sending down its silvery light, the forest below glistening and shimmering with raindrops. I watched the Earth quickly passing as we headed east, away from Aurora and back toward Cynnia's hiding spot. The earth whispered hazy secrets of a dark future that hovered on the horizon. War was so close now, and no matter what plans we made or what allies we found, there was no avoiding it.

Two

Rowe stirred in my arms. I frowned as I twisted to look over my shoulder at him. His muscles shifted beneath my hands as whatever sedative or spell they had put him under finally wore off. I had been hoping to get a little farther before he woke up.

Pulling in my wings, I glided down to the ground, circling as I searched for a good spot near a swath of trees. The wind had been steady and strong, keeping me ahead of the naturi from whom I had taken Rowe. With any luck, I would be able to get him settled and back in the air before they could get a good fix on our location. I also didn't want to meet up with the creature that had succeeded in defeating Rowe just yet. His wounds were still healing. Blood was splattered over his shirt and pants, while a binding on his forearm was soaked with his blood. We were relatively fast healers, but I had a feeling he had been trapped in a particularly nasty battle where he was significantly outnumbered. I almost felt guilty about what I was about to do. *Almost.*

I hit the ground at a run, crushing Rowe as tightly against me as I could while expanding my wings to slow myself. When I came to a stop, I pulled my black wings in against my back, wrapping them close to my shoulders, as if to fight back the chill that hung in the night air. Spring was still newly born, and the nights prone to frosts as temperatures dipped low. I was anxious to get back to Cynnia, where temperatures were somewhat more hospitable, and so was the company.

I placed Rowe on the ground, knelt beside his prone form and dug into the leather pouch at my side. My stomach twisted and churned into a knot, while my breath lodged in my throat. I couldn't believe I was about to do this. I closed my eyes for a second, sucked in a deep breath through my nose and released it through clenched teeth as I reminded myself that I had done worse. Quietly withdrawing the iron collar, I wrapped it around Rowe's neck and affixed the lock. The hope was that the iron would at least dampen his powers, if not completely shut them down.

As soon as the lock gave a soft click, Rowe jerked beneath me. I jumped back, one hand landing on the hilt of the short sword at my waist, as if I were facing a trapped, feral animal—and in many ways I was. His hands automatically dropped to his waist, searching for weapons that were usually close but now were missing. His head swung as he sat up. He looked dazed as he tried to adjust to his new surroundings before his eyes finally settled on me. I forced myself to lift my hand from the sword hilt and straightened my stance, trying to appear relaxed when my heart was actually pounding away in my chest like a thing gone mad. I wasn't going to be the one to make the first threat, even though I had already attempted to take away his powers.

"Nyx?" His voice was rough and ragged.

"Yes, it's just me."

"What happened to the others? Claudia and her bitch pack?"

I fought back a smile at his accurate description of the earth clan members that had been holding him. "Dispatched."

He arched one eyebrow at me skeptically. "You killed them?"

"Knocked them out. Slowed them down. We should have a couple more minutes for you to rest before we need to be moving again. Your wounds are still healing." My gaze dropped down to the arm he was cradling against his stomach.

"You should have killed them," he growled, his eyes darting away from me.

"I am the protector of our people. I won't kill them if I can avoid it."

"Aurora took that job away when she ordered your execution."

"That job was given to me by my father in exchange for my life. Aurora cannot take that away from me so long as I am alive."

Rowe heaved a heavy sigh and shook his head, causing some of his long dark hair to fall in front of his eye patch. There were so many questions I was itching to ask him about his appearance, about his time on Earth when the rest of our people had been held captive, and about his encounters with the Fire Starter, but they all had to wait. When we first met on my initial arrival back on Earth, I hadn't cared about these things. My only concern was for Cynnia's safe return to Aurora and me. But now, as we stood on the cusp of war, I wanted to know these things because I feared I would never have another chance to ask.

"Why did you take me from Claudia?" he asked.

"You are of more use to me alive than dead at Aurora's feet," I told him.

"You don't know that was her intention!"

"She grows more paranoid with each passing day. She thought you would cause no trouble in exile, but I think she has now come to the conclusion that you are too strong to be left alive. Even if Cynnia fails to take the throne, there is always the chance that you might succeed. She can no longer take that chance. Aurora wants you dead for the same reason that she wanted Cynnia and me dead."

"How could you possibly know that? When was the last time you spoke with your sister-queen?"

"I've not seen her since Machu Picchu," I admitted. "But for a time we had spies within her camp."

"Who?"

I hesitated. They had been close companions and follow-ers of Rowe, and aided me in my search for Cynnia. When the two factions formed on that Peruvian mountain months ago, they had gone with Aurora, but always with the inten-tion of reporting back to Cynnia with information.

"Who are the spies?" he repeated. "How do you know you can trust them?"

"Storm and Hale." They were brothers, born more than two centuries apart but nearly inseparable. Where one went, the other followed. They had been devoted soldiers to Rowe during the long years he was trapped on Earth.

Clearing my throat, I pushed out the rest of the words. "Before Hale was killed, he discovered that Aurora was killing off as many of the wind clan as she could get her hands on. She was beginning to notice that most of the wind clan was flocking to Cynnia's camp. It also didn't help that Greenwood, leader of the earth clan, is now taking a close position next to Aurora. It's no secret that he's attempting to acquire your old position as consort, thus elevating the rest of the earth clan."

"And Storm?"

"With Cynnia, grieving the loss of his brother and plot-ting his revenge."

Bending one knee before him, Rowe used his good arm to run his hand through his hair, pushing it away from his face. It was damp hair and slicked back, and now I could see more scars that stretched across the side of his forehead and even into his scalp. Most of them seemed to be on the right side of his body, yet during the fights I had witnessed Rowe in, I never detected any weakness. He was both strong and very dangerous, something I needed to remember at all times despite the sympathy I could feel building inside me for this wounded warrior.

"The only reason you saved me is that you want my assistance in overthrowing Aurora," he said in a low voice that made me want to put my hand back on the hilt of my sword.

"That is my hope."

"No."

"Rowe, the only way to save our people is through Cynnia's plan of coexistence. Aurora is leading us to war and the decimation of what remains of our people."

A sneer curled his thin lips as he clenched his teeth. "I will not help a bunch of traitors to the crown."

"Aurora has betrayed her people. She is leading us to our extinction. The humans outnumber us by frightening numbers. It is my belief that even the nightwalkers outnumber us, and there has even been talk of the return of the bori. We are unable to fight this war that Aurora is leading us toward."

"Aurora's duty is first to the Earth, and the humans have nearly destroyed her. This is our last chance to save our Mother. I believe in her vision of returning power to the Earth," Rowe argued, pushing up with his good arm so he was sitting on the downed tree behind him.

"Aurora has no great vision for the future and protection of the Earth. Do you think after years of living with my sister in captivity I do not know her mind? In her thoughts, there is only the destruction of the human race. There is no thought about how to rejuvenate the Earth."

"I will not side with Cynnia. Aurora is queen," Rowe said, pushing to his feet.

"I'm not giving you a choice. You are going with me and you are going to listen to what Cynnia has to say. Then I will allow you to make your final decision," I decreed.

A smirk lifted one corner of his thin mouth as he raised his hand toward me. "I don't think so."

I stood prepared, tapping the energy of the earth that flowed around me, ready for whatever spell the wind clan master was going to sling at me. Instead, he cried out in surprised pain as he fell backward onto his butt once again. Glaring at me, he reached up and wrapped his fingers around the previously unnoticed iron collar around his neck.

"Iron?" he snarled. "You've placed an iron collar on me?"

"Because I knew you would not come quietly, and we have a long distance to travel."

Pushing back to his feet, he circled around me. "Why do I get the impression that you feel a certain amount of joy seeing me like this?"

I pulled my short sword, hoping it might deter him from attacking. "I should have killed you after what you did at Machu Picchu."

"And how exactly did I upset you at Machu Picchu? We were both in agreement then. We both believed that opening the doorway was our ultimate goal."

"Not at the cost of Cynnia's life!" I shouted, suddenly losing my tight grip on my temper. "When you attacked the nightwalkers during the daylight hours at the foot of the ruins, you not only wasted the lives of our people, but needlessly risked Cynnia's life. You could have come to a compromise, but you are obsessed with destroying the Fire Starter. This personal vendetta will no longer be tolerated."

"Cynnia formed an alliance with the nightwalker. She

deserved what she got. She turned her back on her people and she dragged you blindly along with her."

Rowe lunged at me from his seated position against the fallen log. I took a step back and held my short sword out to my side, careful to keep from impaling him on it. I needed him alive for now. If he didn't side with us, I could always kill him later.

The dark naturi plowed his head and shoulder into my stomach, doubling me over as I slammed to the ground on my back. Rowe instantly rolled off me, ripping the sword free from my hand as he moved away. Stifling a groan of frustration at my stupid mistake, I rolled away from him, regaining my feet while palming a knife at my side.

He didn't hesitate to attack, barely giving me enough time to regain my feet before swinging the sword blade at my throat. I dodged the blow and parried a thrust at my ribs with the knife. A growl escaped him as he continued to launch one slashing move after another, determined to either remove a limb or my head.

A deep calm settled over me as I blocked each attack or slipped away from the reach of a particular thrust. I watched him, his one eye intently focused on me, but something felt off. I knew Rowe and his intense fighting style. I refused to believe that his wounds were slowing him down that much, having seen him in battle with far worse wounds, cutting down nightwalkers as if harvesting wheat. He wasn't throwing everything he had at me. It was as if he knew I would block his every move or at the very least evade him.

However, that didn't mean Rowe wasn't more than willing to leave me horribly wounded and bleeding in the mud so he could go on his merry way. I needed to disarm him so we could resume our flight from the naturi that had been holding him. We were running out of time. Slipping past one lunge, which was an attempt to plunge the blade between my ribs, I slid across the ground under his guard and slammed a foot into his knee, causing the leg to buckle beneath him. The sword he was holding came straight down, aiming for my chest, but I quickly rolled out of the way. As he knelt on the ground, I kicked the hand holding the sword, knocking it loose. The blade flashed in the moonlight as it flew end over end across the open glade.

Rising quickly to my feet, I stood over him, kneeling on the ground, placing the knife against his exposed throat. "Enough wasting time. You come quietly with me now or I kill you, because I'm not allowing you to return to Aurora."

"Afraid she'll welcome me back with open arms?"

"Your best case scenario is that she'll allow you to hunt me down so I can only kill you at a later date. There will be no hero's return for you when it comes to my sister."

A smile grew on Rowe's face, sending a chill down my spine. "It seems you must first save my life."

I was about to ask what that meant when I heard a creak from the tree above us and felt a trembling in the earth. Claudia and the other members of the earth and light clans had caught up with us.

"Damn you!" I lurched away from him and ran across the glade to pick up my sword.

"Aren't you going to give me a weapon as well, Nyx?" Rowe inquired in all too innocent tones.

"I'm no fool. I'll not risk having you stab me in the back while I am protecting you." I tried to refocus my powers, lightning crackling in the air as the wind rose. "Can you fly?" I demanded as wings sprouted from my back, slick with shining black feathers.

"I seem to have an iron collar around my neck."

"Try it! I truly doubt that all of your abilities have been

blocked. Get in the sky and away from here. I will hold them off until I can join you."

I started to send my powers away from my body again to get a sense of where the clan members were approaching from when a large tree limb swung down toward me. I dove for the ground, narrowly missing being struck in the chest, only to have a swath of smaller branches rake across my arms and back. Twisting around while still lying on my stomach, I saw Rowe also diving to the ground a few feet away as a pair of darts pierced the night, aimed for his chest.

"Get out of here. I'll hold them off."

"Last I checked, protector of the people, I was in command, not you," he said as he grabbed the knife at my side.

"Then what are your orders, commander?"

"You take this damned collar off me and we kill my last captors!"

"Not likely," Claudia said, announcing her arrival in the small clearing.

Kill her! Rowe commanded in my brain.

I reacted, not contemplating whether what I was doing was right or wrong. I threw out my arm and a bolt of lightning sizzled from the sky, slamming down into Claudia in a brilliant flash of white light. Her blackened body fell over with a sickening thud in the wet, marshy ground.

My soul cringed at what I had just done, but I took my first step toward the remaining three members of the earth clan, and nearly tripped. A root had sprung up from the ground and wrapped itself around my left ankle. It continued to tighten, biting through the material of my pants and into the soft flesh and muscle. A second root shot from the earth then and wrapped its way around my other leg, holding me in place.

I glanced around and saw Rowe engaged with the one

male earth clan member, while the two females stood off
to the side watched me with grins on their beautiful, elfin-
like faces. Raising my right hand, I started to throw my
last remaining knife at the one on the left when a third root
halted me.

Trapped and certain that they meant to kill me, I had no
choice. I tilted my head back toward the heavens, letting the
rain pelt my face. A peace spread through my body, as if the
water was cleansing me of the act I was about to commit.

The lightning slammed down twice, pounding both of
the earth clan members. The scent of burned flesh drifted
toward my nose.

This wasn't what I wanted. I was the protector of our
people, a title given to me by my father, the king of the
naturi. He had commanded that with every breath in my
body I protect the people and carry out the orders of my king
or queen no matter what. I was to be their great defender.
I was to be the sword and shield my people hid behind in
times of darkness. Now I had become the sword that cut
them down.

Something sharp prodded my neck, compelling me to
open my eyes. Rowe stood before me with my knife point
digging into my throat and a stern look on his face. "You've
gotten sloppy."

"Not at all."

"Four naturi were allowed to sneak up on you. Two earth
weavers captured you with roots, rendering you nearly helpless. I know that I taught you better than that."

"You taught me to fight nightwalkers and bori. Not our
own kind." I pushed back the memories that threatened to
intrude. Rowe and I had trained together many years before
our people were banished to their cage. We knew each
other's fighting styles. We knew each other's strengths and

weaknesses—or at least we had before we were separated by centuries of captivity.

"All the more reason you should know your enemy, far better than any nightwalker or bori," Rowe criticized. "You should never have been trapped so easily."

"I never was," I said with a slight smile. Lowering my eyelids, I stared past him, concentrating on the flow of the earth around me. I murmured a couple words I had been given by our strongest magic weavers, and the roots quickly unwound themselves from around my body and shrank back into the earth.

The moment his gaze shifted to the roots. I landed two quick hits to his wounded arm and another to the wrist holding the knife, popping it loose. The blade still sliced through my skin, but it was only a minor flesh wound that would heal in time. The important thing was that Rowe was no longer holding a weapon. He was dangerous enough without one.

As the hilt of the blade landed in the palm of my hand again, he ducked and rolled away from me. Coming back up on his feet, he was holding the short sword of one of the fallen naturi. We were once again at a stalemate.

"I guess I was wrong," Rowe said, smirking.

"It seems we frequently underestimate each other. It's been too many years. I guess I assumed you grew soft in your years away from the rest of your people."

"Hardly the case, as I have proven. Now give me the key so I can remove the collar."

"You're going with me to speak to Cynnia."

"Even if I wanted to see your traitorous sister, I wouldn't do it as a dog on a leash. Free me now!"

"And risk you killing her at first sight, because she is my 'traitorous' sister? No, I will have you brought before her with your powers held in check. I am more than willing to give my life protecting her, but I prefer to have the odds in my favor where you are concerned. I am no longer sure of what you are capable."

"Anything," he whispered, a dark smile gracing his grim features. He leaned in close to me, the edge of his blade scraping against mine. "I am capable of anything if it means my survival on this rotting wasteland."

"Then come with me, because right now I am the only one who is willing to protect your traitorous hide."

"I'll go, but first give me the key," he said, taking a step backward.

I smiled at him and bravely shoved my sword back into the sheath at my side. "I don't have it."

"What?"

"I don't have it. Never did. It's at our final destination."

"Damn it, Nyx!" Rowe stomped away from me, tightly gripping the sword in one hand while still keeping his sore arm close to his body.

"It was the only way we could be sure you would seek out Cynnia whether I survived the journey or not."

"So I should just kill you now and go alone to Cynnia's location?"

"No, because you'll never be able to defeat the one that captured you in the first place."

Rowe stopped pacing the forest and looked at me, lowering his sword. "What are you talking about?"

"I find it impossible to believe that Claudia and her little band succeeded in capturing you and wounding you so thoroughly on their own. They were just the delivery. Someone else attacked you, and once it is known that you've escaped again, that person or persons will be on your trail. You need me to keep you alive."

"Bitch," he snarled.

"Can you fly?" I asked, ignoring his comment.

Rowe looked away from me as he placed the sword in his empty scabbard. He hunched forward and his brow furrowed in concentration. A low groan escaped his parted lips as a pair of leathery black wings sprang from his back. I bit my lower lip and blinked back unexpected tears at the sight of his wings. I remembered when they were white as newly fallen snow and soft as a kitten's fur. I had been wrapped in those pearly white feathers once, felt their caress. But now they were gone, replaced by something dark and foreboding, as if they represented a stain against his soul.

"We will fly east for the next couple hours and then make camp just before sunrise," I directed, lifting one hand to summon up the winds again.

"We should be moving by daylight. That's when they will be searching for us. We need to gain as much ground as possible," Rowe countered.

"True, but I am the one who is defending you, and I am at my peak strength at night."

He gave a little bow just before he threw out his wings, catching the growing wind. "As you wish, Dark One."

May the earth mother forsake you.

The old naturi curse occurred to me after he used the nickname that had haunted me since my birth, but I regretted the thought as quickly as it appeared. Looking at Rowe now, I had to wonder if the great earth mother had forsaken him already.

Three

Rowe snapped awake with a single magic word. He blinked a couple times before glaring at me. He had been in mid-rant when I laid a hand on his shoulder and cast the spell, sending him into a deep sleep. Of course, I had a feeling that it was effective only because the iron collar was keeping him weak and he was a member of my own clan. For some reason, the sleep spell I cast only worked on members of the wind clan.

"You put me under a spell, you evil witch!" Rowe snarled.

"It's not as if I could trust you to sleep beside me peacefully," I replied, edging toward the entrance of the cave we had found shelter in during the daylight hours. The sun was in the process of setting over in the west, casting the sky in vibrant shades of pink, purple, and orange. I was still waiting for the dark blues and murky blacks to move in before we set off once again.

I removed the barriers and protective shields I had put up as a warning system should anyone get too close to our hiding place. However, I didn't step outside into the open forest. There was something approaching. In fact, I grabbed Rowe's arm as he tried to walk past me into the forest, forcing him to stop.

"Something is coming," I murmured, cocking my head to the side as I tried to listen to what the wind was whispering to me. The Great Mother was constantly talking, revealing her secrets, but only to those willing to listen.

"I sense nothing." Rowe attempted to jerk his arm free from my grip, but I only tightened my fingers around his muscular forearm. Pulling him down to his hands and knees, I forced him to dig his fingers into some soft earth just at the entrance of the cave.

"You may be willing to take chances with your life, but I am not," I said. "Now listen to what Mother has to say. Someone is coming."

"I find it hard to believe that the Great Mother would have anything to say to you, Dark One," Rowe scoffed.

My temper snapped once again, and I shoved him hard in the shoulder so that he landed on his butt. "Have my skills waned?"

"What?"

"Since we've been reacquainted during the past several months, do you believe that my skills have waned from my youth?"

"No," he said, looking more than a little confused. "You're stronger. You're a better fighter, and I did not know you were capable of spell casting until now."

"Then why do you persist in calling me 'Dark One'? You gave up that name when we trained together as youths and I proved myself to you."

"It bothers you?"

"Of course it bothers me!" I paced to the opposite side of the cave and laid my left hand against the wall. "I do not need the constant reminder that I am beneath the touch of the glorious light that comes from the earth and our people. I do not need to be reminded with every breath that my life is an abomination."

I was an abomination. All naturi babies are born during the light of day so that they can be bathed in the glorious light of the sun and the radiant joy of the Earth. Those few born at night were killed immediately. But when I was born just past midnight with my tuft of black hair and wide silver eyes, my father could not bear to lose me. He fought the heads of the clans for months until he finally convinced them to allow me to live, so long as I devoted my life to the protection of my people. And yet, even with that promise, I was an outcast; never knowing the warmth of compassion or love. Only Cynnia saw me as more than the Dark One or the protector of our people. She saw me as sister and loved me. Only Cynnia.

For a time I thought Rowe had been different. We trained together, fought side by side. He was the commander of the naturi armies and I was his second in command. I thought I had proven myself to him as a warrior.

"Look at me, Nyx. Really look at me!" he said now, drawing my eyes back to where he sat on the ground. "Do you think someone who looks like me has a right to judge you?"

"When I see you, I see someone who made a choice, a great sacrifice for the people he was fighting for."

Rowe gave a snort and shook his head. "Don't make it sound so noble. It may have started that way, but my motives weren't always quite so honorable. Sometimes it was just the fastest way to get the job done."

I shook my head, but remained silent as I listened to the wind rush by the entrance of the cave. Night was settling in the woods, filling the open areas between the trees with thick shadows, while the moon drifted in and out from behind the clouds.

"What happened to you after Machu Picchu?"

My gaze shifted back to the naturi sitting on the ground

with his back to the cave wall. Rowe looked as if he was totally relaxed, but I knew he didn't relax if he could help it. He was always ready for the next attack, ready to strike at the next enemy. But then, so was I. Too many years with the same training.

"Surprised we survived?" I asked.

He opened his mouth and then quickly shut it, shaking his head. "No, I'm not. You are a strong fighter. You would have defended Cynnia with everything that you are."

"Thank you," I murmured, surprised by his words. "We traveled northeast, hoping to head in the opposite direction of Aurora. We initially thought she would remain in South America near Machu Picchu. I thought she would remain there and use the strong power of the earth and the forests to rejuvenate, but I was wrong. Our intelligence indicated that she almost immediately headed northwest into a land called Canada. It was like she was mirroring us."

"I'm sure she can sense you."

"As Cynnia and I can sense her in a distant way. There's no hiding. We just hoped to find a spot that she wouldn't immediately attack so we could have a chance to build our army."

"Where?"

I drew in a deep breath and frowned as I released it through my nose. "You'll see soon enough, but we have another stop to make on the way. What have you done since Machu Picchu?"

"Hunted the Fire Starter," he said with a shrug. Unexpectedly, a smirk grew on his lips and he softly chuckled to himself.

"What?"

"When Mira and I last parted, she said that I should seek out Cynnia. Live my life instead of chasing after death."

I gave a little snort as I pushed away from the wall and

walked back toward the entrance. "She's smarter than I would have given her credit for."

Rowe pushed to his feet and shook his head. "And devious. I would avoid her at all costs. She's nothing but trouble."

"Let's get going. They are getting close," I said, letting his comment pass as I stepped slowly out of the cave with one hand on the hilt of my sword. "By the way, who exactly was it that captured you in the first place?"

"Don't worry. They'll be here soon enough. When Claudia failed to report or hand me over to my next escort, they were undoubtedly dispatched to reclaim me." Rowe looked a little too smug for my liking—he was a formidable warrior, and it didn't look as if he had gone along willingly. What would we face?

Stepping clear of the cave, I stared up at the welcoming sky and the growing darkness. The wind was a light caress, carrying with it only a hint of a spring shower. Balanced on the balls of my feet, I inclined forward, allowing my wings to once again sprout from my back. I stretched them to their full length, enjoying the feel of having them free.

"You'll want to put those away," Rowe instructed, coming to stand beside me. "It will only make the fight more difficult."

Looking over at him, I folded my wings so they hung gathered against my back, but didn't make them completely dissipate. I was about to ask him again what I faced but the earth gave me my answer. The ground gave a soft shudder beneath our feet, and the nearby trees creaked and groaned even though the wind had gone still. Around us I could hear the scurry of small animals fleeing the vicinity, running from their burrows while flocks of once sleeping birds took to the skies with loud, fearful cries. Members of the earth clan were approaching, and I could now guess at who had been sent.

As if on command, three willowy women stepped out from behind the trees. They were dressed in tight-fitting buckskins and supple leather boots that allowed them to tread on the earth without making a sound or bending a single blade of grass. They could not be tracked for they were of the earth itself. And I knew they were skilled fighters, because I had been the one to train them for many years. They were Greenwood's three daughters, simply known as the Huntresses among our people. This made the circle complete. If Greenwood's daughters could track down and bring in Rowe for their father, then his place at Aurora's side would be sealed.

"It seems you have stolen something that rightfully belongs to us," Jasmine, the one in the center of the trio, said. Her hands were open and empty, but the same could not be said of her sisters. To her left, Alaina held a short bow with a quiver full of arrows waiting to be set free. On her right, Wyllow held a short blade in each hand and had a large grin on her face. The youngest of the three, she was always eager for a fight. Their eldest sister Jasmine was the diplomat, willing to use words to get close to her opponent before she jammed a knife between their ribs.

"Aurora banished him," I replied. "She had no business with Rowe any longer. She made her choice, and I'm certainly not going to help your father take his place as consort." I drew a pair of knives from my sides as my wings dissipated to mere dust that trickled down to my feet. Rowe had been right. My wings would only be a hindrance in a battle with these three. There were too many trees in the area. Neither of us would get a clear shot to the skies above before we were grabbed.

"Maybe she has rethought her position on the traitor," Jasmine said with a slight shrug. Behind her, Wyllow gave a small snicker, which matched my own sentiments. Aurora was not about to back down—she had been planning this elimination of her allies for months, if not years. At least I believed that to be true when it came to Cynnia and me. Rowe's appearance might have taken her by surprise and she might have decided to sweep him away with the rest of us. Her goal was to begin a new rule on Earth, and she was going to do that with a fresh set of allies.

I placed myself between Rowe and the three women. "Leave here," I told him. "I will find you after I have dispatched these three."

The naturi gave an unexpected snort, drawing my gaze over to find him leaning against the entrance to the cave. "I'm not leaving and missing out on this performance. One way or another, I'm somebody's captive. What do I care who wins?"

"You should have a care since I'm the only one that needs you alive," I grumbled, looking back at the Huntresses.

"We want him alive," Alaina corrected me with an evil grin. "He's got years of torment waiting for him."

Clenching my teeth, I let her words slip away from me as I focused on the coming battle. Overhead, I could feel the clouds moving in and the wind picking up. A low rumble of thunder rolled in from the distance, warning them to walk away now, when they still had the chance.

"It doesn't have to be this way, Nyx," Jasmine said. "We weren't sent after you. We're prepared to let you walk away."

"No, you're not," I corrected before dropping my short sword. As I expected, their eyes followed the blade into the soft ground, allowing me to palm one of the smaller knives from my side and throw it directly at Alaina before she could draw her first arrow. The naturi screamed as the blade found its mark in her right shoulder. She would be unable to use her bow for at least several minutes as the muscles in her shoulder healed.

Wyllow charged around Jasmine, both blades drawn and ready to decapitate me. I reached down for the hilt of the blade I had dropped into the earth, but I could not pull it free. It was as if the earth around the metal had turned to stone, holding it locked in place. I barely dodged Wyllow's first slashing blow, and blocked the second with the blade I had palmed in my left hand.

Out of the corner of my eye I could see Jasmine standing in the same place, whispering a spell. The trees were beginning to sway and it felt as if the earth was growing softer under my feet. I knew this tactic. She was going to pull me down into the earth and bury me alive. It was the quickest and easiest way to dispatch her opponent.

"Don't push me, Jasmine!" I called as I blocked another series of slashes from Wyllow.

"You're the one that has forced my hand," she warned, throwing her empty arms out wide. "You were an excellent tutor, Dark One, but your nights are over at long last."

Gritting my teeth, I finally succeeded in pushing Wyllow away from me and slogged forward a couple of steps as the earth seemed to turn to mush beneath me. I was now sinking down to my ankles in the growing mire. Wyllow rushed me again, both her swords swinging, in hopes of slicing me into two neat chunks. Falling to my knees, I bent backward so I slid beneath the swords. She overextended herself, leaving her stomach exposed. She knew her mistake in an instant and tried to twist out of the way, but it was too late as I slammed one knife into her midsection. The female naturi staggered away from me, pulling the blade from her abdomen while cursing me. I tried to regain my feet but the earth closed in around my calves, holding me in place so I was trapped in a kneeling position.

"Back away, Alaina!" I snarled, throwing out my arm toward Rowe. The other sister had been sneaking around the battle, drawing close to my scarred companion while I was distracted with Wyllow and Jasmine. A bolt of lightning streaked from the sky and pounded the ground between Alaina and Rowe, causing her to jump back.

"Watch your aim, please," Rowe said calmly. He was standing behind me, so I couldn't see him, but I had no doubt there was a smirk twisting his lips.

"A little help wouldn't be unheard of since I am trying to prolong your life," I bit out between clenched teeth as I struggled to pull to my feet. The earth fought me, sucking at my limbs like so much quicksand, leaving me vulnerable.

"You've planned this battle poorly. You're focused on the wrong one," Rowe advised.

And he was right. I was allowing Alaina and Wyllow to wear me down and distract me when Jasmine was the oldest, strongest, and the unspoken leader of the three. She was the one who was going to slowly bury me while her two sisters chipped away at my defenses. In the end they would leave me alive long enough to see them depart with Rowe, then I would die with the taste of failure on my tongue.

Focusing my powers before Alaina could strike at me, I called the lightning. One bolt slammed to the ground between Alaina and me, forcing her to jump backward, buying me a little time. The second struck at Jasmine, who leapt to a thick grove of trees. The old growth reached out its limbs and wound them together, creating a protective canopy over her. It would take several lightning strikes to finally break through the barrier, something that would leave me open to attack by her sisters, who were once again drawing close.

The one positive was that the lightning strike at Jasmine had broken her concentration on the earth. With a grunt, I finally regained my footing, though the ground remained soft like soggy marshland.

Frowning, I resheathed my sword and unsnapped a slender strap on my left side. Grasping the leather handle, I flicked my wrist, allowing the long whip to unfurl before me. It came as no surprise when the three sisters instantly went still, their eyes growing wide as they locked on the new weapon.

"It doesn't need to come to this, Nyx." Jasmine took a step back. "Rowe isn't worth protecting. We don't want to hurt you. You're free to go, I promise you."

"Rowe is worth more than you will ever understand," I said in a low, even voice. I flicked my wrist again, causing the whip to crack like a snap of thunder, warning them.

Wyllow didn't listen. She charged me first, bringing with her the long arms of the trees that surrounded us, hoping to entangle me and the whip. Widening my stance, I swung the whip around, slicing through the tree limbs that drew close, raining down debris on Wyllow before she could reach me. She pushed on, determined to slice through me, but she didn't have a chance. In a flash, I brought the whip down, slashing it across the hands holding her two swords. She screamed, dropping her blades as she pulled her hands in against her stomach.

"Don't turn your back on her!" Jasmine screamed, but it was too late. Wyllow saw the whip coming around for another strike and she naturally turned her back to me, hoping it would take the brunt of the strike. It was what I had been waiting for. The ends of the whip slashed through the thick buckskin shirt and cut grooves in her back.

A sickening scream rose up from Wyllow as she collapsed to the ground, writhing in agony far worse than would be imagined for a simple wound caused by a whip. Desperate to avenge her wounded and dying sister, Alaina charged me next. I swiveled my hips, turning my body to face her as the whip struck out like a venomous cobra. The earth clan naturi managed to stomach three strikes before she finally turned her side toward me, allowing me to rake the whip across her back. She fell to the ground, screaming in pain while Wyllow became horribly silent.

Jasmine took another step backward, shaking her head as tears slipped down her tanned cheeks. Both her hands were balled into fists and trembling before her as she stared at her sisters as they died. For a moment I considered sparing her. I thought about sending her back to her father with a message that I would not allow Aurora to win the fight that she started.

"Mercy is for the weak," Rowe whispered.

Sucking in a deep breath through my nose, I lifted my arm and twirled the whip above my head for a second before flicking it out toward Jasmine. I knew that no matter what I did, she was smart enough not to turn her back on me. I didn't need her to. The whip wrapped tightly around her neck, choking her. Grabbing the whip with my right hand, I gave it a swift jerk, breaking her neck. She collapsed face-down in the dirt.

I released the whip with my right hand and pulled the sword that had been stuck in the earth free. With my teeth clenched, I walked over to where Jasmine lay. Pulling the whip free, I quickly decapitated her, ensuring that she was truly dead, before placing the sword back in its sheath.

I turned back toward the cave and found Rowe standing over Alaina as she writhed on her side, gasping for air as if her throat was closing in. Hatred was splashed across his face as he watched her, and for a moment I had to wonder how far that hatred extended. Did it include all of our kind? Or just those who were hunting him?

"I don't understand," he admitted when Alaina gave her last shuddering gasp and went completely still at his feet. Her green eyes stared wide at the forest, blind forever. "What did you do?"

I finished coiling up the whip as I joined him next to Alaina. Kneeling down, I turned her over onto her stomach and pulled open one of the large tears in the back of her shirt, revealing the tattoo of the tree that graced the back of every naturi. It was a symbol of our tie to the earth, one we were all born with. Rowe bent close to examine her back and then fell to both his knees in surprise, tearing open her shirt so her entire back was exposed. There were five slash marks through the tree, cutting deep within her flesh.

His narrowed gaze snapped back up to my face. "I still don't understand. These wounds aren't deep enough to kill."

"I severed her connection with the earth," I said, hating to utter those very words.

Rowe stumbled to his feet, moving back away from me. "That's impossible. That's just fucking impossible." I noticed that his eyes were no longer on my face, but on the whip still coiled in my hand.

Rising slowly to my feet, I extended my hand to him, offering him the whip. Keeping it coiled, he examined the end and found pieces of iron embedded within the leather straps. But it was more than just the iron that caused their link to the earth to be broken. The whip was imbued with powerful and ancient magic.

As soon as Rowe wrapped his hand around the handle, the whip jerked from his grasp and slithered across the ground. It wrapped around my left leg, the handle coming to rest against my hip. "I'm the only one who can use it."

"Convenient," he replied, twisting the word with a sneer. "You've created an efficient weapon of death that can be used by only you."

"I had no choice."

"No choice? O Great Protector of the people, how could you create a weapon that only kills our people?"

"Because Aurora asked me to."

Rowe's brow furrowed with surprise as he looked at me. I avoided his piercing gaze to coil the whip once again and hang it at my side. I didn't like to think about it. I was the protector of our people. At least I had been. But even before Aurora proclaimed that I was a traitor to the crown, I had become an efficient killer of my people.

"Why?" he asked softly.

I drew in a slow breath but couldn't raise my eyes to meet his gaze. Rowe had this image of our people and what he had been fighting for when he struggled to open the door once again. I hated to be the one who destroyed that image. And yet, hadn't Aurora already tarnished the image when she turned her back on him?

"During the final couple centuries of Aurora's rule," I said, "while we were trapped, the cohesion of our people started to break apart. Factions built among the various clans, questioning her rule. People were dying; our children were struggling to survive birth when we were lucky enough to bear children. Aurora's authority was being threatened."

"She asked that you hunt down anyone who was questioning her rule," Rowe said, finally drawing my gaze up to his face.

"They were accused of treason and immediately dispatched. The old spell weavers helped me develop the whip. I needed something unique and that would immediately strike fear in the guilty. Unfortunately, it was too effective with some of the races."

"What do you mean? It doesn't kill everyone?"

I shook my head. "It doesn't affect everyone equally. It breaks a naturi's tie to the earth. For the earth clan, death is nearly immediate and extremely painful. For the water clan, they can no longer return to the water, which leads to a slower death. The animal clan can no longer shift or call to the animals around them."

"The wind clan?"

"We lose the ability of flight. Our wings are permanently severed."

"But we can control the weather still?"

"Yes, as well as weave other spells if the naturi is strong and old enough."

"You used it on a weaver!" Rowe gasped. The ancient spell weavers of our people were only second closest to the earth next to the ruler of our people. They were held in the highest regard, thought to be untouchable.

"The one who created the whip. Aurora feared his ability to create such a weapon against his own people."

"What about the light clan? What does it do to the light clan?" he demanded.

I shook my head, frowning. "I don't know. Aurora never accused her own clan of treason." I dreaded the day that I would have to discover that bit of information.

"I'm sorry," Rowe murmured, shocking me.

"For what?"

"That you were forced to hunt our people. It would have turned them even more against you."

I forced myself to shrug despite the lump that had grown in my throat. Other than Cynnia, Rowe was the only one to understand what I had been forced to do. I was born to be the protector of our people and had turned into their executioner. And I was good at it.

Pushing such thoughts aside, I focused once again on the mission that lay ahead of me. I hunched forward, balanced on the balls of my feet, allowing my wings to once again spring forth. I stretched them wide, enjoying the feel of the muscles pulling while the wind brushed against my feathers.

Turning around, I saw Rowe struggling to do the same. The iron collar was doing its job by inhibiting his ability to use magic, but it allowed him to call forth the black leathery wings that were a part of him.

"We need to get moving," I said. "You're not the only one I need to convince to side with Cynnia."

FOUR

"Damn it, Mira!" Danaus taunted in a low whisper, a smirk pulling at one corner of his mouth. "Are you going to need a tissue or can you pull it together?"

I threw the hunter a dark look, but otherwise kept my comments to myself. The ceremony in the small clearing in the woods would start soon, and Barrett had generously allowed us to attend since we were the only people James saw as both friends and, in a twisted way, as family. I wasn't going to be the one that started trouble.

Yet, I could understand Danaus's teasing all too well. As we stood there in the quiet forest, a ring of werewolves around us, I tried to focus on the bare-chested James next to Barrett and the rest of the Rainer family. Unfortunately, my mind drifted too often to my recently lost Lily and Tristan. Two people I had taken into my family, into my heart, who were stolen from me through violence and treachery just a few months ago. Watching James being inducted into the Savannah pack, I tried to reassure myself that he would be safe and that no one would strike at him in an effort to get to me. He was now a part of Savannah, but there was a safe distance between me and him.

A hollow ache echoed through my chest. Months had

passed and still I found myself conjuring up ways that things could have gone differently, resulting in Lily or Tristan or both of them being alive today. It was a futile act that only extended my pain, making me more vulnerable to the world around me, but I had Danaus at my side.

The hunter had returned from Venice with me, and moved into my town house in the historic district of Savannah. I had opened my house outside of the city to him, but he proclaimed that living together was a bit fast for him. But even that was said with a smile, as he tended to spend most of his evenings wrapped in my arms at my home. He had left Themis behind, and a part of me was relieved to have him out of Ryan's grasp. The warlock leader of the so-called research society was more trouble than either of us was prepared to deal with. I had no doubt that Ryan still had more schemes that included us, but for now he seemed content to let us live in peace in Savannah.

Determined to earn his keep, Danaus took a job as a bartender and occasional bouncer down at the Dark Room. The exclusive club that catered only to nightwalkers and lycanthropes suffered a bit of a shake-up at his presence, but things had settled back into their normal routine. I didn't have the heart to tell him that as part owner of the Dark Room, I was the one paying his salary each week. Danaus needed to feel independent and yet still connected to the dark other world that pulsed just beyond the notice of humans.

To my surprise, his fingers brushed against my hand, hanging down at my side, before he finally entwined his fingers around mine. *Stop thinking about them. Let them rest,* he admonished in my brain.

Will he be safe?

He will be safe.

Some of the tension finally flowed out of my shoulders and I squeezed his hand as I resisted the urge to lay my head against his hard shoulder. Danaus had become my rock, my one shining lighthouse in the storm, my last hold on sanity in this world. More darkness and evil lay just over the horizon, but I knew that I would at least have him at my side.

Keep thinking thoughts like that and I'm going to need a tissue, Danaus teased.

Asshole, I replied, mentally chuckling at him. I should have known he would be a silent specter in my thoughts. I'd been too dark lately as the world grew quiet. The naturi had left my territory and there was no word from the coven. Not even my father, Nick, had popped in recently to torment me. I paced the floor and stared out the window with my arms folded over my stomach, waiting. I didn't know what it was, but something bad was coming.

At the other end of the circle, Barrett spoke to his pack, fewer than twenty members strong. Their number had been slashed, as they had once been controlled by the animal clan, forced to attack nightwalkers as the naturi searched for me. Barrett had lost two of his brothers, leaving only his younger brother Cooper and sister Erica at his side.

The alpha spoke of unity and family. He spoke of loyalty not only to the pack, but also to their race. He then turned to James and spoke about the young man's accomplishments. He heralded James's unwavering determination and his dedication to understanding the other races throughout his life, as well as James's boundless compassion and fierce loyalty to his friends. And when the vote came down for his acceptance in the pack, it was unanimous. But then, it was rare for anyone to speak out against an applicant when the person had the alpha's full support.

And then it was official. There were no fights. No bloody, exhausting trials in order to enter into the Savannah pack, just a pile of paperwork and a thorough interview with Barrett. James had been considerate enough to ask if I minded if he moved to Savannah before he officially petitioned Barrett. I'd simply smiled and nodded at him.

The only one ever known to skip the formal induction process into the Savannah pack stood on my right, watching the proceedings in silence. Nicolai Gromenko had been a desperate act on my part. Stuck in a bad situation with Jabari as his owner, he was about to be handed over to the naturi as a sacrifice when I finally stepped in and swore to protect him with my life.

Unfortunately, moving the shifter to my domain in Savannah meant that he also had to be accepted by the local pack to survive.

So at my request, Barrett took Nicolai in. But the arrangement couldn't last. Nicolai needed a pack of his own, a place to call his own. He was born to be an alpha, and I knew that a part of him was chafing under Barrett's rule.

"You've brought another sheep into the flock," Nicolai said.

A broad smile finally lifted my lips. "I had nothing to do with this one."

"No, you just look like a proud parent watching her child win his first award."

"Just think of us as friends of the family," Danaus interjected without taking his eyes off James. I inwardly shook my head. Danaus had never truly cared for the shapeshifter, and a small part of me thought it might have to do with my brief past with Nicolai. Of course, that was assuming Danaus was capable of feeling jealousy. I wasn't about to get my hopes up.

At the other end of the clearing a cry of pain rose up, crashing through the air as James began the process of changing into a wolf. A quick conversation with Barrett a few nights earlier revealed that James had spent two months in the winter with the pack, learning what he could do before he briefly returned to Themis with the intention of living without the support of a pack.

While I wasn't thoroughly versed in the lycanthrope world, it was my understanding that transition from man to wolf was painful for the first year, as the person learned muscle control and focus. I squeezed Danaus's hand, a part of me wishing I could take away James's pain. The sweet young man had always expected to be a spectator on the outside of the supernatural world, not a member.

Danaus squeezed my hand back. "He's fine."

"It will get easier," Nicolai reassured me. "In a few months he'll be able to shift anytime that he wants to. For now, he'll be limited to the call of the full moon or the naturi."

Others joined James, the clearing suddenly filled with large wolves of various color. I never took my eyes off of James as I saw the wiry young man change into a wolf with a thick black coat. When the transformation was complete, he shook himself once, as if brushing away the last of the pain, before he trotted over to me.

His long pink tongue lolled out of the side of his mouth as he stared up at me. I could feel his happiness. It seemed he'd finally found his home, and I couldn't have been happier for him. Kneeling down, I plunged my hand through his thick coat, rubbing his ears.

"You're a beautiful wolf," I proclaimed with a grin. "I'm very proud of you."

James nuzzled my arm once before brushing against me and turning back to the rest of the pack, which was milling around the circle. They sniffed and snapped at each other in play, eager to finally be running and hunting on the night of the full moon. As James rejoined the group, I noticed a smaller wolf with a mix of gray and white fur nip at his neck before she trotted off, giving him a little bark as if to encourage him to follow her.

Beside me, Nicolai chuckled. "I wonder how Barrett's going to take that."

"What?"

"That's his sister who's taken an interest in James. I almost pity the boy."

Only Barrett and Nicolai remained in human form. I noted the look that passed between the two men before Barrett finally shifted into a large brown wolf and led his pack out into the woods.

I glanced up at the sky one last time, taking note of the full moon that hung bloated over our heads. "How is it that you're not hunting with them tonight?"

"I will," Nicolai murmured, his direct gaze straying away from my face. "There is something that I wanted to discuss with you first."

"You're leaving, aren't you?"

"You had to know it was coming."

"I did."

"Look, I know you saved my life, not only from the naturi, but from Jabari too. Hell, you've probably protected me from my own kind as well, considering my past. I don't want you to think I'm turning my back on what you did for me."

"But two alphas can't exist in the same pack," Danaus said.

"You knew?"

"Only recently," the hunter admitted. "It's how the others behave around you. You're a natural leader, and it makes things . . . uncomfortable for you when you are forced to constantly heel to Barrett."

"It's not Barrett," Nicolai quickly countered with a shake of his head. "He's a great leader and he has taken amazing care of his people. I . . . just . . . don't belong here."

My brow furrowed. My protection of Nicolai had been

distant at best, but I'd always felt that if he was in my domain, I could reach him in time. I would always be there for him. "Where will you go?"

"Argentina."

"What?"

"To be more precise, Buenos Aires," Nicolai said. "There's a very large concentration of lycanthropes in Argentina. Word has come up through the grapevine that warlocks and witches are going missing from the region and people are starting to point fingers in the direction of my kind. My Spanish is solid and I thought I could go down and see if I could look deeper into the situation before it turns into an indiscriminate hunting party. With the naturi on the loose, we can't afford to have our numbers drop."

"What did Barrett say?" Danaus inquired from behind me.

"Can I help you pack?" Nicolai joked, earning a smack on the chest from me.

"If he ever uttered those words, I would skin him alive and he knows it," I growled.

"No, he said that a place would always be open for me in the Savannah pack should I ever decide to return."

I nodded, shifting my shoulders against the newfound tension accumulating there. "So?"

"So the question has been left up to you. Can I go?" Nicolai demanded.

Feeling distinctly uncomfortable, I paced away from the two men, walking into the open clearing while crossing my arms over my chest. The spring wind was cool and there was still a bite in the air, as if winter were still fighting to hold its grip on the area. But the world was a lush green again and life stirred around us. The earth was awake and alive again. And thanks to my dear father, I could now sense it all, unlike any other nightwalker.

"Why are you asking me?" I said, defensively. "You

know you don't need my permission to leave or stay in Savannah. You don't belong to me."

"You did claim me in Venice before the coven."

I shoved one hand through my hair. "You know that was just for their benefit. You've never belonged to me."

"You might not have seen it that way, but I know that you've been protecting me with your life from that very first moment in Venice. I can't just walk away without . . ." Nicolai's voice drifted off.

"Say the words, Mira," Danaus gently instructed.

"Go, Nicolai. Help the other shifters," I whispered past the unexpected lump in my throat. The lycanthrope walked over and wrapped his large arms around me, pulling me into a tight hug. He was my golden boy, my earthbound Adonis, and he was permanently walking out of my life. "Just don't get yourself killed."

Nicolai pulled away, holding me at arm's length so he could look down and smile at me. "I promise to avoid getting killed."

"And don't go picking fights with any nightwalkers."

"There aren't any nightwalkers in South America," Danaus reminded me, but I ignored him.

"And keep your distance from the naturi. There's no telling where Aurora is right now, and you don't want to go waltzing into a nest of those bastards. Just keep your head down and your nose clean while in Argentina. If you need anything—"

My next words were cut off by Danaus placing a hand on my shoulder and squeezing it tightly while he extended his other hand toward Nicolai. "Be careful," the hunter said, neatly summing everything up when I seemed unable to stop babbling. It felt like if I stopped talking, Nicolai would disappear.

"Thanks. I will," Nicolai said, shaking Danaus's hand.

"I'll leave it to you to keep an eye on things here for me while I'm gone."

"Screw you both," I snapped, turning my back on them. Danaus softly chuckled, while I heard Nicolai shift from human into wolf. I stared off into the woods until I felt something large press against my thigh. I looked down to find an enormous white wolf with a burnished reddish gold streaking his fur. I had never seen Nicolai as a wolf and he was just as beautiful in that form as he was in human form.

"Be safe," I whispered, running my hand over his head. Nicolai lifted his muzzle and quickly licked the palm of my hand before darting off into the woods. I stared at the last spot where I saw him before he disappeared into the thick bank of trees that surrounded us. The hollow ache I'd felt earlier in the evening throbbed to life once again in my chest.

Danaus came up behind me and slid one arm around my waist, pulling me back against him. "He'll be fine."

"In less than a year, I've lost Michael, Lily, and Tristan. I nearly lost Valerio, and I was forced to fight Knox, endangering his life. Now, Nicolai is going somewhere that I can't protect him."

"You can't protect the world," Danaus said, pressing a kiss to the top of my head.

"I'm not trying to, even though it feels like it at times."

Danaus grabbed me by the shoulders and turned me around, forcing me to look him in the eyes. "James is here, safe from the reach of Ryan and Themis. That should make you happy. I am here, out of the reach of Themis, and ready to protect you and the rest of Savannah. That should make you happy. Things are quiet now. Enjoy it."

A reluctant smile pulled at the corners of my mouth as I stared up at the hunter. Less than a year ago we were at each other's throats, looking for the first opening to insert a well-sharpened blade. Now we stood alone in the woods, a deep sense of peace sinking into my bones. While I was reluctant to release Nicolai, I knew it was time for him to go. For now, the others in my life were safe.

Five

Danaus walked over and entwined his fingers through both of my hands before pinning them gently behind my back. I looked up at the hunter, arching one questioning brow at him.

A seductive smile lifted his lips as he leaned in closer, pressing his chest against my stomach and breasts, while my thighs brushed against his. "You do realize that the kids are all taken care of now," he purred.

"The kids?"

"James and Nicolai."

"You mean my responsibilities."

Danaus leaned down and ran his parted lips along my exposed throat so the edge of his teeth dragged across my flesh. There was no hiding my shiver of delight with our bodies pressed so close. "You're not completely free of your responsibilities."

"Really?" My voice was rough and breathless as I pressed closer.

Danaus released one of my hands and cupped one butt cheek, holding me tightly against him so there was no missing the rock hard erection in his pants. I wrapped my free arm around his shoulder while he bit down on some exposed flesh in the hollow of my neck. He was teasing me, pushing my hold on what little self-control I possessed when it came to him. It kept things infinitely more interesting as we danced on the edge of whether I could keep from biting him.

"I'd say that you still have a responsibility to me," he said in a voice so low I could feel it rumbling between us in his chest. "You've been neglectful."

My head fell back with a laugh. "Neglectful? That's hardly true if you consider the two times just the other night."

His hand squeezed my rear end, massaging it. "Yes, but it's been a couple nights. We're overdue."

He was right. It did feel like we were overdue for a little quality time, but I didn't want to just fall too eagerly into his arms. I craved him more than blood most nights and was more than a little frustrated when his job at the Dark Room intruded on our time together, but I kept the frustration to myself, as I knew the job was important to him.

"So you want to just have at it right here in some woods filled with shifters?" I asked.

Danaus's smile widened as his grip tightened and he pulled me into the cover of a line of trees. Pressing my back against a particularly large tree, he grabbed both of my thighs and lifted them so my legs were wrapped tightly around his narrow hips. One hand resumed his massage of my ass while the other busied itself unbuttoning my blouse.

"The shifters are far from here and won't be back for hours," he said in a low, husky voice that sent a thrill through my body. "We're alone."

"We could always just go back to my place and do it," I said, throwing up only a token argument.

"I supposed we will do both, but I want you now."

Danaus captured my lips in a rough kiss that silenced the last of my weak protests. I thrust my tongue into his mouth while tightening my legs around his waist so that my body was pressed even more tightly against his cock. I wanted him just as badly right now, werewolves be damned. A low moan escaped him as his hand slipped inside my bra and cupped my breast. His thumb rubbed against the nipple, teasing it, hardening it into a sensitive little nub. The scent of him danced around me, driving me even wilder as we kissed. I needed him but there were too many clothes in the way. I wanted to run my hands over his warm skin and drag my tongue over his stomach down to his penis. I wanted him wild as well, sweating with need.

Wrapping my arms around his neck, I dropped my legs from around his waist so I was standing before him. I pushed him away from me just a little bit as I dropped down to my knees, my nimble fingers dancing over the button and zipper of his pants. A growl escaped Danaus as his fingers slipped through my hair and he tightened his grip on my head. As I opened his pants, his cock sprang forward, pressing against the fabric of his boxer shorts. I ran my lips against it through the fabric, sending a shiver through his body.

"God, Mira," he groaned, his head thrown back, his entire body clenched and still as he waited for me to finally take him in my mouth.

Shotgun blasts echoed through the silence of the woods then, shattering the calm and startling us both. Danaus and I froze, our eyes searching the area for danger.

"Naturi?" I asked as I extended my powers to sweep over the area while quickly rebuttoning my shirt.

"None. Only the shifters and some humans."

Another set of shots rang out, and this time there was a distinct yelp of pain. My temper surged, sending my hands down to grasp the knives perpetually at my sides as I jumped to my feet. "A hunting party," I snarled. "Stay here! I'll be back in a few minutes."

"Like hell I'm staying here," Danaus snapped back at me, already heading toward the edge of the clearing while closing his pants up. A pained expression crossed his face as he moved, but he said nothing about the sudden interruption.

I grabbed his shoulder, pulling him to a sharp halt. "These bastards aren't going to discriminate between wolf and human at this point. They see you in the woods at this hour and they're going to fire on you as well. Stay here. I can sneak through the woods unseen."

"James is out there along with the rest of the wolves. I'm not going to stand by."

"Bastard," I growled before pressing a quick kiss to his lips, knowing there was no way that he would hold back. He was the hunter, and I couldn't stop him. "Be careful! Don't kill anyone if you can help it. We need information."

We headed in different directions in an attempt to circle around the group of humans who were slowly making their way through the woods. Cloaking myself, I rushed toward a knot of four hunters west of me. The men were trekking in groups of three and four, a total of more than twenty. It made it more difficult for the wolves to strike back when four different guns were trained on them at once.

After a couple of minutes I found four hunters standing over a wounded, naked male who was clasping his side and moaning as blood poured from his body. The wound appeared small enough that he could heal from it, but two of the humans had their guns trained on his head, ready to blow more holes in him if it looked like he was recovering.

"I think you gentlemen are a little in over your head," I announced, leaning against a tree. Startled, the men jerked their guns in my direction. "You should never have come out into the woods tonight starting trouble that you can't finish."

"What the hell—" was as far as one of them got before the wolves attacked at once. No one managed to get off a single shot, and in a matter of a couple minutes, all four men were torn apart and dead.

I stood back with my arms folded over my chest. The pack had only needed a distraction so they could strike at the ones who had hurt their fellow pack member. Despite what I had told Danaus, I knew that these particular men were dead upon discovery. It was the rule of the forest.

One of the larger wolves stepped away from the group and slowly changed back to human form, naked and streaked with blood. Barrett's copper eyes glowed and his handsome face was distorted with rage and confusion. Never had the local pack been hunted by humans, particularly in these numbers. There were stories of wolves being shot by farmers when they ventured too close to human territory, but men never went into the woods looking for wolves at night. It meant one thing—someone was hunting for werewolves.

"How many are there?" he demanded when he finally got hold of his emotions enough to speak.

"Less than twenty now. They seem to be hunting in groups of at least three or more, making it harder for your people to strike back."

"They're hunting us, Mira," he growled, balling his fists at his sides. "They are hunting us!" The remaining wolves that had attacked the humans ventured over to Barrett's side and were milling around, growling and snapping as they sensed his anger and frustration.

"We need to find out who these men are and how they found out about the shifters," I calmly said, knowing that he was going to hate my suggestion. "We need to capture a few of these men alive."

"They're hunting us, Mira!" he repeated, and I knew what that meant. In his mind, it meant that every one of these gun-toting bastards needed to be shredded by the pack. But if we didn't know how the information was leaked, it would never be safe for the pack to hit these woods again on a full moon.

"If we don't get information, more will come. They will keep coming until they pick off every last member of your pack. Some have to be left alive."

"Fine," he bit out after a minute of tense silence. With every muscle tensed in his lean body, Barrett closed his eyes, seeming to block out the world around him. He then opened his eyes and looked down at the smaller wolf at his side. His sister gave a little yip before running off into the woods with a pair of other wolves flanking her.

"I've reached Nicolai," Barrett explained. "He's pulling back some of the pack to the clearing. He will guard my sister and some of the younger members that haven't the strength to change back into human form just yet."

"Do you want me to send Danaus back as well?"

"No, keep him hunting. That's what he does best. Have the survivors brought unarmed to the clearing." Barrett then bent over and turned back into wolf form. As a wolf, he could move through the woods with more stealth, sneaking up on his prey as he blended in with the darkness.

With a quick touch of my mind, I relayed Barrett's instructions to Danaus before setting off myself into the dark woods in search of my own prey. There were only sixteen humans out in the woods with guns. We needed to keep at least some of them alive. I had a dark feeling I knew who was behind this attack. I just needed to know *how*.

With blades gripped in my hands, I slunk through the woods, treading as silently as possible as I headed toward the closest group. A rumble of growling flowed around me as I drew closer to my prey. Wolves circled the group, keeping their bodies hunkered down close to the ground, hidden among the ferns and low-lying brush.

My knives winked in the light of the full moon as I

wiped away the cloak that had hidden me from the view of the humans. I smiled, my pale skin seeming to glow in the light that broke through the trees. They raised their guns toward me but offered no warning as they each fired off a shot. My smile never wavered as I dodged the bullets and then returned to my relaxed stance, casually spinning one knife in my right hand. Humans were an easy target for me after so many centuries fighting nightwalkers, lycanthropes, warlocks, and naturi. Under most circumstances, I could easily let them go with a couple superficial wounds and a good scare. But this time I was struggling to follow my own advice. They had attacked my friends and comrades. They endangered James's life and now they were shooting at me.

"You have no idea who you're fucking with." Lunging forward, I knocked the guns out of the hands of two of the four men before plunging my knives deep into their abdomens. As they bent forward in pain, I pulled my blades free and turned to the other men. One managed to get a point-blank shot to my stomach. I lurched backward a step as the bullet ripped through me and into a nearby tree with a *thunk*.

"My turn," I snarled before stepping forward. I grabbed the end of the gun and yanked it out of his hands before slamming the stock against the side of the man's head, the wood splintering as he crumpled to the ground. With only one man left, the wolves hovering on the fringe of the fight lunged forward, taking him down before he could get off a shot. The two men I had initially wounded with the knives were also shredded into pieces.

Frowning, I reached down and grabbed the collar of the man I had knocked unconscious. A couple of wolves growled at me for taking away their prey, but they quickly backed off. As much as I hated it, we needed to keep a few alive.

Are you all right? Danaus suddenly demanded. I could sense him drawing closer to me, his concern wrapping around me as his powers searched my body. He knew I was wounded.

Just a minor flesh wound. You? I replied, warmed by his concern. It helped to temporarily wash away the hatred seething inside of me, demanding a little more blood of my own.

Couple scratches. I'm having trouble keeping these bastards alive. The wolves . . .

I know, they want blood, and they deserve it.

I've got two that I'm taking back to the clearing, he said.

I've got one. When you get to the clearing, stay there and guard the attackers. We need them alive for at least a little while longer so we can find out what's really going on.

I'm not leaving you out there alone, Danaus warned.

There are only a few left and this is my domain. I won't be alone. The wolves will help me finish this.

When I reached the clearing, I found Nicolai circling a hunter who was seated on the ground clutching his bleeding arm to his chest. The other wolves were hovering close on the fringe, snapping and growling as well. I dropped the unconscious man next to the other man. The wolves' anger and sense of betrayal was thick in the air.

"Danaus is bringing two more," I told Nicolai. "Keep an eye on them. Keep them alive. We need information."

Nicolai answered with a disgruntled snort, but I knew he would follow the orders—he was a good soldier and loyal to his pack, even if he was planning to leave it.

"I'll be back with more," I said, and then smiled as another human cry of pain and horror echoed through the woods. The wolves had struck another blow. Entering the woods, I scanned the area, discovering there were only a handful of scattered humans left. They had disbanded in terror and were now trying to run for safety. Launching myself forward, I flowed through the woods like water through a well-worn riverbed. With a few well-placed hits to the back of the head, I knocked out three more before they could reach their vehicles at the edge of the forest.

I sighed as I tossed the smallest of the three men over my shoulder and dragged the other two back toward the clearing. The wolves would take care of the remaining two. There was no use trying to save them. Barrett's pack never hunted humans. In fact, they were careful to steer well clear of any human territory. The worst that ever happened on a full moon hunt was that they might bring down a buck or flush out a few hares. They ran together as a pack, enjoying the stretch of muscles and the feel of the wind through their fur. They reveled in their connection to the animal that existed within them. The humans had tried to destroy that, and there would be no quarter.

Upon reaching the clearing, I dropped the ones I was carrying with the other survivors, bringing our grand total up to seven of the more than twenty who had gone out into the woods to hunt the shifters that night.

After a few more minutes of waiting, Barrett and the remaining members of his pack trotted out of the woods. A couple of the wolves were moving slowly, limping as they favored wounds. The man who had been shot in his wolf form managed to heal enough to change back into a wolf, though one side of him was covered in blood. His connection to the earth was stronger while in wolf form, and the earth magic had sped the healing process.

Turning slowly around the circle, I did a quick count and then sent my powers out into the surrounding woods. Everyone was alive and accounted for, to my relief. Barrett had lost enough already.

"You're not one of them," one of the captive men bravely said, breaking the silence of the group for the first time. "You're one of them bloodsucking vampires."

"That's surprisingly astute." I smiled wide enough to expose my fangs.

Reaching inside his shirt, he pulled out a large gold cross on a gold chain, dangling it in front of my face. "You're not going to lay a hand on me!"

To my extreme surprise, Danaus stepped forward and wrapped his fist around the chain before jerking it from the man's neck. He tossed it into the woods, putting it a good distance from the man.

"Traitor!" the man snarled, rubbing the back of his neck where the chain had temporarily bit into his flesh. "You've turned your back on the human race. Betrayed us! You're worse than those monsters."

Without a thought, I lunged toward the man who had insulted Danaus, aiming to bury my fangs deep into his throat and rip him apart, when Danaus stopped me. I growled at him as I tried to jerk free. He shook his head.

"I am one of you," Danaus said gently, dousing my anger in an instant. "I want no claim to the human race if this is what they are to become."

A surprised smile tweaked the corners of my mouth as I wrapped my arms around his waist, pulling him close. The time when mankind discovered the existence of nightwalkers and lycanthropes was growing uncomfortably close, and deep down I had always wondered which side Danaus would fall on when the time came. Now I knew—he would remain at my side—and the knowledge was as sweet as the hunt.

"How did they know?" Barrett demanded from beside me, once again in human form.

I released Danaus and looked around to find that most of the wolves had returned to human form. Some of them had pulled on clothes, while others remained boldly naked, staring down the seven men who had hunted them.

There was only silence from the captives who sat at our

feet, not that I actually expected any of them to speak up. Narrowing my eyes on them, I reached out with my powers and rifled through their minds, confirming my fear and guess. My stomach twisted and knotted.

"They're all members of the Daylight Coalition," I said after a couple of minutes. "They were sent out of the Atlanta branch to hunt your pack down. I can see an image of the man who planned the attack, but there's no guarantee that he is the original source."

"Fucking bitch!" snarled one of the men. He pushed up on his knees, and both Barrett and Danaus were there almost simultaneously. The man was dead before he hit the ground again.

I frowned. While I appreciated their overprotectiveness, we did need more information and thus had to keep some of the men alive.

Reaching out with my powers again, I plunged into the minds of the remaining six men who sat before us. With a less-than-gentle push, they all collapsed unconscious, so they could no longer hear our plans. I had a hard enough task ahead of me by convincing Barrett that we needed to release these remaining men alive.

"What are we going to do with them?" I demanded, propping my fists up on my hips as I stared down at the gathering of men on the ground.

"You mean besides kill them?" Barrett said in a low rumbling voice.

"We can't kill any more of them. It's going to attract more attention."

"They attacked us!" shouted one of the werewolves, who stood on the periphery of the clearing. The entire pack agreed that none of these men be left alive.

"Mira is right," Danaus said. "If twenty members of the Daylight Coalition go into the woods, armed to go hunting werewolves, and none of them come back, then it's going to raise more questions. More members of the coalition are going to come looking for you here. Each full moon will grow more dangerous to your kind. They'll start setting traps. They'll send more hunters."

"Then what's your solution?" Barrett inquired, starting to sound calmer. Danaus had brought up a point that could not be easily argued away. While the alpha and the rest of his pack might want vengeance, it was also his responsibility to keep them safe.

"We alter their memories," I offered. "We make them forget about going into the woods or ever hunting shifters."

"And replace it with what other memory?" Nicolai asked as he approached our small gathering around the lump of unconscious men. "And what about the other men who have suddenly gone missing?"

I shoved one hand through my hair and stared down at the men, trying to imagine their evening as they prepared to take on a group of supposedly mythical creatures. They had to have been terrified in the event that they might be right. At the same time, I searched through their minds, sifting for any shred of information I might be able to use to my advantage.

"They stopped at a biker bar," I said slowly as the idea started to form. "Before coming into the area, they all stopped at a biker bar for a drink. The idea was to finalize their plan of attack and get a drink for courage. The only problem was that they got into an argument. Most of them drove off, swearing it was all nonsense and that they were going to leave the Daylight Coalition. The others continued to drink and then left the bar, where the two cars later crashed, which will explain their wounds."

Nicolai shook his head. "It all sounds a little thin, Mira."

"It works off a partial truth. They did stop in a bar before coming to Savannah and they did have a drink to work up their courage. I will just create the image of the fight, and those who died will be remembered as leaving the bar belligerent and determined to leave. It's the best we have to work with at the moment."

"Yes, but who is to say that these six won't return on another full moon with the intent of killing my people?" Barrett interjected. "I still do not support leaving them alive only to fight them again at a later date."

"I understand. I will insert a command deep in their subconscious. At different times during the next month, each one of them will become disillusioned with the coalition and leave it, claiming that it's all nonsense. You will not have to fight these six men again."

Out of the corner of my eye I saw James slowly approaching. He had pulled his pants back on, but both his feet and his chest remained bare. His usually neat brown hair was ruffled and askew, while his ever-present gold-rimmed glasses remained missing. "Can you get any more information about their workings of their group out of them?" James asked.

"I'll see what I can get," I said with a smile.

"That still leaves us with a bigger problem of how they found out about the Savannah pack, how they knew where to attack, and are they planning attacks on other shifter packs around the country," Barrett said, his frown growing deeper.

"We have to take care of one problem at a time," I said with a sigh.

Danaus laid a reassuring hand on my shoulder. "And right now, we have a very large mess to clean up. I say that we take care of the dead and set up the crash scene with this group. Tomorrow, Barrett and Mira can meet to plan how they are going to strike back at the coalition."

Looking over my shoulder, I raised one of my eyebrows

at Danaus. While his plan for the evening was sound, I couldn't even begin to guess at how to handle the Daylight Coalition, though I had to admit that it had been building for some time. Until recently we were content to let the coalition fumble in the dark while making fools of themselves in front of the rest of humanity, which didn't believe in vampires and werewolves. Now they were beginning to act, and if we weren't careful, would take the lead when the Great Awakening finally arrived. Then they would be the ones to offer answers when mankind discovered that nightwalkers were real, and I didn't want to worry about an overzealous, scared human trying to stake me on the street because of the Daylight Coalition.

"Agreed," Barrett reluctantly said, his hands falling limp at his sides in defeat. It was the best he could do tonight. For now, he had to be content that none of his people had been killed and that the attackers were going to be dealt with so they no longer endangered his people.

"Regardless of what we discussed earlier," Nicolai began, laying his right hand on Barrett's shoulder, "I will remain behind if you request it. If the pack needs me . . ."

"No," Barrett replied with a shake of his head. "I am honored by your offer, but you have a new calling that is taking you away from us. You must go. With Mira's help and the plans we set into motion, we will be safe. Just remember that you are always welcome in Savannah. This can always be your home."

"Thank you," Nicolai said, releasing Barrett.

I settled on the ground before the group of six men. We still had several hours before sunrise, but it would take a while to adjust the memories of all six and implant the kind of details needed so they believed what came to mind. In addition, the latent command for them to leave the coalition was even more difficult to accomplish. I was in for a very long night.

Danaus knelt beside me, one hand resting against my back. "Do you need me for anything?"

"No, you can't help me. Could you please assist the pack with disposing of bodies? This is going to take me a while."

He gave a little snort as he pushed to his feet again. "Leave me with the dirty work," he muttered.

Dirty work, my ass. Digging around in the twisted minds of these six men was not how I was hoping to spend my evening, and it certainly wasn't going to be enjoyable either.

Six

Barrett arrived at my town house a couple hours after sunset, giving me enough time to awaken for the night and join Danaus in the city. The lycanthrope alpha was dressed in slacks and a polo shirt, looking once again more like a respectable businessman than a blood-smeared killer.

The shifter had not come alone. Standing behind him with a half-burned cigarette hanging from the corner of his mouth was Daniel Crowley. The detective was one of the few humans within the city of Savannah who was aware of the existence of nightwalkers and lycanthropes, as his sister-in-law was a member of the Savannah pack.

Crowley had been kind enough to help me on a number of questionable police cases that raised more than a few eyebrows. He not only knew about our great secret, but helped to protect it. Yet, I was still more than a little surprised that Barrett had called him in for assistance. That is, unless some questions had been raised about our little two-car crash site, artfully created last night with ample alcohol and a handful of broken bodies who were raced to the hospital with hazy memories.

"It's good to see you Barrett," I said as I motioned for both men to come in. "Daniel, this is a surprise,"

"Drop the act, Mira," the detective said, flicking the butt of the smoldering cigarette into the yard before stepping into my house. He frowned at Danaus, who was hovering just in the doorway that led into the living room. Danaus simply crossed his arms over his chest and said nothing. "After the fiasco with the dead senator's daughter a few months back, I have to admit that I was hoping I wouldn't encounter you two for a little bit longer. I guess my luck ran out."

"And here I was hoping this was a friendly visit. We don't see each other often enough, Daniel. How are Anne and the girls?"

"Wife and kids are perfectly fine; oblivious to the night-mare that has soaked into Savannah."

I shook my head as I ushered the two gentlemen down the hall to the small library on the left. "You're always so chipper." I leaned against the front of the desk while Barrett and Daniel settled in the two leather chairs before my desk. Danaus simply changed doorways to the library entrance. However, he was looking a little more relaxed with his hands shoved in the pockets of his dark blue jeans. I had called down to the Dark Room already, informing the other bartender that Danaus would not be making an appearance tonight. We had darker matters that needed to be handled, and I wanted the hunter on hand for counsel.

"I'm assuming that Barrett has told you about what happened last night," I began, turning my attention fully to the detective when everyone was settled.

"I have the distinct impression that I am getting a cleaned-up version of what truly happened, but I also heard from my hysterical sister-in-law and brother," he admitted, folding his hands over his stomach. "A group of men appeared in the woods with guns and started hunting people down like animals. This will not be tolerated within my district. I won't have my sister-in-law terrified to go outside every full moon."

"Then you do have a full grasp of what is going on," I said with a sigh. "What are we going to do about it?"

"We need to know what they know," Barrett said.

"Last summer, your people were able to hack into their computer systems," I reminded him. A Daylight Coalition member had come into my territory hunting me, and managed to successfully get a picture of me on a digital camera. As a favor, the lycanthropes had hacked their system and deleted the information for me. "You got some information from them. Could you do it again?"

Barrett shook his head. "We monitored their system for a few months before they finally upgraded their security. We have not been able to get back in, and we've been reluctant to try for fear that they will be able to trace it back to us. Their secrets have been closed to us for months now."

"You never discovered anything on who their potential mole might be?" Danaus inquired from the entryway.

"I've spoken with many different clans during the past several hours," Barrett wearily admitted, rubbing the bridge of his nose with his thumb and index finger. "We weren't the only ones attacked. The packs in St. Louis, Austin, and Denver were all hit. We were the only ones that didn't sustain any casualties. However, members of the Daylight Coalition were killed in the various attacks. The bodies of the dead will never be found, but questions will be raised about the large number of men that have suddenly gone missing. The situation is quickly crumbling around us—the police are un-doubtedly going to start looking into the disappearances."

"The lycanthropes will be in the clear during the next few weeks," I ventured, "but when the moon is full again, people are going to trek out into the forests to see if there is a repeat of the same incident that led to the disappearance of so many hunters."

"Is there anything you can do?" Barrett asked. "Anything your people can do?"

"Like adjusting memories?" I said, arching an eyebrow at him. "There are just too many. By now, news reports have hit the air. There are search parties trekking through forests and dogs sniffing the area. It's too much. We would never be able to reach everyone."

"But you managed to cover up the naturi fiasco outside of London last summer, and the human sacrifices at Machu Picchu in the fall," Danaus interjected, causing me to frown at him. It's not that I didn't seriously want to help Barrett. Hell, it was in the best interest of everyone that this was covered up and quickly forgotten about. Unfortunately, if they used the same numbers at the other locations as in Savannah, nearly eighty men had gone missing.

"What about the coven?" Barrett asked.

I shook my head as I folded my arms across my chest. I hated to admit it, "It takes them months to make a decision. They wouldn't be able to help you. However, I can make some phone calls; reach out to the nightwalker keepers in St. Louis, Austin, and Denver. They can do some damage control as best as they possibly can if they haven't started already. We need to take care of the problem at hand and deal with the Daylight Coalition directly. We need to know what they know and take away their information."

"We need a mole in the coalition," Danaus said. He looked over and waved one hand at me. "Want to make a trip to Atlanta? I could get you past whatever security system they have on their headquarters, and you could slip by any humans wandering around the place."

"And what if their source happens to be another lycanthrope, nightwalker, or warlock?" I said. "My cloaking powers would be useless and we would be discovered. We would have no information and I'd be exposed to the group, assuming that they don't know about me already."

"You think one of our own kind has turned on us?" Barrett snarled.

"We already saw a werewolf and a witch traveling with a coalition member last summer," I said, remembering back to the encounter Tristan and I had in a dark London alley just a few months earlier. "It stands to reason that someone has stepped forward to provide them with inside information. Otherwise, they would have never been able to attack four different locations so quickly."

No one said anything for several seconds. Then Daniel spoke, breaking the silence that had grown over the room. "So what you're saying is that you need a human to infiltrate the coalition and report back." It was an uncomfortable truth, but I had a feeling that both Barrett and Daniel had already come to that conclusion before coming to my town house. They were here simply to make sure that we didn't have any other options before taking this very large and dangerous risk.

I drew in a deep breath as I let my hands slip down to the edge of the desk. Staring down at the floor, I wished there were some other option, but if they had someone spying on us, then we definitely needed someone on the inside, spying on their activities.

"A human would make the most sense," I reluctantly conceded. "I could make some minor memory adjustments so that if a nightwalker or warlock read the human's mind, plans for infiltration and betrayal would not be found. At least not right away. This would have to be a relatively short mission. Get in, get access to some basic information—such as the name of the betrayer—and then get out as quickly as possible."

"However," Danaus said, "the person we get to do this

needs to realize it is extremely dangerous. If they are discovered, it is inevitable that they will be killed for their efforts. I'll volunteer for this. I can block my thoughts better than most, and after years of hunting nightwalkers, I think I can be a pretty convincing recruit for the coalition."

I smiled weakly over at him but shook my head. "I'm sure we all appreciate your offer, but if they have a warlock or a witch on hand, it's likely they would be able to sense your powers. You'd be quickly labeled as one of the 'others' and they might not accept you. In addition, there is a chance they already know about me, and if that's true, then it's likely they know about you, considering our frequent association. It's a wonderful offer and idea, but I don't think it would work."

"Unfortunately, I have to agree with Mira," Barrett said. "It's known throughout all of Savannah that you're not exactly human. If it's common knowledge among our people, then we have to assume that the Daylight Coalition is aware of it as well. We need someone who is simply human."

"And that's where I step in," Daniel said with a heavy sigh. "I'm driving up to Atlanta tomorrow morning and renting an apartment. I've already told my wife that I'm going on an undercover assignment and that I'll be out of communication for a while. I've taken some time off work and—"

"Absolutely not!" I declared, springing to my feet. "This is nonsense. You are not to go anywhere near that damned headquarters."

"He's our best and only option at this point," Barrett patiently pointed out.

"Daniel also has a wife and kids to think about," I countered.

"He's also a trained cop. He knows how to handle himself in a dangerous situation," Danaus said, earning a dark look from me. I wasn't expecting him to immediately side with Barrett and the detective. "He knows the workings of the lycanthropes and enough about the nightwalkers to know what he was looking for once he got into the headquarters."

"It also doesn't hurt that I genuinely dislike nightwalkers," Daniel added, grinning up at me.

I shook my head at the human, ignoring his teasing. "I don't like this at all, Daniel. You're taking a big risk. I know we would all greatly appreciate it, but with just a little more time we might be able to find someone else." I jerked my head over to Danaus. "What about one of the hunters you trained for Themis? Are any of them loyal enough to you that they'd be willing to infiltrate the headquarters for us?"

"Maybe, but I wouldn't trust any of them to choose loyalty to me over loyalty to Ryan," he said. "I don't want to push my luck with the warlock now, considering we're not exactly on speaking terms. He may not want to risk the secret, but I don't want to imagine how he could potentially twist this situation to his advantage."

I sighed, pushing away from the desk, but there was no room for me to pace so I fell backward against the front of it, crossing my arms over my stomach. At that point I was willing to risk the life of a human I didn't know just so I didn't have to face the fact that Daniel really was our best choice. He had an understanding of both the nightwalker and lycanthrope peoples. He was grumpy and cranky enough to convincingly appear to be a disgruntled human looking to exterminate the two races. If they did a background check, they would discover that he was a detective, and that would make sense, explaining how he knew about the lycanthropes and the nightwalkers. It all added up perfectly.

"I hate this idea," I admitted.

"But . . ." Daniel prodded.

"It's the best one we've got, particularly since we're short on time," I continued. "We need to get this under control before the next full moon so the local packs can hunt and run without fear."

"Then I leave tomorrow," he declared. "Barrett and I have already developed a reliable way to communicate that should be untraceable. Otherwise, I'll be completely out of contact until I return to Savannah."

"And when you return, you will be under constant protection," I proclaimed.

"That's ridiculous!" he snapped.

I shoved away from the desk front and grabbed the arms of the chair where Daniel was seated, leaning in close enough for the tip of my nose to nearly touch the tip of his. "Is it? What if they find out you were a spy? What if they find out exactly who you are and where you live? Do you really know what you're in for? If the Daylight Coalition discovers that you're a spy, they will strike back at you. I can't allow that. Lycanthropes will watch over you during the day and a contingent of nightwalkers will guard you by night until the Daylight Coalition has been permanently eliminated."

"Mira—" Daniel began, leaning back as far as he could so he could see me more clearly.

I jerked my attention over to Barrett, who sat beside him. "Am I wrong?" I demanded.

The Savannah pack alpha shook his head slowly. "No, you're not." Then, addressing the detective, he said, "We recognize the great risk you'll be taking for both our peoples. You and your family will be watched over while you're gone and following your return."

"And what if I don't come back?" Daniel threw out.

I straightened, took a step back and, frowning, gazed down at Barrett. The lycanthrope spoke up before I could. "Your family will always be taken care of," he said to the detective. "They will be considered a part of the Savannah pack and given all the privileges thereof."

"I don't want my wife and kids to know about . . . about . . . all of this," Daniel growled, throwing out his arms to encompass both Barrett and myself. "They don't need to know about this world if it can be helped."

"They won't know," I quickly said. "Barrett and I have ways of helping. Your wife and daughters will have nothing to worry about, whether it be money or protection from the Daylight Coalition."

"That's all I care about," Daniel said with a slight huff as he pushed out of his chair, followed a moment later by Barrett. "If you don't mind, I need to get home to my wife and girls. I'd like to spend a little time with them before I leave town."

"I understand," I said, showing them to the front door.

"I will keep you updated on any information Daniel sends to me," Barrett offered as I pulled the door open.

I nodded, my hand tightly clenching the doorknob. This was my last chance. Daniel was going to walk out and disappear within the Daylight Coalition in Atlanta. I could stop it all right now with the right suggestion, a brilliant idea that would keep him from sinking even deeper into our world. But I said nothing as both men left. I shut the door then and stood facing it, staring out the glass front. I didn't see them chatting, making plans, as they descended the stone steps. There were only my own swirling thoughts.

Danaus came up behind me and placed a comforting hand on my shoulder, squeezing lightly. "He'll be fine," the hunter said, but I didn't hear his usual conviction embedded in those words. Neither of us thought Daniel was going to be fine. He was willingly walking into the devil's lair because we were desperate.

"I hate this," I said one last time, letting my eyes fall shut, because there was nothing else I could do that wouldn't risk his life more than we already were.

SEVEN

My only warning was a surge of power filling the air in the narrow hallway. Flaring out my own powers, I twisted around in time to see Jabari pop into existence behind Danaus. The dark-skinned nightwalker grabbed a fistful of the hunter's thick hair and jerked him backward, holding him close with his neck exposed.

"It's good to see you, my Mira," Jabari growled. I lurched forward, grabbing for Danaus, as I felt the rise of power, but came up with only empty air and fell flat on my stomach on the hardwood floor as Jabari and Danaus both disappeared. They were gone. Panic filled me as I searched my brain for a way to quickly reach the hunter when the two finally reappeared.

Backyard, Danaus whispered in my brain a second later, sending a wave of relief through my frame. I had expected the Ancient to drag Danaus back to Venice and the Main Hall of the coven. Unfortunately, that relief was short-lived, as I sensed a sharp stab of pain slice through Danaus.

Clenching my teeth in rage, I pushed off the floor and flew through the house, weaving through the rooms and past furniture until I busted out the back door in an explosion of wood and glass. Nothing would keep me from Danaus, particularly when he was in the hands of one of my enemies.

Jabari stood behind Danaus, toward the back of the yard under a large tree, almost hidden within the thick shadows. Yet, the moonlight still danced on the bloody tip of the blade that protruded from the hunter's stomach. Jabari kept one hand on his muscular shoulder, holding him in place.

"Release him," I ordered, my voice cracking like a whip.

"As you wish," he hissed, an evil grin spreading across his thin face. He pushed Danaus forward so that he slid off the sword the nightwalker had plunged through his body. As Danaus staggered forward a couple steps, Jabari raised the blade with the intention of chopping off his head.

Tapping into the energy swirling about me, I located the powers that emanated from Jabari and wrapped them around my fist. With every muscle clenched in my body, I held tight, forcing Jabari to stay his blade. The Ancient fought me, inching the blade slowly closer to Danaus, but the hunter stumbled from the nightwalker's immediate reach as he clutched his wounded stomach.

Nick had given me the ability to sense the powers of others and ordered that I learn to control my two previous puppet masters. During my last visit to Venice, I had used Jabari's powers to kill our mutual enemy, Macaire. Since then I'd been waiting for Jabari to strike back at me. He couldn't afford to leave alive someone who could control him. It went without saying that I felt a certain amount of justice and satisfaction in being able to control him after centuries of being his plaything. Unfortunately, I wasn't nearly as good at it as he was.

A low roar rumbled from his chest as he finally broke free of my hold, pushing my energy back at me with enough force that I hit the back of the house. He glared at me, his arms hanging limp at his sides in exhaustion, while I pushed away from the house and stepped into the yard. Danaus stood off to the side, a hand on his stomach to stanch the bleeding, a knife clenched in the other hand.

Lifting one hand, I summoned up a fireball. "It took you almost four months?" I mocked. "I really expected you sooner."

Jabari stood relaxed before me with his hands clasped behind his back. "Considering that you were successful in destroying Macaire in a rather exquisite display of power and violence, I thought I would give you a slight reprieve. A chance to revel in your brief triumph."

"Yes, I forgot to thank you for the minor assistance you provided." I edged a few feet deeper into the yard, closing the distance between us as I attempted to put myself between him and Danaus. "It certainly made Macaire's demise more entertaining."

"Minor assistance!" Jabari bellowed, his temper finally snapping. "You would never have survived a minute alone with Macaire if you had not learned a new trick."

I chuckled, moving my fingers through the flames. "And that's why you paused instead of killing me immediately. You had to know where I learned my new trick. Couldn't figure it out, could you?"

"I'm not concerned. You'll be screaming it to me before I finally kill you." He raised his hand and I felt pressure building until the fire that hovered above my right hand was extinguished. At the same time, the Ancient pulled a long, wicked-looking knife from his belt and threw it at Danaus. The hunter lunged out of the way, but the blade still embedded itself in his shoulder, rather than his chest.

"Danaus, get out of here," I snarled as I pushed back against the power filling my body.

"I'm not leaving you!"

"He's using you as a distraction! You're going to get me killed."

"I'm ending this," Danaus growled, pulling the knife out of his shoulder. Extending his right hand toward Jabari, I felt a wash of the hunter's powers brush past me as he summoned up his special gift. He was preparing to boil Jabari's blood, ending this stalemate once and for all.

A scream was ripped from my body as Jabari threw more of his powers into me. I tried to grab hold of them and push them out, but there was too much pouring in. The Ancient was too old, too strong. I was still learning how to use my new abilities. I wasn't ready to stand against this monster. I had succeeded against Macaire only because I had both Danaus and Jabari working with me.

"Trust me, hunter," Jabari said in a strained voice. "I'll destroy her before you can kill me."

Danaus immediately dropped his hand, allowing his powers to flow away with an errant breeze. My own screaming stopped a second later as Jabari eased back on some of the power flowing through me. Pain radiated through my entire body, and I knew that the Ancient no longer needed me alive.

"Come now, Jabari," I choked out. "Are you sure you're done using me? Don't you want to go after Our Liege next?"

A fresh surge of energy pushed through my limbs, sending my arms straight out into the air as if I were being crucified. It was one of Jabari's favorite positions, because it left me helpless.

"I have run out of uses for you, my desert blossom," he replied sweetly. "It's time you joined the others that I tried to make to replace you. Time for you to die, but first I'll allow you to watch the painful death of your companion."

With a grunt, I gathered my energy and pushed against Jabari's powers, forcing my arms to lower back to my sides.

I would not be controlled by this bastard any longer, and I wasn't about to allow him to lay a finger on Danaus.

As Jabari reached down and picked up the blade Danaus had pulled from his body, I grabbed his powers once again. Using the Ancient's psychokinesis, I threw him across the yard until he slammed into the brick wall that fenced in the tiny area. I stepped into the yard then, slowly approaching Danaus. The hunter was holding a dagger in one hand and looking more than a little confused. He wasn't sure how to strike when Jabari could so easily rip me apart with his own powers.

"Should we take a chance with Gaizka?" I asked, mentioning the bori that owned part of Danaus's soul.

"Combine our powers?" Danaus said, his lip curling with distaste. "We can't risk setting him free again."

"Then get out of here and let me handle Jabari."

"I'm not leaving you alone with him," Danaus declared, his fist tightening around the knife. "I can try boiling his blood again while you attack."

"You're a liability. A weakness that Jabari can exploit. Go now!"

"Too late," Jabari snarled. At the same time, a dagger flashed through the moonlight and embedded itself in Danaus's chest, sending the hunter sprawling backward under the force of the blow. I twisted around for a second to look down at Danaus to see if the blade had struck his heart, but I didn't have a chance to see anything before Jabari grabbed me with his powers and flung me back across the yard. I slammed into the side of the brick house, causing some of the bricks to crack and crumble under my weight before I slid down the wall to the ground again.

With a scream of frustration, I pushed to my feet and conjured up several balls of fire that circled me while two more hovered above my hands. I waited for Jabari to take a step out of the darkness so I would have a clear shot. I was going to burn the nightwalker to a cinder if it took every ounce of energy I had. My effort produced flickering lights that filled the dark backyard, making the shadows thrown by the large oak trees lunge and sway. Meanwhile, I did what I could to cloak the fight from the view of my neighbors, but with Jabari throwing me around, my concentration had been broken. If I survived the night, I would have to make sure there weren't any memories that needed to be adjusted. We had to protect the secret at all times, even if Jabari was the one picking a fight in the middle of a city.

As the Ancient stepped forward, he raised his hand toward me, sending a painful wave of energy out and into my body. A low whimper escaped me as I fought to keep the flames from going out. But one by one the balls of fire that circled around my frame flickered and then were extinguished with a puff of gray smoke. Clenching my fists and gritting my teeth, I strained, holding onto the ones that hovered above my raised hands. I would not allow Jabari to steal this from me. I was the Fire Starter, and I would fry his sorry ass if it was the last thing I did that night.

Gathering what strength I had left, I pushed back at him, trying to force his powers out of my body without losing my focus on the flames that I still had flickering in the darkness. Unfortunately, I was growing tired and Danaus was not moving on the ground. I was slowly losing this battle. If I didn't finish Jabari off now, I knew that he would have both Danaus and me.

"This is becoming monotonous, Mira." The new voice sent a chill up my spine. Apparently, Nick, my dear father was still watching over his daughter. Or at the very least, he still needed me alive, which was more than what Jabari expected or wanted.

"Now isn't exactly the best time, Nick," I bit out, trying

not to let my focus stray from Jabari. While my father's appearance didn't allow me to gain any ground with Jabari, I noticed that I hadn't lost any either, as the Ancient was now looking just over my left shoulder, where I could only guess Nick stood watching the fight.

"You should have finished with this creature already," Nick said, his voice growing closer. Out of the corner of my eye I could see a figure with wild red hair and pale skin standing beside me. He leaned one elbow on my left shoulder and seemed to scratch his head as if confused by something.

"Jabari is older and stronger than I am," I snarled, frustrated beyond all rational thought. Nick knew that I needed his help, but I couldn't force the words past my lips. I had no doubt that the old god was long accustomed to having his subjects groveling at his feet, but I wasn't going to do it. Jabari had stolen away a chunk of my self-respect and ego when he revealed that he could control me like a marionette. I wasn't going to give that last bit of me away to Nick, even if he was the lost god of chaos.

"And you're my daughter," he replied, as if that was the answer to everything.

Closing my eyes, I balled my hands into fists and turned my entire attention on Jabari, determined to push the last of his powers from my body. "Either help me or go away. I don't have time for you now."

"You're always so determined to do everything the hard way." Nick smacked me across the face, forcing my eyes to pop open again. Unfortunately, the distraction allowed Jabari to gain a fresh foothold. The last of the fireballs were extinguished, and I was left struggling to keep from being consumed by the nightwalker.

"He doesn't seem to be much in your favor, Mira," Jabari taunted. "It's a shame he didn't come along to help you sooner. He would have been great assistance with Macaire."

A low chuckle slithered from Nick and coiled around the Ancient like a fat python, wiping the smile from Jabari's face as he undoubtedly recognized the same laugh he had heard following Macaire's demise. Everyone had assumed it came from an invisible liege lord, but it was Nick's energy they had sensed. "Who says I wasn't there to enjoy my daughter's triumph over not only Macaire, but you and the hunter as well?"

Rage filled the Ancient's face as he threw more energy at me, causing me to stumble back a step. Pain wracked my thin frame as if my muscles and limbs were being pulled and twisted in all directions. I was growing tired, too tired to continue this fight.

"What must I do?" I finally demanded, knowing it was what Nick was waiting to hear. He first needed to know that I was completely at his disposal like an obedient dog.

"Well, since that hunter companion of yours is out of commission for the moment, it seems that you need a new source of energy," Nick said.

"I can only tap Danaus and Jabari," I groaned as my tug of war with Jabari continued. The power from Jabari seemed to have increased in the last minute, as he no doubt realized that Nick was offering me assistance, potentially tilting the fight to my favor. What the Ancient didn't realize was that there would be a price for this unrequested assistance.

"The world lies at your feet, Mira. A sweet plum waiting to be plucked."

"I'm not a fucking naturi. I can't use earth magic like they can."

Nick heaved a heavy sigh, as if I were too stubborn, choosing to ignore the fact that the few times I'd been able to sense earth magic was during special ceremonies at very specific locations. The middle of my backyard was not one of those very specific locations. "Then if you insist on clinging to these nightwalker ways you've chosen to adopt," he said, "I suggest using the blood magic floating in the air. Certainly that will suit your discerning palate."

"You're an ass," I growled, but followed his vague instructions. Closing my eyes again, I extended my focus to include the thick clustering of humans who lived within a block radius of my town house in downtown Savannah. The energy flowed around me, seeming to soothe and comfort sore muscles and frayed nerves. Sucking in a deep breath to steady myself, I felt the energy flow within me, steady and strong like a forest stream, washing away all remains of Jabari.

I opened my eyes and the world seemed to have taken on a fresh luster of glowing silvery light under the caress of the moon. The leaves of the oak tree shimmered and the grass glistened in the growing dew. Colors seemed crisper, and the sound of hundreds of heartbeats pounded away in my brain like a tribal drum.

When I stood among the ruins of Machu Picchu, I had felt the heartbeat of the earth and the great earth mother tremble and sigh as the naturi returned. I felt her rage and her fury. Now, as I stood tapped into the pulse of humanity, I felt a different force—one that at last seemed to be in harmony with my own soul. Nick might have hated my decision to become a nightwalker, but it was who I was, and the source of my power.

Grinning at Jabari, I gathered up the blood magic that flowed around me and shoved it at him, sending him flying back against the far wall of the yard. He gave a soft grunt under the impact but managed to remain standing.

"Who are you?" Jabari demanded, pushing away from the wall.

"The new owner of this lost soul," Nick said with a laugh, which came to a sudden, sickening halt. "Kill him."

"As you wish, Father," I said, a smile widening on my lips. I felt a small pang of remorse and hesitance as I pulled the energy into a little ball in the pit of my stomach. Centuries ago Jabari had been my savior, my mentor, my calm in the storm. He had been the one to teach me and guide me through the dark world nightwalkers inhabited. He had been the one to protect me and teach me how to protect myself. He had always been the guiding hand beside me when others were eager to tear me apart.

Yet, it was only after I teamed up with Danaus at the Themis compound that I discovered I had been little more than an experiment for Jabari. I was his precious puppet for centuries. He spent years controlling me and then wiping my memory so no one would ever know that he had a special weapon tucked up his sleeve should the need ever arise. He never cared for me.

I might have a new puppet master now, but Nick was determined to make me stronger. I only hoped that newfound strength would help me win my freedom in the end. At the moment, it was enough that I would be able to crush my old mentor.

With a laugh, I summoned up a blaze of flames that circled Nick and myself in the center of the yard. With a wave of my hand, the flames streaked across in a straight line and plowed into Jabari, enveloping him. He screamed once and then disappeared.

"No!" I shouted in frustration. I reached out with my powers, scanning the immediate area for the Ancient, but I could sense nothing. Extinguishing the flames, I sent out even more energy in all directions, scanning any part of the globe still bathed in darkness, but I could not sense him.

"Where is he?" I demanded, turning to face Nick.

The old god shrugged his thin shoulders at me, a lopsided smile quirking one corner of his mouth. "Don't know. I guess he got away."

"You guess? Aren't you supposed to be some all-powerful god? Where the hell is he?" I snapped. If I didn't succeed in killing Jabari now, the Ancient was going to come back at a more inopportune time and kill me when I didn't have a fighting chance.

Nick grabbed me by the neck and leaned in close so his nose was smashed against mine. "If I was some all-powerful god, then I wouldn't need you, would I? Jabari is gone, but we'll have another chance at him. Now go check your companion." He released me then, giving me a little shove toward where Danaus lay on the ground, clutching the knife that was sticking out of his chest.

Stumbling to my lover's side, I placed my hand gently on his chest where the knife was sticking out. "Danaus?"

"Took you long enough," he grumbled, wincing as he tried to move. "It's close to my heart."

"Then we need to remove it quickly so this little man can heal up," Nick said, coming to stand over Danaus. Before either of us could react, Nick grabbed the handle of the knife and jerked it from Danaus's body, causing us both to cry out in shock and pain. I quickly put both my hands over the wound and applied as much pressure as I thought would be safe in an effort to slow the bleeding while Danaus's body went about the task of closing the wound.

Nick knelt on the ground beside us and took a closer look at Danaus. The hunter frowned at the thin, red-haired creature with the lavender eyes but said nothing, which filled me with a deep sense of relief. I didn't need Nick requesting that I execute Danaus as well. I had found an edge in a fight with Jabari, but I seriously doubted that the old god of chaos had also given me an edge over himself as well.

"Silly bori scum," Nick snickered. "If—"

"Don't, Nick," I interrupted, drawing his eyes up to my face. "Please, don't." The old god paused as he stared at me. I could feel him rummaging through my thoughts and emotions like someone searching a library card catalog, and I let him. He needed to know how important Danaus was to me. He needed to know that I would not continue without Danaus at my side, no matter what threats he leveled in my direction. Where Jabari had always been my enemy, Danaus was my only ally in this world.

Nick gave a soft snort as he pushed back to his feet and stretched his arms above his head. "For now," he said, then disappeared from sight.

I drew in a deep steadying breath and slowly released it, pushing out all the tension that had filled my shoulders during the past several minutes. It was only when I looked down that I realized the hands pressed to Danaus's chest were trembling, while tears streaked down my cheeks. For a slender moment in time his life had hung by a thread, and he'd been granted a reprieve. For me, that reprieve was time, something I needed as much of as possible. I needed time to become stronger. I needed time to find a way to escape Nick's grasp while preserving Danaus's life.

With a low groan, he pushed off the ground into a sitting position. I slowly removed my hands from his chest, but remained close should he need me. The hunter looked a little pale from the blood loss, but his gaze was as sharp as ever and it was now locked on me.

"So that's your father," Danaus grumbled. "Not exactly what I was expecting."

I tried to shrug, but only one of my shoulders seemed willing to work. "He comes and goes as he pleases in whatever form suits him." I had been relieved to see that he had not chosen to appear as the man I thought of as my real father throughout childhood. Of course, then Nick would have only succeeded in distracting me, which could have cost me my life, thus working against his master plan.

"Your puppet master has changed from Jabari to him? Is that wise?"

"When it comes to your life, it is," I snapped, quickly shoving to my feet.

"What's that supposed to mean?"

"Jabari never saw any reason to keep you alive."

Grabbing my hand, Danaus slowly pulled himself to his feet as well. "And Nick?"

"Sees things differently," I murmured. If Nick was going to continue to use me and keep me cooperative, I needed Danaus at my side. Danaus kept the madness at bay.

Reaching up with a trembling, blood-covered hand, I brushed some of his hair from this face so I could clearly look into his piercing blue eyes. It was his eyes that I fell in love with first. I loved their sparkle and intensity as he searched to see me for what I truly was, beyond the reputation and horror stories. I loved those eyes and didn't want to imagine a night where I wouldn't be able to stare into them.

"I could have so easily lost you tonight to Jabari," I said in a rough voice. "He came so close. He knows that you're my weakness, and you have to run when I tell you to run."

"I will never leave your side, particularly in a battle," Danaus vowed, cupping my cheek with one hand. "And I am only your weakness if you let me become such. Let me be your strength instead."

Sighing, I turned my head in his hand and kissed the palm. "You cannot leave me. The world would never survive my wrath."

Danaus pulled me close, kissing me deeply. I tasted his fear and his love in that moment as we stood in the darkness under the oak trees. I closed my eyes and let myself drift along his emotions, slipping away from the pain Jabari had caused. Pulling slightly away, he whispered with a slight shudder, "I know."

The world was a dark place for me, and after more than six centuries tucked under my belt and more power than I could begin to understand flowing through my fingertips, my grasp on my sanity was beginning to slip. But then there was Danaus. The chaos that occupied my brain seemed to melt and fall away as background noise when he was near me.

After pressing a sweet kiss to my forehead, he stepped back so he could clearly look me in the eye. One hand was still pressed to his stomach where Jabari had initially injured him, while I refused to remove my hand from the wound near his heart. I was sure that both wounds had already closed, but I still could not bring myself to release him.

"Nick is right," Danaus began. "You have to kill Jabari."

"I know. He's too much of a threat, not only to us but to everything that we value. He has to be stopped. And if I know my old mentor, he hasn't traveled far and I will be seeing him soon."

"You have to destroy Nick as well."

"You make it sound so easy. Do you happen to know the best way to destroy a god?" I demanded, unable to halt the sarcasm that laced every word that tumbled from my lips.

"No, but it seems as if we have two choices: we contact an even stronger nightwalker, as in your liege lord, or we find another god that might help us."

"Neither seems to be the wisest of choices, and both could potentially offer more trouble than we've already got. What about Ryan?"

"I would rather not put the power of a god at the disposal of that warlock," Danaus grumbled. "Can you think of any other solutions to our current problems with Jabari and your father?" He slowly turned and started walking back toward the house. I slipped one arm through his, both in an effort to steady his gait and to remain close to his side.

"No," I whispered. It seemed that after all these centuries, I was finally in need of meeting Our Liege. I could only hope that someone with extensive years of experience and power would know exactly how one took on a god and maybe survived to tell the tale.

Eight

Rowe was struggled to keep pace with me. Shifting my wings to the right, I lowered onto a branch, catching the tree trunk with my left hand. The branch groaned and creaked beneath my feet but held. I turned back and watched for Rowe to catch up. Summoning up my powers, I lifted my free hand palm open toward him. A fresh gust of wind not only pushed him in my direction, but also lifted him higher in the air.

Part of our ability to fly came from magic and being able to control the wind. The iron collar around Rowe's neck was inhibiting his ability to control the winds, leaving me to assist him at regular intervals. He wasn't happy about the arrangement, his muttered curses carried to me on the same wind. I could only shake my head. There was no way I could trust him without the collar. I had little doubt he would slit my throat and then be on his way in a flash otherwise, though I wasn't sure he would run in the opposite direction of Aurora, even after encountering Greenwood's daughters.

"Why are you in such a hurry?" Rowe demanded when he drew close to me.

Pulling my wings in for a second, I bent my legs before pushing off the tree and launching myself into the air. The wind swarmed beneath me as I threw out my wings again so I lifted higher, well above the treetops. The full moon was fading slowly, but it still painted the earth below with a silvery light that glistened over small pockets of snow dotting the mountains we were headed through.

"We have someone that we need to talk to before we reach Cynnia." I stretched out my arms and spread my fingers, enjoying the feel of the cold wind threading between them. "You're not my only assignment."

"Who?"

I ignored his question as I scanned the ground for a break in the thick pine trees that covered the earth below us. "There."

I looked over to find Rowe glaring at me, and for a moment I wondered if he would argue with me.

To my surprise, he shifted his wings and started to slowly circle so he could land in the clearing I'd indicated. I followed behind him, giving him a wide enough berth so I would not land on his heels.

The ground was soft beneath my feet from the melting of the last of the snows and from the recent rain that had passed through the area. Folding in my wings, I knelt down and embedded my fingers deep into the earth. I cocked my head to one side and listened with all of my senses. There were other naturi in the area, a lot of them, from the animal clan. We were very close to where we needed to be. In fact, if we weren't being watched and followed already, we would be very soon.

"Where are we?" Rowe demanded. I looked up to find him standing with his hands on his hips, his wings now missing. It was still hours before sunrise, meaning we could still travel by air for quite a while before I called a halt. But he could already tell that I planned to travel on by foot. I didn't pull us out of the air unless it was absolutely necessary. For us, it was both safer and quicker to travel by air. On land, we became the target of too many other creatures I was hoping to avoid until we reached our next destination.

Standing, I brushed off my hands on the legs of my pants before hooking a lock of hair behind my ear. "We're within the Smoky Mountains. We need to head in that direction." I pointed off toward the southeast, deeper into the woods and away from any signs of human life. There were only dots of humanity within the mountains, and all spaced far enough apart that we could tread through the region without attracting their attention even if we weren't cloaked.

"We're walking?"

"For now."

"So we're headed into animal clan territory," he stated, frowning over at me as I started to walk past him.

I continued to walk, leaving him to catch up. "We're going to speak to Kane."

Rowe jogged up a couple steps and roughly grabbed my shoulder, pulling me to a halt. "You're going to get us killed. Since the door was opened, Kane and the rest of the clan have become extremely territorial. They aren't going to welcome you into what they see as their domain—they're going to attack."

"Let them attack. We will defeat them, and then we shall have a personal escort to their leader," I said, pulling free of his grasp so I could resume walking through the forest.

"Confident with your whip at your side that you can take any of our kind down?" Rowe sneered, but I could hear his footsteps on the soft earth. He was at least following me.

"I will not use the whip against the animal clan," I growled. "They are simply defending their domain from trespassers. Jasmine and the others were attempting to steal you from me and were aiming to kill me. They would not see reason. Kane's people will."

"They already surround us."

"I know."

"And yet you're determined to continue on this suicidal quest because Cynnia asked you."

"She asked me to fetch you. This small side trip should not be nearly as treacherous."

"Ha. Ha," Rowe mocked when he realized I was teasing him. I had little doubt that getting in to speak with Kane was going to be dangerous and tricky. Since the opening of the door and Mira's attack on Aurora, the animal clan had largely separated itself from the other clans and gathered in the Smoky Mountains, using the rocky and heavily covered terrain as a refuge from the world. And right now Rowe and I were walking right into the heart of their domain.

We continued on in silence, weaving among the trees as we slowly trekked uphill toward the heaviest concentration of naturi. I could hear animals moving closer to us with the click and scratch of claws moving over bark and through the dirt. A knot twisted tighter in my stomach, and I struggled to keep my heartbeat slow and even despite the fact the animal clan was tightening around us, closing in the circle until we would finally be faced with the voice of the squad that had been sent to defend their territory from interlopers.

As we entered a small clearing, a low growl rumbled around us. Standing with Rowe, I picked out several large wolves, a few bobcats, and a pair of mountain lions. Smaller luminous eyes stared out from the darkness, making me think we were surrounded by a large selection of foxes and raccoons as well. Reaching out with my powers, I discovered that most of the larger animals surrounding us were actually naturi that had shape-shifted into animal form, while the smaller creatures were truly animals that may have been summoned to help with the coming fight.

"We're here to speak with Kane," I announced, holding

my hands out to my sides, open and empty. I wasn't going to start a fight, and I preferred to avoid one at all costs considering that we were severely outnumbered.

Above my head in front of me, a large owl hooted a couple times before it spread its beautiful white wings and glided down. The white feathers melted away to reveal a man with darkly tanned skin and a shaggy mane of blond hair. It looked as if he would have been more natural in the form of a lion, rather than the unassuming and easily overlooked form of an owl. The moonlight gilded his naked body as he took a couple steps toward us. The animals that surrounded us also took a couple steps closer, shrinking the circle. Rowe shifted his stance, bumping his shoulder against mine as I forced myself to remain as still as possible. They were trying to goad us into acting.

Under most circumstances I would have trusted Rowe not to strike, but to calmly brush off their attempts to strike fear in him. However, the iron collar was inhibiting his powers, leaving him weaker and potentially at their mercy. I had put him at a distinct disadvantage; something I'm sure he was unaccustomed to. If he felt too threatened, I had no doubt he would strike first in an effort to save himself.

Steady, I whispered to him in his mind while trying to send comforting waves of calm across his brain.

They're going to shred us before you get the chance to plead your case, Rowe snapped. Yet, at the same time, I felt him draw in a slow, deep breath.

"We have come to speak with clan leader Kane," I announced in a strong voice. "Will you let us pass?"

"I know you, Nyx, and the power of the whip that dangles from your hip," said the gold-haired man. "Great weapon of the queen."

"And I know you too, Locke," I said with a slight bow of my head. "The protector of Kane and second-in-command of the great force that is the animal clan. But you have me wrong. I'm sure you already know that I am not Aurora's weapon any longer. I've been branded a traitor and now willingly follow someone who seeks a life of peace on the Earth."

"And it seems that you keep good company," Locke taunted. "A traitor traveling with yet another branded as a traitor. Starting a club?"

"Yes, I am," I admitted, causing his eyebrows to jump unexpectedly before his head fell back with laughter. I didn't crack a smile because I wasn't joking. It wasn't in my nature.

"And you wish to kneel before Kane and ask that his people protect you and this traitor when Aurora comes for your heads at long last?" Locke said when he saw I wasn't joining him in the great joke that he thought I'd made.

"Rowe is no traitor," I bit out, taking a step closer to Locke so my body was between the two naturi. "He sacrificed everything that he ever was, sacrificed his place among our people so you could now stand on the fresh earth and be wrapped in the warm powers of the Great Mother. Rowe is no traitor," I repeated. "He's your savior and should be afforded the respect he has earned."

Locke stared at Rowe over my shoulder, his full lips pressed into a firm, unyielding line as he weighed my words. To my surprise, he gave a soft grunt and nodded to Rowe, giving what little approval that I could extract from the naturi. I had to win them all over one by one, pulling them away from Aurora's twisted way of thinking. In the heat of battle, many had clung to her skirts, but now that the powers of the earth once again flowed through our starved bodies, our people were starting to think differently. They were a little more open. Cynnia may have set a series of tasks ahead of me, but since looking on Rowe for the first time since Aurora's betrayal, it had become my own personal quest to win him back some of his former honor and glory, as he deserved.

"You make a valid point, Dark One," Locke said, putting my teeth on edge as he used a nickname I seemed to be cursed with for the rest of my life. "I am willing to allow Rowe to pass so long as he immediately leaves our domain and does not return."

"And me?" I asked, cocking my head to the side.

"You have crimes to atone for," Locke said, a vicious grin spreading across his handsome face. "You have slaughtered a number of the animal clan over the long centuries. You have attacked and struck fear in the hearts of our people when you swore to be our protector."

"While I know that you will not believe me, I took no joy in those acts, but was simply following the orders of my queen, as I swore to do. That reason does not absolve me of my crimes, but it does at least explain my actions."

"Convenient answer. Blame it on the queen and wash your hands of the matter," Locke sneered.

"The blood of our people will always stain my hands, and I will pay for those crimes, but now is not the time. Would not Kane like the chance to strike out at the true source of your anger and isolation? Would not your great leader like to take a shot at Aurora?"

"How do you know that we don't already plan against her rule?"

Rowe snorted, stepping forward. "While the animal clan has always been the strongest fighters among our people, you will not get as close to her as you may hope. You need help, and Kane knows it. Otherwise, you wouldn't be hiding out in the mountains, but marching across these great lands to take the battle to her."

"You were told to leave," Locke snapped as he balled his fists at his sides.

Rowe shrugged. "Nyx comes before you, offering you a chance to strike at the one that used you as her dogs of war. Wouldn't it be in the best interest of your people to allow Kane to hear her plan? Besides, wouldn't your leader take more joy in watching her slaughter than just receiving her head after the battle is completed?"

Your assistance is less than heartening, I murmured in Rowe's brain while keeping my face perfectly blank as Locke considered my fate.

If you die now, I may never be free of this damned collar. Furthermore, I would prefer it if Locke and the others don't discover that you have me on a short leash.

After more than a minute one corner of Locke's mouth finally quirked in a half smile. "You make an interesting case. Things have been quiet recently. I'm sure that Kane would appreciate a little entertainment, particularly if it means killing not only a sister of the queen but also the Dark One."

"Thank you," I murmured through clenched teeth. I knew we would not be welcomed with open arms, but I had not expected this level of hostility. Too much time living quietly with Cynnia had made me forget how much I was hated by the rest of our people. Many wanted to see my head on the end of a pike just as badly as they wanted to see either Cynnia or Aurora dead. If I did not believe so completely in Cynnia's vision, then I would have said it was time for another family to rule over the naturi, while Aurora, Cynnia, and I faded from existence and memory.

"You will be led to Kane, where he will decide whether you are to be given an audience or just killed," Locke said.

"And my reprieve?" Rowe inquired.

A fresh smile appeared on Locke's face as he turned his gaze on the one-eyed naturi. "Revoked since you've decided to remain at her side. Your life is now back in Kane's hands." He then returned to the form of an owl and took to the skies again, flying high overhead for a moment before wheeling around toward the east.

You are becoming more trouble than you are worth, Rowe grumbled silently at me as we started walking. The other naturi in animal form drew closer to us, ushering us forward. Our escort continued to snarl and growl, keeping us moving at a brisk pace for fear of someone taking a nip at our legs should we slow too much.

You were facing death at the hands of Aurora when I grabbed you, I replied as I stepped over a log. I jerked my right leg forward as I brought it over the next log, narrowly escaping a fox snapping at my ankle. Its sharp little teeth scrapped along the sides of my leather boot. *Now you're complaining that you face death at Kane's hands. Is there really any difference? Death is death, is it not?*

I find it more likely that I will escape death at Kane's hands but be stuck with this damned collar because you will be killed before I acquire the key.

I'm beginning to understand why the Fire Starter is so determined to kill you.

To my surprise, Rowe looked over his shoulder and flashed a wicked smile. For the first time, I wondered if the naturi was actually teasing me. The Rowe that I grew up with had always been a ruthless killer and brilliant fighter, but in the last months that I'd known him on Earth, I also discovered he had a somewhat unique sense of humor. Was this all a game to him? Did he have some secret that he was hiding away? A chill swept down my spine as I wondered who I should fear more: Kane or Rowe.

Nine

R owe and I trudged nearly five miles through the woods in silence. Only the sounds of the occasional broken branch and the growling of our guards echoed through the dense forest. At the end of our march the dancing light of a fire peeked between the trees, beckoning us forward. My stomach twisted into knots, but I maintained my outward calm. I would not be deterred from my mission. I would not disappoint Cynnia. I would bring back Rowe and win over the animal clan. It was our only hope. Besides, my dear younger sister still had the more difficult task ahead of her.

As we came into the clearing, I paused and blinked a couple times as my eyes adjusted to the bright light of the torches spread about the area. A coyote snarled once and clamped briefly onto my left calf to goad me forward. Without making a sound, I pulled my leg free and continued with Rowe into the center of the clearing.

At the far end, Kane sat on his throne hewn from a giant boulder. The leader of the animal clan was a large man with a massive barrel chest and legs like tree trunks. His body was wrapped in a large bearskin, while his large bare feet were smeared with mud.

The leader of the animal clan always had to be the strongest. He was frequently challenged by other members of the clan in battle. Unfortunately, until Kane, the leaders of the animal clan had not been known as the best strategists in battle. The clan was known as great melee fighters and was usually the first sent into battle against any enemy. It wasn't until Kane rose to power that the group realized exactly how poorly they had been treated by the royal family.

Unfortunately for me, the animal clan had been the most vocal against Aurora's decisions, forcing me to strike against them to protect her sovereignty. They had the most reason to hate me, and I had a dark feeling that I was going to feel the brunt of that hatred tonight.

Our guards had backed away from us, leaving Rowe and myself standing alone in the circle. I glanced around to find many of the naturi changing back into their natural form, while others settled on the ground, still in animal form. Their expressions varied from distaste to outright hostility. Only Kane looked somewhat amused by our presence. Locke took up his position on the right side of Kane's throne with a smug look on his face. Without a doubt, their minds were already made up against me. I had to find a way to not only get out of this alive, but to convince them to take a big risk on a young naturi with a dream.

"I am honored that you have granted me this audience, lord of the animal clan," I said with a bow of my head. I again held my hands out to my sides with my palms open to show that I held no weapons and offered up no threat. At my side, Rowe said nothing as he folded his arms over his chest and glared at Kane.

The leader of the animal clan gave a deep chuckle. "We have been short on entertainment recently, and right now, only Aurora's head carries more value to me than your own."

Suppressing a sigh of frustration, I pushed forward.

"Locke granted Rowe safe passage through your domain so long as he doesn't return. Will you honor that offer?"

"Locke told me of the argument you made for him. Wise words," he admitted, scratching the scraggly brown beard that stretched from his chin. "I will grant him safe passage so long as he never returns to our lands."

All eyes then turned to Rowe, who gave a nonchalant shrug of his slim shoulders. "In truth, I have been short on entertainment as well. I'd like to stick around and see the show, if you don't mind."

Kane gave a deep laugh, slapping one hand on the arm of his stone chair. "Done!" he declared. "I might have been young at the time, but I recall days of you two training together. I would have thought there would be more solidarity between you."

"Things change," Rowe said in a low voice that wiped the smile from Kane's face.

Yes, things had changed for all of us, and none of it seemed for the better. The naturi had been caged, Aurora turned on many of her own people, Rowe branded a traitor, and I'd become a winged creature of death for those I was sworn to protect. The naturi were dangling on the cusp of extinction. Things had indeed changed.

My temporary captive ambled slowly away from where I stood in the center of the clearing and over to a large tree. He leaned against it, crossing one foot in front of the other as he prepared to watch me try to dance my way out of my own death. A part of me wished that Cynnia had not sent me alone into Kane's territory, but I knew that if I had come with more at my back, Kane would have instantly seen it as a threat. I was an emissary, a diplomat. Not a threat.

"Will you give me leave to deliver a final message from

Cynnia before you pursue my death?" I inquired in a calm, even voice, as if I weren't talking about my own bloody end.

Kane arched one thick brow at me and seemed to cock his head to one side in surprise. "The young one lives? Between her run-in with the Fire Starter, the death sentence from Aurora, and her association with you, I assumed that she was long dead."

"No, Cynnia lives, though she is in hiding from Aurora's spies. She has sent me to you with a message. Will you hear it?"

Kane gave a wave of his meaty hand, beckoning me to continue. I once again bowed my head to him, attempting to show a degree of subservience. My people might have hated me from my birth, but until this moment I had been forced to bow to no one but Aurora.

I closed my eyes and drew in a deep breath. My life not only lay in Kane's hands, but also in Rowe's—I needed his cooperation now more than ever before. Unfortunately, it had been many years since we'd last seen eye-to-eye, and Cynnia seemed to forever separate us.

"Cynnia hales your break from Aurora and the independent domain that you have established within these mountains. She wishes you many years of strength and glory—"

"Enough of your pretty words," Kane interrupted as he slouched in his chair. "Surely she has something more important to say, something that just may save your hide."

"Fair enough," I said, my voice taking on an icy chill that had struck fear in the weaker. I straightened my shoulders and crossed my arms over my chest. "Cynnia plans to strike against Aurora. The queen has gone mad. As you well know, she saw treachery and betrayal around every corner. She accused her own sisters of being traitors when we remained her loyal subjects. Aurora plans to continue her campaign against the humans despite the fact that our numbers have greatly diminished. In the end, Aurora will bring about the total extinction of our people. She must be stopped."

"I'm assuming that Cynnia will place herself on the throne should Aurora be defeated," Kane sneered.

"Cynnia has a different vision for our people," I quickly countered, evading his question. "She believes that we can pursue a quiet coexistence with mankind that will allow our numbers to once again flourish. She wishes a peaceful existence that will bring our people back from the brink of extinction. There will no longer be war with the nightwalkers, the lycanthropes, or the humans."

"You paint a pretty picture."

"One that no longer uses the animal clan as its whipping boy." Rowe's interjection surprised me.

Kane glared at Rowe before finally returning his attention to me. "As I'm sure you expected, this plan is appealing after years of being the main force behind Aurora's army. We would like nothing more than to return to the forests and live in peace. However, I'm no fool. What is the catch to this beautiful dream?"

"Cynnia needs to build an army to defeat Aurora and those who have sided with her," I said. "She humbly asks that the animal clan lend their assistance."

"So we are to become the dog soldiers for Cynnia instead of Aurora?" Kane roared. "How is this going to be any different than what Aurora has offered us? We are still under the heel of the ruler and we are *done* with that role!"

"When we go into battle, the animal clan will not be alone," I quickly argued. "They will be joined by members of the wind clan, most of whom have flocked to Cynnia's banner, as well as some members of the earth clan. We will all be equals on the field of battle, taking back our lives from Aurora and securing our future."

Kane shook his head. "Your numbers will still be fewer than those that follow Aurora. You will be slaughtered."

"We will not go down as easily as you expect. Cynnia would like you to lead one battalion of naturi, and should I survive tonight's encounter, I will lead a second. Our commander on the field will be Aurora's former commander, Rowe," I announced, not daring to look over at the one-eyed naturi. I couldn't imagine how he was taking the news that Cynnia expected him to lead the army against his former wife-queen. For now, he remained silent, and I was grateful. "Rowe is unmatched in his fighting skills and a superior strategist when it comes to the battlefield. His leadership along with your own will give us an edge."

"Interesting," Kane admitted. "But I still do not think it will be enough to take out Aurora. Like I said earlier, you paint a pretty picture."

"You need further enticement?" A smile crossed my lips for a second and I chanced a glance over at Rowe, who was frowning at me. I could feel the limb I was walking out on about to break beneath my feet. "As we speak, Cynnia is acquiring the assistance of the Fire Starter and any nightwalkers at her disposal. Mira has come the closest among any of us to killing Aurora. She will give us the edge we need to win."

"Mira has agreed to follow my command?" Rowe smirked, but at least he wasn't falling over laughing. I knew that it sounded ludicrous, and I honestly didn't expect the Fire Starter to obey a single command issued by Rowe. But I did think she would lead the nightwalkers in an attack against Aurora. That would help regardless of what Rowe believed.

"Mira will lead the nightwalkers in battle. She will not strike against our fighters. There will be a truce."

I will believe it when I hear the words spoken from Mira's very lips. I was grateful for the silent communication from Rowe. For now, he wasn't willing to sabotage my efforts to win Kane's assistance.

The animal clan leader sat forward in his chair, leaning his elbows on his knees as he threaded his fingers together before him. "Rowe, the Fire Starter with her nightwalker army, and the animal clan," he slowly listed. "That is an impressive gathering. Word recently reached me that the nightwalker defeated a bori. She may actually give a valuable edge to this battle. The animal clan is . . . interested."

"What more can I say that would win you and the animal clan to our cause?"

Kane smiled broadly at me. "A place of true leadership in the new regime should Cynnia become the next queen of the naturi."

I knew it would come to this, but I didn't hesitate: Cynnia understood the duties that came with being the queen. "She has given me permission to say only this. If both you and Locke are amiable to the idea, she would offer Locke the position of consort should she ascend to the throne."

"Locke? Not me?" Kane demanded, sounding surprised.

"She would prefer that you remain close to your people in the animal clan, while Locke would learn to take on the role of leader of the entire clan armies. You would undoubtedly still hold considerable influence over Locke for many years." I paused and shrugged my shoulders, loosening my arms from their tight fold over my stomach. "And to be completely honest, Cynnia is attracted to both Locke's appearance and personality. She feels that not only would the animal clan be pleased by the arrangement, but that she and Locke may actually have a happy life together."

Kane twisted in his chair and gazed over his shoulder at his second in command, who seemed more than a little stunned by this development. He had just been offered the second highest position in the naturi royal family. I knew that Locke and Cynnia were familiar with each other, but I didn't think Locke was aware that my sister actually had some feelings for him.

"Would you accept such a duty?" Kane asked of Locke.

"I would if it is your wish," Locke said, staring down at his lord. It was a dangerous position. He would be taking a higher position over Kane, and yet would still feel compelled to answer to him for the first few years of the new regime as he became acclimated to his new position as consort.

Kane nodded. "It would be nice to see a member of the animal clan back in the royal family. Of course, there is a catch, isn't there?" Kane narrowed his gaze on me. "Should Cynnia die in battle and Aurora is defeated, won't you be next in line for the throne?"

"No, I hold to my father's promise—I will never be eligible for the throne. If both Cynnia and Aurora are killed in battle, our people will need a new leader, not me or Rowe. If Cynnia requires it, Rowe and I will remain on in an advisory capacity, but our days as members of the royal court are over."

Kane sat back in his chair, stroking his beard as he turned over my proposition in his mind. While I was bringing danger to his people, I was also offering them prestige and a new position of power within the naturi hierarchy. Was he willing to take a chance on a new life for his people, or would he prefer that they spend their last days hiding in the mountains away from Aurora?

"Let me just add a bit to chew on that Nyx left out," Rowe said unexpectedly, strolling out into the clearing. "Assume that you don't join Cynnia. Eventually, Aurora will come looking for her darling sisters, and without the help of the animal clan, she will wipe them out. And when our queen is done, she will turn her attention to the rest of the groups who have broken from her. At that point you will either be forced to bow before her, just before she removes your head for treason, or you will be forced to fight her without the assistance of Cynnia's army. One way or another, you will fight Aurora." With his piece said, the dark-haired naturi sauntered back over to the tree he had been leaning against as if he hadn't spoken at all.

After a couple minutes of tense silence, Kane finally looked up at me with a dark grin crossing his face. "My people will join Cynnia in her fight against Aurora. We would like a new place within this world we have returned to. We would like to finally live a life of peace. But nothing is given without it first being earned among our people."

"And how do I earn your assistance?" I dreaded the response.

"Beat me in a fair fight and the animal clan will join your growing armies."

My stomach dropped and my heartbeat suddenly began to race as I looked over Kane once again. He was a behemoth, and it had been too many years since I had taken on someone like him. The animal clan members I had been forced to pursue recently were lean, sinewy creatures, with speed but not strength. Kane could crush me without straining himself. But I had to agree.

Ten

Hardening my jaw, I reached down and unsnapped the loop that held the whip at my side. I walked across the clearing and placed it in Rowe's hand, who looked at it with confusion filling his one good eye. But he said nothing as he tightened his grip around the horrible weapon. Kane had said a fair fight, and that wasn't possible with the whip.

As I returned to the center of the clearing, Kane pushed out of his seat, letting the bearskin slide off of his back to reveal acres of tanned skin and hard, bulging muscles. I could only hope that all those muscles would steal his speed from him, giving me a slight edge in that category. Otherwise I might finally be outmatched. Until this moment only Rowe had ever been able to beat me in a fair fight. But then, that had always been simple sparring as we honed our skills.

"What are the rules of engagement?"

"Rules?" Kane repeated with a chuckle. "There are no rules. We fight until one of the combatants yields or dies."

"May I use a weapon?"

"I'll permit you two daggers." Kane waved his hand. "No swords. No crossbows or any other little tricks that you might have. No magic."

I removed the two swords hanging from my body and

tossed them to the side of the clearing, out of my reach. "Agreed."

That one word was all he was waiting for. With a great roar that seemed to make the air tremble, Kane launched himself at me. Within two steps he had gone from running on two legs to four as he shifted into an enormous black bear. I gasped before diving to my left. I hit the ground and rolled to my feet with a knife in each hand. Clearly, Kane could shapeshift into any creature he wanted, and in the blink of an eye.

The bear growled as it turned and charged again. I scampered out of the way as one massive paw swiped at where I'd been kneeling. Black claws slashed through the air, the tips catching on the edge of my shirt before I could escape. I pulled free and ran to the far end of the clearing. Around me, members of the naturi clan were hooting and cheering their leader on, calling for my head. This wasn't a simple fight where I would yield if I was trapped and couldn't escape. I either beat Kane or I was going to be killed. I needed to end this as quickly as possible.

Unfortunately, Kane didn't give me time to think or formulate a plan. As soon as I got my feet planted with my weapons at the ready to take on the massive black bear, the black bear melted away to reveal a sleek mountain lion with some of the sharpest fangs I had ever seen.

Lightning might make him a little wary of you. Rowe's suggestion surprised me. But then again, he would never be free if I were killed.

I streaked to the other end of the clearing as Kane ran at me. He missed me again, sending up a spray of dirt as his back paws dug into the earth and quickly changed directions. In the form of the cat, Kane had the advantage of both speed and strength. He lunged at me with both paws extended, claws ready to rip my face open. I knelt down on one knee and dug my feet into the earth as much as possible to steady my position. With my right hand, I blocked one paw, while I dodged the second so it only scraped along my shoulder. At the same time, I buried my blade into his side, sending a feral scream through the night. Kane snapped at me with his strong jaws, narrowly missing my throat. His hot breath danced across my cheek and a quick look in his eyes revealed that there would be no last minute act of mercy. He was going to kill and eat me.

Pulling my blade free, I pushed the giant cat off me with a grunt, but the growing pain in my shoulder weakened me. Kane's paws slid a little in the dirt, but he was already catching himself for another pass. I remained kneeling on the ground, waiting for the attack. As he launched himself into the air, I pushed upward, jumping as high as I could while forcing my wings to explode from my back. The pain was excruciating. Between the wound in my shoulder and the force needed to expand my wings so quickly, my body screamed. In fact, the pain nearly kept me from summoning up the wind I needed to lift me a few off the ground and out of Kane's reach.

I circled the clearing, blood dripping down on the field of battle as it rolled from my shoulder. For now, I was buying myself time, which was exactly what Kane didn't want. Overhead, the clouds began to churn and the sky grew dark as the moon was blotted out. A storm was brewing, though the first rolls of thunder had yet to be heard. It took time, energy, and concentration to summon up a lightning storm, something I couldn't do while I was running from Kane every second.

Unwilling to give me even a moment's rest, Kane quickly switched forms again, stunning me. I had assumed that the animal clan leader would go for something large like a condor or some other taloned raptor. But Kane was trickier than I gave him credit for, flashing into a griffin. With the body of a lion and the wings of an eagle, the creature was able to easily launch itself into the air after me. My only advantage was that I was the one controlling the wind. I swooped away from the beast as its talons streaked two long gashes along my legs.

Reaching upward, I gave a large sweep of my wings, pulling me straight up into the air. At the same time, a large beak clamped onto my right ankle, snapping bone. I bit back the scream as I focused my attention on the storm. I was taking a big risk, but I didn't have much chance of winning this battle otherwise. As I exhaled, a lightning bolt sizzled down from the clouds. It washed straight over me and down through Kane before it finally pummeled the ground. Kane immediately released me and fell.

Spreading my wings, I glided slowly down to the earth, where I landed on my left foot while keeping my right foot up in the air. My wings were spread, holding me balanced, as I couldn't put any weight on my broken ankle until it mended.

Kane lay in his natural form in the center of the clearing. Smoke rose from his large naked body as he slowly shifted. I had no doubt he was merely stunned, but a part of me was hoping that this was enough to win him over to Cynnia's camp.

"Do you yield?" I demanded, trying to keep my voice even and free of the pain pulsing through my frame.

"Kane will never yield to the Dark One!" shouted one of the members of the animal clan that surrounded me. The cry was repeated by several others, until two coyotes finally ran onto the field of battle. Knife in hand, I managed to slash one in the chest as he lunged at me, but I couldn't reach the other as it jumped onto my back and bit deeply into the bones of my wing. My scream echoed through the forest as pain filled my frame. The wings of a wind clan member were some of our most sensitive parts. Broken wings were nearly impossible to mend and could not be fully retracted until they were.

Blinded by pain, I slashed again at the coyote before me, gutting him up the center. I tried to reach the other one on my back but stepped down on my right foot and crumpled to the ground with the coyote on top of me. I was preparing to shove my knife into the stomach of this creature as he opened his jaws and dove at my throat. But before either of us could act, a large black boot caught the coyote on my back under the chin, sending it flying across the clearing. I looked up to see Rowe standing over me, my whip tightly clenched in his right fist and one of my swords in his left.

"I thought this was going to be a fair fight," he shouted. "Do you doubt the abilities of your leader so much that you must break the rules of engagement?"

"Kane?" Locke asked.

Kane was pushing into a sitting position as I saw his second in command step around the throne. Kane had started this fight, and right now he was the only one that had the power to keep things from turning ugly. I had a dark suspicion that Locke would let the animal clan tear us apart regardless of any earlier agreements. The scent of blood was in the air, and they were ready for the attack.

"Just a scratch," Kane growled. I looked up at Rowe and nodded, signaling that I was still strong enough to continue. Not that I had much choice. I had to beat the leader of the animal clan or die.

We both pushed to our feet. For now, Kane remained in his natural form, eyeing me warily, while I still balanced on my left foot. The bone in my right ankle felt as if it was mostly healed, but it was still too weak to put any pressure on. At the same time, my right wing hung limp at my side.

The hollow bone had not been broken, as I initially feared, but the wound was deep and throbbing painfully. It was going to be a while before I had the ability to completely retract my wings again.

"You wish to continue?" Kane asked, one side of his mouth quirking in a smile. At the moment I was the only one who was bleeding, since the single knife wound I inflicted had already healed on him.

I tightened my grip on the knife. "I will not fail Cynnia. She wishes to have the animal clan at her side, and that is what I will deliver no matter what it takes."

"That's what I thought," he grunted. "The Dark One did not become a proficient fighter because she backed down when the odds were against her."

Still grinning at me, Kane transformed into the shape of a mountain lion again, knowing he had the advantage of both dexterity and speed in that form. He stalked me, circling to my left, forcing me hobble away in an effort to keep a comfortable distance between us. The skies overhead gave a foreboding rumble and lightning flashed as it streaked between clouds. Kane snarled, but hunched away from me as if expecting yet another strike. He was at least wary of me, but that only meant there was a fresh urgency now to take me out before I had a chance to call down more lightning.

A low growl rumbled from Kane as he shifted his weight to his back paws. I knew what he was going to do and I was prepared for it. The mountain lion leapt at me, claws extended as he aimed for my upper body and face. At the exact moment, I fell flat on my back. Pain screamed through my system as I smashed my wounded wing into the ground with my body weight, but I pushed through it as the mountain lion overshot me by nearly a foot.

As his paws hit the earth on either side of my head, I plunged one knife deep into his stomach and pulled upward, opening up a long wound. I pressed the other knife against his throat with enough force that blood splattered down on my forehead. If he moved the wrong way, I had the ability to gut him and slice his throat all at the same time. He was trapped.

"Do you yield?" I asked in a deceptively soft voice. The clearing had becoming eerily silent as I held the life of their leader in my blood-covered hands. Kane growled softly at me but didn't move a muscle. "How are you going to call this one, Locke?" I called out. "If he moves the wrong way, I will kill him before he can get a tooth or claw on me."

Locke paused for only a moment. I didn't know if he was either communicating telepathically with Kane or honestly weighing whether he wanted his leader to live. A few quick slashes from me and he could not only claim leadership of the animal clan, but also consort to the next queen. Luckily, Locke didn't strike me as the power-hungry type. Otherwise, I don't think Cynnia would have offered herself up so quickly to what could become a very dangerous situation.

"The fight is over," Locke declared in a loud voice. "You have defeated Kane."

With amazing slowness I withdrew both weapons from where they were pressed within the mountain lion. However, they were still tightly clenched in my hands and held at the ready as Kane looked down at me with his narrowed gold eyes. He was not happy about the outcome, and I was waiting to see if he would abide by Locke's declaration. He paused over me for a tense moment, then limped into the center of the clearing.

I painfully pushed up into a seated position in time to watch Kane shift back into his natural form. There was a long cut along his stomach, while a second wound stretched across his neck, leaving his front covered in blood. There was a low murmur of conversation among the other naturi surrounding me, and none of what I could catch sounded good. Kane was the one that had demanded this fight. He had promised that his people would help Cynnia if I were to win. Now they seemed extremely reluctant to accept that I had beaten their leader.

A frown pulled at the corner of my lips as I tried to weigh my next plan of attack. If the rest of the animal clan attacked, I wasn't sure I was strong enough to fight. I wouldn't be able to take to the sky and I still couldn't run, so I would be forced to fight every last one of them, along with any animals in the area they might summon.

Call forth your wings. I don't trust Kane, I whispered across Rowe's brain.

You can't fly, Rowe countered.

I'll manage.

Pointing to the bearskin draped over the chair, Kane waved to Locke to bring it over to him as he pushed to his feet. The beast of a man was still shaking his head as he walked over to his throne. He wrapped the warm bearskin around him and resumed his seat before his eyes finally fell on me. I had yet to rise from the ground, and my face remained smeared with his blood.

"You have lived up to your reputation," Kane said with a heavy sigh and a slight groan as he shifted in his chair, trying to find a more comfortable spot, considering his wounds. "You are fearless, quick, and smart. And despite the . . . zealous nature of some of my people, you also kept it a fair fight. I didn't think the Dark One was brave enough to allow the whip to leave her side."

"At Aurora's command, I put aside what honor I had so I could abide by her wishes," I admitted. "I am now trying to take a little part of that back each night. The whip would not have been a fair weapon in a fight that was not supposed to be to the death."

Kane smiled broadly at me. We both knew he would have killed me the first chance he got. I was just lucky that I was a little faster and maybe a little smarter.

With a laugh and a clap of his hand, Kane announced, "You have won back a shred of your honor tonight. You have beaten me, and we will join Cynnia in her fight against Aurora as I promised."

I regained my feet with some struggle and returned my blades to the sheaths along my body. I felt broken and sore in too many places. My right wing hung limp on my back, while my left wing was folded forward around my left shoulder as if protecting me. Kane's blood had soaked into my clothes and covered my exposed hands and face. I was a mess, but I had completed one of my tasks for Cynnia. However, as I glanced over at Rowe, I wasn't sure that I had completed all of my tasks. The powerful naturi still needed to be won over to the young princess's side.

"Thank you for your promised assistance, Kane," I said with a bow of my head. "Please bring your people to the outskirts of the city called Savannah, where the Fire Starter makes her domain. Rowe and I will meet you there. When I sense you have arrived, I will arrange a meeting for you with Cynnia so the proper planning can begin."

"Agreed," he said, thumping the arm of his chair.

I bowed my head to him one last time and started to limp across the clearing toward Rowe. I was exhausted and sore in too many places to count, but we had to get out of Kane's immediate domain before sunrise if we were going to find a safe place to spend the daylight hours. I didn't think Kane would send his people after me, but I didn't trust some of his more zealous followers not to come looking for me.

"You're leaving?" Locke demanded, surprise filling his voice.

"It's best that we make some further progress tonight," I replied. "We will make camp at sunrise."

"We are comrades now!" Kane declared, pushing carefully to his feet as the last of his wounds healed. "We will fight Aurora's army together! That means that you will make camp with us tonight. You must heal so that you are at full strength when you continue your journey."

"We are traveling at night when I am at my strongest," I hedged.

"Then we will protect you both while you sleep during the day, and have food for you when you awaken tomorrow night," Kane quickly offered.

I resisted the urge to look over at Rowe, who was now standing beside me. If we were staying in the animal clan camp, I wouldn't be able to use the sleep spell on him or they would know he was my prisoner rather than my comrade in arms. In my moment of weakness, I might not only lose Rowe, but also the assistance of the animal clan.

I'll behave myself for now, Rowe promised as if reading my thoughts. *Besides, a weak you means that I don't have proper protection. We rest. You heal.*

"We are honored," I said, forcing a weak smile on my lips as I looked up at Kane. "We accept your offer. Cynnia will be most grateful that you have looked after us during the daylight hours." I just hoped that we survived without any new problems.

Eleven

My right wing screamed with pain as I tried to fully extend it. I had walked nearly a quarter of a mile from the main camp of the animal clan to a wide stream. Stripping off my clothes, I tried to rinse out some of the blood before stepping into the icy water myself. In the center of the stream, the water rushed past my calves, numbing any lingering pain I might have felt in my right ankle. Now I was only left with the wound in my right wing, which seemed reluctant to fully heal. I knew it would be completely fixed by the following evening, but I didn't want to wait that long. I wanted to go to sleep at sunrise knowing I was back at full strength.

I had been somewhat reluctant to leave Rowe alone with the animal clan, but he'd already promised to behave himself, and for now that was the best I was going to get. I could only hope he was intrigued by the promise that the Fire Starter planned to join our little uprising. At the very least, he now knew we were headed for Savannah, and the one-eyed naturi could take another swipe at her if he had it in mind.

Bending down, I cupped the cold water and splashed it on my face a couple times before wiping away the excess.

Kane's blood had covered my face and hands, leaving me feeling sticky and dirty. I pushed the cold to the furthest reaches of my mind as I scrubbed my hands together, washing away the last of the blood. Before rising, I ran my wet hands over my legs and the rest of my body. It had been too long since I'd properly bathed. Too many nights of running and hunting. Cynnia had kept me on the run for the better part of the past month, seeking out any who might join our cause. Savannah held the promise of a day's sleep on a comfortable bed and a warm bath.

There was a subtle shift in the air, a slight change in the energy that had me jerking upright. I was completely unarmed in the stream, leaving all my clothes and weapons on the bank. I thought I would be safe so far in animal clan territory, that I could sneak a few private moments to myself. Of course, the alliance with the animal clan was shaky at best, and I wasn't sure everyone agreed with the idea of working with Rowe and me. Someone could be looking to strike while I was at my weakest.

When I scanned the immediate region, my heart stopped beating for a second. Rowe had sought me out. The area was thick with trees, blotting out the moonlight, but after a moment I could pick him out on the rise leading down to the stream, leaning against one of the trees. He hadn't been standing there long since it was impossible for him to sneak up on me with the iron collar around his neck. He couldn't cloak his presence.

"What do you want?" I demanded. I pulled my left wing around my front, blocking his view of my body as best I could while my right wing continued to hang limp at my side. I turned in the stream so I was facing him, taking an unsteady step backward on the slippery rocks.

"How is your wing healing?" he asked, descending the rest of the way to the bank of the stream.

"Fine. It will be just fine," I snapped, taking another step back. "Return to the camp. I will be right behind you."

"It's not fine," he growled back at me. "You can't retract your wings yet. It's not healing properly." He took a step into the water and I took a wobbly step back as my left foot settled on some shifting gravel. "Stay still! I'm not chasing after you. I just want to look at your wing."

"And I said it's fine! I don't need you looking at it!"

"Look! If your wing isn't properly mended, we're not flying out of here tomorrow night, and I'm anxious to set foot in Savannah," he admitted. "Now let me look to make sure that it isn't broken."

"It's not broken. Please, Rowe, don't come any closer."

The naturi shoved his hands through his shaggy black hair, pushing it away from his one good eye. For just a moment I could clearly see the scars that stretched across one side of his face, disappearing under the eye patch and down his neck into his shirt. "What? You make these grand speeches about me being the savior of our people and you don't trust me! I'm not going to hurt you. If I was going to do that, I wouldn't have bothered to walk out into this icy water."

"I trust you," I whispered, staring down at the water, wishing it was darker out, but it didn't matter. His night vision, like mine, was perfect.

"Then what? You're embarrassed about being naked in front of me? We're soldiers, Nyx, tending wounds. That's all. Besides, it's only your back."

"I know." And that was where the problem lay. He was going to see my back and I was afraid of taking the risk.

"Will you hold still?" he asked after a long tense moment.

"Only if you promise to never breathe a word of what you see."

"This is ridiculous—"

"Promise me!"

"I promise," he grumbled as he trudged out into the icy stream to where I stood. It wasn't until he was almost directly next to me that I finally turned around so he could look at my injured right wing.

His touch was amazingly gentle as his fingers first glided over the feathers in a soft caress before slowly moving up along the bone. I flinched beneath that touch as he neared the wound and his hands stopped until my wing settled again.

"The bone might have been initially cracked, but it feels solid to me," he announced after completing his inspection. "You'll probably have to sleep with them out today to allow the healing to finish, but you'll be in the skies again by sunset. I've seen far worse."

I watched him out of the corner of my eye as he bent down and cupped his hands together so he could capture some water. He poured it over the wound, washing away some of the dried blood that was sticking to the feathers.

For a second I thought I was in the clear. Then he repeated the process a second time, pausing to stretch the wing out.

"Great Mother forsake me," he swore, his hand stilling on my wing while his other hand rested on my left shoulder. At that moment I knew he had finally caught sight of the tree tattoo on my back.

"You promised, Rowe," I reminded him desperately.

"Nyx," he whispered in return. He released my shoulder and I could feel the cold tips of his fingers tracing down my spine along the massive tree that covered my back. "I don't understand. You're younger than I am. Younger than the ancient weavers, and yet . . ."

"I know," I murmured, hanging my head. I could only envision what he was seeing. I hadn't seen a reflection of my back in more than two centuries, but I could guess what was there—the branches now stretched over my shoulders and were starting to creep down my arms.

All naturi were born with the tree tattoo. It was a symbol of our connection to the earth. As we grew in age and strength, the tattoo grew as well, stretching across our bodies and gaining more details. My father had not kept me alive because of some deep love for his daughter. He had kept me alive because my tree had been more developed than any other child he'd ever seen. In me, he saw great possibilities, a deeper connection to the earth.

Unfortunately, it all had to be hidden. I was the Dark One. If anyone suspected that I might be stronger, more powerful, than some of our ancient weavers, I would be killed on the spot.

The fingers on both of Rowe's hands traveled up my back again. He gently forced me to lower my wings so he could see the branches starting to stretch down my arms.

"The roots have reached the backs of your knees," he whispered in awe. "At this rate, in a few years, the soles of your feet will be covered in the roots. You will be in constant contact with the earth and her powers." His warm breath brushed against my neck, sending goose bumps down my arms. I could feel his body heat against my exposed back and the gentle brush of his shirt.

"If I live that long," I muttered under my breath. With the war coming, I was no longer counting my remaining expanse of life in years.

Rowe abruptly stepped away from me, dropping his hands back to his sides. "Your tree is more advanced than Aurora's," he declared. "That's why you've always dressed like you have. You've had to hide."

"It was for the best," I quickly argued. "Our people needed to believe in Aurora, and it would not have helped their faith in her if they knew that her younger sister had a stronger connection to the earth. She would have been dethroned."

"And you would have been killed," he said, finishing the thought to its natural end, but he quickly continued. "Why hide it now? Let the world know that you are stronger than her."

I twisted around to look at him, holding my left wing to my front with my left arm. "I'm still the Dark One. They don't follow me. They follow Cynnia. Our people still need the promise that I will never be their leader. No matter what strength the Great Mother may give me, I will always be in the shadows."

"That's wrong."

We stood in silence, embraced by the darkness. Only the sound of the stream flowing around us filled the night air. He knew my great secret; the one thing I had hid my entire life from my people, and I felt that I could trust him. I just wondered how far he trusted me.

"Will . . . will you show me your back?" I asked.

"Why?" he demanded, suddenly very defensive.

"I can guess that the scars stretch across your body. I want to know if they had hindered the growth of your tree," I admitted.

"Growth?" he scoffed. "Our Great Mother abandoned me centuries ago." Yet as he spoke, Rowe grabbed the top back of his shirt and jerked it over his head. He stood with his back to me, facing the thick woods that surrounded us. Even in the darkness I could easily make out the white lines of the scars that crisscrossed his arms and went over his shoulders. There were a few that streaked through his tree, but I was relieved to find the tree tattoo had grown over the scars, indicating that his connection to the earth had not actually been damaged. It didn't seem as advanced as it should have been, considering his age, but I could still spot bits of new growth near his shoulder blades.

"Do you trust me?" I asked.

"Why?"

"Because I want to help you."

"How?"

Instead of answering, I placed both of my hands against his warm back. Muscles danced and flexed under my touch, but he didn't move. Closing my eyes, I spread my wings as far as I could, ignoring the pain that shot through my right wing. I reached out, pulling the energy straight from the earth and through my body. It left through my hands and poured into the limbs of the tree that graced Rowe's strong back. He jerked once and then a low groan escaped him as relief rolled through his body.

Unfortunately, it wasn't just the power from the earth that was flowing through me and into his body. My own thoughts and emotions poured unbidden into him no matter how I tried to control the flow. I had admired and cared for Rowe for as long as I could remember, but was careful to hide all those emotions deep inside as I fought to become his strong comrade in arms. I was his second in command of the armies, the weapon of the queen, the protector of our people. I was the Dark One. I wasn't permitted my own feelings.

After nearly a minute my hands began to tremble under the weight of the energy flowing through me and my knees buckled. I collapsed down into the icy water so it flowed around my hips. The cold water helped to clear my head from the fog that seemed to have grown around my thoughts, but fatigue still kept me on my knees.

Throwing his shirt on the nearby bank, Rowe turned around and knelt in front of me. He gently captured both of my upper arms in his hands, his thumbs slowly caressing my flesh as if he could push away the growing cold. My wings hung limp behind me and I no longer cared what he could see of my naked body. I was too drained and emotionally embarrassed.

"What did you just do to me?" he whispered.

I kept my head down, staring at the water that flowed between us. "I strengthened your connection with the earth. It had grown weak because of all the trials you've been through. It was like I rejuvenated your tree."

"You can do that?"

A half smile twisted on my lips. "I learned long ago that I had more skills as a healer than as a soldier. Unfortunately, my father only saw my strength with the earth as a weapon of war."

"I'm sorry." He lifted his right hand and pushed some of my hair away from my face.

"It's no matter," I replied brusquely, lifting my eyes to meet his. "The important thing is whether I have won you. Will you help us?"

A smirk danced across his face, lighting his expression. "My brain still rebels at the idea of fighting against the woman I still see as my queen, but I cannot just simply bow down and die for her, because she does not see my work in a positive light. I struggled and gave her freedom, and yet she calls me a traitor. But I will be accepted in Cynnia's world, once again given a place as commander of armies." He paused and his smile grew even wider. "I will be once again faced with the Fire Starter, allowed to be close to her as she is forced to work with me. It will be an interesting experience, and I wouldn't miss it."

With rubbery, tired legs, I pushed to my feet and stepped around him as I walked back to the shore. "I'm realizing that this is the best answer I'm going to get from you." Shuffling through my clothes, I picked up my left boot and opened a small compartment in the heel where I withdrew a small iron key. I walked back out to where he was standing in the water, watching me.

"You had the key?" he demanded.

I reached up and inserted the key into the lock, trying to avoid his gaze. "Of course. I had to be able to set you free if you saw reason."

"And what if you were killed?"

"Cynnia has a second. You would have had to go see her," I replied as I removed the iron collar and tossed it out into the water.

"I should have suspected as much," he grumbled.

"I'm sorry, but keeping you weak was the only way of keeping you from killing me in my sleep."

A weak smile crossed his mouth for a second as he reached up and let his fingertips stray across my cheekbone. "I don't think that I would ever be able to do such a thing to you, no matter how bad things became."

I shook my head, my cheek brushing against the palm of his hand. "You would have done so to protect yourself. It would have been understandable."

To my surprise, Rowe continued to stare at me with his piercing gaze roaming over my face. "I always suspected that I married the wrong sister."

I tried to form the words that Cynnia would have been a wise choice, but the words grew stuck in my throat because I knew without a doubt that he was talking about me. I knew by the softened gaze and his hand lingering on my face. Also through the infusion of power from the earth that I had given him, he now fully knew my feelings for him.

"You look at me with the same compassion in your eyes that you always have. You don't see the monster that I've become. You don't treat me like an outcast like the rest of our kind."

"Because you're not," I argued, cupping his cheeks with both of my hands. "All I see is a man who has sacrificed more for us than anyone else. You only wear the scars to prove the trials you've been through."

"And you wear your scars on the inside. We are a pair."

Rowe pulled my face closer to his and kissed me gently on the lips. My eyes fell closed, basking in the feeling of being touched by another; to feel such warmth and intensity toward another creature was new to me. No naturi had ever touched me in such a way. They had used weapons to hurt, but I'd never been touched with compassion and what could only feel like love.

Threading his fingers through my hair, Rowe pulled me tighter against him, deepening the kiss. My hands slid from his cheeks to his chest as his tongue slipped into my mouth, tasting me. I moaned against his mouth, enjoying the feel of his warm chest pressed against mine. I traced his scars with one hand, trailing from his shoulder down to the top of his pants.

Rowe gave a soft chuckle as he slid his mouth away from mine and down my neck to my shoulder. "You taste sweeter than honey and your hands are driving me more than a little mad."

"Should I stop?" I whispered, stilling my hands where they rested on the sides of his stomach.

"I don't think there is any stopping now. We owe each other this after so many years," he admitted. "You're not the only one who has been watching from afar, admiring but remaining silent."

This time I leaned in and pressed my lips to his mouth, kissing him deeply. We had done our duty to our people. We were owed this moment, no matter how brief it might be. Without breaking the kiss, Rowe scooped me up in his arms and carried me out of the stream to gently lay me down on the soft earth of the bank. He pulled back and looked at me laying beneath him in the pale moonlight. My black wings were thrown out to either side, like two dark glistening sheaths of night, while my pale white body shone like a grounded star. A small sharp pain intruded into the moment from my wounded wing, but I paid it little heed as I focused on him.

"I've watched you grow as a warrior," he said. "I've admired your determination and your strength, but I never for a second expected you to be so beautiful."

Kneeling beside me, careful so his knee did not crush any of the feathers on my wings, he drew his hands slowly over my naked body. His fingertips danced over my thin waist and cupped my breasts, drawing a soft moan out of me as my back arched.

Rowe pulled away from me for a second to remove the last of his clothes and then gently spread my legs so he could kneel between them. My heart pounded in my chest as a mixture of fear and longing raced through my veins. I had never been with a man. I wanted his touch more than I wanted my next breath, and yet at the same time I feared what was about to happen. What if I couldn't perform as he hoped? What if I disappointed him? What if . . .

Everything will be fine. There was a slight chuckle of amusement lacing his words, but there was also warmth and concern.

His hands resumed their roaming on my body, but this time there was a new sense of urgency. His mouth followed close behind his fingers, washing my body in a series of long wet kisses that left behind a trail of fires. My legs shifted around his waist, pulling him closer to me. His hand finally dipped between my legs as one of his fingers slid deep inside me, wringing a low moan from me in the sound of his name.

My body writhed beneath him as he moved his finger slowly in and out of my body.

"I'm trying to take this slowly for you, Nyx, but you're breaking what little willpower I have," he said in a rough voice.

In response, I reached out with one hand and slid it down his body until I finally reached his hardened member. My fingertips grazed the tip and his whole body jerked between my legs.

Yes, he hissed in my mind with near desperation.

Rowe put his free hand beside my head, moving his body closer to me so I could more easily reach him. I wrapped my fingers around him, slowly stroking him, drawing a low groan out of him that seemed pulled from his very soul. He was rock hard within my hand and yet the skin was velvety soft. None of his scars reached past his waist, leaving him perfect, but only for me to see.

"I can't wait any longer," he moaned as he once again shifted his position between my legs. Grabbing both my wrists, he held them over my head as he slowly guided his body toward the entrance of mine. He pressed slowly inside and then pulled out again, bringing a whimper of need from my throat. I didn't want slow. I wanted him inside of me. I needed this feeling of desperation to be squashed and his body deep inside of mine.

"Rowe," I moaned, shifting beneath him in an attempt to press more of him inside of my body.

"You're going to be the death of me," he groaned before plunging deep inside me. There was a flash of pain as my body struggled to expand enough to accommodate his size. He paused, unmoving inside me, as he leaned down and kissed me. His tongue swept through my mouth until I was moaning again. It was only then that he started moving, sending the first waves of pleasure through my body.

"Release my hands," I pleaded, squirming beneath him as I raised my hips to meet each of his thrusts. It took me only a second to catch his rhythm, driving a fresh moan from his body.

Rowe forced out a chuckle and shook his head, sending his long black hair cascading around his face. "If you start touching me, I'll lose what little control I do have."

"I need to touch you, Rowe." My breathing grew heavier and my eyes closed as I concentrated on the feeling building between my legs. "Rowe?" I said in a fractured voice.

"Just let it come," he whispered in a husky voice. At the same time, he picked up his speed, pounding inside of me a little harder. He released my wrists and let his hands sweep down my flushed body. Each touch only added to the feeling, until the dam finally seemed to break. A scream was ripped from my throat and my body arched beneath him. Muscles clenched around him as he slid in and out of me, sending fresh waves of pleasure through my frame.

As the last ripples of pleasure ran through my frame, Rowe let out a low groan. I could feel him expanding within me before he finally exploded with a gush. He fell forward, his hands on either side of my head as he finally grew still inside me. His breathing was heavy and a bead of sweat trickled down from his temple. A slow grin grew across his face as he leaned down and pressed a slow kiss against my lips.

"So that's what sex is like," I murmured, feeling completely relaxed.

"You haven't been missing much," Rowe teased, kissing me again before slowly pulling his body out of mine.

I sat up as he sat beside me, flexing my wings. The pain was gone from my right wing completely, allowing me to slowly and carefully dissolve them into a fine black dust. I reached across and touched his arm with my fingers, drawing him out of thought. I wasn't sure what this meant between us, if things had changed forever or if this had simply been a release of built-up tension.

"Things are different," he admitted.

"Do you just live in my thoughts?" I demanded, pinching his arm.

A crooked smile lifted his lips as he looked over at me. "That time I wasn't in your mind. It was just a guess because I was wondering the same thing. Things are different between us now. I'm not sure what's going to happen, but I do know that I'm not going to let you out of my sight. Unfortunately, for now, we have a new duty before us."

"Cynnia," I murmured.

"And the defeat of Aurora. We can't be free until Aurora is gone."

"I know. You're right."

Rowe reached over and took my chin between two fingers, turning my face toward him. "But that doesn't mean we can't steal a few moments to ourselves when we can."

I smiled as I leaned in and pressed another kiss to his lips, my fingers straying across the scars that crisscrossed his beautiful face. The Fire Starter was right. There was something evil about this one-eyed naturi, but I welcomed that sinister grin and his nimble fingers.

We finished dressing but lingered by the side of the stream, watching fractured bits of moonlight dance across the water as it splashed within its banks. We talked softly of our time apart, of the years that had passed, separated on two different worlds. Unfortunately, there was one reoccurring thought eating at my mind. I was reluctant to bring it up and spoil our companionable moment but afraid that it had a bearing on what we faced.

"What happened to Nerian?" I found myself softly asking when a long silence settled between us.

"The Fire Starter killed him."

"I know how he died, but I am more concerned with how my brother lived. I spoke with a couple survivors of the first trip to Machu Picchu those many years ago. They told me how Nerian tortured Mira, and deep in my heart I can't fault her for wanting revenge."

"If you're going to pity Mira, then you should know that Nerian wasn't alone in her torture," Rowe stiffly said, looking over at me with a stern expression. "We needed her to be our protection when the nightwalkers came. And as it turns out, we needed her more when it came to opening the door."

"I know about your role in Mira's torture as well," I replied in a soothing voice. "You and I are no different in the duties we've had to fulfill during our long lives. However, the others spoke of the twisted joy that Nerian took in Mira's torture."

Rowe heaved a heavy sigh and his shoulders seemed to slump under a new weight. "I know where you are going with this, and I have to admit that your suspicions are correct. Nerian had gone mad. At first I thought it was just an obsession with the Fire Starter and getting her to do exactly as he commanded. I thought it was just a need to break something that he perceived as weaker than him. But even after our defeat at Machu Picchu and we became more concerned with simple survival, his obsession never waned. In the last years that I knew him, he no longer followed orders; he mumbled constantly to himself and accused others of helping Mira to escape him. I was finally forced to banish him from the rest of the group that remained under my command before he killed someone."

Pulling my knees up to my chest, I rested my chin on them while wrapping my arms around my legs. "During the brief time that I knew him before the wars, I could see flickers of moments where I knew his thoughts were in a dangerous place. He looked at Aurora with envy and I heard him utter traitorous words about our father. I think if he had remained with the royal family, he would have tried to kill Aurora in an effort to steal the throne."

"It is a possibility," Rowe said, slowly scratching his jaw.

"And now I'm only left to wonder," I sighed, letting my eyes fall shut.

"Wonder what?"

"Has the same madness that struck down my older brother come to claim my sister as well? During the past century, Aurora has come to see conspiracy against her around every corner. People were killed by me in the name of treason, and there are some that I struggle to believe would harbor a single treasonous act against her. And then she turned on Cynnia, who wanted nothing more than to find a peaceful solution instead of pursuing a route that will ultimately lead to our extinction."

"She also turned against you, her one and only true champion through it all," Rowe added.

"Is this madness that is eating away at her brain? She was always a cold, distant person, but in the past years I've seen her act in the name of sheer cruelty. Has the same madness that afflicted Nerian taken hold of my sister?"

Rowe reached out and ran his hand down my back in a soothing caress, wiping away some of the tension that seemed to be growing in my shoulders. "Aurora is not the woman I remember or the person I agreed to be consort to. She is power hungry and obsessed. While I have no love for the humans, you are right that she will lead our people to extinction if she continues this course of action. She's not thinking clearly."

Rowe paused abruptly, and I lifted my head to look over

at him. He was staring into the woods but I don't think he was actually seeing the world around him. Without reading his thoughts, I could feel the pain of him reviewing that night on Machu Picchu when his wife-queen rejected him despite everything he had done for her. I could feel the heavy weight of that rejection and his own self-doubt over his appearance, though he hid both very well from the world around him with a thick veil of confidence and sarcasm.

"I think you're right," he whispered, still not looking at me. "I think she has gone mad."

Reaching up, I placed my hand against his cheek, startling him back to look at me again. "Then we have to stop her. We have to protect what is left of our people before she kills us all."

A crooked smile crossed his lips and then he turned his face and pressed a kiss into the palm of my hand. "I may not agree with the idea of giving the throne to someone as inexperienced as Cynnia, but she will be better than the madness of Aurora."

"I wouldn't worry about Cynnia," I said with a smile. "She may be young and inexperienced, but she will have us as counsel at her side during her first few years. I feel confident that between the three of us, we will find a way to rejuvenate our people."

"And what of her new consort Locke?" Rowe asked, arching one brow at me.

"I am hoping that he proves to be more than just eye candy for Cynnia."

Rowe lunged at me, knocking me on my back while grabbing my wrists with both of his hands so he could properly hold me down. "Eye candy? Where would you learn such a phrase as that?"

A soft giggle escaped me as I stopped struggling against him. "Cynnia has made a friend with a human witch. I overheard them talking and they used the word eye candy when referring to the man Cynnia has chosen to be her consort."

"Are you . . . disappointed? I mean, I'm not the man you came to care for those centuries so long ago. I'm not . . ." he stammered, his grip loosening on my wrists as he started to straighten.

Pulling my arms free, I sat up and cupped his face so he could not pull away from me as I forced him to look me in the eye. "I would change nothing." And that statement went for my entire life. There were things I regretted and many things I was sorry had to happen, but somehow that connection of events led me to this moment alone in the woods with Rowe. I would not risk changing anything and miss out on this exact moment. I would change nothing.

Twelve

Danaus softly snickered as he stood by the window looking out of my office in my town house. I glanced up from the financial paperwork that my human assistant Charlotte had recently sent me to find the hunter standing with his hands in his pockets as he shook his head at whatever he was watching outside. A frown started to pull at the corners of my mouth, as a feeling crept over me that said nothing good was arriving on my doorstep. Following the brief chaos caused by the Daylight Coalition and Jabari, everything seemed to settle back into an easygoing quiet, and I was hoping that Danaus and I could spend a little time enjoying that quiet uninterrupted.

"I'm afraid to ask, but what are you looking at?"

"It seems that you're possibly about to have a visitor, if she can make up her mind," Danaus replied, his gaze not wavering from the scene outside the window.

I pushed out of my chair and started to walk around my desk, closing the distance between us. Pressing my head between his strong shoulders, I wrapped my arms around his waist from behind, holding him tightly against me. "What are you talking about?"

"She approaches the front steps then stops, and paces

away talking to herself. She's done it three or four times now."

"Who?"

Danaus twisted around to look down at me, a smile growing on his handsome face. "The one person that can make you feel uneasy."

Ignoring his ominous, teasing comment, I peered around him to look out the window and saw a woman pacing the sidewalk in front of my town house, talking to herself as if trying to give herself a pep talk into ringing my doorbell.

"Shit! It's Shelly!" I hissed between clenched teeth. I grabbed Danaus's arm and tried to pull him away from the window, but he wouldn't budge. "Come on and move. Maybe she hasn't seen you yet. We can pretend that we're not here. She'll go away."

As if it were a sign that my luck really had run out, the front doorbell rang, echoing through the town house.

"Damn it! We don't have to answer it," I said in a hushed voice, as if she could hear me through the thick brick walls.

"Mira, we have to answer the door," he replied in a firm voice, though the corners of his mouth were twitching with suppressed laughter as he stepped around me and starting walking toward the front hall.

"You don't have to enjoy this so much. It's not like you're all that comfortable around the witch either," I muttered under my breath, but I had no doubt the hunter with the superior hearing heard the comment.

Reluctantly, I followed him into the hall, but hung back several feet with my arms folded across my chest as Danaus answered the door. He didn't hesitate, didn't bother to ask what she wanted; he simply guided her into the house, grinning up at me over Shelly's head as she glided across the doorstep.

The pert blonde beamed at me in her pretty white slacks

and yellow top as if she were a fresh spring flower. She quickly rushed across the short distance that separated us and captured me in a tight hug that didn't seem to end until I finally patted her on the back a couple times. When she pulled back, she grasped both of my hands in hers and released a heavy sigh.

"Oh, it is so good to see you again!" she crowed. "After all that mess at Machu Picchu and the stories I heard about what actually happened at the ruins, it just gives me nightmares. But you and Danaus made it out safely and that's all that matters. And you look fabulous! Well, of course you look fabulous. You're a nightwalker. Have you ever seen a nightwalker that didn't look fabulous? But really, you look just great after everything you have been through."

"Shelly, would like to come in and sit down?" Danaus inquired when she finally seemed to take a breath.

"Yes, that would be wonderful!" she said, giving my hands one final squeeze before releasing me. She preceded Danaus and me into the parlor, giving me a chance to throw the hunter a dark look behind her back.

I hadn't seen Shelly since we'd left her at the resort at the foot of the Machu Picchu ruins months ago. Danaus had initially contacted her when I expressed an interest in trying to learn how to use earth magic, since Shelly was an earth witch. Unfortunately, it seemed that being a nightwalker was effectively stunting any hopes I might have of becoming a great user of earth magic. However, she had been key in protecting the nightwalkers during the day from the naturi that had surrounded us. She had also been instrumental in keeping a close watch on Cynnia when Danaus and I were otherwise preoccupied with staying alive.

After Machu Picchu, I heard that Shelly returned to her home in Charleston and possibly traveled a little farther north in search of fresh, welcoming earth to recharge, following the violence and bloodshed that washed over the peaceful Peruvian mountain.

In truth, I expected never to hear from her again. She and I were as opposite as two people could be. She was an eternal optimistic who saw only the good in people she encountered. She was a powerful witch in her own right and yet struggled to use her powers against anyone else, even if they were aiming to harm her or those she was sworn to protect. I had no doubt she fully believed in the creed that many magic users initially swore by: "Do no harm." Unfortunately, as I learned the hard way, the more powerful a magic user became, the easier it was for them to forget that little promise.

Shelly perched on the edge of one of the chairs, as if her excitement threatened to send her back to her feet again in a fit of joy. I chose the corner of the sofa farthest from her, while Danaus chose the other end of the sofa, directly across from her. But then, I think he was confident that she was there to visit me and not him, which would mean he would be able to beat a hasty and obvious retreat.

"I ran into Knox a few days ago," she started as soon as we were all seated. She shifted so she was fully facing Danaus, and the hunter slid back in his seat, suddenly looking extremely uncomfortable. It was all I could do not to laugh out loud. "He told me that you've left Themis and you're now staying permanently in Savannah. That's wonderful!"

"Thank you," he said in a low, gruff voice. His eyes shifted to me for a second, as if seeking help, but I only grinned at him.

"Knox also mentioned that you're working at the Dark Room. That has got to be a strange switch for you. I mean, one minute you're hunting down nightwalkers and now you're serving them drinks. How did you make such a switch?"

"I look at it as he's keeping the peace," I smoothly interjected before Danaus could take a breath to answer. I worried that this was still a sore subject with the hunter after spending so many centuries hunting nightwalkers; that his new position at the Dark Room chafed more than he was willing to reveal to me. "That has always been Danaus's job, to keep the peace. He did just that for Themis for centuries, and now he is helping to maintain the peace in one of the most dangerous places in all of Savannah."

That seems a bit of a stretch, Danaus silently said. *She's more correct. I serve drinks instead of removing heads now.*

The Dark Room is a safer place for both nightwalkers and humans now because of you.

That might be true, but you're stretching the truth, he pressed, but I could feel the underlying laughter in his mind, which only made me long to lean across the sofa and press a long kiss to his full lips. For now, the hunter was happy in his new life with me and Savannah. I planned to bask in that happiness for as long as it lasted. In time, I knew he would grow restless again and keeping the peace at the Dark Room wouldn't be enough for him. But considering his long life, I was hoping he would at least stick around for a few decades before the boredom kicked in.

"Is the Dark Room really that dangerous?" she asked in awe-filled tones. "I mean, I don't know a lot of nightwalkers. Just you and Tristan, which I am really, really sorry to hear about. I don't know what happened—"

"We don't discuss it," I said sharply, slashing cruelly through her apology.

"I am sorry, Mira," she continued after a tense moment of silence. "He was a wonderful person. Tristan, and you, and Knox, are the only nightwalkers I really know, and I never saw you as all that dangerous. I didn't know that the Dark Room was such a scary place. I guess it is a lucky thing that Danaus is there now."

"Shelly, what brought you to Savannah?" I suddenly demanded, causing Danaus to wince as I cut straight to the heart of the matter. The mere mention of Tristan's name had dissolved the last of my patience. Now was not the time to give the little earth witch a lesson in exactly how dangerous nightwalkers could be. She had seen the violence with her own eyes, and yet it seemed she had chosen to whitewash the memory so that nightwalkers didn't come out looking half as scary as we truly were. Of course, if she was willing to face the fact that she was sitting with one of the most dangerous nightwalkers in all the world, I truly doubted that she would have come on this little visit alone. On the other hand, she had been smart enough to pick a night that Danaus was free from his duties at the Dark Room. She could have been counting on the hunter acting as a buffer, as he always did.

"I'm actually here on someone else's behalf," she admitted slowly. Leaning forward, she placed her elbows on her legs and twisted her fingers together as if knotting them in her growing anxiety. It was one of the few times I saw a frown cross her small, bowlike lips. Her long blond hair fell forward, framing her heart-shaped face, accenting the flush to her cheeks, which I hadn't noticed there a moment ago. In the silence of the room, I could hear her heart pounding in her chest.

"Who?"

"We need your help, Mira," Shelly evaded, raising her wide eyes to me as to somehow weaken my will.

"Who?" I repeated, my voice growing harder and colder. A knot twisted in my stomach the more anxious that she became.

"Cynnia would—"

"No, absolutely not!" I said, coming out of my seat. I paced to the far end of the room, shaking my head while clenching my teeth. I wanted absolutely nothing to do with that renegade princess. Sure, I admired her for the gutsy way she used me as protection against both nightwalkers and her own kind. But that admiration only stretched so far. Trouble followed that naturi no matter where she went. And after the rough several months I'd spent fighting against and with Danaus, I thought we both deserved a little peace and quiet. Cynnia would not allow such a thing.

"Please, Mira. She only wants to talk to you," Shelly said, rising to her feet as well when I paced back toward the sofa.

"I'm no fool, Shelly," I snarled. "Cynnia wants more than just to talk. She used me as her own personal bodyguard last fall. I wouldn't be surprised if she's come back looking for a repeat performance."

"Actually, that's been my job." Shelly tilted her head up a little as she spoke, pride filling her words.

"What do you mean?" Danaus asked. I leaned against the arm of the sofa and crossed my arms over my chest as I watched the witch through narrowed eyes. She stared back unflinchingly, head held high.

"I encountered Cynnia and Nyx not long after Machu Picchu. There were looking for someplace to stay hidden while they formulated a plan to stay alive against Aurora. Since that time, I have been acting as Cynnia's personal bodyguard along with her sister Nyx."

"They're going to get you killed."

"They're fighting for a good cause. If you have to die, isn't it best to die fighting for a good cause?"

"Dead is dead. Glory and honor are just pretty ideas that don't exist anymore," I whispered, talking mostly to myself. Honor was a concept I still clung to, though mine was more than a little tattered and torn these days.

I stared at Shelly in silence for more than a minute, dark thoughts swirling through my head. Just a couple centuries ago I would have told her to bring Cynnia forward and the consequences be damned. I was always searching for the next fight, the next adventure that led me so close to death that I could kiss the grim reaper.

But now things had changed. I had seen more than six centuries pass before my eyes. I had watched people I loved greatly fall at my feet and die. I had been washed in the blood of my comrades and my enemies more nights than I ever wanted to count. A part of my soul was tired of it all. Besides, now I had Danaus to help soothe the ache when the memories came to haunt me. I had Danaus's gentle touch and teasing smile. I had his wisdom and experience to help guide my decisions and to drive me insane when we didn't see eye-to-eye on a matter. I had Danaus now, and I no longer wanted to chase after death. For the first time in more years that I could count, I was ready to live.

"She does need your help," Shelly said gently when I finally seemed to calm down, "but for now, she would be content with a meeting. She just wants you to hear her out. Cynnia has already sent Nyx out to speak with someone else. It's my job to convince you to at least meet with her, listen to what she has to say with an open mind. That's all we're asking."

"If Nyx is away and you're here with me, then who is guarding the little princess? That's not being a very good bodyguard," I taunted.

"It was a risk Cynnia was willing to take. She knew that I would be the only one you'd listen to for even a few minutes, so she is taking a big chance by allowing me to leave her alone for a period of time."

Staring at Shelly, I furrowed my brow before glancing out the window behind me. Cynnia didn't take big chances. She took calculated risks. Right now she was being hunted by Aurora's followers, and there was only one place nearby that they might fear to tread.

"Damn it, Shelly! She's already in Savannah!" I shouted, throwing my hands up. Pointing at Danaus, I growled, "Check the area! How many naturi are lurking in my city?" I could have tried to complete the search myself, but while Nick had given me the ability to sense all the different types of power, I still had trouble distinguishing the naturi from the lycanthropes, and I wasn't very good at estimating their numbers.

Frowning at me, Danaus nonetheless pushed his powers out from his body and through the house. I closed my eyes and was swept along in the wave as it washed through my city. I could feel the soothing vibrations of the nightwalkers across the landscape and then the jarring sensation of the naturi.

"There are seven," he replied, pulling his powers back into his frame. "They are sticking to the outskirts of town, possibly across the river in lycan territory. None in the city proper."

"That's not good," Shelly murmured, balling her hands into fists before her. "When I left, Cynnia had only three guards with her. I don't know who the other three are."

Sucking in a slow breath and releasing it to cleanse my mind, I looked over at Shelly as she was torn between her duty to convince me to listen to her charge and her duty to protect the princess. It was a position I could understand.

"Does Cynnia's need to talk to us have to do with her sister Aurora?" I asked in a low, even voice, which made me sound more reasonable that I was feeling.

"Yes, I'm afraid it does."

I looked down at Danaus, who simply shrugged his broad shoulders at me. "You knew it was coming."

"I foolishly wanted a little more time."

Turning my back on Shelly, I glanced out the window into the large park square opposite my town house. Cars swooshed by, their lights dancing across the trees so the shadows lunged about the open area. I sensed no nightwalkers close to my home, only humans enjoying the warmer than usual spring evening. There were still many hours until the sun rose. Plenty of time to hear the plea of a naturi princess.

"If Cynnia is talking about engaging Aurora and is thinking of potentially using Savannah as a battleground, then Barrett Rainer, alpha for the Savannah pack, should be involved in this discussion."

"I don't think she wants to use any city as a battleground," Shelly quickly countered. "However, there is always the chance of Aurora coming after her."

"Barrett should be involved," I pressed. That was my first big mistake when dealing with the naturi. I had made it a nightwalker issue and kept the shifters in the dark in an effort to protect our own shame and secrets. In the end, many good lycanthropes had died without knowing why. I'd learned my lesson the hard way. Barrett deserved a voice in what was going to happen next.

"All right," Shelly said. "I don't think Cynnia will be averse to your suggestion. We shall meet—"

"Tonight," I finished. "I want this over as quickly as possible. We are currently faced with another pressing problem, and I would prefer not to have the naturi in the region causing problems as well." Danaus was frowning at the callous way I was treating Shelly, but I didn't care. She was bringing a threat into my domain and it was my job to protect my people, not bring them more harm. "We need a neutral location. I'm not holding the meeting here."

"The Dark Room?" he suggested.

"No naturi will ever step foot in the Dark Room again," I said, glaring at him. The last time such a thing happened, Knox had nearly been killed and several other nightwalkers and lycanthropes in fact had.

"The Docks?" he tried again, mentioning the newly restored nightclub that I favored down on River Street.

I shook my head. "Too loud and too many humans."

"Then how about the tunnels?"

A smile lifted the corners of my mouth and I resisted the urge to kiss him. It was brilliant. It was a favorite haunt of the shifters during the day when they needed to take care of a little business, while other nightwalkers used it as a daytime lair and a secret way of sneaking around the city.

"There's an entrance to the tunnels just off River Street where it meets up with Bay near the shipping yards. Tell Cynnia to meet us there in two hours. I'll bring Barrett."

"Thank you, Mira," Shelly said in a rush. She unexpectedly closed the distance between us and wrapped me in a quick, tight hug before she was out of the room and out the front door, heading back to the naturi she was supposed to be guarding.

Threading the fingers of my right hand through my hair, I bent my head and stared at the ground. I was trying to convince myself that it all wasn't crumbling away beneath my feet. I had worked so hard getting my life back in order, putting some distance between not only myself and the naturi, but myself and the coven as well.

"You will just go and listen to what she has to say," Danaus said. I could hear the leather creaking beneath him as he pushed off the sofa and approached me. He laid his large hands on my shoulders and squeezed, attempting to ease away some of the tension.

"The war with Aurora is coming, and Cynnia needs our help if she is going to survive. We're getting sucked into another battle with the queen of the naturi," I said, my voice trembling.

"Look deep inside yourself, Mira. Tell me there's not a part of you longing to take another shot at her."

A slow chuckle rose from my lips as I dropped my hand back down to my side. Danaus knew me too well. Aurora and Rowe were the reasons I had been tortured so many years ago. Aurora was the one who nearly had me killed among the ruins at Machu Picchu just a few months ago. Destroying her would mean that her people would be weakened, and in time they could slowly be picked off. Destroying Aurora would be one of my most favorite kills of all.

"The cocky bitch has been causing too many problems in my domain for too long."

"All you need is Cynnia to point you in the right direction and potentially provide you with a little bit of an army," Danaus whispered in my ear. "It could be fun."

"You're a deliciously evil man, Danaus, but you're right," I said, twisting my head so I could press a kiss to his hand. "Killing Aurora, and if I'm lucky, Rowe, would finally cleanse me of the naturi. I could restart my life again without this shadow from my past hanging over me."

"Just one more battle and then it will all be over with the naturi," Danaus said, pressing a kiss to the top of my head.

I jerked around, a smirk twisting my lips. "I seriously hope you don't believe that. Nightwalkers and naturi living in peace? Now that's the stuff of fairy tales."

"I find that idea no different than our situation."

"Ours is different. You came to your senses. The naturi will not," I teased, slipping away from him before he could grab me.

"I hope you are wrong," he called after me as I headed back to the office to call Barrett.

"Me too," I whispered. I wanted Aurora's head clasped firmly in my hands, but I didn't want a war with the naturi. There would be no hiding it. The humans would see it, and our world would be thrown open at last. No more hiding in the shadows, only the Great Awakening.

Thirteen

The only thing keeping me from pacing the open tunnels was the fact that both Barrett and Danaus were perfectly still despite the growing tension. Like any potential meeting, we brought along our respective seconds in command. Cooper, Barrett's brother, leaned against the car that had carried the lycanthropes, while Knox leaned against one of the brick columns that stretched up to the ceiling of the tunnel. Danaus was both my lover and my confidant, but in the nightwalker world, Knox would always be my second in command in Savannah. However, I had a slight suspicion that Knox would just as willingly take orders from Danaus as from me. That's why I trusted Knox so much. He was smarter than most nightwalkers.

"How do we know this isn't some naturi trap?" Cooper suddenly demanded, shattering the silence that had filled the tunnels. His voice echoed off the stone walls, carrying deep into the thick darkness that hugged close. "I mean, we've got the leaders of the vampires and the lycanthropes right here. What better way to take over the city than to kill them both in a single fight and then move into the city?"

"Danaus, how many naturi are in the city?" I asked, looking over my shoulder at the hunter.

"There are four naturi approaching us, but there are at least a dozen on the outskirts of the city," he replied a couple seconds after the warmth of his powers had swept past me.

I frowned. There had been only seven naturi in the region when we spoke to Shelly earlier. I wasn't comfortable with how their numbers were growing, but for now I was more concerned with the contingent of four approaching our location. With any luck, that would be Cynnia and her honor guard.

"I truly doubt that four naturi is enough to kill us all," I said blandly.

"And if they're members of the animal clan?" Cooper shot back at me, anxiety creeping into his voice. Two of his brothers had already been killed as the result of fights caused by the naturi animal clan.

"We'll handle it," Danaus said.

"She's late," Barrett muttered.

Folding my arms over my chest, I leaned my hip against the side of my car, keeping clear of the headlights pointed toward the doors that led into the tunnels. "She'll be here. This is too important a meeting for her to miss. She knows this is her only chance to win our support."

Luckily, we had to wait only a couple more minutes before one of the large metal doors leading to the tunnels creaked open. Shelly entered first, raising her hand against the blinding light of the two sets of car headlights aimed at her. We wanted the advantage when our opponents entered the tunnels. For several minutes they would be blinded while we were hidden deep in the shadows that filled the tunnels.

"Mira?" she called out, blinking her eyes rapidly as she struggled to adjust to the light.

"We're all here," I confirmed.

Shelly slowly walked into the tunnels with her hands raised to her shoulders, open and empty, to show that she wasn't holding any weapons. I was about to tell her to drop her hands, but I felt that the submissive stance put the others at ease. Cynnia followed close behind with her three guards. They were armed, but with their arms raised and away from their weapons, in a neutral stance. They needed to protect their princess so they had to remain armed, which was fine, because we were all armed as well. Trust was definitely thin on the ground.

Cynnia looked much the same as when I had last seen her among the ruins of Machu Picchu. She had a slight frame, while her tanned face was framed by a wealth of dark hair. She still appeared to be little more than seventeen to nineteen, but I knew her to be several centuries old. Young to take the throne, I suspected, by naturi standards. Nyx looked to be older than her sister Cynnia, and yet the younger sister was the one stepping forward. I knew there had to be more to the story behind that arrangement, but it had nothing to do with us. I didn't care to become involved in naturi politics. It was enough that I was up to my eyeballs in nightwalker politics with the coven.

"I see that you're keeping one step ahead of Aurora," I called out to the group as they slowly moved out of the direct line of the headlights and into the darkness so they could start to pick us out of the shadows.

"Not exactly an easy task," Cynnia admitted, dropping her hands limply to her sides. "But then, we quickly noticed that she seemed content to remain on the West Coast, well away from your territory. We decided to take advantage of that interesting affinity."

"So you've been hanging out with Shelly in Charleston these past few months," Danaus concluded. "I would have thought you would have remained in South America. Even I know that the earth magic is thick there. It would have been to your benefit."

"We assumed the same thing of Aurora, so we immediately headed north to get away from her." Cynnia shrugged her thin shoulders. "And with nightwalkers dominating most of Europe, we decided to head for some safer territory."

I frowned, clenching my teeth slightly. "So you used me once again to act as your protector against your own kind."

"Just your reputation," Cynnia hedged, but a grin widened on her lips.

"Be careful or I might decide to take that protective umbrella away from you," I warned. It was enough that she had tricked me into protecting her the first time: I respected her ingenuity and daring, but that respect only went so far, particularly when it threatened the safety of the people in my domain.

"In truth, I have come hoping to acquire the help of more than your reputation, as I'm sure you have guessed," she said. The female naturi took a step closer, while her bodyguards stayed a few steps behind. Only Shelly remained directly behind her shoulder, potentially to help add her voice to Cynnia's argument.

"I can guess where this is leading, but I've come willing to hear your side of the tale," I said, sliding my hands into the front pockets of my leather jacket. The air in the tunnels was several degrees colder than the air outside, and the thick leather added an extra layer of protection should this meeting come to blows.

"Since the doors were opened around the world in the fall," Cynnia began, "allowing the naturi people to return to Earth, Aurora has been building an army. While some have flocked to my banner, I know that my numbers are not as great as hers. It is only a matter of time before she decides it is time to finally wipe out not only me but my sister Nyx as well."

Beside me, Knox shifted from one foot to the other, betraying a surprising lack of patience. "If you'll forgive me, why do we care? The naturi have done nothing but slaughter both the shifters and the nightwalkers."

"Because the world faces one of two futures, depending on who lives and who dies in the battle that is coming," Cynnia said, unmoved by his gruff comment. "Should Aurora win, she will continue her campaign to wipe out mankind in an effort to 'save' the Earth from the destruction man is causing the Great Mother. Along the way, she will destroy every nightwalker she runs across and turn every shifter she finds into her slave."

"Lovely picture," I murmured sarcastically.

"Indeed," Cynnia sighed with a shake of her head. "One of the reasons for the falling out between me and Aurora was due to my vision for our return to Earth. I wanted peace." She paused for a minute, balling her small hands into fists at her side as she searched for the right words. "I wanted peace not only with the humans, but with all the races. If I can take Aurora's place as queen, I will take the remaining naturi deep into the wilds that are left around the world and we will exist there in secret. We will find ways to secretly strengthen the earth despite the interference of mankind. We will coexist."

"That's an interesting promise," I said when the others remained silent. "Considering the centuries of war that were waged with the naturi before they were finally caged, I find it hard to believe they would agree to coexistence with their enemies, particularly with the humans."

"I will admit that many will resist this idea at first, but I fully believe that once Aurora is defeated they will come to realize how truly dire the situation is," Cynnia said.

"And what is that?" Cooper prodded.

"The naturi are nearing extinction," Cynnia admitted.

Surprisingly, those words did not bring the smile to my

lips as I would have expected. If those words had been uttered by Rowe or Aurora, I would have hooted with joy while promising to wipe out the last of them. But as they were whispered from a heartbroken Cynnia, standing before me with the weight of an entire race on her shoulders, I could only feel . . . sympathy.

The young naturi princess continued. "During the final centuries in our cage, the naturi had trouble producing children, and many died due to a growing weakness we can only guess was caused by a weak connection to the earth. Furthermore, Aurora directed those loyal to her to cleanse the ranks of anyone who might not agree with her rule. Our numbers have been decimated, and I fear with the war that will inevitably be waged between Aurora and me, our numbers will be cut even further."

Barrett pushed off the car door he had been leaning against and rubbed the bridge of his nose between his thumb and index fingers before he finally spoke. "Why should we care? You've spent centuries subjugating and slaughtering us. Why shouldn't we let you have your civil war? Wipe as many of each other out in war and then let nature take its course with the rest of your dwindled race."

Barrett had voiced the thought running through the mind of everyone there. While Cynnia was seen as more of a neutral entity because of her stance toward coexistence, she was far from a welcome sight. Just being naturi still made her the enemy of all those who had come to meet her in the abandoned tunnels.

"The Great Awakening," Danaus proclaimed, drawing all eyes over to him. "Aurora plans to wage war on the humans anyway; she's not going to care about who sees the battle that is looming on the horizon. Should there be a great battle between Aurora's army and Cynnia's army, there will be not only witnesses, but also innocent victims. She will force the Great Awakening upon the world despite the plans of the coven, lycanthropes, and the magic users."

I frowned. Danaus was right. The Great Awakening was something we had been planning for during the past several centuries, the day when we let humanity know of our existence. It was our hope that if we controlled the release of the information, we had a better chance of easing them through what was going to be a rough transition period. With the exception of Our Liege, who wanted the Great Awakening to happen this year, it wasn't supposed to occur for at least another fifty years at the earliest. The human race wasn't prepared to know about our existence just yet.

"He's right," Knox conceded, shoving his hands into the pockets of his slacks as he stared down at the rough dirt floor.

"Is that part of your goal?" I inquired, pinning Cynnia with my narrowed gaze. "Will you keep this war quiet and hidden from the humans?"

"We have to." She took a tentative step toward me. "We won't be able to slide quietly and secretly into this world if the humans have discovered our existence."

"So if we leave you alone, not only do we risk Aurora winning this war, but we also risk the coming of the Great Awakening in the worst possible way," Barrett summarized. "And if we side with you, what? Peace and harmony."

"As much as I can manage among my own people," she quickly countered. "However, that's not to say people will not die. We are fighting a war with Aurora against some powerful clan members. There will be casualties, but sometimes we must take these risks for the greater good."

"Casualties come with war," Danaus agreed.

"The Savannah pack has already sustained more than our share of casualties when it comes to the naturi," Cooper snarled, taking an aggressive step toward Cynnia. The young princess didn't move when faced with the virulent hatred rolling off the lycanthrope, but I have to admit I was more than a little pleased to see Barrett place a restraining hand on his brother's shoulder. While I'm sure he agreed with Cooper, he still had not walked out of the meeting.

"I'm not sure what the Savannah pack can offer you in the way of assistance," Barrett said neutrally as Cooper took a step back so he was standing next to his brother again. "As you well know, we can be easily controlled by the animal clan. We would be nothing more than mindless pawns in battle, and I will not allow that to happen to my people again."

"I understand your concerns, and at the moment my sister Nyx is negotiating an alliance that would ensure that would not happen to your people. If the shifters of Savannah will join our fight, it will be of their own free will and it will remain that way until the end."

Barrett nodded thoughtfully and then turned his questioning gaze on me. In fact, I could feel everyone staring at me. With nightwalkers easily outnumbering lycanthropes in the city, I had at my disposal the largest army. In addition, I was the Fire Starter. Whether I wanted it or not, I was the leader of Savannah, and Barrett was waiting to see which way I was going to fall on this issue before he was willing to make any final decisions for his own people.

"What are you bringing to the table, Cynnia?" I demanded, crossing my arms over my chest again.

The naturi princess looked at me, confused for a moment, and then glanced over her shoulder questioningly at Shelly, who frowned. "The army," the earth witch said. "She wants to know what you're offering besides the nightwalkers and shifters you're trying to recruit."

"The animal clan within the naturi people has long been seen as the foot soldiers, the lowest of the clans, and they've grown weary of this position," Cynnia said. "As a result, their leader and most of the clan has broken off from Aurora. Nyx is negotiating an alliance with them. When we go to war with Aurora, one of the strongest groups of fighters will be among our warriors. From them, I will gain a promise that the shifters will not be controlled in any way."

"A decent start." Inwardly, I hoped she had more up her sleeve than just a pack of mongrels.

"For the most part, the wind clan has also joined my cause, leaving only the light and earth clans at Aurora's side," she continued. She clasped her hands together before her. "Her numbers are still large, but the presence of the Fire Starter will help to keep the light clan under control somewhat."

"What about the water clan?" I demanded. "I've seen them come ashore."

Cynnia's hands stilled as her gaze dropped down to her fingers. "Nyx has managed to contact some of them. Their numbers have been decimated. What few remain exist in only the deepest ocean trenches or in the most northern territories, living half-lives between humanlike creatures and a creature of the ocean. They cannot help us in this battle. They want nothing to do with either side and I respect their choice."

Unfolding one arm, I started ticking off each point on my fingers. "Wind clan. Animal clan. In addition, you want all the nightwalkers and lycans that can be pulled together so we can go after Aurora in some remote location hidden from the human populace. Should you win, there will be a *permanent* truce between the naturi and the other races."

"That is correct," Cynnia replied, flashing me a fragile smile as she tried to look reassuring.

"There's only thing that you're missing," I said with a frown.

"What's that?"

"You're creating this great army, but who will be leading it? You? An untrained warrior who has never seen a night of battle?"

"I helped you at Machu Picchu!" she snapped.

"But you weren't leading the charge or calling out the commands. I was." And when it came to going up against Aurora, I wasn't going to follow just anyone. In fact, I wasn't sure I was all that willing to follow anyone she named.

"You're right," she agreed in a soft voice. "I haven't proper battle experience. Kane, the leader of the animal clan, will lead his people into battle, while my sister Nyx will be the leader of the wind clan armies. And if she succeeds as I know she will, both Kane and Nyx will be following the final direction of Rowe in battle."

I made a small choking noise as both my hands slammed into the side of the car and I tried to lurch back away from Cynnia.

Follow Rowe? Every fiber in my being rebelled at the very idea. So much so that my stomach churned until I thought I would vomit up blood. Rowe was my enemy in every sense of the word. We had managed a temporary truce when both our lives were on the line, but it was made with the understanding that we would soon find ourselves on the opposite sides of the battlefield again.

"No!" I snarled. "Absolutely not! It will never happen." I jerked around and placed my hand on the handle of my car with the intention of pulling the door open and driving out of there so I could put as much distance between myself and the idea that I would once again work with my former tormentor. Before I could open the door, Danaus placed his hand over mine while placing his other hand on the door over my shoulder, pinning me gently in place.

Just hear her out.

Rowe nearly destroyed me, I snarled back. As the memory flashed to life in my brain, my temper snapped again. At the same time, balls of fire popped into existence in the wide entryway that led to a series of tunnels under downtown Savannah. There was a soft cry of surprise and distress among the gathered group, which only helped to feed my anger and the flames.

"Mira?" Shelly softly inquired.

"I won't do it," I repeated through clenched teeth, holding my body painfully still as every muscle in my frame tightened.

"Please, Mira," Cynnia said in an amazingly gentle and beguiling voice. "I fully know the history between not only you and Rowe, but also with my brother Nerian. I have spoken to other Machu Picchu survivors, and you of all people have no reason to help us other than the fact that it will help your own people in the end."

"You're asking for the impossible," I hissed, looking around Danaus at the naturi princess. "Rowe is loyal to his precious wife-queen. He will never come to your side."

"I am confident that Nyx will change his mind. She will make him see reason."

"And if she can't?" Knox interjected.

Cynnia paused and heaved a deep, slow sigh. "Then she will kill him. We can't afford to have him as an enemy. In truth, I fear his fighting prowess and experience more than Aurora's army. If we can get him to lead our armies, I am confident we will be victorious, however."

"Then you will have to achieve your victory without the help of the nightwalkers because I will not follow a single order uttered by that monster."

"You won't have to," Cynnia quickly said. "You and Barrett will lead your own people in this fight. We will tell you our plans for the encounter and you will place your own people into the battle as you see fit. You will not have to follow a single order from Rowe, I swear to you. I would never ask that of you."

Turning back to face the car, I closed my eyes. Danaus's thumb stroked over my hand, trying to ease away some of the tension. I pulled back some of the power that filled the flames that dotted the cave so that the light dimmed slightly. I hated Rowe. I hated him with everything I was, but I was making a selfish decision to turn my back on Cynnia and her cause because of my own past. Her goal, if she succeeded, would not only put off the Great Awakening, but also stop the constant battles with the naturi and my own people. To make matters worse, I had a feeling that Barrett would follow me if I decided not to help the naturi. It was going to be an all or nothing game when it came to the involvement of the lycans and the nightwalkers.

When Cynnia spoke again, she sounded a little closer than she had been only a couple seconds earlier. "I know that you will never forgive him, and I will not try to ask that of you. I am just looking for a temporary truce for the good of both our peoples."

"Rowe bears no love for mankind," I said, refusing to open my eyes. "What does he care if Aurora wishes to continue her campaign?"

"I believe that Rowe cares first for our people and he will not allow Aurora to pursue our extinction," Cynnia pressed on. "He will help us, and when we succeed, he will slip away into a silent, secret existence away from mankind with the rest of us. I am offering him peace and acceptance after centuries of struggle and hatred among our people."

Gritting my teeth, I reached out to Knox, letting his perpetual calm sweep over me before I spoke to him. I could feel his concern for me, but he did not outwardly display it. *What is your opinion?*

I believe that we must do what is best for our people. We will follow you regardless of what you decide in the belief that you are protecting us in the best fashion that you see for us, he honestly answered, but I could tell he was already leaning toward Cynnia's camp. He was only twisting it to make it sound like I actually had a choice when I really didn't. If I left Cynnia to go to war with Aurora without our help, we risked the complete destruction of our way of life. If we helped, we at least had a chance at peace.

You're a real bastard sometimes.

I don't know about this Rowe, but I know that the night-walkers will follow you anywhere, Elder. We will fight and defeat Aurora if we are to maintain our secret.

And that was the important part. Protecting the secret.

I pulled in several cleansing breaths through my nose and pushed them out through my clenched teeth before I finally released the door and turned back to face Cynnia. Danaus stepped back but still remained standing close to me should I need his support. My rock.

"You will have the support of the nightwalkers," I agreed, "but Rowe must keep his distance from me. My temper is a tenuous thing and I would hate for your great commander to go up in a puff of smoke before the battle has begun."

"I understand," Cynnia said with a relieved sigh before she turned her eyes on Barrett.

"We will stand with the nightwalkers and I will follow Mira's lead," Barrett agreed, as I expected. "She has more experience than I in battles such as these. I look for you to hold to your promise about controlling the animal clan. Should it be broken, my people will leave the battle at the first opportunity."

"Thank you for your assistance." Cynnia bowed deeply at the waist to both Barrett and me. "When Kane, Nyx, and

Rowe arrive, I will contact you again so we can plan how we will deal with Aurora."

Behind me, I felt Danaus stiffen and his powers flare from his body. I slipped into his mind and could feel the bulge of earth energy approaching our location.

"Cynnia, have you sent for more guards?" Danaus demanded.

"No, the rest of my armies still remain near Charleston. I didn't want to risk bringing more of my people into Mira's domain until we had settled matters," she said.

"Then we have a problem."

"They've been hunting me," Cynnia admitted with a weary shake of her head. "I thought we had lost them long enough that I could have this meeting without endangering you."

"Can you tell what clan they are from?" I inquired.

"Earth clan, mostly," Cynnia said. "But there appears to be at least one from the light clan."

Looking over at Barrett, I smiled widely enough to expose my fangs. "Are you in the mood for a little warm-up? Some practice for the battle to come?"

Barrett smiled back as me as he started to unbutton his shirt, preparing to shift into wolf form. "I welcome it," he said, his voice a deep growl in his barrel chest.

So did I.

Fourteen

Danaus stepped away from me, giving us plenty of room to fight in as he pulled a gun from a holster at his back. Knox palmed a pair of wicked looking blades as he shuffled a little closer to me. Meanwhile, both Barrett and Cooper shifted into wolf form, giving them the advantage of speed, stealth, and stability in the somewhat rocky terrain.

"Cynnia, hang back toward the tunnels with your guards!" I commanded, easily slipping into the role of leader as the battle hung before us. "Shelly, if things start to look like they're not going our way, take Cynnia straight down the far right tunnel. It will take you up under the Pirate House. From there you should make it out of the city without further problem."

"You think things are going to be that bad?" Knox inquired, twirling one blade in his hand. "I mean, you've fought worse odds than just a dozen naturi."

"It's earth clan naturi and we are somewhat underground at the moment," I reminded him. "It's not the best place to be holding this battle if I had a choice."

"But you and Danaus can just cook them all as they come through the door, ending this battle in the blink of an eye."

"That's the whole plan at the moment, but the light clan

member could make things difficult for me." Turning my attention to Danaus, I asked, "Do we have any time to change locations?" The hunter only shook his head, which was for the best. While the earth clan had the advantage with this location, it was at least removed from the eyes of any humans. A fight here was unlikely to endanger our secret being exposed to the rest of the world.

I could feel the swelling of earth energy growing closer. With a wave of my hand, I extinguished the flames hovering in the air, leaving the tunnel lit by only the headlights from the cars we'd arrived in. With any luck our attackers would be blinded when they entered the dark cave, giving us the advantage for a precious few seconds.

Edging over to where Barrett, in wolf form, was anxiously pacing, I knelt down and placed a hand on his head, my fingers sinking into his thick fur. "When the light clan naturi has been identified, I need both you and Cooper to focus on him or her as I try to keep it occupied. Once the light naturi is killed, it will be easier for me to end the fight quickly."

Barrett gave a quick snort, which I took as agreement. It was dangerous. If I didn't keep the light clan naturi busy, Cooper and Barrett were toast.

Glancing over, I found Cynnia surrounded by her honor guard. With short swords in hand, the three were crouched in an aggressive position, ready to protect their future queen. Shelly stood positioned in front of Cynnia. I could feel the energy sparking around her, mixing with the energy coming from the naturi as the earth witch drew her power from the ground beneath her feet.

A loud creak at one of the metal doors drew my attention back to the entrance. The door was opened wide enough to allow one naturi to slide through. She raised her hands in front of her eyes to shield her from the glaring bright light coming from the cars. Instantly, I summoned up my powers and engulfed the naturi in a ball of flames. Unfortunately, they had been smart enough to send in the light naturi first to keep me occupied and essentially out of the battle until she was killed.

The light clan naturi threw out her arm as she dove out of the way and tucked into a neat roll, sending a large fireball in my direction. I quickly captured it and caused it to dissipate harmlessly as the rest of the attacking naturi followed her into the cave, using the safe cover she had created.

A low growl filled the enormous cave, echoing down the various tunnels, as Barrett and Cooper prepared to strike. Unfortunately, getting to the light naturi meant going through the eleven others surrounding her.

"Danaus, can you get rid of her for me?" I asked, hoping that a quick use of his powers would save the lycanthropes from what was proving to be a suicide mission.

"I'm having a little trouble at the moment," he grumbled. For a second I wondered why, but my question was quickly answered when a dart embedded itself in my left arm. Pain screamed down my left side, burrowing down under my shoulder blade and throbbing in each of my fingers. I'd been so focused on the light naturi that I hadn't noticed the earth clan naturi opt for poison darts to keep us at bay.

Pulling the dart out of my arm, I slipped behind one of the cars and turned my attention to Cynnia. I was about to tell that group to seek cover when I discovered that Shelly had already erected a magical barrier around her group. A half smile lifted one corner of my mouth. She was learning faster than I was giving her credit for.

I peered out from the safety of the car in time to see a series of fireballs hurled at my group. Kneeling down, I lifted my good right arm and called the fire to my side instead. Barrett and Cooper were lunging in and out, attempting to harry the naturi, but the circle around the light clan naturi was not wavering. In fact, we were at a standstill. They were not taking a chance at moving closer in, while we were not succeeding in killing them or pushing them out. What disturbed me most was that I wasn't hearing any gunfire from Danaus. I tried to look around the car to see what the problem was, but the light naturi succeeded in keeping me too occupied to allow my attention to divert to the hunter.

Unfortunately, I felt the tide begin to change when a sickening yelp filled the air. I couldn't afford the chance to look around to see who it came from, but I knew that one of the werewolves had been injured. The growling grew louder and I sensed them both retreating toward our group. Another round of fireballs were launched in their direction, and again I caught them, protecting the lycanthropes while they found a safer location. For now, they were out of the fight until the wounded werewolf healed. His companion would protect him until he was on his feet again.

With them temporarily taken out of the fight, and the wind clan naturi defending Cynnia, that left only Danaus, Knox, and me to wipe out the naturi that were creeping closer to our position. It wasn't the best odds I'd had in a while, but I was unwilling to accept that they were impossible. I had to get through this fight to get my chance at Aurora's head.

"Can you boil any of them now?" I asked Danaus. The darts had stopped flying and the naturi were now running toward us with short swords drawn.

"Not a problem," he said as he rose from behind the large rock he had been using as a shield. With lightning speed he pitched two silver blades at the approaching naturi, catching two of them in the throat and sending them choking to the ground. He lifted his right hand and I could feel the energy surge from within him to sweep out toward the approaching naturi, and then it stopped just as suddenly. I twisted around, daring to look at him for a second, to find him staring at the ground.

"What's wrong?" I demanded.

"I'm sinking," he said, confusion filling his voice. Both of his feet were already covered in wet earth up to his ankles. He lifted one leg, trying to pull it free, but the quickly rising earth seemed to reach up and pull him back down. The earth clan had stolen away my other weapon by pulling him down into the earth. I needed to kill these bastards fast before Danaus was buried alive.

I turned back in time to see three naturi, and taking position directly in front of Danaus, raised my short sword in time to block a series of blows aimed at removing some critical body parts. While fending off the naturi, I continued to try summoning up flames to ward off my opponents, but every flicker was quickly doused by the light clan naturi, protected at the back of the cave by a small contingent of the earth clan.

Burn them! Boil them! We're losing this one, Knox cried in my brain. And he was right. I could feel the panic rising in Danaus behind me as he continued to sink. He was so completely distracted by just trying to survive that he didn't have a chance to use his powers, and I couldn't harness his powers because it would sap him of the strength to fight the sinking earth.

"Shelly, get out of here!" I shouted, hating to admit defeat. The wind clan surrounding Cynnia had no magical edge under the earth, and we could only fight off the earth clan naturi with swords. If they turned their magic on the princess, we would be buried alive unless Shelly had a fresh trick up her sleeve, and I wasn't willing to bet on that just yet. With Cynnia and her pack out of the way, we might at least get rid of some of the naturi should they turn their attention to the fleeing group.

However, luck just didn't seem to be on my side. The earth clan naturi continued to come at us. I killed one of my opponents, but another took his place. Growling intensified from the far corner, indicating that some of the earth naturi were approaching the two lycanthropes. It wasn't going to be a fair fight with one of them still wounded.

For the first time since the return of the naturi, I had to admit I was outgunned. I had spent most of my time going up against light and wind clan naturi, finding ways around their powers and keeping the fight on a physical level. I wasn't prepared for a combination of earth and light clan in an area that gave them a distinct advantage.

"Mira! Can't breathe!" Danaus gasped.

I didn't need to look around to know that Danaus had sunk down into the earth to the level of his chest, the naturi using the dirt to crush him, keeping his lungs from properly expanding.

"Knox!" I screamed. I needed help. Someone had to free Danaus.

"I'm trapped," he shouted back.

"I'll see if I can help!" Shelly replied, stunning me.

"I told you to get out of here," I snarled. I ducked low to avoid a sword aimed at my throat while blocking a second sword aimed at plunging through my heart. A few glancing blows had left me bleeding in a few places along my arms and legs, but nothing that had me concerned.

"Cynnia said that we won't abandon you," Shelly said, sounding distinctly closer.

I wanted to open my mouth to argue with her but said nothing as I continued to fight with the three naturi that stood before me. If Cynnia wanted to take this risk, it wasn't my place to try to stop her. I was more concerned about saving Danaus, and I didn't care where the help came from.

A scream from near the entrance of the tunnels seemed to draw everyone to a halt. I quickly looked over the heads of the naturi facing me to see a group of figures dressed all in black moving into the tunnels with amazing speed. A quick scan revealed that they were nightwalkers, but I was not at all familiar with them. And at that moment I didn't care. The tables had finally turned.

"Shelly, shield me!" I commanded. In a blink of an eye a blue shield popped around me, protecting me from the swords of the naturi. Safe from my closest opponents, I turned my full attention to the light clan naturi, throwing fireball after fireball at her so she was preoccupied when the unknown nightwalkers finally plunged a knife into her chest and cut off her head.

The light clan naturi finally eliminated, I pulled more energy to my side and set aflame the remaining earth clan naturi that filled the cave. With the arrival of the unknown nightwalkers, the fight was over in a couple minutes. But now I was faced with the question of who our saviors were and what I owed them for their much needed assistance.

Fifteen

Shelly immediately dropped the shield from around me and rushed over to the deep shadows where the lycanthropes were hunkered down. I turned to find Danaus chest deep in the earth, struggling to get a full breath of air. The earth clan naturi had essentially turned the earth around him into a somewhat hard quicksand so he sank down, but as the pressure increased, the earth was crushing him.

"Knox! Help me free him!" I cried, falling to my knees before the hunter. My hands trembled as I dug into the dirt around his chest, breaking fingernails and tearing my fingers up as I pulled the earth away. Knox dropped to his knees beside me and quickly joined me in freeing the hunter.

"I can breath," Danaus proclaimed after nearly a minute of digging. He sucked in a few deep breaths as Knox and I paused.

"Do you think we can pull you out or is it hardened completely around you?" Knox asked, clamping his left hand over a cut on his right arm that was struggling to close.

"You can try to pull me out," Danaus said, twisting his body as much as he could, trying to free up some space. "Just don't pull my arms out of their sockets."

"Gee, thanks for the warning," I groused as I pushed

wearily to my feet. Then I grabbed his left arm while Knox got on his right. On the count of three we pulled as gently as we could, slowly lifting Danaus out of the earth and back onto solid ground. The hunter immediately collapsed to his knees and sucked in more air.

"Take a break," I murmured, running my fingers through his hair before turning my attention to Knox. "Keep an eye on Cynnia for me as well as our new companions. It seems that Cynnia's witch bodyguard is somewhat preoccupied with the shifters."

"Got it."

Watching the nightwalkers that continued to hover near the entrance to the tunnels out of the corner of my eye, I walked over to the lycanthropes. Both Cooper and Shelly were kneeling beside Barrett, who was sprawled naked across the ground. Shelly had her hand pressed tightly against his stomach, while Cooper, who was also naked, had one hand pressed to his brother's right arm, attempting to stanch the bleeding. The witch was chanting softly with her eyes closed. I could feel the energy swirling in the air around her as she attempted to heal the worst of Barrett's wounds.

"You seem to be in safe hands," I said, resting my fists on my hips as I stared down at the alpha of the Savannah pack.

A crooked smile lifted the corners of Barrett's mouth and he shook his head. "They are making much of nothing. I've seen worse wounds."

"But never from a naturi blade," Cooper snapped. "We can't take any chances."

"Who are our unexpected guests?" Barrett asked, ignoring his brother's comment. He wasn't about to show more weakness than he already displayed. He was more interested in directing the conversation away from himself.

"That's what I'm about to find out," I admitted with a soft sigh. "I wanted to make sure you were all right first."

"With this angel working on the worst of my wounds, I think I shall be fine," Barrett said, smiling once again.

"Done!" Shelly announced, allowing her shoulders to slump wearily. She rubbed both her hands across Barrett's flat stomach, smearing away most of the blood to reveal what appeared to be a long red scratch.

"I didn't realize that your skills included healing," I said, gently pulling on a chunk of Shelly's blond hair.

"They apply to only earthbound creatures such as lycanthropes," she admitted, lifting her head to look over her shoulder at me. "There's nothing I can do for nightwalkers, which are bound by blood magic."

"Convenient," I grumbled.

"We couldn't take a chance with a wound from a naturi weapon. Cynnia warned me that they use all sorts of poisons and spells on their blades."

"Have you even met Barrett before this moment?" I asked on an impulse.

"Not formally," she said, a deep blush stealing to her cheeks. "I was at the town house when he stopped by before our trip to Peru last fall, but there was no time for introductions."

Barrett made a sound of disgust in the back of his throat as his eyes fell shut. It had not been a good moment between us. He'd accused me of betraying both our peoples to the naturi because I had chosen to protect Cynnia. And now he was fighting for her as well. Oh, how the wheel of fate turns.

"Shelly, this is Barrett, the alpha for the Savannah pack," I said, introducing them with an even voice despite the fact that I was laughing on the inside. "And this is his brother Cooper, his second in command."

"It's a pleasure to meet you both," the witch replied as if she were not kneeling beside two naked men. "I want to thank you for your agreement to help Cynnia. You—"

"Shelly, you may want to save it for another time," I interrupted. "I want you to get Cynnia and her people out of here through the tunnels before I go meet our new companions."

The earth witch nodded up at me once and then turned her attention back to Barrett, smiling at him. "I wouldn't shift for a little while if you can help it. I don't think the wound will tear back open, but it would be better if you didn't take any chances."

Barrett caught her left hand as she tried to rise and gave it a quick squeeze before letting go. "Thank you," he murmured in a low rough voice that surprised me. I raised one eyebrow at the lycanthrope but said nothing as he watched the witch quickly pick her way across the cave and return to Cynnia's side.

I waited until the naturi party had begun to head toward the tunnels before stepping away from the lycanthropes and walking toward the center of the cave. The nightwalkers that unexpectedly joined the party had been considerate enough to wait at the far end as I checked over the health of my people. We were all battered, bruised, and cut, but nothing that wouldn't heal with a little time.

As I reached the center of the cave, Danaus joined me, standing just a step behind my right shoulder. His breathing had evened out and I could feel his powers sweeping around me in great waves as he prepared to protect me. And for once I appreciated his overprotectiveness. I didn't know these nightwalkers. I had never sensed them in my area before. Hell, I had never sensed them before at the coven or throughout my travels in Europe. The only thing I could tell for sure was that they were old. Very old.

And then a human stepped out of their midst and bowed deeply before me. My bodyguard Matsui! I knew then that members of the Soga clan stood behind him. I'd had a feeling this day would come, when I would finally meet the Japanese nightwalker clan that he had spent years protecting. Unfortunately, I did not expect it to be under quite so dire circumstances. It wasn't heartening to know that not only was Jabari lurking around my territory, but that there now were unknown nightwalkers within my domain.

"It's a surprise to see you here, Matsui, considering that neither you nor Gabriel was summoned to my side," I started, trying to maintain my confidence despite the fact that we'd been getting our asses kicked before they arrived.

"Visitors from the Soga clan have come to speak with you," he said, bowing his head to me. "We did not mean to intrude, but only wished to help in your struggle against the naturi that have also been causing the clans in Japan some problems. Would you allow me to introduce the head of the group that has come to your domain?"

"I would be honored," I said with a nod.

Matsui stepped to the side and motioned for a nightwalker to step forward. He looked to be in his mid-twenties, with hair cut short and somewhat fashionably spiked. In contrast, his traditional dress was completely black, allowing him to easily sink into the dark shadows of the caves.

As he came to stand before me next to Matsui, I bowed deeply to him, placing my hands flat against the sides of my legs. I bid him both welcome and thanks in Japanese. It was all I knew of the language, but he seemed pleased enough when he bowed slightly back at me with a smile on his face.

"I am called Hideo," he said in a low, soothing voice. "Matsui has told us many great things about you, and it is I who is honored to meet you."

I held back a frown, struggling to keep both my face and tone neutral. "While I am pleased to hear that Matsui has reported back positive things, it was my understanding that he had left his place within the Soga clan and was exclusively my bodyguard. I didn't realize that he was also acting as a . . . scout for the nightwalkers of Japan."

It had been on the tip of my tongue to call him a "spy," but it would be stupid and rude to immediately pick a fight with a group of nightwalkers that had just come to our aid, especially when each of the four was older than me by many centuries. One surprise battle a night was my limit.

"We apologize for any confusion," Hideo replied. "Matsui is your bodyguard and will remain so as long as you wish him to be at your side. He is an excellent fighter and will die protecting you if it comes to such a thing. However, he was sent into your domain with the intention of procuring more information about the infamous Fire Starter before we made the trip ourselves. If one wishes to form an alliance, is it not best to get as much information as possible about the person with whom you may be placing your life?"

"I understand. Matsui has performed admirably for me and I have been very pleased to have him working as one of my bodyguards," I said. Matsui had knowingly acted as a spy while under my employ, and now I had to decide whether I would keep him. I didn't like being spied on. It was bad enough that the coven was keeping tabs on my ac- tivities. I didn't need to worry about a bunch of Japanese nightwalkers half a world away.

Heaving a great sigh, I shoved my hands into my pock- ets and relaxed my stance. We were on my turf now and it was time to push formality aside. We had all been through enough tonight already, and I had a feeling my night was far from over.

"While I am grateful for your impeccable timing tonight and your assistance in dealing with the naturi, I have to wonder why you have chosen now to come into my domain," I said. "In fact, for as long as I can remember, the nightwalker clans of Asia have shown no interest in the occurrences of the West."

"True," Hideo conceded. "Many centuries ago we struck a deal with your coven Elders that my people were to be apart from their rule. We had our own structure, our own lifestyle that did not fit within their world. Unfortunately, it now seems that the problems of the West have leaked into the East."

"The naturi," I muttered with a shake of my head. With the many doors that had opened around the world following the sacrifice at Machu Picchu the past fall, I had little doubt that even Japan was now seeing its share of problems with the naturi. In truth, I hadn't given it much thought since Aurora had made her base here in the West, but the repercussions of our failure in Peru were being felt everywhere.

Hideo nodded as he folded his arms across his chest. "Yes, those earthbound creatures that you call the naturi have been attacking our clans both day and night. We have never had such a problem before, so we came to you after Matsui told us of your many battles with their type."

"But why me?" I said, shaking my head, as I hoped to dodge responsibility for this lonely group looking for a little direction. I had enough of my own problems without adding an entire new set.

"Besides your personal experience with the naturi, Matsui informs us that you recently achieved a position of Elder on your coven, Fire Starter," Hideo carefully said. He was good. He was not only calling on my fighting experience but also using this as an opportunity to formally address a representative of the coven. And as if that wasn't all, he was invoking my position in the nightwalker world as the Fire Starter. Yep, I was screwed.

Do you think they would help us? Danaus whispered in my brain.

Against Aurora?

It seems they can handle themselves in a fight, and taking down Aurora could ease their problems at home.

But would they accept an alliance with their enemy? I wondered to myself. It was something I was still struggling with, and I wasn't sure that I would be able to sell such a plan to a group that already shunned its own kind under most circumstances.

"We have much to discuss, and I would prefer to spend that time in more comfortable quarters," I announced, loudly clapping my hands together. "Matsui, will you please bring our guests to me in one hour? That shall give Danaus and myself time to clean up here and check on a few matters before we have our meeting. They will be able to sense my location, I am sure."

"Is there anything we can assist you with?" Hideo offered, but I quickly waved him off.

I snapped my fingers and a small teardrop flame appeared above my hand. "Most of what needs to be done can be finished in a flash. I just need a little time to freshen up." And develop a new game plan, I thought.

For now, Daniel and the Daylight Coalition were forgotten. Cynnia and her troubles with Aurora had slipped away. Even my struggles with both Jabari and Nick had fallen by the wayside. The mysterious Soga clan was in my domain, and I was certainly not the best emissary for my kind here in the West. For once, I wished the damned sun would finally rise.

Sixteen

Danaus bade me to stop pacing for a third time, but I
wasn't listening. My mind kept turning over the fact
that I was suddenly being thrust into talks with a clan of
Japanese nightwalkers; a significant and completely unexpected event. I was a fledgling the last time a member of the
Far East nightwalkers appeared before the coven, and the
meeting did not go well. After centuries of silence, I knew
that the naturi were the reason for their appearance. But did
they also know that I was partially to blame for the failure
to prevent their return?

To further complicate matters, I was now aligned with
members of the naturi in hopes of killing their queen so I
could place a different naturi on the throne. And the best
part: I was expected to play nice with the naturi that had
been trying to destroy me for most of my existence. How
had things gotten to be so bad so fast?

Leaning against a tree at the edge of the clearing, Danaus
watched as I swung my katana through the air, slicing at
the wind that was beginning to stir. After a brief trip to my
house, where we took the opportunity to rearm with an as-
sortment of blades, we traveled out to the clearing the Savannah pack used during the full moon for its meetings. Out

here, we were hidden from the view of humans in the event that this conversation went as poorly as their last visit to the coven.

"Are these Japanese nightwalkers really that tough?" Danaus inquired as I carefully slid the sleek sword into the sheath hanging across my back, then ran my hands down over the knives strapped to my sides.

Keep your voice to yourself. You don't know how close they are. They could be listening.

A little paranoid, aren't you? Danaus asked in a mocking tone. But his sense of humor didn't keep him from being just as prepared as me. The hunter had grabbed his favorite sword with the rune inscribed along the blade, as well as a collection of knives that were secreted about his person.

They are in a foreign land and may be looking for an advantage over us. It's enough that they had to step in and save our hides from the naturi. They need not hear our private conversations about them as well.

Why are you so concerned?

I finally stopped pacing and stood in front of the hunter. *Because I am completely unprepared for this. I don't know what they want. They've not spoken to anyone outside Japan in centuries. These nightwalkers are also centuries old. Ancients! I'm half tempted to go track down Jabari since I know he's still lurking in the region, but I fear he would make a bigger mess of things.*

We're better off without him.

I— The words halted in my brain as I felt a swell of power drawing near. A car had stopped less than a mile away from the clearing. They weren't attempting to cloak their appearance any longer. There were three nightwalkers approaching, along with one human I could only presume was Matsui. A ball of anger flared. I had trusted my bodyguard to protect me. I have to admit that I had always suspected he was a spy,

but I'd hoped I was wrong. After I was finished with the
Japanese nightwalkers, Matsui was getting on a plane with
them. Gabriel would have to find another replacement for
my poor Michael.

Unfortunately, I was also coming to the realization that
I would never find a replacement for my fallen bodyguard.
Michael and Gabriel had been the perfect combination.
Their experience, wisdom, and just general common sense
allowed them to survive at my side for several years. Finding another that would protect me with his life and wouldn't
betray me was proving to be difficult.

Danaus sensed our approaching company as well and
pushed away from the tree to slowly walk out into the clearing. With a wave of my hand, a large fire sprang to life in
the center of the clearing, deepening and pushing back the
shadows to the surrounding woods. Several other fireballs
burst into existence around the clearing, hanging in the air
like oversized fireflies. We all had perfect night vision, but
I wanted nothing to be hidden here. I wanted to remind the
Soga clan exactly who they were dealing with. The Fire
Starter.

The hunter came to stand beside me, a frown pulling at
the corners of his mouth as his hands rested on the hilt of
two knives strapped to either side of his waist. "You're right.
They are old. Ancients at least as old as Jabari, if not older."

"You should never have come," I whispered, angry with
myself for not considering it sooner. His life had already
been at risk when we faced the naturi that evening. I didn't
need to add to it by pitting him up against a trio of nightwalkers that were significantly stronger than me. I should
have handled this alone.

"Don't start this now," Danaus growled.

"I've risked your life enough tonight. You should be
home—"

"Doing what? Baking a pie in the kitchen? Your laundry?"

"This is nightwalker business—"

"And as your consort, that makes it my business as well," he snapped. "I was handling nightwalkers long before we met, Mira, and I'm going to continue to handle nightwalkers regardless of whether we are involved. You have to stop trying to protect me."

Clenching my teeth, I closed my eyes for a second while I dragged in a deep breath through my nose and released it through my mouth. He was right. I was being overprotective. If there was anyone among my acquaintances that could handle himself in a fight, it was Danaus. Since taking him as a lover, it had become easier to forget that first and foremost he was an efficient killer.

"Stay behind me," I grumbled, refusing to vocally acknowledge that he had a valid point. That didn't stop him from chuckling softly at me as he took one step back so he hovered just behind my left shoulder.

Hideo was the first to step out of the shadows and enter the clearing. He raised one hand to shade his eyes against the bright light of the dancing flames that filled the immediate area. The ancient nightwalker was followed by two of his companions, on either side of him. Matsui stepped around them and briefly bowed to me before turning back into the woods. I could only guess that he was going back to wait at the car. My greatest concern, however, was the one missing nightwalker from their group.

"Thank you for agreeing to meet me here. I thought the added privacy would be most beneficial to our talks," I said, forcing a smile onto my lips.

"We are honored that you have agreed to speak with us during this most trying time. We are sure that you are quite busy with your own troubles," Hideo stated with a nod of his head. He glanced around the clearing and I could hear him sniffing the air. "This is an interesting location."

"This is actually the meeting spot for the local lycanthrope clan. Since the full moon has already passed, I thought it would be the one remote location in the city where we would be undisturbed."

"And the scent in the air . . . ?"

"Yes, it is human blood," I confirmed. The smell of dried blood lingered. Considering that we spent centuries hunting down and ingesting the delicacy, it was no surprise that most nightwalkers could easily discern between human blood and the blood of other races simply by smell, even if it was a day or two old. "During the full moon there was an altercation between the lycanthropes and a group of humans determined to hunt them down. Members of the Daylight Coalition."

"I fear we have not heard of them."

"You will," Danaus grimly interjected, drawing a frown to Hideo's mouth. I saw him cock his head ever so slightly toward the nightwalker on his left as if he were listening to something the nightwalker was silently saying.

"I was unaware that one of your companions was injured in the battle," I stated, changing the subject to the more important topic of the location of the missing nightwalker.

"Not injured," Hideo corrected with a wave of his hand. "I hope that you don't mind, but it was a very long journey here. He was in need of sustenance. I apologize for not seeking your permission first."

It was an excuse. Not a particularly good one, but one I could not argue with at the moment. I held up my hand and smiled at my companions. "Please say no more. I understand your situation and you are welcome to feed in my domain so long as you abide by the coven's rules of discretion and protection of the secret."

"Of course. Thank you," he agreed with a slight bow of his head. He then turned his attention to Danaus, who was just behind me. I could easily imagine the grim, disapproving expression etched in the hunter's hard face. I had little doubt he was also disturbed by the missing nightwalker. "Despite the lycans' recent problem with the humans, we find it reassuring that you have chosen to keep a human close to you in the form of a companion, as well as the human bodyguards that you keep on staff."

"Apparently you have not been fully informed. Danaus beside me isn't a companion. He is my consort on the coven," I replied with a growing grin that allowed my fangs to peek out. I was waiting for their shock but was ultimately disappointed.

"Matsui had mentioned his increased importance in your life," Hideo admitted. "We have long seen it as essential to have a strong relationship with humans. It's reassuring to see the West adopting a similar mentality."

"Mira remains very unique in her stance toward humans and their place in her life," Danaus said blandly.

"But as an Elder, she could represent a positive influence for others," Hideo countered with a small confident smile.

"I hope so," I said.

"Please allow me to introduce my companions." Beside Hideo on the left, a nightwalker who appeared to be about the same age and yet felt several centuries older stepped forward. "This is my second in command, Tetsuya." The nightwalker quickly bowed to us and then stepped back behind Hideo's shoulder again while the other nightwalker stepped forward. "And this is my close advisor, Kojima." The final, remaining nightwalker at least had a few flecks of gray in his hair, but his face still looked relatively young and fresh. However, Kojima felt as if he were the youngest of the trio.

"It is both an honor and a surprise to meet you," I said. "If my memory serves correctly, I was but a weak fledgling when an emissary from the East met with the coven, and the purpose of that meeting was to break all ties with the coven and the nightwalkers of the West. If you'll forgive my bluntness, why the sudden break from the silence?"

Hideo's earlier smile widened and I saw only the barest flash of fang, as if he were trying to hold it back and was failing. "I was forewarned of your bluntness and have been told you appreciate it in those you deal with. Of course, I'm sure you must know what would drive Japan's nightwalker clans into breaking their centuries of silence."

"The naturi," Danaus said in a low growl.

The smile melted from Hideo's face at those two words. We had expected as much. Since the opening of the doors following the battle at Machu Picchu, the world had been flooded with naturi. Even the Soga clan, after centuries of isolation and silence, were looking to me to clean out this nest because I was the famed Fire Starter. But fame was not going to help me survive the nights ahead of me.

"Yes, those earthbound monsters have been hunting down my people these past several months. Our human daylight guardians are no match for them. Two entire clans have been completely wiped out. Another lies on the verge of extinction. These clans are nearly as old as the people of Japan themselves, and now they are gone forever."

I nodded once, chewing on my lower lip. "Yes, we have lost many nightwalkers and lycanthropes as well due to the increased presence of the naturi."

"We have come to find out what the coven plans to do about the naturi threat," Kojima stated.

Frowning, I stared down at the ground, weighing my next words carefully. I had little encouragement to offer them, but then, I had to remember that they'd turned their back on the coven and our ways. Was it really my job to offer them a hand of assistance?

"As of my last meeting with the coven, the naturi threat was being handled by the keepers of the individual domains. The coven itself is not acting beyond the occasional incursion," I explained in a firm, even tone. "For now, it is seen as the job of every nightwalker to rein in and hunt down the naturi."

Hideo looked over at Kojima and then at Tetsuya before leveling his narrowed gaze on me. "And that is the coven we remember. Unwilling to act to save its own; concerned only with hiding from humanity so it does not have to answer for the lifestyle with which it has become so enamored."

I merely shrugged my shoulders at his correct assessment. "It is not in the nature of the nightwalker to change. We are as we have always been."

"Ahhh . . . but you are different," Tetsuya replied. "You were reborn differently than the rest of us. You are the Fire Starter."

"Little more than a parlor trick when it comes to fighting the light clan," I said with an absent wave of my hand. At the same time, the flames around us shifted and flicked brightly, as though a breeze had swept through the woods and disturbed them. It seemed they were starting to move in for the kill, and I had to fight the urge to reach for my nearest blade. It wasn't that I was a coven Elder that attracted them to me in the first place. It was the fact that I was the Fire Starter and had survived multiple encounters with the naturi. I was a survivor, which was what they needed when it came to defeating the naturi at last.

"But you must have some plans for your own domain," Hideo pressed. "Matsui spoke of one naturi in particular, Rowe, who has been hunting you. We have even heard that the queen of the naturi has made it a special mission to acquire your head since you were so instrumental in stopping their return many centuries ago."

Kojima stepped forward to stand in front of Hideo. His hand slid down to his side where I could only guess there was a concealed blade. The soft sound of earth crunching beneath Danaus's feet drifted up to my ears as the hunter restlessly shifted his stance. "We're under the impression that you may be under increased pressure here and planning something that could alleviate some of that pressure for your own kind and the shapeshifters."

A smile toyed with the corners of my mouth as I looked over at Danaus. The hunter was watching me closely, waiting to see if I was willing to reveal my own plans for Aurora to our visitors. In truth, I couldn't decide. The Japanese nightwalkers had turned their back on us. They had left us to lead our own lives and demanded that there be no interference in their lives from the nightwalkers of the West.

Desperation had drawn them back to our side, but I didn't expect them to agree so easily with what we had planned, no matter how desperate they were. In fact, I was more concerned with them becoming a hindrance if they didn't agree. Hell, I wasn't banking on the coven to back me on this, so I wasn't telling them either. How could the Japanese clans go along with my plans?

"You are correct in that we have plans for my domain of Savannah," I admitted with a sigh as I finally decided to step out on this limb. "Unfortunately, you have to keep in mind that my main goal is not the preservation and protection of our people while eliminating the naturi threat. I am aiming for something far grander. I want a permanent peace. That is what we were meeting about in the tunnels when you aided us tonight."

"A permanent peace?" Hideo repeated. "You have found a way to return the naturi back to their cage?"

It was a tempting idea, but one doomed to failure in the end, as we had already proven with their escape. The cage that held the bori was enduring, but I wasn't willing to put my money on the idea that it would last indefinitely either. Putting the naturi back in the cage was not only impossible because I had no idea how it was accomplished in the first place, but also impractical. I didn't want to have to fight another Rowe years from now as he completed a list of sacrifices in order to free his people. Like I had said, I wanted something more permanent, even if it meant a sizable sacrifice and a change in mentality for us all.

"There will be no return of their cage," I said grimly with a shake of my head. "We do not know how it was formed. Furthermore, the naturi have been scattered to the four winds, and we would never get them gathered together so they can be recaptured."

"Then how would we achieve this permanent peace that you spoke of?" Tetsuya inquired.

"We first need to get rid of Aurora."

"Stopping Aurora would bring us peace? We would still be overwhelmed with naturi," Hideo said.

"Stopping Aurora would be the first step in the process of achieving peace," Danaus said, drawing all eyes over to him. "She maintains her plan to destroy not only nightwalkers but humans as well in her effort to save the Earth. She is single-minded in her plan, and she has begun to turn on her own kind. She is alienating those she would need to accomplish her grand scheme."

"There is a fissure that is growing among the naturi," I added. "We should be able to use that break in their solidarity to our advantage."

"How?" Tetsuya asked warily.

I smiled at him. "An alliance."

"With the naturi?" Hideo demanded, his soft voice hardening for the first time. "You are planning an alliance with the naturi?"

"Yes," I said with a slight hiss of warning. I wanted to keep this meeting as civil and calm as possible, but I knew that what I was suggesting now was treasonous among the nightwalkers. We had spent too many centuries fighting against the naturi. From the very birth of our race, they had been our enemy. There was no reconciling your differences with your enemies. At least, not when it came to the naturi. What I had said earlier was too true. Nightwalkers didn't change. But then, I guess Tetsuya was right; I was different.

"Aurora has tried to kill both of her sisters in the name of treason. The younger of the two sisters, Cynnia, wants to establish a coexistence between naturi and nightwalkers. A number of naturi have already rallied to her side, and she aims to take on Aurora. If we can get Cynnia named queen of the naturi, we have a chance at creating a permanent peace between our two peoples."

Danaus stood beside me with a hand resting on the hilt of one dagger at his side in the form of a warning.

"From what we have come to understand, the naturi are weary of war. The race is slowly dying off. Cynnia is offering them a chance at survival by simply blending into the background, a return to the forests of the world where they can live in peace."

Kojima shook his head and paced a couple steps away from his companions, edging a little farther into the clearing. He was clearly the most emotional of the trio, struggling to maintain the same outer calm as his companions. "If they are already facing eventual extinction, why do we not just take advantage of it and kill them off?"

"Because their numbers are still great," I said, closely watching the pacing nightwalker for any sign that he was reaching for a weapon. "The war that would ensue would place us against all the naturi, and no matter what you may hope, we would never be able to rally the nightwalkers together to defeat the naturi horde."

"You would also be faced with the Great Awakening if you attempted to wage such a war," Danaus reminded us.

The Great Awakening. I liked to think it was something that nightwalkers from both the East and the West were trying to avoid. Especially since we still had to deal with the naturi epidemic first. I could only manage one thing at a time.

"My people are ready for the Great Awakening," Hideo firmly said.

I shook my head. "But the world is not. If your people are struggling with the naturi, then you are not ready to face a world that knows about nightwalkers and lycanthropes. Those humans you are so eager to call your friends are just as likely to turn on you the moment they begin to see you as a threat—which you are."

"Coexistence is the only way we can hope to continue our current life while remaining hidden from humanity," Danaus said. "Cynnia wants peace between the two sides, and it is the wisest choice at this juncture."

"Do you seriously think peace with the naturi is possible?" Kojima demanded, glaring at me. I didn't blame him for his doubts. He was only voicing the same thoughts that I had. The only difference was that I knew what had truly happened among the Machu Picchu ruins. Cynnia wasn't just trying to save her own skin; she was trying to save her race from an even bigger war that Aurora was planning. We didn't need to turn the humans against us just yet. That would come soon enough, I was certain.

"With Cynnia as their leader, yes," I replied. "I'm not so blind as to think that all the fighting between the nightwalkers and the naturi will stop. There will be small branches that are determined to keep the war going even after Aurora's defeat, but that is nothing in comparison to the war Aurora is determined to wage."

Hideo scratched his chin as he silently stared at me. "This Cynnia was the one you were meeting with tonight?"

"Yes. The leader of the Savannah lycanthropes, me, and my associates all met with her tonight to discuss her plan. In truth, I have just now agreed to go along with her plan. There is still much planning and strategizing that needs to be done, but I believe in her vision for our two peoples. After countless centuries that have cost us too many lives, I believe that Cynnia can finally bring the war between the nightwalkers and the naturi to an end."

"If Cynnia is for peace between our races, why were there naturi attacking you tonight?" Tetsuya inquired.

"Because Cynnia is being hunted by her sister Aurora. The queen has become paranoid and insane with power. At Machu Picchu this past fall, she branded Cynnia and her sister Nyx traitors. She banished her consort Rowe. She has made enemies of the very people she needs most at her side to succeed in defeating the nightwalkers and the humans. Those so-called traitors are now gathered together to bring her down."

"And they have won over the Fire Starter as well," Danaus added with a smirk. "The odds are starting to tip in our favor. Aurora may have greater numbers, but we just need to take down the queen to finally quell the naturi nation. Cynnia will lead them into seclusion while the nightwalkers and the lycanthropes return to their previous way of life."

Hideo shook his head at me. He paused and threaded his fingers through his hair, pushing it away from his eyes. "And what happens if this Cynnia succeeds and takes her people away from the human world? What if the naturi are allowed to return to the woods where their numbers are permitted to grow once again? Won't we be eventually faced with a new, stronger threat?"

An evil grin slipped across my face, and I could feel a lavender glow filling my eyes. "The peace that I speak of is merely a temporary one in hopes of avoiding an even greater and more dangerous war that will rip away our veil of secrecy. The fight between Cynnia and Aurora will cut into their numbers, leaving the naturi weakened. It will take them a long time to replenish themselves. That will give us time to train our own death squads to specialize in hunting down the naturi in their own territory. At the moment, we haven't an edge when it comes to fighting them in the woods. Time and research will give us that edge. Do not mistake my decision to agree to a truce with the naturi. My ultimate goal will always be their complete extinction."

Mira! Danaus exclaimed in my head, though there was no outward signs that he was stunned by my admission.

It is better to kill them off before they get the chance to kill us off, I coldly replied. *Cynnia has some pretty ideas, but the truce between the two races will always be temporary. She can't rule forever, and I know Rowe. He won't allow the coexistence to stretch indefinitely. He is a soldier and he has been trained to kill nightwalkers.*

But you agreed to a truce with Cynnia!

I will not be the one to break that truce, but make no mistake, it will be broken eventually, and we will be prepared for it.

"Your plans are interesting," Hideo conceded. "We are reassured by the fact that your end goal remains the elimination of the naturi race. However, we cannot accept a temporary truce with a group that we plan to ultimately destroy. The naturi are our sworn enemy and we cannot agree to work in harmony with them."

"Even if it means avoiding the Great Awakening?" I asked, cocking my head to one side as I stared at him.

"This just may be a sign that it is finally time for the Great Awakening to happen."

"I can't accept that." I crossed my arms over my stomach and glared at Hideo. "If it is within my power to delay that horrible event, I will do everything I can to delay it. Humanity is not ready."

"And we cannot accept such two-faced betrayal," Hideo countered, looking completely at peace with his decision. It was all I could do not to snicker at him.

"The clans of the East truly are different," I said. "Here, betrayal is a way of life. It's a survival mechanism."

"We are not like you," Tetsuya said, looking more than a little offended.

"And yet you came here looking for my help. I may be different, but I was raised by the nightwalkers of the West. I'm not that different."

"We cannot help you," Hideo firmly said.

"Because of my ultimate plans of betrayal?" I raised one eyebrow at him.

"Because working with the naturi would be a betrayal of our promise to fight them," Hideo corrected.

"Then maybe it's time to rethink that promise, if you have any hope of protecting your people in the long run," I said, and held up my hand to stop his next comment, which I knew would be a rejection of that very suggestion. "Remain in my domain for a few nights. It is a long flight back to Japan, and you and your people will need some time to regain your strength. Think about what I have told you. If you would like an audience with Cynnia to further discuss her vision, it can be arranged."

"And the coven's position on your plans?" Kojima asked.

"The coven has no position on my plans because I am

handling this as the keeper of my domain. If we succeed in ridding the world of Aurora, I will then deal with the coven."

Hideo frowned at me, his dark eyes narrowing. "While we appreciate your offering and the position that you find yourself in, we believe that our situation is direr at the moment. We politely request that you accompany us back to Japan where you will aid us in ridding our lands of the naturi pest."

My voice dropped to a low warning. "I'm afraid that I can't do that. My job is to protect my domain, not yours."

"And I am afraid that your refusal is not an option," Tetsuya countered.

I took a step backward while both my hands dropped down to the knives on either of my hips as I waited for the attack. "You can't force me to assist you. My work is here."

"We are confident that you will come if it means coming for your consort," Kojima said with a dark grin.

It was then that I finally felt it. He had been cloaking himself deep in the woods, but now that he had drawn close to the clearing, I could sense his power clearly despite his efforts to hide himself from me. I growled, stepping in front of Danaus to block the other three nightwalkers in front of me from approaching.

The other one is here. He's going to attack you from behind, I warned Danaus silently.

It's too late, Danaus snarled in my brain. *He's already done it.*

I twisted around to find the smaller man hanging onto Danaus's back, his legs wrapped around the hunter's slender waist while holding a short blade to his throat while his other hand held a knife close to Danaus's heart.

Boil him, but don't kill him. I will handle the others.

The fireballs that circled the clearing crashed to the ground in an explosion of sparks and debris as I launched myself at my three opponents. It wasn't that they had hoped to kidnap me for their own ends. I was pissed over the fact that they thought for even a second that they could lay a hand on Danaus. It would not be tolerated.

Knives spun out of my hands in a flurry of glinting silver across the clearing. They were easily blocked by my skilled opponents, but it gave me enough time to draw my sword. As it cleared the sheath, I coated the sleek blade in dancing flames. The trio hesitated to approach, allowing me to back to them to the edge of the woods.

At the same time, the screams of their secret companion echoed through the clearing, bouncing off the trees and soaring into the black sky above. There was a heavy thud as the body hit the ground behind me. I could hear the scrambling in the dirt as he writhed about, undoubtedly clawing at his flesh.

"Drop your weapons now, or your companion will be boiled from the inside out," I threatened.

"Nomura," Tetsuya whispered, his gazed locked over my shoulder.

"Do it now! He doesn't have much time!"

"Agreed," Hideo said, throwing down the sword strapped to his back. His companions quickly followed and then held up their empty hands in acquiescence.

Turning sideways, I looked over at Danaus, who released the Japanese nightwalker from the ugly grip of his powers. The nightwalker named Nomura stopped writhing about and curled up into a tight little ball on the ground, moaning.

"In case you were wondering, Danaus can more than take care of himself," I said smugly. "Touch him again and he will not hesitate to kill you all. Touch anyone else in my domain and we will both hunt you down. I can sympathize with your desperation, and that is why I have spared your companion's life."

"How?" Hideo whispered.

"That's my secret," Danaus said in a low voice.

I took a step backward and put my sword in its sheath on my back. "Take your companion and return to your daylight resting place. My offer stands. You may stay in my domain for a few nights to give your companion some time to recover. Consider my plan. The elimination of Aurora may also succeed in helping your own people in Japan."

"We do not welcome the Great Awakening, but working with the naturi to avoid such a fate is equally abhorrent to us."

"I'm not thrilled with the idea either, but we have been backed into a corner." I frowned. "It's time to make some tough decisions."

"Agreed," Hideo said with a slight sigh, sounding tired for the first time. I couldn't blame him. Dawn was drawing close and it had already been a very long night.

Cautiously, the three members of the Soga clan approached their fallen member and carried him from the clearing, keeping as much distance from Danaus and myself as possible. Kojima paused long enough to pick up their weapons at the edge of the clearing.

When my eyes finally fell on Danaus, I considered rescinding my offer and burning all four of them to a crisp, but I got hold of my temper at the last second. Hurrying to the hunter, I put my hand over his, resting on his throat. He had been cut deeply enough that blood was leaking between his fingers, while a second more shallow wound had sliced through his shirt and cut through the flesh over his heart.

"I'm fine," he reassured me in a low voice that danced across my skin.

"You're not. That bastard cut you. He could have seriously injured you. I thought their goal was to kidnap you. How could I possibly agree to help them if they killed you?" I ranted.

"I honestly think it was an accident." Danaus weakly smiled at me, trying to ease my fears and cool the anger bubbling just below the surface. "When I started to boil his blood, he jerked away from me, pulling the knife across my throat as he rushed to get away from me."

Danaus lifted his hand, wiping away the blood to reveal a long, angry red cut, but at least the bleeding had stopped. I pulled away my own hand, covered in his blood, my fingers trembling. A deep, unrelenting longing rose in my chest, nearly dragging a whimper from my throat. I wanted to lick my fingers clean of his blood. I want to suck the blood from his fingers and run my tongue along this throat to clean away the last of his blood. And if I was honest with myself, something dark inside of me longed to sink my fangs in his throat and finally drink deep.

With jerky movements I grabbed the edge of his cotton shirt, wiped my hands clean of the temptation, and took a step away from him. It was more than the fact that Danaus would not let me drink from him. It was that I refused to ever allow a nightwalker to feed from him, including myself. Danaus was above such things. He was my lover and constant companion. He was too precious to ever become a source of sustenance. I wouldn't allow it.

But that didn't mean my instincts didn't scream for his blood. Danaus understood that longing and was smart enough to give me space when I needed it.

"It's been a long night. You need to feed," he murmured.

"Yes," I reluctantly admitted, looking away from him.

He placed his hand under my chin and tipped my head so I couldn't hide from his direct gaze. "Go feed. I will take the car back to the city. Do you want me at the house?" His thumb gently stroked across my cheekbone, and my eyes slipped shut for a moment, easing some of the hunger pains.

"No need. It's late. I will go directly to bed when I return to the house. I have much to think about tonight."

"As you wish." He leaned in and slowly pressed a kiss to my forehead. His motions were slow and controlled, careful not to set off any of my more predatory instincts when the smell of his blood was still wafting through the air. I could feel the turmoil churning within him as he walked away and I remained a silent ghost in his thoughts. He still struggled with my need to ingest human blood, but he was fighting to accept it. This relationship was not an easy thing, but we were trying.

Seventeen

Danaus found me seated on the floor in the sunny yellow bedroom at my house the next night. A shaft of thick moonlight shone through the open curtains, cutting a square on the ground and glazing the furniture in an ethereal silver glow. After Lily's death, Danaus and I had pulled the sheets and blankets off the bed and washed them. We opened the windows, welcoming in a chilly early spring breeze in hopes of the fresh air washing out her scent. But no matter what we did to cleanse the room, I swore I could still smell her presence in there, even after the past few months. I closed my eyes and drew in a slow deep breath so the air filled my useless lungs. I held it, picking apart the scents of dust, laundry detergent, lemon-scent cleaning product, and finally Lily.

She had been so briefly in our lives. A child of the street with an amazing gift to see the auras of the people around her, Lily had been special to me. She had spirit and courage. She was quick and resourceful. She should have survived. At that moment she should have been safely ensconced at the Themis compound, being taught by the paranormal researchers in a positive environment. Instead, she now lay in a cold grave in a distant cemetery because a bori had used her to get to Danaus and me. We had failed her.

But then Lily wasn't the only one haunting me. Just down the hall, Tristan's room remained completely untouched from when he was last in there. When I returned home from Venice in December, I locked the door to that room and allowed no one to touch his things. I didn't even go inside, but I could imagine the unused bed, rumpled from where he would lay on it as he read. The computer on his desk would be sitting in sleep mode, waiting for its master to return home so he could resume his search for new music. Books and magazines were haphazardly scattered about the room, while a pile of laundry lay in one corner, waiting to hit the washing machine. I knew his unique scent would be thick in the air. If I entered his private domain, I would be lost to the horror of our past.

I replayed that night in Venice and doubts ate at me. I couldn't convince myself that I had done the right thing. Macaire had shattered his mind, so that Tristan would look straight through me, never seeing my loving face or the tears streaming down my cheeks as my heart broke in bitter shards. I should have found a way to save him. If I had taken another minute and not been consumed by rage and despair, I might have come up with a way to save him. Vainly I reminded myself that his mind was broken: he was locked in a world of perpetual torment, and it had been my responsibility to set him free. Killing Tristan might have been the kindest thing I could have done for him, but it was slowly destroying me.

Heavy footsteps creaking on the wooden stairs helped to break my destructive train of thought, but it didn't completely free me of the two ghosts that seemed to be clinging to me. I had come into Lily's room to hide from the rest of the world as I tried to think about the chaos swirling around me. But my thoughts were stuck on my two dead companions.

I didn't need to reach out with my powers—I could feel

Danaus's energy swirling up the stairs like the tentacles of a sea creature to search me out. Warm and comforting, they wrapped around me, beating back my demons before he leaned against the door frame to stare down at me with a frown marring his handsome face.

"What are you doing?" he demanded as I looked up at him.

"Thinking."

"I can't imagine that any productive thinking can be done in here."

"I never said it was productive thinking. I'm just thinking."

"About what?"

"All the ways in which I went wrong."

"Mira . . ."

"No, Danaus, think about it. I mishandled things, and now Michael, Thorne, Lily, and Tristan are all dead. My judgment is off. And now I've gone and made a pact with the naturi. I have agreed to be Rowe's ally, of all people! The creature that has been torturing or trying to kill me most of my life!"

Danaus heaved a heavy sigh as he leaned his shoulder against the door frame. "Michael and Thorne were lapses in your judgment. You didn't think ahead and bad things happened. But you've learned, Mira. You've grown more cautious and you're thinking things through instead of rushing headlong into a situation. Valerio and Stefan could have easily been killed in Budapest, but your careful planning saved them on more than one occasion."

His words stung a little as my own fears were validated, but I respected Danaus's point of view and his honesty. He wasn't going to lie to me to make me feel better. "What about Lily and Tristan? Maybe if I had—"

"There is no 'maybe' with Lily and Tristan," he interrupted. "The situations were far beyond your control. Gaizka got the better of us when it came to Lily, and we didn't anticipate the depths of Macaire's depravity when it came to Tristan. We lost them to bad people. It happens no matter how hard we try to protect everyone we love."

I took another deep breath and slowly released it as I stared straight ahead into the room, trying to force some of the tension out of my shoulders. My ass was getting sore from sitting on the floor for the past couple of hours and my back was stiff. However, I still wasn't ready to move. I felt as if I had managed to find a hiding place from the world in this bright little bedroom, and I wasn't ready to leave it.

"Why does it feel as if the world is falling into chaos?" I murmured, talking mostly to myself. "The Daylight Coalition has decided to strike now, endangering countless nightwalkers and lycanthropes in my own domain. I can't shake the feeling they have been drawn to this city because of me. As a result, Daniel has been put into an extremely dangerous situation in hopes of garnering information. To make matters worse, Cynnia comes to me with a plan to get rid of her sister by teaming up with Rowe and the rest of the naturi. It's the very thing I swore I would never do! Ally with the naturi!"

"You're trying to do what is right for your people," Danaus reminded me.

"Right for my people? Can I even be trusted to judge what is 'right for my people'?" I snapped, twisting around to stare up at him. "I'm romantically involved with a nightwalker hunter that is part bori—the sworn enemy of the nightwalker nation! I've agreed to an alliance with the naturi in an effort to stop a war that would bring the Great Awakening. I feel as if I've killed more of my own kind during the past several months than I've saved."

"Think of the faceless numbers you've saved by your actions," Danaus calmly said, to which I only gave a derisive snort.

"And to add to my fun, members of the Soga clan are here trying to drag me back to Japan in hopes that I will solve their problems."

"You can't help everyone."

"At this point I don't feel I can even help myself," I groused, falling deeper into self-pity. The situation truly was growing more and more out of control, and it was only going to get worse when Nyx and Rowe finally arrived in my city. I would have to find a way to work with Rowe without trying to kill him at the first opportunity. Not the easiest of tasks.

"Enough," Danaus growled. Pushing away from the door frame, he stepped into the room and stood before me with his feet wide apart and his fists on his hips. "Stop the whining. Stop the complaining. Stop the self-pity." Grabbing my left upper arm, he hauled me to my feet and then bent low enough to drop me over his shoulder while wrapping his free hand around my legs.

"Danaus!" I shouted, struggling to get into an upright position as he walked out of the room and headed for the stairs. He bounced me once, causing me to lose my balance. I flopped back down so I was lying over his shoulder. My hair felt forward, partially obscuring my view of his nice ass as we slowly and steadily descended the stairs.

"You need some distraction. Clear your mind."

"If you want to distract me, we could have stayed upstairs and used one of the other bedrooms," I suggested.

"This is better," he firmly said as he hit the ground floor and made a sharp turn around the banister. He paused long enough to open the door under the stairs that led down the basement.

"Better than sex? I really doubt that," I replied, pushing some hair out of my face as he started to descend yet another set of stairs.

Danaus said nothing in reply. He just silently continued

down into the basement. Once in the center of the room, he none too gently dropped me on my ass on a thin mat. I gazed around the room in the bright overhead lighting. A couple months ago we had removed all the furniture, the wet bar, and the big screen TV. It had all been a facade in the first place to convince anyone who came into the house that there was nothing out of the ordinary.

In place of the items of leisure, Danaus and I had ripped up the carpet and replaced it with a covering of thin sparring mats. The walls were covered in a wide variety of weapons and sparring shields. The room was now a big open space for us to practice our fighting techniques. In here, blood was spilled and bones broken, but since we healed so quickly, the wounds were only a temporary distraction before we were back at it again.

As I sat in the middle of the mat, I watched Danaus walk over to the far wall containing the various staves and other blunt objects, all arranged according to discipline. I frowned as he paused, looking over the broad selection.

"What are you in the mood for?" he called out as his hand passed over a quarter staff and headed toward the Far Eastern fighting style weapons. As I watched him, I kicked off my shoes and pulled off my socks, preferring to be barefoot on the mat to give me better grip.

"For beating your skull in? Give me the jō staff," I replied. My aikido was far stronger than some of my other training, giving me what I hoped would be an edge. Danaus picked the jō staff off the wall and threw it at me as I pushed to my feet. I caught it over my head and frowned as he pulled down a pair of eskrima sticks, as I expected. His kali training had proven to be much better than mine when we'd both fought with the medium-sized rattan sticks in the past, leaving me with more than a few welts and a broken forearm. I had learned that opposing him with the jō staff tapped better into my aikido training, which was also complemented with more than a little Jeet Kune Do training. In this sparring session, it appeared we would be evenly matched. A small smile grew on my lips as he settled the two sticks in his hands and gave them a few lightning quick swipes through the air.

"What? No kalis or bankow?" I mocked, referring to the wavy blade and the spear that were commonly matched with one of the eskrima sticks in a traditional kali fight.

"Just blunt objects tonight. We're playing a slightly different game," he said with a smirk.

"Different scoring system? We going to twenty points instead of ten?"

"Better. If a hit is scored, the loser takes off an article of clothing."

My eyebrows jumped and my mouth fell open as I stared at him for a second. "Strip sparring?"

"You needed a distraction and a way to burn off some steam."

I gave a small chuckle and shook my head at him as I turned my jō staff over in my hands, getting ready for his attack. "Grand Masters are rolling over in their graves right now."

With my feet planted on the mats, I clenched my muscles and tightened my grip on the red oak staff as Danaus closed the distance between us. His face was completely expressionless, and I could feel the calm sweeping through his mind and down through his body as he settled into total focus on knocking the absolute crap out of me. I, on the other hand, was a ball of energy waiting to explode. I could find no calm, no center of peace, as thoughts of the Daylight Coalition, Rowe, Cynnia, and the Soga clan all danced through my head.

The second he was within striking distance, Danaus

pounded me with a flurry of hits I barely managed to block. The hunter was a blur of motion, aiming striking blows from the top of my head to the inside of my thighs as he searched methodically for an opening. The speed at which he came at me kept me on the defensive, but I didn't back up an inch, refusing to give him the satisfaction of overpowering me with his speed and skill.

After more than five minutes of nearly nonstop blows, Danaus stepped back and wiped the sweat from his left temple. He wasn't breathing heavily yet, but the flurry of strikes had taken its toll. I took the opening and launched my own attack with the jō staff. He caught a strike aimed for his neck with his eskrima stick, but before I could sweep the staff down to knock his legs out from beneath him, he hit me with a punyo, slamming the end of one of the eskrima sticks in the dead center of my forehead.

Dazed, I stumbled backward a couple steps until I finally landed on my ass in the middle of my mat. With my left hand, I touched my forehead to find a steady trickle of blood starting to slide down to the bridge of my nose. I wiped away the blood as the wound quickly closed. I had a feeling I would have a bruise there for several more minutes. My thoughts were scattered and my head throbbed, making me wonder if he'd succeeded in cracking my skull.

"I want your shirt," Danaus proclaimed.

Frowning, I put down my staff, pulled my black cotton T-shirt over my head and tossed it at him. The hunter caught the shirt with one of the sticks in his hand and tossed it to the side of the room as if putting aside his prizes. I was beginning to wish I hadn't bothered to take off my shoes. My focus wasn't on the fight as it should have been, and I was going to lose quickly if I didn't get centered.

Grabbing up my staff again, I rose to my feet with a push of my powers. I stuffed all my stray thoughts down into a

ball in the pit of my stomach so my mind was finally clear.
Before I had my feet properly set, Danaus came at me again
with sticks flying. I beat them back, and actually managed
to overpower him enough to forced him to take a step back.
My usual vampire speed was returning as I focused on the
fight before me. Danaus struck out with his right hand, and
I easily blocked it, but it was a feint. He jabbed with his
left hand, hoping to catch me in the middle of the chest. I
twisted out of his reach, balancing most of my weight on
my right foot. As he started to pull back from the missed
blow, I once again swept down with my staff. This time the
jō staff hit its mark, slamming into the back of both of his
legs. Danaus hit the mat flat on his back, knocking the wind
out of his lungs.

Grinning, I stood over him with the jō staff pointed at his
throat. "Shirt, please."

"I'm still wearing my shoes and socks," he patiently
pointed out.

"And I said shirt. Now."

I stepped backward, returning to my side of the sparring mat so he could sit up and pull his black T-shirt over
his head. He tossed it to me and I caught it with one hand.
Bringing it to my face, I pretended to take in a deep whiff.
"Ahhh . . . I smell fear," I said before tossing the shirt over
to the side of the room.

Danaus gave a deep chuckle as he pushed to his feet
again. A new feeling twisted in my stomach as I watched the
play of muscles before me. His stomach was flat and lined
with thick muscles, while his arms bulged as he flexed the
muscles and took up position with the eskrima sticks. The
shirt had been a mistake. I now had a new distraction, and
this one wasn't as easy to push away as it danced before my
eyes. Damn it, I should have said shoes. I could only hope
standing before him in a lacy red bra was having a similar

effect, but I wasn't willing to rely on it. Danaus had an un-nerving focus when he wanted to win.

As we stepped back into the fight, I struggled to clear my mind so I could focus solely on the blur of eskrima sticks. As Danaus started to circle me, I thought I had an opening at last. I raised my jō for an overhead blow, but he blocked it with one hand striking me with a redondo by whipping the free stick about to slam against the back of my head. My head jerked forward, but I had enough focus still to snap the end of my staff forward in hopes of catching him in the knee with the end. Unfortunately, he shifted out of the way in time and took a step back.

"Jeans," he said, ignoring my attempts to strike when we were supposed to have already separated.

Temper and frustration rising, I threw my jō staff down to the ground with a loud clatter while I unbuttoned and jerked off my pants. I threw them at Danaus and quickly picked up my staff. He had enough time to toss them over to where my shirt lay before I was attacking again. I was half naked and feeling more than a little vulnerable, but my temper was also flaring. Danaus and I were usually evenly matched in most of our sparing matches, but I was letting him take advantage of my distraction and losing to him in a most embarrassing fashion.

We exchanged strikes back and forth for several min-utes, neither gaining the advantage over the other. I blocked one of his strikes with my staff, but his eskrima stick slid down the pole, smacking into my hand with enough force to bloody the knuckles. I didn't release my jō.

Danaus took a step backward, lowering his guard. "Bra."

"That doesn't count as a strike! You didn't mean to hit me!"

"A strike is a strike."

"I'm not giving it to you."

"I think you will," he said with a narrowed gaze. He dropped the eskrima sticks and approached me. I backpedaled, but was unwilling to strike at him if he was unarmed. As he reached me, he grabbed my jō, pulled it out of my hands and dropped it on the ground. He wrapped his right hand around the back of my head, grasping a handful of hair as he pulled me roughly against him, locking his lips over mine. I didn't hesitate, kissing him back with the same passion as my eyes fell shut. The fingers of his right hand tightened in my hair while his other hand cupped one of my breasts. His thumb brushed over the nipple, causing it to harden beneath the thin layer of lace.

I fought back an evil smile as I suddenly grasped both of his arms and swept my leg behind both of his, taking him to the ground. I landed on top of him, laughing. "I think that officially counts as a strike," I announced with a smile. "Give me your pants."

"I'm still wearing shoes and socks," he pointed out with a smug smile.

I shrugged as I moved to straddle his lower hips. "I guess you'll just have to lose them along with your pants." Reaching down, I unfastened the button on his jeans and pulled down the zipper before he grabbed me. He flipped me onto my back and came to kneel between my bent knees.

"I think that counts as—" he started to say, but I halted the words in his throat by rising up on my elbows and kissing him. I got the point—he wanted me to relax and stop second-guessing myself, but now I was ready to get down to business.

Shifting my weight to my left elbow, I reached up and ran my hand over his chest, loving the feel of his warm, smooth skin lightly laced with dark hairs. I deepened the kiss, tasting him, memorizing him the same way I did every time I made love to this man. I wanted him burned into my brain so there was no getting him out. I wanted him so deeply ingrained in me that I walked around with his scent wrapped through mine. A part of me still longed to have his blood filling my veins, but I refused to feed off him. I wanted Danaus to remain pure and untouched by my kind. He was to remain above the reach of the food chain.

Danaus reached behind me and with one hand unsnapped my bra. He quickly swept the bit of fabric aside so my breasts were free. My nipples brushed against his chest, teasing us both before he finally lowered his head and took one breast into his mouth. My head fell back and a low moan rolled from my throat as the first wave of delicious sensations slipped through me. My knees on either side of his hips tightened, holding him in place.

With my right hand, I slid my palm down his flat stomach and inside the waistband of his boxers. The tips of my fingers teased across the head of his hardened member, causing it to jump at my touch while his hips jerked forward. I tried to slide lower so I could run my hand down his shaft, but Danaus caught me by the hips and held me in place. His mouth switched to the other breast, while his hands started to pull my panties down off my hips.

Reluctantly, he pulled away from me so he could completely pull off my red panties, leaving me lying completely naked before him. The hunter stared at me with dark hungry eyes. Putting his hands on my knees, he spread my legs apart, leaving me vulnerable and aching for his touch. His right hand slid down my knees along my inner thigh to settle between the sweet folds of flesh to touch my clitoris. My hips instantly rose off the mat as I jerked at his touch. His finger easily slid deep inside of me, earning him another moan before he slid it back out again.

"You're wearing too many clothes," I choked out when I could think clearly again.

"I guess you should take care of that," he murmured, sliding his finger inside of me again to erase all thought. His hand left me and I prepared to move when his mouth settled over the same spot his hand had been only a second earlier. His tongue invaded me, pushing me past all rational thought as a part of me hovered on the edge of an orgasm, but I wasn't willing to give in just yet. I wanted him panting and desperate as well.

Grabbing a fistful of hair, I pulled him up so he was nearly lying on top of me, and then I slammed him down on his back. I quickly climbed on him so I was facing his feet, allowing me to jerk down both his pants and boxers to his knees. He was partially trapped by his clothing, limiting his movement and leaving him at my mercy. I wrapped one hand around his hard penis and raised it up so that I could run my tongue along its long length. Danaus groaned and bucked beneath me, then clenched my hips with both of his hands as I carefully took the entire length of him in my mouth.

He grabbed me and pulled me backward so he could return his tongue to my clit while I sucked on his hard cock. My thoughts swam in a warm pool of pleasure, pulling me back toward the orgasm I had been fighting moments earlier. I was close, but I needed more.

Sensing my physical frustration, Danaus lowered his head and focused on kicking off his shoes. I gave his cock one final suck before letting it go. The hunter jerked off the last of his clothes in one quick motion then pulled me beneath him. He entered me in one thrust, causing me to scream in pleasure.

Foreplay was over. No more teasing. No more taunting or gentle touches. With his hands braced on either side of my head, Danaus pounded deep inside of me while I wrapped my legs around his waist, lifting my hips to meet each of his thrusts. After only a couple of minutes I was crying his name as the orgasm ripped through me like a hurricane pounding the shore. My body gripped him buried deep inside me, squeezing him tighter until he finally exploded as well, wringing a groan of pleasure from him before he finally collapsed on top of me, his body trembling.

We lay together in silence for several minutes with him still deep inside me. I listened to his breathing slowly even out while his heartbeat returned to its normal rhythm. To my surprise, Danaus started chuckling. I looked over at him, raising one eyebrow, but he only motioned toward the wall closest to me. I turned my head to see the private bedroom I used during the daylight hours.

"So close to a comfortable bed, and yet so far away," he said wearily.

I snorted, looking back over at him. With my hand, I moved some hair from his face so he could see me clearly. "Yeah, but this was more fun."

"True."

"Besides, we had yet to properly christen this room," I teased. To our mutual delight, we discovered that we both had a ravenous sexual appetite, and during the past few months we had taken the time to have sex in most of the rooms of the house as the moment struck us. For some reason, the sparring room had been left out until now. It proved to be far more comfortable than the kitchen, but still not as nice as my bed in my private chamber.

I smiled at him, letting my fingers run down his hard jaw to rest for a second on his chin. "Thank you," I whispered. Between the sparring match and the sex, he had managed to distract my thoughts and in some strange way restore my confidence. He believed in the decisions that I was making and the direction I was heading. Danaus believed in me.

"We'll get through this. Nick, Rowe, and all of them. I'm

here with you. I'm here to stay," he said, leaning his head down to press a kiss to my fingers. "I just ask that we use a bed next time. I'm getting too old for this shit."

Arching my back, I threw back my head and laughed. Danaus laughed as well, letting the sound bounce off the walls and fill the house, holding the darkness at bay.

Eighteen

Anxiety clawed at Rowe. While he had never been particularly talkative during our journey east, he seemed to grow even quieter as we approached the edge of the city of Savannah. This was the Fire Starter's domain, and during our recent time together, he had made no secret of his animosity for the nightwalker. With her alone lay all his frustration and rage regarding his attempts to free the naturi from our cage. I wondered whether he was truly capable of working with her in an effort to stop Aurora. Did his need to protect and save his own people outweigh his hatred for Mira? Doubt ate at me.

Fully cloaked from the view of humans, we drew in our wings and settled lightly in a small opening that appeared to be a park in the middle of the city. I took a couple steps away from my companion and shook out my wings, giving them one last good stretch before allowing them to completely disintegrate.

When I awoke at sunset, he was already speaking with some of the other animal clan members while eating a quick meal. Rowe and I never spoke of what happened down by the stream, but then, I didn't know what to say. Had it only been a splinter of time never to be repeated? Had we both

suffered a moment of weakness and simply needed the physical closeness of another damaged creature? I didn't want to
consider whether there was something more. Didn't dare to
hope.

But none of that mattered now. I had to get him to Cynnia
and focus on the coming war with Aurora. If either of us actually had a future when this was over, we would face those
questions then.

"Where is she?" Rowe demanded in a low, rough voice.
His question startled me after the long silence, causing me to
flinch. Closing my eyes, I reached out—despite all Cynnia's
cloaking and protective spells, I could find her no matter
where she was. After only a couple seconds her energy
popped into existence for me on the other side of the city.

"She's not too far from here," I said, starting to walk in a
direction that took us deeper into the city.

"Is she with the nightwalker?" Rowe's voice grew harder
and colder.

Gritting my teeth, I fought to keep my tone calm and
even as I continued through the park. "I can't tell, but she
will be able to sense that I am back in town. She will know
that it is best that we not meet with the nightwalker present
for the first time."

Rowe gave a soft grunt, which brought me to a sharp halt.
I spun around and pointed an index finger at him, poking it
into the middle of his chest. "You agreed to this. You agreed
that you would not only hear Cynnia out with her plan, but
that you could work in concert with the Fire Starter. Was that
all a lie?" Something else stirred in the pit of my stomach as
I wondered if there was more that he could be lying about. I
knew Rowe, I knew the manipulation he was capable of, and
I would not be used by him so he could get close to Cynnia.

"I can't wipe away centuries of animosity just because
your sister hopes to save our people," Rowe snapped.

"Well, you're going to have to find a way to handle it." I was beginning to regret taking the iron collar off before he had his meeting with Cynnia. I was always so careful, but he had successfully overcome my methodical logic and caution in the name of . . . what? Companionship? Compassion? A connection with another creature I had never felt before?

I was losing my edge, my focus. I lived for one reason only: to aid Cynnia in any way possible. And now I was letting Rowe distract me. Tightening my fists at my sides, I started to turn my back on Rowe and to resume walking across the park when he stopped me by laying his hands gently on either side of my face, forcing me to meet his gaze.

"Mira and I have a long, dark past. I can't just push those emotions aside no matter how dire the circumstances," he said as he ran his thumbs across my cheekbones.

I took a step back, away from his touch and nodded once, fearful that he was attempting to manipulate me through my emotions for him. "And I will not do anything that will allow you to jeopardize Cynnia's life. You agreed to listen fairly and with an open mind to her argument. If you do anything that I deem a threat to her safety, I will not hesitate to kill you."

A smirk curled one corner of his mouth and he leaned in toward me. "You think it will be that easy?"

I smiled back at him as I placed my hand over where my whip was clipped to my hip. "It's never easy, but I don't miss when it comes to Cynnia's safety."

"After what happened with Aurora, your loyalty to your younger sister is . . . interesting," Rowe said, taking a step back to allow me a little more breathing room.

"Cynnia believed in me first and she has always believed in me. I will not abandon that trust and faith."

Rowe spread out his arms and bowed his head to me. "I will listen to what she has to say."

I believed him. If Rowe was going to attack Cynnia, he was going to go through me first, and we both knew it. After what had happened at the stream, I didn't feel this was the best arrangement, but at least I could say it was an honest one and I knew where we all stood. The weight on my shoulders was no lighter as I led Rowe through the city toward my sister, but it was something I finally understood. Questions regarding the two of us after the events at the stream still hung heavy in the air, but now was not the time to bring up such seemingly trivial things.

We finally stopped at a narrow town house in the heart of the historic district of Savannah. There was a For Rent sign leaning up against the side of the front porch, where the owner had left it following Cynnia's recent arrival. Her witch companion Shelly was handling all the human details of renting safe residences and procuring some basic foods, while Cynnia was supposed to be hidden at all times and guarded by her contingent of followers.

When I scanned for Cynnia, I had picked up the presence of four other naturi near her, while a larger gathering waited on the outskirts of the city for a signal from the young princess. Kane and his people would be moving more slowly through the woods, but I knew they would be there soon enough. We needed to secure both the assistance of the nightwalker and Rowe as quickly as possible so that everything I had told the lord of the animal clan didn't turn out to be a lie.

As I put my foot on the first step leading up to the house, the front door swung open and Shelly stepped into the doorway with a broad smile. The young human woman seemed to be a perpetual ray of sunlight streaking across the land, no matter how bleak the circumstances. Despite her constant chipper attitude, I believed in her sincerity when it came to protecting Cynnia. From what my sister told me, both of them had been through a great deal when they traveled from Savannah to Machu Picchu. Cynnia trusted her, so I did as well.

"There you are! We were beginning to get worried," Shelly announced, plopping both of her hands on her hips as she stepped out onto the porch. "Cynnia seemed to be expecting you a few days earlier."

"There were some complications," I murmured as I mounted the steps. A new weariness crept into my bones as I reached the front door landing. A breeze blew from inside the house, carrying with it the scent of wild flowers. There was a feeling of safety in that smell. I had completed the first leg of my mission and I was tired. Cynnia and I were a long way from accomplishing our goal, but at least I was back with my sister. The nagging fear of something happening to her while I was absent could fly away for the time being.

As I passed Shelly, I noticed her smile wilt as her eyes shifted to Rowe. Her shoulders stiffened, but she remained determinedly chipper as she greeted the other naturi and welcomed him into the house. I didn't know what Mira had told her about the rogue naturi, but there was little that could have been positive.

"Where's Cynnia?" I demanded as I paused in the foyer. The town house was sparsely decorated with a couple of landscape paintings hanging on the pastel walls. The floors were covered in a honey wood, and each of the rooms seemed to spill forth warm light to beat back the night. Dawn was only an hour away and yet I could sense people moving about. I had a feeling Cynnia and her guardians were sleeping little these days, as they not only worried about a strike from Aurora, but she was also now deep in Mira's territory. Any truce with the Fire Starter would be an uneasy one.

"She's sitting in the parlor," Shelly replied, stepping in front of me to motion toward the room off to the right.

"Were there any problems?"

Shelly's smile crumpled completely and her eyes quickly darted away from me. But as she opened her mouth to answer, Cynnia's confident voice floated from the parlor. "Nothing that we couldn't handle."

"By your friend's expression, I struggle to believe that," I replied, following the voice into the room that held my sister. I found her curled up at one end of a sofa, her feet tucked into the side of the cushion, one arm comfortably on the couch armrest, the other resting in her lap. She wore a pair of jeans and pale pink T-shirt, making her look like a teenage human rather than the next queen of the naturi people. But for now we needed her to blend as much as possible with the rest of the world and escape the notice of anyone who could be potentially looking for her.

"We were attacked by some earth and light clan members during our meeting with Mira and the leader of the local lycanthrope pack," Cynnia finally admitted with a shrug of her slender shoulders. "We had some troubles at first, but we were victorious in the end."

"And the Fire Starter?" Rowe demanded as he came to stand beside me, just past the entrance into the room.

"She and the lycan alpha Barrett have agreed to side with us against Aurora," Cynnia said with a bright smile.

Shelly shimmied into the room and clapped her hands together as she heaved a heavy sigh. "You two have got to be famished and exhausted. I can get you some food, or show you where you can freshen up or maybe just get some rest for a while."

"We need to talk," Rowe said in a low voice, his eyes never wavering from Cynnia's face. I watched as my sister leaned back and folded both hands in her lap while her eyes locked on my face. It was an old signal we had developed years ago. We could speak telepathically, but we discovered early on that Aurora could also hear our thoughts since she was our sister. To protect our little secrets, we developed a series of hand gestures that signaled a variety of questions, answers, and emotions. At first it had been nothing more than a little game done to amuse ourselves as we snuck behind Aurora's back. Now it had become an invaluable tool as we struggled against our once beloved sister.

Without saying a word, she was asking if I had succeeded in bringing Rowe willingly to her. I lifted my right hand and grasped my left elbow, signaling that I had succeeded in my mission. Cynnia gave a little sigh and shifted position, resting her hands on either side of her body. She was open and ready to proceed with her plan to win Rowe over to her side.

"We will meet now," I said to Shelly, barely glancing over at her.

"Are you sure?" Shelly asked in low voice. "Cynnia said that you had been on a long trip. I just thought—"

"It's okay, Shelly," Cynnia gently interjected, trying to soften the blow as we brushed off her offer of hospitality. "It's best if we talk now. Could you leave us and shut the doors behind you?"

Shelly gave a quick stiff nod before she left the room. I could almost sympathize with the human. She had been involved in a great deal of the protection of Cynnia and the planning to overthrow Aurora. It would be difficult to now be excluded from what was obviously an important meeting. However, things were different with Rowe, more delicate. I had no doubt that Rowe still harbored ill feelings toward the humans, and I didn't want one lingering about, cluttering up what was going to be a difficult discussion. Cynnia and I both knew that we needed his help if we were going to succeed against Aurora.

As soon as the door closed to the room and we were alone with Rowe, the naturi arched one eyebrow at Cynnia and demanded, "Pet?"

Cynnia calmly shook her head and looked him in the eye. "No, she's a good friend and protector. Not all humans are useless."

Rowe gave a little smirk. "I never claimed that humans were useless. I've found many uses for them."

"Yes," I said with a slight hiss. "I heard of your harvest in a land east of here. I've heard of several harvests that you've led in an attempt to achieve your goal." A harvest resulted in the slaughter of humans and the harvesting of their organs for a series of blood spells that Rowe shouldn't have been casting in the first place. Of course, he was not the first of our people to lead a harvest, and I knew without a doubt that there would be more one day. There was power to be found in the human soul, and the easiest way for us to harness that power was through their organs.

"My task was to free Aurora and our people at whatever the cost," Rowe said through clenched teeth. "When the regular methods didn't work, I pushed the limits of my knowledge. I sought out new layers of power. I knew that I could not fail our people."

"And you didn't fail," Cynnia said in a gentle voice. She motioned with her left hand for him to sit on the sofa beside her. The naturi hesitated, his body stiff and his expression unyielding before he finally softened enough to take a seat on the sofa. I moved opposite him, leaning up against the fireplace mantel. Despite my sister's attempts to create a warm and inviting atmosphere, I couldn't relax. It was my job to stay focused and protect her from any threats, even those that came from our so-called allies.

"As I was saying," Cynnia said, shooting me a dark look for a blink of an eye before she finally looked over at Rowe again. "You have saved our people. As I am sure Nyx told you, our people were languishing within our cage. We were no longer growing; our connection with the earth had been nearly severed."

"Nyx told me things were grim," Rowe admitted, earning a frown from me. I thought I had clearly spelled out that our people were dying. However, before I could chime in, the evil bastard flashed me a quick grin to indicate that he was only teasing me. If I didn't know better, I would have suspected he was trying to push every last one of my buttons.

"However, things have not gotten better with the release of Aurora," Cynnia continued, oblivious to the play between myself and Rowe.

"I gathered that much when she ordered both your death and Nyx's at Machu Picchu," Rowe blandly commented while scratching his chin. A growth of dark stubble was starting to gather there, giving him an even more menacing look. "Most people don't like to be faced with their own death."

"It's more than being faced with your own death," I snapped. "It's about being betrayed by the person you have sworn to protect and obey under any circumstances. It's being called a traitor when all your actions have been for the good of your own people. I have no fear of death, but I will not go quietly into that dark embrace if I have not earned it."

"Aurora is the queen," Rowe said with a shrug.

"And she's gone mad," I countered.

"She's turned on you as well," Cynnia interjected, turning Rowe's attention to her in an attempt to keep us from going at each other's throats. "You gave everything to the naturi. You sacrificed everything for our kind. You followed her command to free us and she turned on you. Banished you."

I crossed my arms over my stomach and leaned my right

shoulder against the wooden edge of the mantel. "You owe her no loyalty."

"But that's the funny thing about loyalty," Rowe replied with another dark grin. "Once it has been won, you must stick with the one that you have sworn your fealty to."

"She betrayed you, Rowe." Cynnia shook her head, closing her eyes. "She has done nothing to deserve your loyalty any longer."

"And it's not just you that she has betrayed," I added. "She has also betrayed the trust of our people. She is supposed to be our protector. She is supposed to lead us toward a safe and secure future, but this obsession with destroying mankind will only lead to the destruction of our own people. Our people are no longer strong enough to face such a task. The humans have grown stronger over the centuries while we have grown weaker. Their weapons have improved, while we have stagnated and lost touch with the earth and our powers."

"A war with humanity means an end to our people," Cynnia said simply. "We will not win that war."

Rowe leaned back and crossed his legs at the ankles, stretching out his long, lanky frame. "So what do you suggest?"

"Peace."

"That can only be achieved through war with Aurora," he said.

Cynnia nodded, a frown pulling at the corners of her mouth. "True. Aurora will not willingly turn away from her plans. She will not stop in her determination to destroy mankind. Our only option if our people are to survive is to stop her."

"You seem eager to turn on your sister," Rowe said.

"The only eagerness we feel is to finally have this ugly task done," I commented.

"Our people are running out of time," Cynnia said. She reached across and laid her hand on the sofa cushion near to Rowe. "We can't afford to have a long drawn-out battle with her. And we believe that with your help, we can end this quickly and quietly."

"Along with the help of Mira and the nightwalkers," Rowe sneered. The words seemed to twist around in his mouth before sliding past his clenched teeth.

"Yes, I believe the Fire Starter will be an asset to this endeavor," Cynnia stated. "She has faced Aurora in the past and nearly succeeded in defeating her." Cynnia neatly left out the fact that Rowe had been the only thing that stopped Mira from killing Aurora when the naturi shoved a knife in the nightwalker's back. "I think with our combined strength, we will have a better shot at defeating Aurora than we did at Machu Picchu."

"And you think that the Fire Starter will abide by whatever agreement you have forced her into?" Rowe demanded with a slight chuckle.

"It's not about getting Mira to obey," Cynnia said, pulling her hand back. "She needs peace with the naturi as well. If Aurora forces us into a war with the humans, then it will bring about the Great Awakening—something the nightwalkers and the lycanthropes are trying to avoid at all costs. And in truth, I would prefer to avoid it myself. Mira will help us fight Aurora because it is in her best interest to do so."

"And after?"

"When it's all over?" I said. "When Aurora has been defeated and our people are finally safe to live their lives? We will return to the forests that protected us at one time and we will grow strong once again. Our people will flourish. Our children will not die at birth and they will renew their connection with the earth. And I believe that with our return, the earth will grow strong as well."

"And then what?" he pressed.

Cynnia turned her worried gaze on me for a second before she looked over at Rowe again. "There is nothing else. We live in peace and harmony with the earth. We remain hidden from the humans. For the first time in countless centuries, our people will thrive. Can you be happy with such a life?"

Rowe stared straight ahead of him, seemingly blind to his surroundings as he honestly considered Cynnia's question. It would mean giving up his personal vendetta against not only the Fire Starter, but all nightwalkers and humans. It would mean finding another purpose for life after living so many years as a warrior of the naturi people. I understood his hesitation, because it was the same change I faced. My role of protector would end, and I had to wonder if the naturi people would accept my existence if I was no longer their protector.

"I would like a moment alone with your sister," Rowe said without raising his eyes. I hated to leave Cynnia alone and vulnerable with a skilled killer, but I had to show him some trust if I was to win him over to our side. With a nod from Cynnia, I turned and started to walk toward door that led to the foyer.

"No, I meant a moment alone with Nyx," Rowe corrected, stunning me into immobility. I twisted around to look at Cynnia, who was eyeing me silently. Yet in the end she simply shrugged and pushed off the sofa. She walked out of the room, throwing me one last questioning glance while I returned to my spot in front of the fireplace.

Rowe waited until Cynnia had closed the door behind her, leaving us alone in the room. I could feel his powers sweep around me as he checked to make sure that my darling little sister wasn't listening at the door. He pushed off the sofa and walked over to stand directly in front of me. I could feel his body heat radiating off him, bouncing off my own flesh.

"She paints a pretty picture," he said just above a whisper.

"It's the truth." I forced the words out, trying to sound calm and unmoved by his proximity despite the rapid pounding of my heart. A part of me longed to reach out and run my fingers along the scars that crisscrossed one side of his face.

Rowe shook his head. "It's her vision of the future. It's a peaceful place where our people will thrive and grow once again."

"And you have a problem with such a concept?"

"I think such a concept will have a problem with us. Cynnia may be able to lead her followers against Aurora, and she may even be able to lead them to victory with our combined help, but do you honestly think that she will be able to force them to accept us?"

"Possibly," I hedged, struggling to keep my gaze locked on his.

"You had to convince Kane to join our side by promising that we would lose our place in Cynnia's court should she become the queen. We will have no place in Cynnia's world."

"I know my sister," I vehemently argued, leaning a little closer to him. "She will not abandon me."

"The same way you knew Aurora?"

"Aurora never approved of my existence and used me only as her enforcer. She was never a sister. Cynnia is my sister."

"So you will have a place in the world that Cynnia is creating."

"Yes, but that's not what this is about, is it?" I said, tilting my head to the side as I looked at him. I could see the concern in the corner of his one good eye as I stared past the cold resolution and determination. "It's about you having a place in this world. You're confident that since Aurora already marked you as a traitor, you will always be marked a traitor of our kind."

I could feel a rare smile slipping across my lips as I raised my hands to cup his face. He didn't jerk out of my touch, but actually leaned in closer while his eye fell shut. "I have little to offer you but myself and my protection," I told him. "While Cynnia will promise you protection and a place among our people, I will promise you a place at my side."

Rowe's eye popped open in surprise and I felt him stiffen in my hands. "A place at your side?"

"So long as I have a place in Cynnia's world, so shall you. They will accept you or we will leave together."

"And you would be content with this quiet, peaceful lifestyle that Cynnia seeks for us?"

"It will not be as easy as it sounds, but I have a new . . . interest . . . to keep me occupied, I believe."

Rowe smiled at me. "A new interest? Yes, I think life could suddenly become interesting with you free of Aurora." Leaning in close, he brushed his lips against mine in a light kiss that left a tingling in my body all the way down to my toes. I tightened my grip on his face and pulled him closer, deepening the kiss, tasting him as flashes of the previous night flooded my brain. I wanted to touch him again, to relive the stolen moment we had enjoyed, but now was definitely not the time.

When I pulled away, I could feel Rowe's heavy breath across my lips, and his one good eye was nearly black with desire. Without touching his mind, I knew that the same thoughts were running through his head.

"We're in this together," I murmured, brushing my lips against his. "But I will not choose between you and Cynnia. You can't win that battle."

A smirk twisted his lips. "I never expected to. However,

do you believe we can honestly live in peace away from the humans?"

I let my hands slid down his chest and shrugged my shoulders. "For a time, maybe. But there will be a point where we will have to fight them. Cynnia's plan is simply buying us some time to strengthen our forces."

A new wicked grin spread across his lips. "So you are planning to resume Aurora's campaign once she is defeated."

"The humans are destroying the Great Mother. This cannot be allowed." I shook my head, the smile slipping from my face. "However, we can do nothing to help her if we are weak."

"Then you have won me to your side," Rowe said, leaning in for one last kiss that was only broken by a resounding knock at the front door to the house. We had a visitor, and it was time to return to the business of saving the naturi from destruction.

Nineteen

A pair of lycanthropes was ushered into the parlor by Cynnia and Shelly, while Rowe and I separated. The one-eyed naturi moved to the far edge of the room and lounged against a doorway leading to another part of the house, and I remained leaning against the mantel. A look of deep concern filled Shelly's eyes as she gazed on the older of the two shifters. An uneasy feeling twisted in the pit of my stomach as I watched these two newcomers. This wasn't a social call.

"Nyx, Rowe," Cynnia began, capturing our attention. "This is Barrett Rainer, alpha for the Savannah pack, and James Parker, one of the pack's members."

I nodded to the two men but otherwise remained silent, waiting to hear what had brought them to Cynnia's doorstep at such an early hour. The sun had yet to creep over the horizon, though I could see through the nearby window that the sky was slowly changing from its midnight blue to slate gray as dawn approached.

"We've come to ask for your assistance," Barrett said, taking a seat on the sofa. To my surprise, Shelly settled on the sofa beside him, while Cynnia returned to the other end of the couch she had been sitting in earlier. James hovered nearby, fingering his gold-rimmed spectacles while pacing with the pent-up energy of one with too much anxiety to settle in any place for long.

"What has happened?" Cynnia asked, bringing a frown to my lips. We had enough problems of our own. We didn't need to be dragged into the problems of the local lycans after just winning Rowe over to our side. I needed him to stay focused, not distracted by minor scuffles with the shifters or even bigger fights with Mira and the nightwalkers.

"The Daylight Coalition has been harassing the lycans and nightwalkers of Savannah recently," Barrett explained, resting his forearms on his knees. He looked tired and more than a little haggard, as if he had spent too many sleepless nights worrying about something. "They knew where to hunt us during the full moon. They knew too much. We deduced that they must have some kind of insider providing them with information, so we decided to send our own mole to infiltrate their ranks."

"Who went?" Shelly inquired.

"A local police detective by the name of Daniel Crowley," the lycanthrope replied. "He has long been a supporter of our kind, and we needed a human who could sneak into their ranks. I promised his sister-in-law—a member of my pack—that he would return to Savannah safely."

"I don't know this Daylight Coalition," Cynnia said with a shake of her head as she looked over at me.

"It's a human group of mercenaries," Rowe said, unexpectedly speaking up, but then I was forgetting that he had been alone on earth for centuries while I was locked away. He would naturally be more familiar with what was happening among the humans and the other races. "They made it their mission to hunt down anything they don't classify as human. For now, they seem content to set their sights on the nightwalkers and the shifters."

"But should they discover that there is someone else out there in their world, I am sure they will be happy to expand their focus," James added.

"Is that a threat?" I demanded, pushing away from the mantel. The young man with the copper-colored eyes met my gaze and pressed his lips into a firm line in attempt to hide the fear I could feel rattling around in him.

"It's a statement of fact," Barrett said calmly, ending the standoff. "They think they are protecting the purity of the human race. The lycans and the nightwalkers have been betrayed by someone to this group, so it is not a stretch to believe that the naturi are not safe either."

"How long has Mr. Crowley been with the Daylight Coalition?" Shelly inquired.

"He left three days ago," Barrett said with a shake of his head. "He reported back that he made initial contact with the group, and we have since heard nothing from him. He was supposed to report in each night and retreat to Savannah if things started to feel bad. Daniel is an experienced cop and a good detective. Something has happened to him."

I shifted from my left foot to my right, crossing my arms over my chest. I didn't like where this was leading. "But it's only been a few days. He may not have a good opportunity to report in if he's being closely watched by the coalition. I think you should give this more time before acting."

"There isn't time," Barrett growled. "We had an agreement that he was to report in every day. If he went silent, we would come in to get him. We made a promise."

"Then I guess you should go," Rowe said with a shrug of his shoulders.

"No, you need help," Shelly snapped, throwing Rowe the darkest look I had ever seen cross her sweet face. "That's why you came here. You can't go in there alone."

Barrett flashed Shelly a weak, grateful smile while

wringing his strong hands together with worry. He didn't seem to be the type accustomed to asking for help. In fact, lycanthropes didn't like to help anyone outside their own pack. "I would have gone to Mira and her nightwalkers, but the sun is rising and we need to leave now if we are to have any hope of saving Daniel."

"I will help you," Shelly offered.

"You can't," I immediately cut in.

Shelly's head snapped up and she pinned me with wide blue eyes filled with hurt and desperation. "What? Why?"

I frowned at her. "You've already promised to act as the personal bodyguard to my sister. Are you going to abandon her to help these animals?"

Her face crumpled as she looked from Barrett to Cynnia. She knew I was right, and I didn't think she would willingly abandon Cynnia after making such a pledge. It was clear that she was attracted to the alpha and wanted desperately to help him, but she was trapped by her own words.

"If you believe so deeply in this cause, I will release you," Cynnia said gently. She kept her face perfectly blank, but the witch stuck to her word as she shook her head slowly.

"No, I can't. Nyx is right. I made a promise to you. I will not leave your side until we have taken care of this matter with Aurora."

"While we appreciate your offer," Barrett began, patting her hands, which were fisted before her. "We were looking for the help from a naturi or two."

"What can we do for you?" I demanded.

"Like the nightwalkers, you can cloak yourselves from sight. You would have a better chance at sneaking into their headquarters undetected. We don't know if it's a lycanthrope or a nightwalker that has betrayed us. Either way, you can at least cloak yourself from the view of humans in the headquarters, allowing you to sneak in and dispose of the traitor. You would give us a needed edge as we searched for Daniel."

"We can't help you," I said firmly.

"Excuse me?" James demanded in a harsh voice before Barrett could speak.

"We can't help you," I repeated, narrowing my gaze on him.

"Nyx—" Cynnia started, but I quickly cut her off.

"Our numbers are not so great that we can sacrifice anyone for a mission that does not exclusively put us closer to taking care of Aurora. We have to remain focused."

"I can respect your need to remain focused on your plans," Barrett said calmly, though I could see the anger and frustration growing in his eyes. "But my people cannot move forward if we have someone at our backs waiting to kill us while we attempt to help you. We need to know we are safe on that front before we enter another war."

"We all have our problems," Rowe said with another shrug.

"Then you have a new one," Barrett said, pushing to his feet. "Because the lycans are no longer available to help you in your war."

"Barrett, please, wait!" Cynnia said, jumping to her feet at the same time Shelly rose, a look of panic shooting across her face.

Barrett raised one hand, halting her words. "You want us to put our lives on the line for your war against Aurora. I agreed to risk my people for you in a war that currently has nothing to do with us. Now when my people need help against a much smaller but equally deadly enemy, your people are unavailable to help. That is not how you treat an ally." He shook his head as he balled his fists. "If the timing had been different, I would have gone straight to Mira. She would have helped me without question, but even she has her limitations. I thought after pledging my assistance in your war, I could rely on you to help my people in the name of maintaining the fragile peace we had established."

"We'll help you," Cynnia agreed, stunning me.

"Cynnia!"

"No, Nyx! He's right," she said, glaring at me because I failed to see the need to risk our few men in an attempt to save a few lycanthropes when we had a bigger problem on our hands. "We came before him and Mira asking for their assistance, asking them to risk their lives in a naturi war. The least we could do for our allies is to help them with their own threat. We owe them that."

"Is this what you really want?" I asked, fighting back the frown trying to pull at the corners of my mouth.

"Yes. You and Rowe will go look into this matter for me," she announced. "The lycans deserve our help after promising to come to our aid."

I bowed my head to her, wiping my face clean of all expression. "As you wish."

Cynnia turned her attention back to Barrett and extended her hand to him in friendship. "Barrett, I am offering up to you my two strongest and most skilled warriors. They will help you get your friend back and take care of the Daylight Coalition threat."

Barrett nodded, quickly shaking her hand. His entire body was stiff, his ego clearly bruised from having essentially come begging for assistance. The lycans had their own skills, but if there was a traitor in the Daylight Coalition, that person would likely be able to sniff out a lycan in a heartbeat. They would have no edge in a stealth attack. "I appreciate your assistance in this matter."

"Where are we going?" I asked, drawing his dark eyes back to me.

"Outskirts of Atlanta," Barrett replied. "That's their nearest headquarters and where Daniel went. It's about a four hour drive, but I'm confident we can make it in less time."

"What's the plan?" Rowe interjected, pushing away from where he was leaning against the wall. Now that he had been elected to join in this little mission, his mind was more focused on the logistics of what lay ahead of us.

"We sneak in as best we can, locate Daniel, and destroy their computers. If we can locate the identity of the traitor and take him out, it would be an added bonus."

Rowe scratched his chin and nodded. "How big a team is going?"

"The smaller the better," I said, looking over my shoulder at him. "Easiest way to make a quick in and out."

"If you want it small, then it can be just the three of us," Barrett said. "You two can sneak in and out quickly and quietly, but you will need me to identify Daniel."

"I want to go as well," James added, rushing over to stand next to Shelly. "I can fight."

"Not this time," Barrett said with a shake of his head.

"Daniel is a friend of Mira's, and I owe Mira and Danaus a great deal," James pressed, pushing his glasses farther up his nose. "It is important to me that I be able to help him."

"Yes, but Mira and my sister would never forgive me if I allowed you to put yourself in this kind of danger without proper training first. You remain behind and that is an order," Barrett commanded. James clamped his mouth shut and walked away, hands fisted at his sides in frustration. He accepted the orders of his alpha but obviously didn't like them.

"Do you also have to go?" Shelly asked, putting one hand gently on the crook of his arm. "Isn't there someone else you could send? You're the alpha for your pack. What would they do if something horrible happened to you?"

"I'm confident they would find someone to fill my place,

and he would hold to the promise I made to assist the naturi in their battle against Aurora."

"Yes, but have you completely healed from the wound inflicted on you by the earth clan? If you're not . . ." Shelly's voice trailed off when Barrett covered her hand with his large one and smiled at her.

"I am completely healed because of your help. I am the best choice for this mission. I will be fine, but I appreciate your concern," he murmured in a low, deep voice.

Like James, Shelly didn't seem too thrilled with this decision, but she would have to accept it because it was Barrett's will. I resisted the urge to roll my eyes when I caught Rowe smirking at me.

Will you show such warm concern for me when I finally go after Aurora? he silently demanded.

I won't have the chance since I will be ahead of you with a blade aimed at her heart, I replied.

Assuming Mira doesn't beat us all, he reminded me.

Yes, it was going to be a three-way race to see who would have a chance at killing my older sister. The odds were in our favor that at least one of us would survive long enough to have a reasonable shot at her.

I cleared my throat when I noticed Cynnia watching us a little too closely. "We should get moving soon," I announced, louder than I meant to. "However, Rowe and I just returned from a long journey. We need a little time to eat and for him to grab some weapons. We should be ready to leave within the hour."

"I understand. We will take my car," Barrett said, then turned to James. "Return to my house and tell my family what has been decided. I will be in contact later tonight to report the result of our incursion. If I don't survive, I am confident that the naturi will contact Mira, who will pass along the information. My people will know what to do."

"Barrett . . ."

"Go, James, and follow my orders to the letter," he said in a near growl.

The young man nodded once and quickly left the house, closing the door softly behind him. It was an ugly task he'd been handed, but one that had to be done. Cynnia had told me of the numerous lycanthropes killed in battles in the city. Now they were at risk of losing their alpha. They would not be thrilled to know that his only form of assistance came at the hands of a pair of naturi.

"Everything has been decided," Cynnia suddenly proclaimed. "Shelly, please take Barrett to the kitchen and get him some coffee while he waits for Rowe and Nyx to prepare." A knot twisted in my stomach as I watched the witch lead the lycanthrope out of the room. There was something on Cynnia's mind. Considering that I was exhausted and had just been volunteered for yet another mission for her, I really didn't want to hear it.

When we were alone again, Cynnia smiled at Rowe. "I am assuming you are now willing to work with us against Aurora."

"You have my sword at your disposal," he said with a bow of his head. However, there was still a smirk twisting his lips, as if there was some secret joke teasing the back of his mind.

"Very good. Nyx's room is at the top of the stairs on the left. You will find her stash of weapons there. When you come down, I will have someone fix you some food." There was no question that he was being dismissed, but Rowe merely nodded once and left the room, closing the door behind him.

"What's going on?" Cynnia demanded in a low voice the second the door closed.

"Nothing."

"I'm not a blind fool any longer, Nyx."

"I never said you were."

"There's something going on between you and Rowe. What is it?"

"My goal was to win Rowe over to our side. I have done exactly that. You shouldn't question my methods, little sister."

"Don't patronize me!" she snapped, nearly stomping her foot on the carpet-covered hardwood floor.

"I don't mean to. Things are settled with Rowe. He is with us."

"Is he? Is he with us? Or is he with you?"

"Is there a difference? I am with you and we have the same goal."

"There is a big difference to me," she argued, pointing at herself with her index finger. Her face was becoming flushed with a mix of fear and anger. "You could have promised him something I can't or won't deliver. I want Rowe fighting at our side, but not at the risk of what I'm trying to create for the future of our people."

"I know your vision for the future, my sister. I would not do anything to jeopardize that. Do you trust me?"

The question made Cynnia pause, the anger draining out of her eyes as she stared at me. "Yes, of course I do. I trust you with my life."

"Do you trust me with the future of our people?" I pressed.

"Yes," she replied without hesitation.

"Then you have nothing to fear from Rowe," I said, and briskly walked out of the room and closed the door behind me, ending any further discussion. Regardless of what feelings I had for Rowe, my devotion to Cynnia and our people ran deeper. I knew that at some point our visions for the future of the naturi would diverge, but for now Cynnia and I were on the same path. We would deal with the future when the time came.

Twenty

Calling up a brisk wind, Rowe and I flew easily to the top of the plain two-story office building that was home to the Daylight Coalition. The tan stone structure looked more like a fortress, with narrow slit windows coated in a black film so no one could see inside. I sensed at least a dozen humans, which was confirmed by the scattering of cars that filled the large parking lot.

I rubbed my eyes against the bright sunlight after I landed on the rooftop and pulled in my wings. I had become accustomed to sleeping during the day, and this job was wearing me more than a little thin. Rowe and I had taken turns sleeping, while Barrett drove the car. During the last half hour, the lycanthrope told us what little he knew of the building we were attempting to infiltrate. In his one and only communication with the Savannah pack, Daniel had been able to reveal that the first floor was filled with offices and there was a receptionist in front. A set of stairs at the far western part of the building led both to an underground basement and to the second floor. Daniel was unsure what was on either of the other two floors, but he hoped to infiltrate one of the two during the next few days. Barrett feared that the detective had succeeded in doing just that, and now we were there to rescue him.

"There's two lycans inside," Rowe murmured as he also drew in his wings and came to stand beside me. I nodded, a frown pulling at the corners of my mouth. I had sensed the same thing. It meant that our traitor or traitors were likely inside, but also that they could potentially sense Barrett sitting in his car a short distance off, waiting for us to signal him with the walkie-talkie attached to my belt. We needed to move fast before someone came out of the building to look into the matter of the unexpected lycanthrope in the parking lot.

Rowe stood on the roof and looked around the area with his hands propped on his hips. "Do you know how to take down the security system to the building?"

"Not a clue. I am assuming we can just rip out some of the wires sticking out of the building in the box over there. That should knock the power out, right?" I replied, pointing toward a large metal box with several thick wires running from it to power lines farther out in the parking lot.

Rowe shook his head and smiled at me. "You really haven't spent much time in this world. Your suggestion is a good way to get yourself killed and potentially set off some alarms. How about a sudden spring thunderstorm?"

I gave a sweeping bow and threw out both arms to him. "I concede to your greater experience regarding the workings of human security systems and their destruction."

Rowe said nothing as he stretched his arms toward the sky while his power filled the immediate area. I also tapped into the powers of the earth swirling about me and reached toward the clouds that were starting to churn. Adding my own powers to the mix, it took only a moment for black clouds to gather directly overhead. Lighting crackled as it jumped from dark cloud to dark cloud, followed by a deep rumble of thunder.

My companion lowered his arms long enough to physi-

cally move me away from the metal boxes and to the far
end of the roof, while I remained concentrated on the storm
we were creating. With one hand still resting on my shoulder, Rowe reached up with his free hand and called down
a thick string of lightning. It pounded into the rooftop and
caused the metal box holding wiring that led into the building to explode in a shower of sparks. A second lightning bolt
slammed into the pole holding up some wires. The wooden
pole split down the center in an explosion of shards of wood
and sparks from the snapping wires. Standing on the rooftop, I could see the lights going out in the surrounding area
as we succeeded in knocking out the power for many busi-
nesses and homes. It was a good start.

"Should we contact Barrett now?" Rowe asked, squinting
at me as the rain finally broke in a heavy sheet, clinging to
his eyelashes and running down his nose.

"Let's get inside first and clean out some of the humans,"
I suggested, and started to raise my hand to end the storm.

"Leave it," he said, capturing my hand before I lifted it
above my head. "It will act as a good cover when we enter
and leave."

"How do you want to enter?"

"Through the roof. We'll work our way down, killing
humans as we go," Rowe said with a wicked grin.

"How will we know if we run into Daniel?" I asked. "We
need to call Barrett so he can identify him."

"And let the lycan give us away the second we enter the
building? Not a chance!" Rowe paused long enough to wipe
more rain out of his eye and slick back his hair so it wasn't
obscuring his vision. "We'll just take our time and read
their thoughts as we go. Anyone named Daniel gets to live
for now. We'll contact Barrett when we have the first and
second floors under control. I've got a feeling that the basement level is where all the fun is going to be."

I frowned. I had not hunted humans in a long time and
wasn't sure how I felt about it. When I had returned to Earth
after my entrapment, I'd been indifferent about their existence. My main focus was on protecting Cynnia's safety, and
killing nightwalkers as I went.

Rowe grabbed my left shoulder and gave it a hard squeeze.
"Stop thinking about them as helpless little animals. They
are going to hunt us eventually. Let's stop them before they
get the chance. It's just one more speed bump on the road to
Cynnia's vision for a peaceful existence."

"Nicely put," I muttered under my breath. I didn't think
he actually believed a word of what he said. He enjoyed killing humans.

Raising my hand toward the sky again, I called down a
large bolt of lightning to slam down on the opposite end of
the roof. The building trembled beneath our feet. I called
down a second and a third bolt before I could see a hole
finally appear in the concrete. The air smelled of burned
ozone and smoke, but it was quickly overwhelmed by the
rain that continued to come down in buckets.

With a knife in either hand, I paused at the hole in the
roof to look over my shoulder at Rowe, who was holding
a short blade and a knife. His gaze was narrowed on the
opening into the building. Energy flowed around us both as
we cloaked ourselves against the view of any humans. The
room below me was pitch-black, but I could see that there
was nothing below me but open floor. I jumped into the hole
and landed silently in a crouched position, waiting. I didn't
expect anyone to attack, as I didn't sense any creatures on
the second floor, but I wasn't going to take any chances.

When I was confident we were alone, I moved away from
the opening and stepped deeper into the room, allowing
Rowe to jump down. My eyes quickly adjusted to the darkness, and I could make out massive piles of boxes lining the

walls. The coalition seemed to be using the second floor of the building as storage. I walked over to one of the open boxes and pulled out a thick stack of pamphlets that decried a plague of nightwalkers and other dark creatures lurking in the shadows. They espoused the coalition's ideology and included quotes from religious scripts in an effort to strengthen their argument.

"What is it?" Rowe whispered, looking over my shoulder.

"Leaflets and pamphlets for their cause," I murmured, dropping them back into the box. "This floor seems empty to me."

"Then let's give them a reason to not return to it," Rowe said, grinning at me.

"A fire?"

"Sounds good to me. All this stuff will go up easily."

"Too easily. We have to get through the first floor and the basement. I don't want to get trapped in the basement when we're trying to get out of this place."

"Just a small fire that will spread. The chaos will work in our favor while we get through the area."

I shrugged my shoulders as I walked back over to the opening where the rain was pouring into the room. I placed my knives in their sheaths and lifted one arm and pointed at the opening while pointing with my other hand at a pile of boxes at the far end of the room. Closing my eyes, I summoned up another lightning bolt. However, this time the energy surged straight through me and exited my other hand to slam into the boxes. Paper and cardboard exploded in a shower of ash and flames.

"Holy shit!" Rowe gasped, surprising me. "I've never seen anyone do that."

"Yes, I'm quite unique," I bitterly muttered, letting my arms fall limp at my sides. That particular trick took a little bit out of me, but I was regaining my strength as the fire started to grow. Pulling my weapons back out of their sheaths, we jogged toward the door marked EXIT and quietly eased out to concrete stairs blanketed in thick darkness. I was forced to pause as my eyes struggled to adjust.

Sliding along the wall, we quickly descended to the first floor and stopped. I frowned, noticing a dim light coming from the basement level, when there should have been no light at all. There was a great deal of shouting going on from that level, but things seemed to be relatively calm outside the stairwell door to the first floor. I was tempted to say to Rowe that we should continue to the bottom floor, but I didn't want to leave potential enemies at my back. We needed to clean out the first floor before moving on.

As I reached the door handle, an alarm went off in the building. I looked over my shoulder at Rowe in confusion. I thought we had taken out all the power.

"It's the smoke alarm on the second floor," he explained. "They'll be calling the fire department soon if we don't take care of the first floor employees."

I nodded, pulled the door open, and was immediately faced with a tall, lanky man in a suit. He was staring straight through me with a confused look on his face. He couldn't see me because I was cloaked, but was confused as to how the door opened on its own. Rowe reached around me and pulled the man into the darkness, plunging his knife into the man's throat before he had a chance to give a shout of surprise. We left him gurgling on the stairs leading to the second floor before we tried again to enter the first floor.

Dripping wet, we stood in the dimly lit office building. The few windows that dotted the building had been blacked out for privacy, but it also left them blanketed in darkness when the power was out. I felt like another shadow lost in the darkness. Around us I could hear nervous voices raised as people huddled in various offices in hopes that being in a group would protect them from the darkness as they waited for the power to return.

"Take the right," Rowe said, jerking his head in that direction. "I'll go left. Kill anything that moves. We'll meet up on the other side. Don't let anyone make any phones calls. They could call up some assistance from the ground floor. I'd rather keep this a private party."

"See you on the other side," I said, clinking my knife against his raised blade before heading to the right, disappearing into the deeper shadows.

My footsteps were silent across the carpet. In fact, the only sound I made was the occasional splat of water hitting the floor as it dripped down from my face and hair. The air was cool, raising goose bumps on my flesh, and I was forced to clench my teeth to keep them from chattering. With my heart racing in my chest at the thrill of the hunt, I knew my body temperature would soon rise.

I paused at one small office whose door was open. A man sat in a chair in front of a desk, while another man lounged in his leather chair behind the desk. Both were wearing white shirts and ties. I edged into the room and stood there in silence, watching them. It almost seemed wrong to kill them as they sat so innocently, but I reminded myself of the tenet that had guided the sword of so many naturi over the years: humans were destroyers of the Earth. And worst of all, these humans were going to be destroyers of my kind when they were given the chance, simply because we represented something different.

A low growl gave me away, but it wasn't enough to give them a chance to protect themselves. I threw one knife, which buried up to the hilt in the throat of the man behind the desk while I turned my attention to the other man. Gripping the handle of the second knife, I plunged it directly into his chest, piercing his heart, while my free hand went over his mouth and nose, blocking any noise that would escape him. In one quick motion I jerked the knife free and slashed his throat. The spray of his blood across my cheek and arm somewhat warmed me while silencing the man. Retrieving my other blade, I slipped out of the room and closed the door behind me.

I was in and out of two more small offices in the same fashion in only a couple minutes. Blood was splattered across my arms and face and starting to take on a pink hue in my rain-soaked clothes. With knives still gripped in both hands, I turned a corner, heading toward the front of the office, when I heard a woman gasp in horror. She sat by candlelight at her large desk, her hands tightly gripping the arms of her chair as she stared wide-eyed at me. Confused, I did a quick scan of myself to find that I was indeed still cloaked. However, I discovered that I wasn't the only one emanating energy. The woman was a witch.

Raising my hand to throw one of my knives at her, I saw her reach out with one foot and step on a red button on the floor. I knew that couldn't possibly be a good thing. I flung the knife at her with all my strength, but she had already succeeded in throwing up a magical force field around her so my weapons couldn't penetrate.

We have a problem, I said, reaching out mentally to contact Rowe.

What?

The woman at the main desk in the office is a witch.

The receptionist is a witch? His voice sounded amused in my head, and I felt the need to punch him in the arm so he would be serious again. *You think they'd screen for such things since the coalition doesn't like nonhumans.*

This is serious. I think she alerted someone to our presence.

They still won't be able to see us.

They will with her help.

Then make sure she can't help them, he admonished before cutting off the connection between us. A part of me wanted to snap at him. It was as if we were back in training together with him issuing all of the orders. But in this case I knew that he was right. I had to get rid of the witch before she could assist anyone who might be banging up the steps from the basement.

"Wh-What are you?" she demanded, keeping her back pressed into her chair.

"The person sent to kill you for betraying your people," I murmured as I walked toward her. I raised one hand and rested it against the bubble of energy that sizzled around her. I couldn't physically penetrate it with my body or my knives. However, I suspected that magic would do the trick. I stepped backward again to give myself some room while I unhooked my whip from my side. Snapping it once, I flicked it at her to see if it would penetrate her bubble. She was smirking at me until the tail of the whip snapped around her knees, leaving behind a trio of long, deep scratches. The end of the whip was imbued with magic, allowing it to penetrate her bubble of protection.

Anger warped and twisted her features as she threw out her right arm toward the front of the building. The glass in the front door shattered into a thousand pieces, as if an explosion had gone off. Yet, instead of falling to the ground, the glass pieces hovered in the air in the door frame. The witch then pointed her extended arm, sending the shards flying directly at me. I had enough time to throw up both arms to protect my face. However, the rest of my body was exposed. I could feel a hundred little cuts across my body as sharp pieces of glass scraped along my flesh and embedded deeply. Little rivers of blood ran down my body and started to soak into my clothes. I was tempted to give a little shake and brush off the glass but suspected that would only push the shards even deeper into my skin. The pieces would need to be picked out one by one.

Out of the corner of my eye I saw her glance at the remaining window at her disposal. I snapped my whip and swirled it over my head once, sending a wave of pain screaming through me as I moved. I wrapped the length of the whip around her neck and gave a sharp pull, jerking her out of her seat and to the floor in a crumpled mess. She grabbed the whip and pulled desperately on it, trying to create some slack so she could breathe. I tightened my grip on it, wrapping a section around my upper arm as I took a step closer. The bubble of energy that had protected her was gone.

Kneeling on the ground behind her, I tightened the whip around her neck again, slowly choking the life out of her. I watched as her lips turned an ugly shade of blue and her eyes began to bulge from their sockets. Her long red fingernails clawed at the leather whip before finally dropping limp at her sides. I remained on the ground, holding her tight until I heard her heart stop beating at long last.

Unwrapping the whip, I stood, letting her fall to the ground in a heap next to her chair. She was hidden behind her large, tall desk and would go unnoticed at first glance. But I was running out of time. As I replaced the whip at my side, I could hear heavy footsteps pounding up the cement stairs toward the first floor.

Coming out from behind the desk, I continued toward my right to finish off the last of the offices so I could meet up with Rowe. Unfortunately, the doorway to the stairway exploded open and men with guns poured into the office building. I paused where I was, trying to decide whether I should continue with my extermination or stop the men who offered the greater threat. Rowe could undoubtedly finish off the office workers without a problem or help from me. I needed to cover his back so he could work quickly.

Pressing my back to one wall, I waited for the footsteps to get closer. I clenched my knives in my fists, sending another streak of pain through my hands from the shards of glass still embedded there. Blood dripped from me, staining the carpet in a motley spotted pattern. As the first man appeared around the corner, I swung both of my arms out. One knife buried deep in his muscular gut while the second one hit him in the throat. I continued to rip through his body, pulling the knives free as he collapsed to the floor in a convulsing, quivering mass of spurting blood.

The man behind him paused in horror. Like the others who had just burst in from the stairwell, he was dressed differently than those men I'd encountered so far in the office building, with their white shirts and striped ties. These men wore black pants and shirts in an effort to blend in with the darkness. Weapons were openly strapped to their bodies, as if they were the ones selected to wage the coming war against the different races. If they were looking for a war, then I was willing to give it to them. Placing my hand over that of the man who clutched a gun, I forced it up to his temple and pulled the trigger, blasting his brains against the opposite wall. He gave one last scream of terror before he slumped at my feet, dead, drawing more attention in my direction.

Flashlights flicked on, bright spotlights through the darkness, in an effort to spot their attacker, but I pulled back around the corner. While still cloaked from their view, I was dripping blood onto the carpet, which was bound to give me away eventually. Wiping my knives clean on my pants, I ducked low and swung around the corner. I took down one armed man after another. Gunfire filled the air as they frantically searched for the creature killing their men with amazing speed. A couple bullets skipped across my leg and another plunged through my shoulder, clipping my collarbone before I managed to finish them off.

Rowe appeared a couple minutes later, covered in blood, to find me sitting against the wall in the middle of a hallway filled with dead bodies. I once again wiped my knives clean on my clothes and shoved them back in the sheaths on my body. Most of my wounds had healed, but I was moving a little slower than I had minutes earlier. I had lost a lot of blood, and the glass still needed to be removed from my skin. I felt bruised and more than a little worn from the fights, but I would be able to manage as we headed down to the basement level. Below us, I could still sense a pair of lycanthropes, which I knew would be of interest to Barrett.

Smoke was starting to hang in the air on the first floor, and the temperature was steadily rising. The fire we started on the second floor had grown and was now determined to make its way down to the first floor. While it had set off a panic among the humans, giving us the ability to easily sneak up on them, it was now cutting our time short.

"I think it's time to call in Barrett," I said as I slowly eased back to my feet by sliding my back up the wall.

"You're hurt?" Rowe asked, looking more than a little surprised.

I shrugged and immediately regretted the action, as my collarbone was still struggling to mend. "It was a narrow hallway and they got in a few lucky shots."

"And the glass? You're sparkling in the light," he said.

"The witch got in one spell before I could kill her. You have any problems?"

"Nothing worth mentioning. The humans are dead and the naturi are alive. Just as it's supposed to be," he said with a wide grin.

"Don't get too excited," I growled. "We still need to get down to the basement and see what the coalition actually knows. The witch could see me, but she didn't know what I was. It might mean they don't know about our people yet. We need to be sure before we leave this place."

Rowe turned serious as he pulled the little black walkie-talkie off the waist of my pants and pressed the button. "Any problems?"

"None." Barrett's voice came back scratchy but easily understandable. "However, smoke is pouring out of the roof. I imagine that the fire department is going to be here soon."

"Then you better haul your ass in here fast so we can get this done. There are two lycan waiting for you to play with."

"I'm coming," Barrett replied. And with him would be the entire fury of his pack.

Twenty-one

Rowe took the point going down the stairs while I headed up the rear, with Barrett sandwiched between us, his guns drawn. Rowe and I remained with our knives, preferring to stick with the old ways. We were faster that way. Rowe paused at the bottom of the stairs and pointed toward the light coming from under the door.

"Private power generators," he whispered, answering his unspoken question. "They're ready for us."

I didn't doubt it. They had sent a dozen armed men up to the first floor and not one of them came back alive.

Standing back against the wall, Rowe pulled the door open. A barrage of gunfire flew in, peppering the staircase and far concrete wall. Rowe looked over at me and raised an eyebrow while smiling mischievously. It was a look that didn't fill me with confidence.

"Don't shoot! Please, don't shoot!" he cried in a wavering voice, as if terrified. He even changed the pitch and tone, removing any potential threat from his voice. "I only came here to bring you one of these dirty werewolves when the lightning storm started."

"Bring out the dog!" ordered a harsh voice. Rowe pulled me behind him, motioning for me to hold the door open.

In one smooth motion Rowe pushed Barrett down to his knees with guns in both hands. As I moved into the doorway, Rowe stood behind Barrett, who fired while Rowe flung knives at the visible enemies. Screams of pain went up for a couple of seconds in shock before the armed men answered with their own gunfire. I put one foot on Barrett's hip and slid him out of the way while slamming the door shut. Bullets pounded against the thick metal door before they finally gave up.

"How many did you get?" I demanded, holding the door closed with my shoulder.

"Two," Rowe replied.

"Four," Barrett added as he changed the magazines in each gun so they were fully loaded again. I quickly scanned the basement area and sensed only ten more men, at least three of whom were wounded. The lycans were still there, toward the back of the building.

"Do you think we should try that trick again?" Barrett asked.

"They've already moved away from the entrance to the other rooms," I said, pulling one of the knives from my side. At the same time, the light seeping from under the door went out, plunging us into total darkness.

"They must have night vision goggles if they hope to take us in the dark," Barrett grumbled.

"Night vision goggles?" I repeated, looking over at Rowe.

"Devices to allow humans to see in total darkness," he replied quickly as he grabbed a fresh knife.

"Can you see anything at all, Barrett?" I demanded. My vision was fine. It had taken me a second to get readjusted, but I was accustomed to the darkness of the night.

"I'll be able to in a minute," he replied as he stepped away from us. He quickly stripped off his clothes and laid them in a rumpled pile at the foot of the stairs before changing into wolf form. There was no mistaking that this wolf was a shapeshifter. He was simply too large. I frowned. While he would have the edge in speed and added dexterity, he couldn't wield a weapon beyond the massive jaws and sharp teeth he possessed. All told, I wasn't sure that he had an advantage in his wolf form. However, I suspected he wouldn't be able to see his opponent otherwise, and Barrett wasn't about to allow us to leave him behind when we finally took down the last of the coalition members.

"Barrett, we're going to leave the lycans to you to take care of," Rowe directed, edging closer to the door again. "We're going after the humans. If you can sniff out Daniel while you're at it, give a howl and we'll come running. Otherwise, we'll have to beat it out of a couple survivors."

"Hopefully he's here," I muttered before Rowe jerked the door open again.

He walked out first, scanning the area with both his eyes and his powers. No one was in the immediate corridor except for the prone bodies of six dead men leaking blood across the tile floor. Rowe and I moved silently down the hall, while Barrett's claws clicked across the floor behind us.

We turned a corner and came upon a room with a set of windows in the wall, revealing men seated behind a series of glowing blue screens, furiously typing in away while glancing continuously over their shoulders.

"They're trying to delete their information from the computers," Rowe said. "I'll take care of them. Continue down the hall and don't get yourself killed."

"As you wish," I muttered under my breath while Rowe slipped like a ghost into the room, then quickly proceeded to kill every human inside. Three down. Just a few more to go.

Barrett accompanied me down the long hall to a pair of double doors. Gripping the blades tightly in each hand, I drew in a slow, steadying breath. My powers were completely useless, considering how far underground we were. I had to rely completely on my training as a killer. But then, Rowe had been very thorough in my training as a defender for the queen and a protector of the people. Yet, after spending most of my life trapped in a cage, I had begun to wonder if I would ever get the chance to try my skills out on armed humans.

As I edged the door open, I heard the ominous click of weapons being cocked and locked into position. Not hesitating, I dove into the room and leapt behind a tall set of crates off to one side. Gunfire filled the air, lighting up the black room. Barrett scampered after me and settled behind the boxes. Bullets chipped away at the wooden crates and pinged off the concrete walls near us. We were pinned down, but that would only last for so long. It was only a matter of time before they started their approach and took aim from a significantly shorter distance.

"If I draw their fire," I said to Barrett, "can you get behind them?"

The wolf nuzzled my arm for a second before turning in the opposite direction to poke his nose out from behind the box. He was ready for me to draw their fire.

Pushing my back away from the crates, I rolled my shoulders and closed my eyes for a second as I summoned my wings. They sprouted from my back, tearing through the soft material of my shirt. The thick blackness of the wings blended with the darkness of the room, allowing me to stretch them to their full length before drawing them in again. Climbing carefully to the top of the stack of crates, I slithered across on my belly, then balanced on the edge with my wings extended. The ceiling was just high enough to allow me to glide a short distance. Unfortunately, I would reach the ground a few feet directly in front of them. Barrett only had one shot to get at them before I was torn to shreds by their weapons.

Clenching my teeth, I launched myself off the crate and glided across the room. I threw three knives down on them before they even took notice at the attack from above. Screams of horror went up and they moved their weapons so they were now pointed at me. Just before reaching the ground, I jerked my wings in and tucked my body into a ball so I rolled forward, making myself a smaller target.

Luckily, more screams went up, accompanied by a low growl as Barrett struck. To lend him a hand, I rolled back to my feet and jumped over the table the men who took refuge in the room had been hiding behind. With my knives slashing with frightening speed, I dispatched the last of them, while Barrett tore another man apart with his teeth.

The lights suddenly flicked on as we finished with the bloody work. I raised one hand to shield my eyes from the overwhelming glare, blood dripping on my nose and running down my cheek. I blinked a couple times and twisted around toward the entrance to find Rowe standing in the doorway, looking a little bloodier than he had been only a few moments earlier.

"Finished in here?" he inquired in a light voice.

My wings settled around my shoulders as I looked around at the carnage. An array of black and lethal-looking weapons was spread out on the table I'd leapt over. The four men in the room had been hacked to pieces in a matter of seconds and were now lying in pools of their own blood. "Just finished," I replied.

"I took a peek around the place," Rowe said, keeping his eyes on me as Barrett wandered off to a corner to change back into human form. "There are three locked doors. Two with lycans behind them and one with a human."

"The human has to be Daniel," Barrett said in a low, rough voice, just barely back in human form.

"What do we do about the other lycans? Are they prisoners as well?" I asked as we headed toward the door Rowe was holding open for us.

"Doesn't matter," Barrett said with a shake of his head. "They betrayed their people. They could have taken their secrets to their grave and they didn't. They deserve death. But right now my main concern is getting to Daniel. We need to reach him before the fire department arrives and this place caves in around us."

Rowe silently led us to the room that held the presence of a human. One well-placed kick near the doorknob sent the door flying open and banging against the wall behind it. In the center of the empty room a haggard, beaten man was taped to a metal folding chair. He was slumped over, looking as if he were barely holding onto life.

"Daniel!" Barrett cried, rushing over and kneeling beside the man. Rowe and I quickly set to work cutting the thick silver tape that bound him to the chair. He reeked of urine, sweat, and dried blood. He might have been held captive for only a couple days, but it appeared that he had spent most of that time being beaten into a bruised and bloody pulp.

"Barrett?" Daniel said in a dazed and rough voice as he tried to lift his head to look around.

"Yes, it's me. I came to take you home."

"How did you know?" Daniel asked, his voice cracking.

"You haven't contacted us in days. I promised that we would come after you."

"I didn't tell them anything, I swear. I didn't say anything," he continued. Tears started to stream down his face, and I was forced to look away, focusing on the last bit of tape at his ankles.

"I know you didn't say anything," Barrett said, squeezing both of Daniel's shoulders. "You would never betray us. What about the other lycans?"

"I never saw them, but I could hear them being tortured."

Daniel gave a shudder before falling forward to lean heavily on Barrett. "I could hear the screaming through the walls next to me. I think they're from Charleston. They're not from Savannah."

"We'll take care of them before we leave."

"I've got it," Rowe said, snapping my head up. The naturi disappeared from the room without a whisper of noise. We didn't move as we listened to him kick in each door and quickly dispatch the other two lycanthropes quickly and mercifully.

"Let's get out of here," he commanded, sticking his head back in the doorway. "Smoke is starting to fill the hallways. The first floor may be impassible now."

"This used to be a parking garage," Daniel said. "They took me out a back underground entrance one night. We can use that."

Putting one of his arms over my shoulder while Barrett took the other, we helped Daniel back to his feet. We moved as quickly as we possibly could, but he stopped us once again as we passed the room where the men had been working at the blue glowing screens.

"The computers! We need the computers!" he shouted.

"There isn't time," Barrett argued.

"It's full of information on everyone," Daniel pressed. "We need it. We need to know what they know. Otherwise, this whole mission was for nothing."

Barrett looked over at me and Rowe for a moment in indecision. "I've got him," I said. Rowe and the shifter didn't hesitate to dart into the room. I watched as they pulled cords out of two metal containers and hefted them up on their shoulders. I didn't know what kind of information resided with these computers, but apparently it was important enough to risk everyone's life.

We paused one last time so Barrett could run back and

grab his pants before Daniel directed us to the enclosure where Barrett and I had encountered the last group of Daylight Coalition members. At the rear, we saw a plain white van. We loaded Daniel into the back while Barrett worked on getting the van started. Rowe pushed open the gate and I slammed the back doors shut when it growled to life. Then Rowe hopped inside as Barrett idled by the gate.

In the parking lot, Barrett stopped next to the car he'd driven up to Atlanta. Rowe hopped out with instructions to follow us back to Savannah. We were pulling out of the business complex just as giant red trucks pulled in with sirens blaring and red lights flashing. I took one last look out the back window of the van to see flames poking out of the windows of both the first and second floor. The rain had stopped but the clouds still hung black and heavy in the sky.

We'd succeeded in our rescue mission, but I had the distinct feeling that we hadn't heard the last of the Daylight Coalition. We had merely slowed them down a bit.

Twenty-two

During the next four hours, Daniel hovered between consciousness and uneasy sleep in the back of the car. We threw an old cloth tarp we found over the floor for him to lie on. It didn't provide any cushion, but after everything he had been through, he didn't appear to notice the hardness of the car floor.

"Thank you for coming with me," Barrett said after we rode for more than an hour in complete silence. "I know that neither you nor Rowe wanted to help, but I am grateful that you did. Daniel would not have survived much longer in their hands."

Sitting in the back of the van beside Daniel, I looked up to meet Barrett's hard gaze in the mirror. "You're welcome," I murmured.

We fell back into another long, uncomfortable silence before the lycanthrope finally spoke again. "Does it bother you that much to be helping someone like me?"

"Someone like you?" I repeated warily, unsure of where he was headed with this conversation.

"Yes, a shifter. A lycanthrope. Mira says that at one time we were like pets to you and your kind."

I frowned. He was determined to bring up a past that

seemed ancient history, and unlike him, I'd been around to live it. Barrett was only feeling an echo of ache for his ancestors. I was reluctant to proceed, as it seemed the only outcome would be an argument.

"Soldiers, actually," I corrected him in a soft but firm voice. "The lycanthropes were created as soldiers to fight against the nightwalkers and the bori. You were too valuable to be kept as pets, though some were kept as personal guards for elite members of the naturi clans. The better question might be how you feel about working with a creature that was born to be your natural enemy?"

"What are you talking about?" he snapped.

"During the last days of the wars, it was the nightwalkers and the lycanthropes fighting. Not the naturi and the bori. The bori created the nightwalkers to fight the naturi and the lycanthropes," I said with a shrug. I gazed back down at Daniel, who had fallen asleep again. "Your two races have now seemed to overcome your past and are working together. You should be proud of that accomplishment. It is something that can never be achieved between the naturi and the bori."

"Why?"

Again I shrugged, but I didn't think he could see it. "We want the same thing, but are unwilling to share."

"What's that? What thing?"

"Dominance over the world."

"That's not what Cynnia has been telling us," Barrett argued, looking over his shoulder at me, the wheel of the vehicle jerking. He twisted back around and tightened his grip on it. "She promised that the naturi would leave and live a life of solitude in peace."

"Cynnia is trying to rewrite the goal of our existence. She still desires to possess the world and strengthen the powers of the earth. The only difference between her and our ancestors is that she believes it can be done with the coexistence of humans and naturi."

"Do you think she's right?"

"I am willing to help her achieve her goal any way I can."

"But do you think she's right?"

"In all honesty, I do not know. Our people have been trapped for a very long time, and now there is a fight for the throne for the first time in our history. Things are changing rapidly for us, which is very unusual. If Cynnia is to succeed, now is the best time for that to happen."

"If the Daylight Coalition has its way, you may never have a chance to find out if she's right," Daniel said, speaking up suddenly. His voice was rough and ragged from lack of use.

Squatting down in the back of the car, I edged closer to the human who lay prone before me. His eyes were still closed and his breathing was heavy due to the pain I could imagine still wracked his frail human body. I doubted he had eaten or slept much during the past couple of days. His face was swollen and bruised dark shades of blue and purple. There was a long cut along his jaw that stretched down his neck. His clothes were splattered with his blood and torn in places, revealing more cuts and bruises.

"What has the coalition planned?" I inquired.

"I'm not sure, but they're well-informed," he said with a soft sigh. "They seemed to know who I was and my connections to the Savannah pack almost immediately."

"What happened?" Barrett asked, looking up in the mirror again as he tried to see his friend.

Daniel licked his lips and took another couple deep breaths, his face twisting as if the pain of the memory made it difficult to speak. "They attacked shortly after I checked in with you the first night. They sent nearly a dozen men. They gagged and tied me up before bringing me back to their headquarters. I was locked in that room almost constantly. They took me out to show off their weapons and brag about how they are going to destroy both the vampires and werewolves. I guess they never imagined I would survive long enough to escape."

"What about the two lycans being held next to you? Do you have any sense of how long they were there?" Barrett pressed.

Daniel shook his head and then flinched at the motion. "None. Longer than me. I could hear them through the walls. The spoke mostly about the pack in Charleston, but they gave up information about Savannah. They mentioned Mira by name. Even went so far as to tell them to stay out of Savannah because of her."

"Did they give a physical description of her?" I asked.

"No. Just a name and that she was a nightwalker that protected the city." Daniel opened his eyes, looking at me for the first time. "We need to warn her. They'll be coming after her next."

Oddly, I found myself taking the man's left hand in both of mine and squeezing it reassuringly. "We will."

Daniel had risked his life for both the nightwalkers and the lycanthropes, and he was just a human. He could have easily been killed for a cause that was not his own, and I could not help but respect him more for his bravery and selflessness. I'd spent little time around humans in my life and even less time actually speaking to them. This one in particular surprised me.

I looked up at the back of Barrett's head, turning my attention away from the human. "What I don't understand is how members of the Charleston pack knew anything about the Savannah pack. Wouldn't that kind of information be private to each pack?"

Barrett shook his head and made a sound of disgust in the back of his throat. "Because of the geographical closeness of the two packs, we have always tried to maintain a somewhat open relationship so that neither side became too territorial. We've even used the same hunting grounds in the past during a full moon. However, all shifters swear to the same code of silence when it comes to outsiders. The penalty is death to anyone that betrays our secret."

"Barrett, if they know about me, then they'll be able to find Annie and my girls!" Daniel said with sudden urgency. He tried to twist around to look at Barrett in the front, but his face contorted in pain and he slumped back onto the floor of the van.

"I've had people watching them very closely at all times since you left. We will continue to do so," Barrett firmly said.

"We're going to have to leave Savannah," Daniel said softly, closing his eyes again. His hand slipped out of mine and he lay limp as his breathing grew more ragged. "It won't be safe for us any longer if they know about me."

"I understand," Barrett replied in a low voice, sounding saddened by the loss of his friend. "I will contact the local pack wherever you go and have them extend the same protection that I am offering you now."

"Barrett, you can't ask—"

The lycanthrope quickly cut him off. "I can and I will. Any pack will be happy to help your family after what you have sacrificed for our people. You will be protected. In the meantime, you will call Annie when we reach Savannah so she knows you're safe. You will then stay with my family until you're properly healed."

"I can't," Daniel argued. "I need to get home."

"You are a mess, my friend. You haven't the strength to protect anyone. You need time to heal or you will only terrify Annie."

A lengthy silence settled into the car again, with everyone

lost in their own thoughts. I stared down at the human, looking to see signs his wounds healing, but nothing changed
as I expected. I was not accustomed to such a slow healing
process. Again, I found it astounding that humans had survived for so long.

"Who is Annie?" I asked, breaking the silence.

"She's my wife," Daniel murmured.

"And you have girls? Are there other wives?"

"No." Daniel gave a small chuckle and looked up at me,
cocking his head to one side. "You're not human, are you?"

"No, I'm naturi."

"And I thought you were everyone's enemy," Daniel said
with a slight smirk.

"Apparently not any longer."

Daniel fell silent again, and his breathing seemed to even
out for the first time as he relaxed. When he spoke again, he
sounded somewhat distant, as if falling asleep again. "I have
daughters. Five daughters."

"How?" I found myself whispering in awe.

A blush stole to Daniel's cheeks and he cracked one eye
open at me. Even Barrett chuckled at me from the front seat.
"The old-fashioned way," he uttered before closing his eye
again.

"Most of our females will never hold their own child,"
I said in a low voice. "Five is . . . unheard of among my
people."

Daniel blindly reached out with his left hand and
squeezed one of my hands. "I'm sorry."

"So am I," I whispered in a voice so low I wasn't sure
that even Barrett with his keen hearing picked up my words.

Yet, even as the sad thought passed through my brain, I
had to question the wisdom of ever reproducing. Despite my
constant training and work as protector of my people, even
I felt the occasional stirrings inside me, the longing to hold

my own flesh and blood. But as I sat in the back of the dirty car with a lycanthrope and human, covered in blood of my enemies, I didn't think it was wise to attempt to bear my own children. What kind of an influence would I be?

What's wrong? Rowe demanded suddenly in my brain, his voice like a gentle caress across my brow.

I fought back a surprised smile, as I had not thought he would pick up on my change in emotions. Drawing in a slow breath, I released it through my nose, pushing away the temporary melancholy I felt for both myself and my slowly dying race.

Nothing now, I replied, making sure to wipe the voice in his head clean of any traces of sadness. His concern for me was enough. There would be time enough later to worry about myself and my people. For now, it was enough to know I was not alone in this world.

Twenty-three

Danaus had not arrived at my home yet when I felt a shift of power in the air. The feeling built slowly, like a spider crawling up my flesh until it was squatting at the back of my neck. I knew what it was. Or rather who it was. Frowning, I left my sanctuary in the basement and climbed up the stairs before crossing through the underused kitchen to exit out the back door. My nearest neighbors were several acres away, with trees surrounding my property in all directions, obscuring the view. It was the safest place for facing Nick, and it protected my house in some small way. I had just finished rebuilding my study following his destruction of it and was in no mood to rebuild any more of the house. I had spent too many years moving around, and I liked it and its contents as they were.

Standing unarmed in the middle of the yard, I raised my arms out to my sides and stretched out my powers so I could feel the various energies swirling around me. Nick had opened up my senses. Before, I could only sense the soul energy that emanated from humans and lycanthropes, as well as the thin, wispy presence of nightwalkers. Now, it was as if a great door had been opened before my eyes. I could sense the energy of the earth along with the beating pulse of the naturi. I could sense other strange powers I couldn't identify and seemed indeterminate, as if trying to cloak themselves yet unable to completely hide from me.

In the mix of it all, I had learned to identify my father's unique power signature. Most of the time he seemed distant, content to simply watch the show that was my life from a comfortable chair in some hidden theater of the cosmos. However, when I strayed from the direction he thought I should be headed in, my dear parent intervened. Apparently, I wasn't on the track he deemed proper for me. Or in truth, for him.

Still tapped into the energy around me, I summoned up a ring of fireballs the size of baseballs in a large circle around me. Shadows lunged and danced from the nearby trees as the night came alive with motion due to the flickering lights.

As I expected, Nick accepted the invitation and appeared in my circle, transforming one of the fireballs on the far side of the circle into the form of a tall, lean figure. After a couple of steps toward me, the flames subsided to reveal a man in a dark maroon suit with a crisp white shirt and tie. His hair was black and slicked back, while his features had become sharp and hawklike. I had never seen him in this form before. Usually, he appeared looking like the kind, sweet man who had raised me from birth in the belief that I truly was his daughter. He had also appeared as a goth teenager full of angst and piercings, and as a man with red hair and lavender eyes like myself. But this was new and strangely disconcerting. Not for the first time, I felt as if my soul were on the line as I stared at him, unflinching.

"I'm assuming that you wanted something," I said with as much distain as I could muster without betraying the fear twisting into tight knots in the pit of my stomach.

"Can't a father pay his loving daughter a social call?" he asked, extending his arms as if he meant to embrace me. I took a step back before I could catch myself, not wanting to be anywhere close enough so he could actually touch me. That path only led to excruciating pain and broken bones.

"You're not the social type," I sneered, forcing myself to remain still at the edge of my circle. My knees were like water and I could feel my fingertips trembling. I needed him gone as soon as possible. I didn't want another fight I couldn't win, and I definitely didn't want him anywhere near Danaus, should the hunter suddenly appear at my house now that the sun had set. "What's with the new appearance? I thought you preferred to look like my father."

"I grew bored looking like a common fisherman. I thought I would come looking like someone you might encounter in your business dealings," he said, running his hands down the front of his suit jacket with a look of pride. However, that look was instantly wiped away, replaced with an appearance of ominous threat. "Besides, I am the true father that you need to concern yourself with. Not that distant and dead memory."

I gave a huff and shoved one hand violently through my hair, which gave away my growing anxiety. I didn't need Nick in a bad mood. I needed him amused or focused on an important issue. Not angry. "Fine. What did you come here for?"

"I'm not happy with how things are developing within your domain. You are not handling things how I would have hoped."

That was way too vague to be considered helpful in any fashion. I was dealing with the Daylight Coalition poaching lycanthropes outside of Savannah, the Japanese nightwalkers were attempting to drag me kicking and screaming to Japan, and the naturi were expecting me to side with them in the coming war against their queen. What part of that complete mess was not to his liking? Because at that moment I could have done without all of it.

"Jabari, that nightwalker that has the ability to control you, is still hanging around in your domain," Nick declared, nearly causing me to laugh out loud with relief. He had chosen to focus on what appeared to me to be the least of my concerns.

"Jabari? You're worried about Jabari causing problems?" I demanded, unable to keep the sarcasm out of my voice. I was playing with fire when it came to mocking Nick, but then I was never very good at bowing to anyone, however much more powerful they were than me.

Nick shoved his hands into the pockets of his slacks and settled back on his heels as he shook his head at me. "You have not tamed this one. He still thinks he can control you at any moment. He wants you in the palm of his hand or dead. Neither suits my needs."

"I'm sorry to hear you're not pleased. What can I do to rectify the situation?" I inquired in my most patronizing tone. I knew I had overstepped what Nick was willing to tolerate when he immediately disappeared. My stomach dropped and my throat felt as if it had closed in on itself. I twisted around, trying to spot where he would reappear next, while at the same time scanning the region for his powers. I felt him, but there was no exact location until it was too late.

A hand clamped on the back of my neck in a viselike grip, while a hot breath brushed against the hair that covered my left ear. "Now see, that's the kind of attitude I'm looking for. I just want your complete cooperation and total obedience. Is that too much to ask?" he growled at me.

"Considering what you're asking for most of the time, yes it is," I said through clenched teeth. I was too stubborn for my own good. I was literally in the hands of a god and still picking a fight because I was unwilling to bow to his every wish.

"Well, this time I think you'll be in complete agreement

with me," he said. He tightened his grip on my neck long enough to pitch me forward. I caught myself with both hands and tucked in for a quick roll on the ground before popping back up to my feet. I jerked around and remained in a defensive stance as I waited for him to strike again. "I want you to finally kill that nightwalker."

My head fell backward with laughter and my hands unconsciously dropped down to my sides as I lowered my guard against him. I couldn't help it. It was as though he'd asked me to take an afternoon stroll in the sun. He wanted the impossible.

"Kill Jabari?" I repeated as if my hearing had suddenly gone fuzzy. "Don't you think that if I could, I would have done so already?"

"You haven't been trying hard enough," Nick said in a low growl.

"He's thousands of years old! I can't beat him. I can only control him when he lets me, when it's to his advantage. He's not going to stop doing that just so I can kill him."

Nick waved his hand toward me and a surge of energy knocked into my chest. I fell to the ground, my butt slamming against the earth. "He may be an Ancient, but you are my daughter."

"Some daughter." I gave a soft snort as I moved some hair out from in front of my eyes. "You toss me around like a rag doll. Do you honestly think it's going to be any different with Jabari?"

"You have more powers to call upon now. You have an edge over him at last."

I pushed off the ground and brushed some bits of grass and dirt off the seat of my leather pants. "Why now? If you haven't noticed from all the gatherings I've been attending recently, we're facing a multifront war, and me picking a fight with Jabari now isn't the best timing."

"I see this as the next stage of your training," he offered.

There were times when Nick was willing to provide me with information, and there were times when he simply wanted to knock me around. This seemed like one of those times when he needed me to know something—or at least I hoped it was.

He paced a little closer to me. "Training that provides you with the strength and ability to regain my place as a true god once again."

I crossed my arms over my chest, suspicious of that statement in too many ways. "And what does that mean for everyone else? We spent a lot of energy and lives getting rid of the naturi and the bori so the humans would be safe. Are we now going to suffer under your rule once you regain your place as a true god?"

"You spent a lot of energy and lives!" he screamed, his hands balling into fists as his face flushed red. There wasn't a second to guard against the attack. He was simply there in the flash of an eye. The back of his right fist slammed across my face and I fell to the ground in a heap. As I rolled onto my back, Nick was on top of me again. Kneeling at my side, he placed one hand against my chest, but I could feel his energy plunging deep inside me. It felt like his fist was wrapping around my soul and trying to pull it from my body. He was trapped in a blind rage, and he was going to kill me if I didn't do something to stop him.

Closing my eyes against the wrenching pain, I focused all my energy inside of myself and wrapped my own pull of power around my soul, attempting to hold it in place. I tapped into the swirling energies around me, strengthening my hold so he could not pull my soul free of my body. If he removed it from where it resided in its little hole deep within me, he could set it free, instantly killing me, and yet I had a feeling that my soul would be trapped forever on this plain, never able to move forward to the next level of existence.

After more than a minute of tug-of-war with my soul, Nick finally released his hold and lifted his hand from my chest. I remained perfectly still on the ground with my eyes closed and my powers wrapped tightly around the remnants of my soul in case he should try to attack me a second time. Energy flowed into me from all directions, from the earth and nearby humans. I could even feel some of Nick's powers mixing with the other energy pouring into me. I felt stronger, more powerful, than I ever had before. I felt as if I could take on Jabari and at last crush him like an insignificant insect.

While I lay there, I felt Nick's powers increase again as he prepared for another attack. Balling my hands into fists, I pushed the power deeper inside of myself and then I disappeared. Stunned shock gripped me so quickly at the unexpected ability that I immediately reappeared exactly where I was, which did me little good against Nick. My eyes popped open and my mouth formed a perfect O in surprise. The only time I had been able to disappear and reappear before was when I tapped into Jabari's powers. Now I either had the power to do it on my own or I could simply tap into Nick's powers to do it.

"You can do it on your own," Nick said.

"What else can I do?" I demanded with an eagerness I couldn't hide. The world had suddenly opened up to me in a new way, and I needed to know the extent of what I was capable.

Nick gave a slight shrug of one shoulder as some of the anger started to drain out of his expression. "You will never know until you try."

With a small smile, I wrapped a ball of energy tight within my chest, gathering together as much energy as I could stand. It crawled along my skin like a millipede and pounded against my chest like a heartbeat, but it was nothing more than power looking for an outlet, and I was willing to give it one.

I directed the energy at Nick, sending it crashing into the center of his chest, throwing him several feet backward across the yard. As soon as he was standing again, I hammered him once more, knocking him off balance while I set him on fire in a towering inferno that threatened to light the nearby trees. I paused long enough to watch the flame-cloaked figure brush off his jacket and take a few easy steps toward me.

"The fire bit is getting old and stale, Mira," Nick said in a singsong voice.

"Then how about this?" I said. Pushing to my feet, I directed my hands down to the ground, feeling the pulse of the earth beneath me. Straining to maintain the flames, I directed the roots of the surrounding trees to explode from the ground and wrap around his ankles. The roots pulled and slammed him to the ground again as he extinguished the flames. Pulling in different directions, I attempted to split him into two different pieces, but he disappeared before I could even get a grunt of pain out of him.

Nick instantly reappeared before me and cocked back his fist to punch me, but I was gone this time before he could touch me. I reappeared a few feet away, my mind scrambling for some new way to attack him that could make some kind of impact when it dawned on me: use the same attack that had been so effective on me. Gods had to have souls as well, right?

Gathering up as much powers as I could possibly stand before a scream could be torn from my throat, I reached out toward the energy flowing from Nick. I plunged the powers inside of him, searching for that faint wisp that was his soul.

I found it in a heartbeat, but it was like trying to wrap my arms around an angry grizzly bear. The energy thrashed about, shoving me away anytime I grew too near. His soul could actually fight me, where mine lay limp and helpless against his attacks.

"And that is why you should never have become a night-walker," he calmly said, before finally brushing me and my powers aside like an annoying fly. I was thrown back again, slamming into the ground.

I pulled the energy back to me and disappeared again before he could attack me. However, it felt as if a hand grasped me around the neck and pulled me back so I was standing directly in front of Nick.

"Enough playing for one night," he declared. "I think you've begun to understand exactly what kind of power is at your fingertips if you only try." To my surprise, his words sounded heavy, as though he was struggling to catch his breath. There was a slight flush to his cheeks, indicating that he might actually be tired from all the exertion of fighting me. I tucked that little mental note away in the back of my brain and kept my face clean of any expression.

Of course, it was only after I released the powers I'd been holding onto that I felt a wave of exhaustion pour over me. My knees turned wobbly and threatened to buckle under me, while my arms felt as if lead weights had been tied to my wrists. I needed to sit down and wait for the feeling to pass, but was unwilling to show any weakness to Nick, knowing that he could potentially take advantage of it.

"Do you think you can handle Jabari now?" he demanded.

"It feels as if the fight will be a little more even," I admitted. "He can still control me, which gives him an edge."

"And you can stop him from doing that if you truly want to. Take care of this, Mira, because you do not want me to," he warned. Nick took a step back, and I did the one thing I thought I would never do. I stopped him. My curiosity had gotten the better of me.

"The nightwalkers didn't really cage the naturi, did they?" I quickly blurted out when I sensed he was preparing to disappear.

The energy in the air seemed to dissipate with the spring breeze. He frowned at me, and I felt myself clenching all my muscles as I waited for him to strike me again. It was that statement earlier that had set off his temper in the first place. For reasons I didn't understand, the story that had been told to me centuries ago about how the naturi and bori were caged was proving to be false. I had a feeling that only a creature as old as Nick might hold the truth I wanted.

"No, the nightwalkers were not the ones to cage the naturi," he said with a sneer. "Nor were the lycanthropes the ones to cage the bori. I will give you that both races aided in the capture of the naturi and the bori, but you were not the force behind the act."

"Then what happened? How were the two races drawn into their cages?" I asked, still inwardly cringing as I waited for his temper to explode again.

"They both chased after the one thing they want most in the world."

"Control of the Earth?"

"More power."

"I don't understand."

Nick sighed and rubbed the bridge of his nose with his thumb and index finger. He wandered over to the patio at the back of my house and silently settled into one of the wrought-iron chairs around the table. He waited until I slowly walked over and took a seat opposite him. It was the first time either of us had come close to a civil conversation, and I had a feeling it might be the only time. Nick's temper was too like my own and could flare up with the smallest provocation. I was treading on thin ice.

"The naturi and the bori are attracted to power. They believe that more power is the only thing that will give them an edge over the other, and thus the ability to wipe out the other," Nick explained.

"So what kind of power could have attracted them both into a cage?"

"How about a pair of fallen gods?"

I sat back in my chair, speechless as I tried to wrap my brain around the thought. "You sacrificed two of your own to capture the naturi and the bori?"

"No!" he shouted, slamming his fist on the table. "They made the sacrifice. They made the choice to go into the cages and act as bait for those bastards. It's their powers, their souls, that are keeping the cages from breaking down."

"But the naturi cage is breaking down," I said, hating the words as they came out of my mouth. I didn't need to throw more wood on the fire burning in his glowing lavender eyes.

"That's because she's dying without her mate."

"Which gods were they?"

"The creator gods. The first gods." Nick looked down at his hands, which were folded in his lap. "They need each other for strength and stability. They have been separated for a very long time."

"They were the first?"

"Born from the Earth herself," he declared with a faint smile. "The Pagans referred to them as Freya and Woden, but they truly have no names. They were simply the first gods, and then came the other gods, and then the humans. The naturi and bori were later created to keep a balance with the humans, but it was a mistake. The two were constantly at war with each other no matter what the gods ordered. They had been made too powerful in their own right."

"So the first gods sacrificed themselves by locking themselves with the naturi and bori in cages. The cages have been feeding off their powers. The naturi and bori have been feeding off their powers, weakening because they've been kept apart from each other and the earth."

Nick gave a short little chuckle. "There is hope for you yet."

"Will they die?"

"Eventually, if someone doesn't take their place."

"And if they die, then the cages will break and the remaining naturi and all the bori will be set free again."

"Yes."

"But you said that the gods were half dead. How can anyone take their place?"

Nick gave a twisted little smirk and shook his head at me. "They can't." My father pushed out of his chair and gave a pull at his jacket to straighten it. I remained lounging in my chair, turning over the dark information he had already handed to me. "And before you can ask, yes, the reason the gods are half dead and nearly forgotten from this world is because the first gods are gone from it. Their sacrifice nearly killed us all as well."

"But you're looking for a way to make a comeback," I said, bringing a smile back to his lips. "And I'm sure that you're not the only one."

"Definitely not. But I wouldn't get any ideas of finding some outside help. None of the other remaining gods are half as forgiving or generous as I am."

"I'm sure," I said sarcastically.

Nick started to turn away from me, but paused and turned back, scratching the tip of his nose. "And before I forget. Your nights with that bori bastard are growing short."

"What?" I demanded, trying to lunge out of my seat, but a wave of his hand succeeded in pushing me back down. I started pulling the energy back toward me again, ready for another fight with my father, but he only shook his head in warning.

"He can control you, and I won't allow it."

"Danaus won't control me," I argued, tightly gripping the arms of the chair. "We're on the same side. He doesn't want to control me."

"You're on the same side for now. Considering your past relationships, I have a feeling that truce could end very quickly, and then you will have no choice but to kill him."

"Then let's wait for that truce to end naturally," I argued, inwardly confident that such a day would not come between Danaus and me. "There's no reason to kill him now."

"He's a distraction."

"He's a needed ally in the coming war."

Nick shook his head at me, refusing to budge from his stance. "He's a distraction and a threat. His days are numbered, but my main concern is Jabari. Take care of him." And then, without another word, he disappeared from sight. I scanned the immediate area, but his distinct signature of power was gone. I was alone.

I remained sitting on the patio for several minutes, turning over all the information that Nick had delivered as well as the new extent of my powers. He was right in that I needed to finally be rid of Jabari. The Ancient was not only a threat to myself, but to Danaus and anyone else that mattered to me. I couldn't allow him to continue to risk their lives just so he could use and manipulate me. It was time for it to end.

But then, Jabari wasn't my only problem. I needed to get rid of Nick as well. I couldn't be his pawn any longer. For that matter, I couldn't be allowed to make him a more powerful creature than he already was. The world was far too fragile at the moment to stand the shake-up he would create. What I needed was someone else that had a similar problem as myself. Nick had intimated on more than one occasion that I wasn't the only offspring of a god wandering the earth. There had to be another like me, with their share of impressive powers that could aid me in getting rid of a god. And in truth, I already had a solid guess as to where I could find one. The only problem was getting him to go along with any plan that I managed to weave into creation. It was one thing to take on nightwalkers, lycanthropes, and the naturi. It was a completely different story to stand toe-to-toe with a god and expect that you just might live through it.

Sitting on the back patio, I closed my eyes and listened to the breeze as it swept through the trees, rustling the leaves. Crickets chirped softly now that Nick had left and I'd gone completely still in my chair. Around me, energies swirled and flowed, carrying with them burbles of emotions and broken thoughts. I could feel the soft swell of the powers that flowed up from the earth like a mother's gentle reassuring caress. I knew what I had to do for the first time in my life. The only problem was that I couldn't bring myself to move. I had so much to lose now. Danaus, Knox, Valerio, all of my people. The Savannah pack. My home here in Savannah. The quiet peace that existed between the occult and the humans. It all was balanced on a precipice, and I knew that if I failed, I would lose it all. It was time to act for the final time.

Twenty-four

Jabari was at the Dark Room. I hadn't needed Knox to call me with the information as I was driving into Savannah, but the tenseness in his voice told me he was hoping I would do something. When I parked in my usual spot outside the club, I found both the bouncers missing from the front door and a small splatter of blood running down the door frame and pooling on the ground. A frown pulled at the corner of my lips as I wished I had heeded Nick's advice sooner and dispatched Jabari when I first encountered him. I should have found a way to deal with the Ancient much sooner, despite my lingering feelings for my onetime mentor.

Upon entering, I found the Dark Room nearly deserted; only Danaus and another bartender remained stubbornly at their posts. I had forgotten that it was Danaus's night to work there, and need not have worried about his imminent arrival while I was with Nick.

Knox was hovering in the doorway that led to the back rooms of the nightclub. He was leaning against the wall with his arms folded over his chest, a grim expression stretched over his handsome face. For the most part, Knox saw the Dark Room as his little domain within my territory. I left him to maintain the peace within the club when I was not present, and in many ways that peace extended out to most of Savannah. He was my second in command and always would be, despite Danaus's new position within my life. He not only knew me and my temperament, but also knew Savannah and her nightwalkers very well. Knox was the perfect moderator between myself and the rest of the *others* that inhabited my domain.

Without letting my gaze travel around the club, I walked over to where Knox stood, knowing that Jabari and some others were at my back on the far side of the room. I would deal with them when I was ready. First, I wanted to speak with Knox.

"What happened outside?" I asked.

He glanced over my shoulder for a second before directing his gaze back to me. He spoke in an extremely low voice, but we both knew that Jabari could hear us. "He killed the two bouncers, Clay and Karl, when they asked for some kind of identification. They didn't realize who he was. I sensed him, but I didn't get outside fast enough to warn them." Knox hung his head and squeezed his eyes shut. I could see the memory as clear as day running through his head. He opened the door in time to see Jabari ripping both the lycanthrope and the nightwalker to shreds in seconds. Neither had enough time to react.

It wasn't their fault either—they were simply doing their jobs and didn't realize that they were faced with a short-tempered member of the coven. If I or Knox or Danaus had been present at the door, we would have stopped them from questioning the Ancient, but things just hadn't worked out that way.

"Did you contact Barrett?" The alpha of the local pack needed to know that yet another one of his pack members had been killed while working at the Dark Room. Something that was happening far too frequently for my liking.

The Dark Room had once been a very peaceful, pleasant place for nightwalkers and lycanthropes alike.

"I left a message with his sister. It seems that Barrett has returned with Daniel, but the human is in rough shape. He's going to need some time to heal. Barrett also appears to be worried about Daniel's family."

"Offer to send some nightwalkers over during the evening hours. We can remain hidden better than the lycanthropes."

"Already done," Knox replied with the first shadow of a smile I had seen on his face since I walked into the nightclub.

"Good. Then I guess I'll go do my job and take care of this matter," I said, not caring if Jabari was listening to the conversation.

Before turning around, I glanced over at Danaus and winked at him while a little smirk danced across my lips. He didn't smile in return. He had eyes only for Jabari and wouldn't relax so long as I was within the Ancient's reach. There was no question that the Ancient had come to my domain with the simple intention of killing me, but he seemed content to drag out my execution and torment the members of my domain. Danaus was willing to hang back in the shadows for now, but he would be watching closely. If the talks seemed to turn sour, I knew he would be over the bar and at my side in a couple of heartbeats.

I walked across the nightclub, crossing the empty dance floor to the large booth that Jabari inhabited alone. At the entrance to the booth, two humans lay sprawled on the ground. Their breathing was labored and they were a sickly shade of pale—the nightwalker had drained them of too much blood. If they didn't get some help soon, it would be a miracle if they survived the night.

"Knox, get these two to a hospital now!" I shouted, stepping over them so I was standing just outside Jabari's booth. His feet were propped up on the table and his back was pressed against the back of the booth, looking for all the world as if he was the king of all he surveyed. Not quite.

"I wasn't finished with them," he said lazily.

"They're nearly dead. You're finished," I snapped. For the first time, I noticed that his dark skin looked a little singed and he was keeping his hands curled close to his body. In our last fight, I had managed to score a hit with my blast of fire before he escaped. It had been enough to hold the night-walker at bay for a few nights as he healed.

Sliding into the seat opposite him as Knox picked the two nearly dead humans off the floor, I crossed one leg over the other, affecting the same nonchalant attitude. "What are you still doing within my domain?"

"I need to finish killing you. You've grown too powerful for your own good."

"Tipping the scales on the coven in the wrong direction, am I?" I mocked. The only reason Jabari had supported my ascension to the coven was because he saw me as a puppet he could easily wield, thus giving him two seats on the coven instead of just the one.

"You always had to know that your life span was limited," Jabari taunted. "Hated by one and all in the night-walker community. Hunted by the Ancients. And once it was known that I would no longer be willing to protect you, it was only a matter of time before others came hunting for you. The ultimate prize."

"But none of them have been successful, and now you've been forced to do your own ugly work," I said with a growing smile. "Only problem being, I'm stronger than you anticipated and now you can't finish the job."

Jabari gave a slight shrug of his shoulders, but by the tension that slipped across his face, I could tell he was still in pain. "A minor setback. You seemed to have acquired a new guardian of sorts."

It was a struggle to maintain my nonchalant tone when a part of me longed to smash his face into the glass table between us. "Yes, I've found another to pull my strings. Of course, the difference between you and him is the fact that he's trying to make me stronger, while you're only concerned with how I can be used by you."

Jabari and I had too much history for both of us to remain living. Nick was right—my creator was a threat to everything I was attempting to do to save both the nightwalker and human races. Jabari's only concern was himself and how he could increase his own powers, which was accomplished only through manipulating me.

"And I'm guessing that your master's first command is to get rid of me," Jabari replied blandly, as if this were all a big joke.

"Actually, that's his second command." My sneer seemed to take some of the laughter from his expression. "His first command was to learn how to control both you and Danaus. Now we've moved on to the next stage."

"And you think you're capable of succeeding?"

"Quite confident."

Jabari glared at me with cold black eyes. I met his unblinking gaze steadily, mindful that Nick offered up a worse hell than Jabari could even imagine.

To my surprise, I blinked first despite my growing hatred for the monster that sat across from me. No matter how much I despised him or how much he threatened all my plans, I still had need of him for one last task.

"However, I'm willing to grant you a temporary reprieve," I ventured slowly.

"Already bucking against your new master? You won't last long that way," he growled. A faint glow gave his eyes an almost golden tint.

"No, I'm willing to take this chance because I'm aiming

for something greater than either of you two bastards." I clenched my fist at my side, but managed to keep my voice low and even as I continued. "War is coming."

"It seems I've heard this speech before," Jabari interrupted.

"Yes, it's been nearly a year and nothing has really changed in our world." There were a hundred accusations waiting on the tip of my tongue to explode. If he had only sent more nightwalkers to Machu Picchu months ago, we would not have found ourselves in the current mess against Aurora. If he had been more honest and forthright with me sooner, I might have been better prepared to deal with Rowe and the other naturi, instead of blindly believing along with the rest of my race that the naturi were near extinction and content to live out an isolated existence.

But I swallowed those words, choosing to focus on the imminent problem rather than dwelling on the past. "A war is coming between Cynnia and Aurora. If we're not careful, the war will bring about the Great Awakening. Aurora does not care who will get killed as long as she wins. And if she does win, she will continue her campaign to rid the world of humans, which is naturally not to our benefit."

"So you're asking for the nightwalkers to take a side in this matter," Jabari said with a slight incline of his head.

In response, I gave a light chuckle. "A choice has already been made. The nightwalkers of Savannah, and any other nightwalkers I can summon, will be fighting alongside Cynnia and her army," I informed him. "Cynnia seeks a truce between the races so her people can resume the peaceful, isolated life they once led before Rowe went on his crusade to set the naturi free. Cynnia plans to kill Aurora and take the throne. I will be there to help her destroy her older sister."

"You want to get in the middle of a blood feud between a pair of naturi? Let them fight it out and then just kill the survivor," Jabari said with a dismissive wave of his hand.

"It's far worse than that. The Daylight Coalition has become aware of certain lycanthropes and nightwalkers within the immediate area, as well as in other regions around the country. The humans have begun to actively hunt us. From my understanding, we've struck out and destroyed their Atlanta headquarters, but we need to make another strike against their group, gather more information on exactly how much they know about us and our identities."

"It seems as if everything has been decided. What could you possibly need me for?"

"I want you to arrange a meeting with Our Liege. I have something of great importance to discuss with him," I started with a certain amount of glee. I was reducing this powerful nightwalker and Elder of the coven to nothing more than messenger boy, and I loved it. "He needs to know that the Great Awakening is looming on the horizon along with other greater problems if something is not done. Our people need to know what lies ahead of them so they can prepare any way possible."

"Times have changed if I am to be running errands for you now." Jabari folded his arms over his chest.

"Yes, it was not quite so long ago that you were sending me to one distant location after another with little explanation and no hope of success. Well, your odds are slightly better. I'm sure you can also dig up Our Liege if you really wanted."

"If you survive this disaster that you're planning, I'm confident you will have his full attention. Of course, that's assuming you get past me tonight."

Frowning, I lowered my gaze on the old nightwalker and

clenched my muscles as I prepared for the attack. "Don't fight me tonight. I have plans for you and really would prefer not to kill you now."

I wasn't surprised when Jabari disappeared before my eyes. I had expected as much from him. It was a scare tactic, but after facing Nick earlier in the evening, it was going to take a little more than that to get the adrenaline pouring through my veins. Reaching out to grasp hold of the powers that flowed around me, I instantly sensed Jabari hovering close by, waiting to strike. I slid out of the booth while wrapping Jabari's powers around my fist. I jerked him back into existence before me and slammed both my fists into his chest as he reappeared, sending him flailing across the room until he finally hit the far wall of the nightclub.

"We don't have to do this now," I said, brushing my hands off. "We can wait to kill each other until after Aurora is dead."

"I would much rather kill you now," Jabari said in a low voice that seemed to creep across the dimly lit expanse separating us.

"I'm sure you would." I was preparing to summon up more energy to attack Jabari when the nightwalker sent his own powers rushing through my frame. A surprised scream was ripped from my throat as the pain overtook me. He held me locked in standing position with my arms thrown helpless out to my sides, leaving my heart vulnerable for the plucking if he decided to do so.

Do you want my help? Over the pain, I could feel Danaus's powers brushing against me, waiting to push their way in so he could force Jabari out of me. But Jabari had spent most of my life as my puppet master, and I was going to defeat him on my own terms at last without the aid of the hunter.

Not right now. Thanks for the offer, I replied, forcing

the words out as if through clenched teeth. *I'll handle this myself.*

Digging deep inside, I grabbed hold of Jabari's powers as they seeped through every limb and organ of my body and started to push them out again. His powers were no different than those I had learned to wield under Nick's *gentle* tutelage. I could feel Jabari pushing back at me, forcing more energy into my frame until I was sure I would soon be torn into a million pieces. Clenching my teeth to stop another scream of pain, I finally succeeded in pushing his presence out of my body and mind for the first time by myself.

"Enough!" I shouted. Exhilarated and furious, I summoned up my powers again and threw Jabari back against the wall. "Enough games from you." I took one step forward and disappeared, only to reappear again directly in front of him. Reaching back, I pounded my fist into his left jaw.

Lifting his right hand, he raked his long sharp nails across my face in a single, brutal swipe that left behind four long scratches. I stumbled back a step, putting some distance between us as I blinked away the blood dripping into my eyes. Jabari immediately came at me, grabbing the front of my shirt and throwing me across the room. I crashed to the floor in a clatter of tables and chairs.

As I pushed back to my feet, I grabbed one chair and ripped two wooden legs off. They weren't quite the eskrima sticks Danaus had used earlier in our sparing session, but they would do for now. With weapons in hand, I approached Jabari again, knowing full well that his fighting style was more hand-to-hand combat and swords. I was hoping to have a slight edge over the Ancient, considering all the fighting styles I had studied over the years and honed more recently with Danaus at my side.

Staying in constant motion, I landed several sharp hits to his body and head with one of the sticks while blocking his attempts to strike at me with the other stick. We circled each other, both bleeding lightly from a variety of wounds, but nothing that was strong enough to end this stalemate as we moved like tigers looking for an opening.

"Come on, Mira," Jabari said in a low, ragged voice. "Just burn me. You know you want to."

"Not this time." I laughed as I hit him on the back of the head, then slid out of his reach as he attempted to retaliate. "I want to take you down with my bare hands." Besides, the old nightwalker knew I would need to pause for a second to conjure up enough power to nail him to the wall with flames. He was looking for that opening to plunge his hand through my chest and take me out first. If I kept moving, it was harder for him to strike at me.

Unfortunately, Jabari had other tricks up his sleeve. Sliding backward out of my immediate reach with the sticks, the nightwalker plunged his power back into my frame. My feet turned to lead and I stumbled so I was kneeling before him. My hands remained tightly wrapped around the sticks but I couldn't lift my arms.

Jabari's dark laughter swirled around the room, brushing against me as I struggled to push him out of my body once again. He had his claws sunk deep this time, and it felt as if he was tearing away at my organs and muscles.

"I have you this time, my desert blossom," he gloated. "It seems our relationship is finally at an end. It has been . . . amusing." He made a fist and pulled it back to plunge it into my chest. My stomach twisted as my eyes locked on that fist, knowing that any second it was going to be deep within my chest cavity before his fingers wrapped around my motionless heart.

"I'm not through with you yet," I snarled through clenched teeth. Gathering what powers swirled around me, including Danaus's seductive strength, I shoved the energy against Jabari. His feet slid across the smooth floor until he was pinned against the wall. Freeing myself of his hold, I plunged my own powers into his body, holding him completely still. At the same time, I lifted to my feet as if pulled up by a pair of invisible wings.

Gliding inches above the ground toward him, I raised one of the chair legs I was still holding and plunged it into his chest, purposefully missing his heart. Jabari screamed in pain and rage as he fought my hold. The great Elder no longer held terrible fear over me. That was Nick's job now. I had finally taken back a part of my life, if only to hand that part over to another.

"Now, as I was saying," I started when Jabari stopped screaming. He was growing weak from the blood loss and had gone completely still, no longer pushing against the powers that kept him completely immobile. "You will travel with Danaus and me to Venice. The night is young enough here that the dawn should not have risen over the city just yet. Danaus and I will speak with Our Liege. And then you will step down from the coven. If you are there when I return to Venice, I will finish what I started here." To punctuate my point, I jerked the stick in his chest so it scraped against his heart, wringing another scream of pain of out him.

Soft footsteps drew my attention for a second. I glanced over my shoulder to find Danaus standing close to me, waiting for my next move. With a weak smile that I hoped was somewhat reassuring, I threaded my sticky, blood-covered fingers through his while I tightly grasped Jabari's shoulder. I nearly closed my eyes as I delved deeply into Jabari's mind, pulling forth an image of the Main Hall that was home to the coven. I could disappear and reappear over short distances, but I had never attempted anything quite so far as jumping from Savannah to Venice in a single motion. I needed Jabari's crystal clear memories to aid me.

Unfortunately, with those memories came a wealth of hatred that churned and seethed around me. During the long century that I had spent at Jabari's side in my youth, I had only sensed feelings of warmth and love from him. I'd been convinced that he cared only for my well-being and that I was fully aware of my importance within the nightwalker nation. I had no memory of his experiments to learn how to control me. I could not help but wonder if he had also hid this deep well of hatred from me as well.

It was hard to hate him with the same vehemence. He was my father, my mentor, my creator. He had been a guiding light and a pair of strong arms when the world became too overwhelming for a creature that struggled to understand her own powers.

But I had to hate him, because if I didn't, it would get me killed.

We reappeared in the Main Hall with its expanse of black marble floor and raised dais. The four golden chairs of the coven Elders shone brightly in the overhead candlelight. All were currently empty as dawn was quickly approaching. If Stefan and Elizabeth were in residence in Venice, both would be in the catacombs below, unaware of what was happening just a few floors above them.

As soon as I felt the floor firmly below my feet, I released Danaus's hand and gave Jabari's shoulder a shove away from me. The Ancient stumbled backward until he finally fell on his backside. The shaft of wood still protruded from his chest, while his shirt was soaked with his blood. If I left him as he was, there was a good chance he would die during the day and not awaken the next night because of the continuous blood loss. I wasn't willing to take that chance.

Stalking him, I smiled wide as he pushed backward, trying to escape. My eyes glowed brightly and the blood lust was on me. I needed this. I knew that I'd promised him a reprieve, but I also knew that I had been lying the moment the words left my tongue.

"Mira!" he screamed. Despite the immense pain he had to have been in, I felt his powers surge toward me in an attempt to control my actions, but I was wholly focused now. There was no penetrating my defenses as before. I brushed his attempts aside like swatting an annoying fly. Dropping suddenly to my knees, I jerked the stick out of his chest and immediately plunged it through his throat, limiting his cries to a low gurgling. Using the hole I had created in his chest, I reached inside and easily plucked out his heart. Jabari's body went instantly limp before me. At long last the Ancient was dead and could no longer haunt me or threaten those I loved.

Clutching his heart tightly in one hand, I grabbed the shoulder of his shirt while I stood. I dragged him across the shining floor, leaving a smear of dark black blood. I placed the heart on my seat and left the body at the foot of the stairs before my chair. In the event that I wasn't around the next day to speak with members of the coven, the Elders and their lackeys would all know who had finally disposed of Jabari.

As I stepped away from the body, relief hit me like a runaway train, leaving me weak in the knees. Danaus laid his large hands on my shoulders and squeezed gently, holding me steady so I wouldn't fall to the blood-covered ground. As it was, my clothes were already splattered with it, and blood was smeared across my arms and face. I was grateful that he'd respected my wishes to face Jabari alone. It was only fitting that I fought this demon alone at long last. It was the only way I could finally purge my fear of him.

In the end, I finally saw Jabari as he truly was: an extremely old nightwalker afraid of the bright future that lay before him. He was no longer concerned about himself and how to best protect his interests. And I had finally become too powerful for him to control. I was only useful to him as a puppet and a frightened fledgling.

"Are you all right?" Danaus demanded. It was only when his hands slid down from my shoulders to grasp my hands that I realized they were violently trembling. A shiver wracked my body as I dragged in a deep breath and slowly released it. As the air escaped my useless lungs, the power I had been holding onto also escaped me, seeping back down into the earth and swirling once again around the creatures it emanated from. Danaus's powers hugged close to my shaking frame, like a warm blanket pulled around me. He was there now, when the battle was over, to ease my wounded psyche and protect me as I licked my wounds.

"I'll be fine," I murmured in a low voice.

"I thought you planned to let him live," Danaus said, sounding more than a little surprised.

A small smile tweaked the corners of my mouth. "Yeah, well, I decided that I could most likely accomplish everything I needed to without his assistance. Besides, the monster had already lived long past his usefulness."

Danaus smirked on me in return. "I could have told you that months ago."

"Thank you, smartass." Leaning against his chest, I raised my face up to his, and he met my lips with a melting kiss that succeeded in wiping away the last of the fatigue and confusion in my brain. As I reluctantly broke off the kiss due to the rising of the sun, I rested my head against his chest, letting the sound of his beating heart rumble through my frame.

"So, what's the plan now that we are in Venice?" he inquired as he pressed a kiss to my forehead.

"Sleep," I sighed wearily.

"And then?"

"A meeting with Our Liege. Jabari was the oldest and

strongest member of the coven. I also succeeded in taking out Macaire just a few months ago. If that doesn't catch Our Liege's attention, I don't know what will. We will get our meeting."

"Are you hoping he will help you raise an army to fight the naturi and Aurora?"

A frown pulled at my lips as I turned my face against his chest. "It's too late for that now, I think. We're on our own. If he still stands by what Macaire told me, Our Liege will welcome the Great Awakening. I'm hoping I can get his help to get rid of Nick. I can't do it alone."

Danaus grasped the sides of my waist and moved me away so he could look me in the eyes. "You're taking on Nick?"

"He's not content with Jabari's death. He wants you dead as well."

"Mira—"

"It's not just that. We can't allow him to regain his former power. He's the god of fucking chaos. The world simply can't handle his presence when we still have to face the Great Awakening."

Danaus closed his eyes and frowned as his head dipped lower. He knew I was willing to risk everything so he could live, but he didn't want me taking those risks. I laid my hand against his cheek, and his eyes opened. "Dawn is close. We both need to sleep. Return to the main islands and get a hotel room. Sleep and eat. Return here at sunset. We will begin our search for Our Liege then. With any luck, Our Liege will come to us."

"What about you?"

"I'll remain here during the day. It will be safe enough."

Danaus looked more than a little doubtful, but in the end he pressed another lingering kiss to my lips before he left the Main Hall. It felt as if a part of my heart followed him, leaving me feeling hollow and worn. I needed Danaus like the earth needed the sun and the rain. I needed him like a nightwalker craved blood. He was all the sustenance that my soul craved.

As the sun crept closer to the horizon, my feet turned toward the door in the far wall. With a shove, the door loudly creaked open like in one of those old horror movies, sending an echo down the long stone staircase that led underground. Closing the door behind me, I followed the staircase down into the darkness until I reached the ground floor. A handful of torches danced with firelight around the large room filled with stone and wooden coffins to protect us from the world like some hidden graveyard for the living dead.

A quick glance around the room revealed that more than twenty nightwalkers were either sitting up in their resting place or standing beside a coffin, watching me with intent stares. I was covered in blood, and it was widely known that I had not been in Venice earlier in the evening. Something dark had happened. To make matters even worse, I was seen trudging toward my private room, among those reserved for each Elder of the coven. I had not slept in the underground tomb of the coven in centuries, rarely even when I was on good terms with Jabari during my youth.

Leaning against the entrance to the room beside mine was Stefan. I paused in front of him, watching him emotionlessly drag his eyes from my feet to the top of my head. "So you've finally done it," he announced.

"Yes, it seems the coven is once again short another Elder," I said blandly. "I'll leave it to you and Elizabeth to see to his replacement." Then without further comment, I entered the room and closed the door with a hard thud.

The room contained a wash basin and a pitcher of water, as well as a large, four-poster bed. I looked down at my hands briefly and decided there wasn't enough water to even bother trying to wash up. Besides, it seemed fitting that I would spend the daylight hours washed in Jabari's blood.

Exhausted down to my very soul, I crawled into the bed and collapsed against the pile of pillows. I closed my eyes and wiped my mind clean of thought, brushing aside the last broken bits of worry that had plagued me over the past several nights. As the sun peeked over the horizon, I felt my soul finally fly free of my body and sleep overcame me at last.

Twenty-five

Before opening my eyes the next evening, I knew something had gone terribly wrong. I could feel the air charged with energy until I thought I could hear it crackling like a loose tension wire snapping in the wind. Keeping perfectly still, I focused on reaching out to Danaus, but felt nothing but a gaping nothingness that threatened to consume my soul. Danaus wasn't there. I should have felt him somewhere in Venice. Of course, that was assuming I was even still in Venice.

There was no putting off the inevitable. I drew in a slow breath, taking in the soft smell of burning wood and the fake pine scent from some kind of cleaning product. Releasing the breath, I opened my eyes and soaked in my surroundings. The austere stone walls of the coven underground were replaced with a soft mauve damask wallpaper and cream-colored furniture. A fire burned brightly in a large fireplace in the far corner, warming the room in both temperature and spirit.

I sat up in bed and found myself facing a man sitting in a high-back leather chair near the foot of the king-sized bed. He wore a dark suit with a pale blue shirt, the collar open to reveal a long pale throat. Dark brown hair feathered away from his lean face and curled at the collar of his jacket. His face was expressionless except for the fathomless dark eyes that watched me with a frightening intensity, a tiger watching its prey as it took its first few steps into the open clearing.

An uneasiness settled deep into my bones. The sun had settled below the horizon less than an hour ago. I had not overslept by that much, and yet it felt as if I'd been in this room for much longer. This creature must have gone into the coven crypt during the daylight hours, but everything in my mind screamed that it wasn't possible. Sure, there was an extra aura of power circulating around him, reminding me too much of myself, but I could still tell without pulling apart his lips to see his fangs that he was a nightwalker.

"Good evening, Mira," he said in a deceivingly soft and gentle voice that seeped into my brain and wrapped around my thoughts. "I hope your rest was a good one."

A shiver ran through my body before I could catch it. His voice was hypnotic. It was both terribly frightening and completely comforting in the same moment. I felt as if I were wrapped in the warmth of the summer sun while at the same time shaken down to my very soul with its awesome power. Dread gripped my stomach, twisting it into knots. I wasn't faced with some unknown nightwalker with a few interesting parlor tricks up his sleeve. This was Our Liege.

Swinging my feet off the edge of the bed, I slowly walked over and knelt before him while placing one hand on the arm of the chair. "My Liege," I murmured, humbled to finally be in his presence. I was faced with the most powerful nightwalker among our people. He was the one all nightwalkers answered to under all circumstances. And despite my general lack of respect for any and all authority types, I could not help but feel a quake of fear run through my body now that I was facing with him. He was the only one I had known of that both Jabari and Macaire feared.

And yet, now that was I kneeling so close to him, wrapped even tighter within his power, I could start pulling apart the various layers. He had the same ability to pull the energy that circulated naturally in the air from both the souls of all living creatures as well as the power emanating from the earth. He was in contact too with that even more ephemeral energy I could sense when I was near Nick. Below it all was his own natural power, which came from being a nightwalker. As I mentally touched it, I realized that he was even younger than me.

A light chuckle escaped him, surprising me as it rippled along my flesh like a wave across the shore. My bent head snapped up and I met that dark gaze, for a moment getting lost in the deep pit of his eyes. The smile that crossed his lips didn't completely reach those dark eyes.

"The great Fire Starter kneeling before me," he commented with a mocking grin. "I didn't think that such a thing would ever happen for anyone, including myself."

"You are Our Liege," I countered in a soft voice. I was unable to judge whether he thought I was skating on thin ice or just a passing amusement. I had suspected that my destruction of Jabari and Macaire might finally bring him out of hiding; however, I had not paused long enough in my plan to consider whether he would be pleased with my actions or angered.

"That is true. You may call me Adio," he said, briefly laying his hand over mine on the arm of the chair. His touch was surprisingly warm, perhaps because he'd been sitting near the flickering fire. The decision to have a fire in the fireplace struck me as more than a little odd. As nightwalkers, we weren't typically bothered by a little cold air, and none would usually brave enough to start a fire. There were just too many odd things about Adio that my brain struggled to organize.

"I am honored. I am Mira, and I am at your service."

Again he chuckled, drawing my eyes back up to his lean face and dark gaze. "We shall see, won't we?"

"You don't think I would obey your wishes?"

"I know that you are one to follow your own wishes more than the wishes of others who would seem to be more powerful than you. Of course, Jabari and Macaire dearly paid the price of believing otherwise, because there is no one more powerful than you."

At that I could not stop the soft snort that escaped me. "I think I may have finally met my match."

"In me?" he inquired with one arched brow.

"I—I—"

"You don't know. That's a true and honest answer, which I can respect." Adio smiled down at me. He waved one hand toward the second chair that sat at the foot of the bed, hidden somewhat in the shadows. "We know so little about each other, so how can we gauge each other as proper opponents?" he continued while I rose and sat in the chair, facing him again.

"Are we opponents?"

He gave a slight shrug of his slender shoulders. "That is another thing that time will only tell."

"Where is my consort? Where is Danaus? I cannot contact him. Am I still in Venice?"

"He is safe with a friend of mine, I swear to you. You are in one of my secret sanctuaries within Venice. I wanted only a few undisturbed moments with you alone."

I didn't like the answer, but for now I knew it was all I would get. Safe didn't mean that he was happy or comfortable or even uninjured. At best, it meant he was still alive, which I would just have to accept. The sooner I got through this interview with Adio, the sooner I could get back to Danaus.

Pursing my lips together, I stared at Adio as he lounged in the chair, but focused on the energy that swirled around him. He reminded me too much of myself, which only meant one frightening thing.

"You're like me, aren't you?" I demanded suddenly.

"How is that?"

"One of your parents wasn't human."

"Mother actually. Her name was Eos," he said with a smirk.

"The Greek goddess of the dawn. Also known as Aurora to the Romans. How ironic!"

"Yes, I've heard of your troubles with the naturi's queen Aurora. The coincidence is quite unfortunate."

"But your mother was a god, just like my father. That means you were born differently."

Adio smiled broadly at me. "Yes, but my differences were not as openly apparent as your own. I've heard the rumors. Born as a human with the ability to create and manipulate fire—a unique power that you carried with you into your rebirth as a nightwalker."

"What of yourself?"

"I found that being the nephew of Helios gave me a certain invulnerability to fire, though I can't control it like you."

"And?"

Adio's smile broadened. "And when I became a nightwalker, I quickly discovered that I was more appropriately called a daywalker."

I came out of my chair, sliding it back a few inches as I tried to move away from him in shock. "What do you mean daywalker? You can be in the sun? You're awake?"

"I sleep when I wish and I can walk about in the sun, but like any nightwalker, I am still dependent upon blood to survive."

I stared at him a moment longer, as if frozen in place with

the thought that this nightwalker had come to me during the middle of the day and stolen me away from my resting place. It was the idea that he could go to anyplace where a nightwalker rested and quickly see to their demise.

Adio motioned for me to return to my seat. "You're looking at me much the same way that prior coven regarded me when I first appeared."

"With horror?"

"Pretty much. One day, I swept in and killed two of their members as well as the previous liege. The remaining two were Jabari and Macaire. I took them to a place much like this and informed them that I would be taking over as liege."

"But that was so long ago. You had to have been so young," I said softly as I slid back into my chair.

"I was, which was why they were less than pleased with the idea, but after waving my hand through a flame a few times I think I convinced them they might have another Fire Starter on their hands. For the time being, they were unwilling to cross me. And in the end it all worked out for the best. I mostly kept to myself while the rest of the coven managed the night-to-night activities of our people."

I shook my head in disbelief. "But there has to be more to it."

"Why do you say that?"

"By the energy I can feel swirling around you! You're not just drawing from the blood energy in the region, but also from the earth and the other energy that even the gods seems to be in touch with. How long have you been in touch with that?"

"Most of my life."

"Your mother, Eos," I whispered. "She's been in your life. She taught you."

"From a very early age."

I shook my head and closed my eyes, cursing my luck.

I didn't know if Eos had been a patient, loving teacher and mother, but at least she was there to teach him exactly what he was and what he was capable of from an early age. She'd given him a distinct edge his entire life, where I had been forced to learn everything the hard way, particularly during the past few months under Nick's painful tutelage.

"But if you always knew that you were the child of a god, why make the decision to become a nightwalker?"

"Because I believed in being in a position of power when the time came for the humans to know the truth. What my mother made clear to me was that the gods were in no position to reassert themselves as the power players in this world. It would be the nightwalkers and the lycanthropes that stepped forward as the dominant races when the Great Awakening happened."

"Did she take into account the naturi?"

"No," he sighed softly. "I don't think she did, but then I didn't think she expected the goddess of that cage to weaken so quickly without the constant contact of the earth or her mate."

"I also don't think she took into account the plans of my father," I grimly admitted.

"Yes, I have to admit that I am curious as to your parentage," Adio said, sitting forward. "I suspected that a god had a hand in your unique qualities, but I have been reluctant to let my interest be known lest it draw more attention to you than necessary."

"You shouldn't have worried. I've done a good enough job on my own drawing attention to myself," I muttered.

"Yes, but I didn't want Jabari or Macaire drawing any connections between you and me."

"I'm grateful. I didn't have the kind of training that you were lucky enough to receive."

"I noticed."

"You've been watching."

"Through a friend and from a distance. But things have changed recently."

"My father has suddenly stepped into my life." I sat back in my chair and rested my head in my hand while propping my elbow on the arm of the chair. "It has not been an easy transition."

"And will you be kind enough to finally tell me who your illustrious father is?"

"When you bring me Danaus," I stated firmly, narrowing my gaze on Adio. I had spent the past several minutes sizing up his powers and didn't feel like I was at a distinct disadvantage. Eos might have spent more time training him, expanding his powers, but Nick's training had been thorough if not life-threatening, in its own right. Adio didn't need to have Danaus secreted away.

"You don't trust me?"

"I don't trust anyone. I'm sure you'll get used to the feeling."

Adio laughed softly as he sat back in his chair again. "And that humbleness that you were so eager to grace me with has already melted away. So fast."

"You have something that is known to be important to me, and you are asking some very intimate questions. I will not sit here and allow my hands to be completely tied when I can start making some demands of my own."

Adio seemed to consider my request for a moment before he finally nodded. A couple seconds later I could hear heavy footsteps in the hallway approaching the room. I knew the weight and the cadence. It was Danaus. Just before the door opened, I was able to finally sense him as if a veil had been lifted, but at the same time I could still sense a second magic user in the area beyond Adio. Danaus was not alone.

As the hunter opened the bedroom door and walked in,

I jumped to my feet, but didn't step forward because close behind him I saw Ryan. I tore my eyes from the white-haired warlock to focus on my dear companion.

Are you all right? I demanded silently, Adio and Ryan not needing to hear our conversation.

I'm fine. You?

Safe for now.

Our Liege? Danaus inquired, his eyes briefly dropping to the top of the seated Adio's head.

Yes, and obviously in league with Ryan. Not a positive development.

Nope, we're screwed.

It was a struggle to force myself to sit back in the chair facing Adio. My eyes moved over to the warlock and I unclenched my jaw. "It's been a while, Ryan."

"It's always a pleasure to see you, Mira," he replied pleasantly.

"How long have you known Adio?"

"A few years," he nonchalantly replied.

My mouth twisted into an ugly smirk. "So you never really needed me as a contact with the nightwalkers or the coven. You already had the ultimate contact."

"True, but he needed someone to keep a closer eye on you. I agreed to assist."

"How convenient," I sneered.

"Now, Mira," Adio chided. "Let's keep this pleasant. No harm has come to Danaus or you while in our care. Now that you can see that Danaus is perfectly healthy and safe, will you please answer my question? Who is your father?"

I hesitated. It was an ugly answer, a fact I hated to admit to even if I had no control over such a thing. It wasn't as if it was my fault that my father was a monster, only that others didn't need to know about it. But then, if anyone had a chance to help me get rid of him, it was Adio, and it certainly didn't hurt that he had Ryan in his back pocket.

"He goes my several names."

"Pick one."

Again the names were stuck in my throat. "Coyote," I finally said, but their faces were blank at the Native American reference to their trickster god. "He has probably also gone by Puck, Hermes, Eshu, Anansi, Set—"

"Loki," Adio breathed in fearful tones.

"Yes, but he's going by Old Nick now. Or rather, just Nick."

"That explains a few things," Ryan said grimly. "The fire, the appearance, the tendency toward chaos over order. You are your father's daughter—the god of chaos."

"Yes, that does explain a few things," Adio murmured, folding his hands in his lap as he sank deeper into his chair while staring intently at me. "Your powers have grown exponentially recently. A year ago you would never have taken on a member of the coven such as Macaire, and now you have killed both him and Jabari. There are also rumors that you've defeated a bori. And now you're plotting to destroy the queen of the naturi."

"You're certainly well informed," I snidely replied, crossing my arms over my chest.

"I've survived this long by staying well informed," Adio snapped. "With the destruction of the two most powerful members of the coven and the ascension of your own friend to the coven, one has to wonder if your next step is my seat."

A bark of laughter escaped me before I could catch it. "I never wanted a seat on the coven in the first place. I fear that was mostly Jabari's maneuvering, which only succeeded in backfiring on him. You can keep the position of Our Liege. Just leave me to my domain of Savannah."

"We want to be left in peace," Danaus added.

"And wouldn't that be a danger to the world?" Adio inquired. "The daughter of the god of chaos and an ageless man with bori-laced powers left to run wild."

I smiled at Adio, my fangs poking out beneath my upper lip. I leaned forward, gripping both arms of the chair. "I'm not your biggest problem, not by a long shot."

"What would my biggest problem be?"

"Nick."

"What are his plans?"

"He's never been entirely clear with me, but it sounds like he wants all of his old powers back and to return to his place as a powerful god and not just be a minor player. He plans to use to me to those ends."

"Then we simply need to kill you to stop those plans," Ryan offered.

"Not a chance," Danaus growled, which only caused my smile to widen.

"Thank you. It's nice to know there is at least one person alive who isn't eager for my death," I teased. I then turned a serious gaze back on Adio. "I was thinking more of a trap. Would your mother aid me?"

Adio shook his head. "She is no match for the god of chaos in this world. She is simply the goddess of the dawn, fragile and fading in strength as the day passes toward its apex. Eos would not help you."

"Then would you help me? You said that you became a nightwalker because you wanted to be a part of the dominant species when the Great Awakening happened. If Nick succeeds, we will all be subject to his whims."

"I will consider it."

"What will it cost me?"

Adio smiled. "Very wise."

"You can't get something for nothing in this world. What would you want in return? My chair on the coven? Exile?"

"I had . . . something . . . in mind when I brought you here, but now that I know the source of your blood, I am hesitant," Adio admitted.

"What?" Ryan suddenly cried. "You promised me!"

"Promised what?" Danaus demanded. He took a step closer to the warlock, but Ryan didn't seem to notice, as his angry gaze was focused entirely on the top of Adio's head.

"I'm having second thoughts," Adio admitted.

"You promised!" Ryan shouted.

I looked from Ryan's flushed face to Adio's look of distress. There was only one thing a nightwalker could offer a warlock of his strength and power. My stomach churned. "You promised him that I would change him," I softly said, drawing Adio's gaze to my face.

"Both of our bloodlines combined in his body to bring about his rebirth," Adio said.

"Absolutely not!" Danaus declared.

"It won't work," I stated firmly.

"It worked with you," Ryan quickly argued. "You had three makers."

"I also had the blood of a god already running through my veins," I countered. "I was different to start with. Underneath all your powers, you are still human at heart, Ryan. Your body will glom to the first drop of nightwalker blood that enters your system and will ignore any other that enters."

"How can you be sure?" Adio asked.

"I'm not, but do we want to risk not only changing him into a nightwalker, but using the diluted blood of both the goddess of the dawn and the god of chaos?"

"It seems there is much that we must still discuss," Adio announced as he pushed out of his chair. "I will leave you here to come up with your proposal to get rid of your father while we discuss what I will choose to be my payment should I elect to aid your endeavors."

"You know, you could always just do it out of the goodness of your heart," I pressed, rising from my chair as well.

Adio turned back to look at me, pausing as he tried to leave the room. "My mother was the goddess of the dawn, not the goddess of love."

"True," I murmured as he left the room, followed by a somewhat irate Ryan who slammed the door shut. We could have done well if the goddess of love had decided to have a few children in the world. We might have been a little better off, but then I guess I should have been grateful that the god of war hadn't been particularly prolific. At least, I didn't think he had been.

Twenty-six

"You can't be seriously considering this?" Danaus raged the second we could no longer hear Adio and Ryan's footsteps in the hallway.

I swallowed a sigh as I crossed the distance between us and wrapped my arms around his waist, laying my head on his shoulder so my forehead was pressed into the hollow of his neck. For now, I didn't want to think about Nick, Adio, or Ryan's frightening demand. I just wanted to hold the hunter and know that he was safe.

"Did he harm you in any way?" I asked, avoiding his question.

Danaus heaved a deep breath before finally wrapping his arms around me and holding me tightly. "Ryan appeared a few hours before sunset and politely escorted me to a house near the outskirts of the city. I was allowed to briefly look in on you. At the time, you were alone and there wasn't a window in the room, so I decided that he needed you alive for the time being. We simply sat in the parlor not speaking, waiting for the sun to set."

"Sounds like fun," I murmured against his neck before pressing a kiss against his warm flesh.

"I wanted to rip his head off the entire time, but he didn't say anything so I held my temper."

"Smart man."

"I also didn't know what kind of danger you were in or how you had been brought here, so I didn't want to take any chances."

"Again, smart man."

Danaus grabbed both of my upper arms and held me out away from him so he could look me in the eye. "Then listen to this smart man and don't agree to this. You can't give Ryan the kind of powers you have. He would be just as great a danger as Nick."

"Not at first. I wouldn't make him a First Blood, but simply chum—weak and helpless for the most part. It would be centuries before he truly came into the bulk of his powers."

"Mira, you can't!"

"I have to consider it. Adio is a child of a god, like me. He's the only one that might be powerful enough to help me trap Nick. I need his help."

"You sound like you have a plan."

"Something that I have been slowly developing."

"How dangerous?"

"Oh, it wouldn't be one of my brilliant plans if it wasn't extremely dangerous and somewhat stupid," I teased with a wide grin.

"And I won't like it, will I?"

"You'll probably hate it, I'm sure, but I think it's going to be the best shot we have."

"When do you plan on telling me about this brilliant plan?"

"Soon. I hate to even breathe the words out loud since it's hard to guess how close Nick is at any moment. I want it to be a surprise for him."

"Naturally."

"For now, our main focus has to be Ryan and his request to become a nightwalker. I can understand his need to not be at the bottom of the nightwalker food chain when he is turned, but I'm not comfortable with the idea that he would have my blood flowing through his veins."

"Beside the fact you also swore that you would never make a nightwalker of your own."

It was a struggle not to roll my eyes at him. Yes, I had sworn that I would never make a nightwalker, and Ryan was the least of all people that I wanted to have my blood. But I also had a feeling that this was no fragile relationship between Ryan and Adio. There was a firm understanding between the two men after years of collaboration. I had been picked because of my strength and powers, but now Adio was having some doubts about the idea of another child of chaos potentially running around. The bloodline would be even further diluted when it passed from me to Ryan, but it wouldn't be enough. There were still risks.

What worried me the most was the same vein of darkness that ran through me also plunged through Ryan. The warlock would not be able to keep his powers in a positive place, but would have to let the darkness consume him. Adio might be able to control his fledgling for a while, but that would only be a temporary solution. In the end he would have to kill Ryan or I would have to come hunting for him, assuming I survived my attempt to take out Nick.

"The only thing we have on our side at the moment is the fact that Adio and Ryan don't completely see eye-to-eye on this matter." I moved away from Danaus and sat on the edge of the bed, hanging my hands between my legs.

"How do we take advantage of that?"

"We try to quickly reason with Adio while we are in the process of making Ryan into a nightwalker," I suggested.

"And if he doesn't listen to reason?"

"Then Adio will be forced to change Ryan over himself, and then kill me for disobeying him."

"What I don't understand is why Adio *didn't* change Ryan over himself," Danaus said as he sat on the bed beside me.

"I have a feeling it's for the same reason I don't want to change him over. Ryan is already a powerful warlock, and neither of us is sure what powers he's going to retain when he is reborn. Neither Adio nor I want to make an even bigger monster by giving him access to the blood of a god. Unfortunately, Adio didn't realize what he was dealing with until he had me in his grasp. Now that he's made his mistake, he has to find a way to gracefully back out of his agreement with Ryan without upsetting whatever arrangement the two men now have in place."

Danaus scratched the dark stubble that had grown on his chin. "Could we secretly find a surrogate to take your place? Would Ryan be aware of the difference while in the process of being remade into a nightwalker?"

"That's my hope, but we need to get Ryan drained first," I said, rubbing my hands together. I couldn't help but feel a little pleasure at the thought of digging my fangs back into the warlock's neck. Not only would the revenge be sweet after he attempted to manipulate me, but the warlock's blood carried with it an extra little bonus—I could be awake during the daylight hours as long as I was drinking his blood. I was still vulnerable to the rays of the sun, but to be awake and alive for those long hours and not vulnerable was too precious to pass up.

"You're getting normal blood back into your system as soon as we get home," Danaus sternly said without needed to read my thoughts.

"A few days wouldn't hurt."

"Yes, they would." I looked over at his face and saw the

resolve in his beautiful blue eyes. I had a feeling I would
be feeding off a normal, everyday human before I had the
chance to even leave Venice. The last time I'd fed off Ryan's
blood, the results had not been pretty. In fact, they nearly
cost Tristan his life and me my sanity. Yes, Danaus was
right. Never again.

A knock came at the door, and Danaus jumped to his feet
and placed one hand on the knife at his side as he stepped
in front of me. A part of me was pleased to discover that
neither of us had been divested of our weapons during the
day, but then, we were faced with a powerful warlock and a
powerful nightwalker. They could easily find ways around a
sword and knife if they wanted to.

"Come," I called, resting a reassuring hand on Danaus's
arm for a moment as the door swung open. As the two men
reentered, I let my hand drop back down into my lap. The
awe I felt less than an hour earlier when I first met Adio had
melted away. I had expected a nightwalker that was older
than Danaus and radiated more power than I could com-
prehend. Instead, I was faced with someone who was something of a charlatan. He had gotten his seat as Our Liege
through his special powers and then sat back, leaving the
coven to protect him out of the fear that he would kill them
all in their sleep. The biggest problem when I looked at Adio
was that I saw myself reflected back, except I was infinitely
more devious and dangerous.

"You've had some time to consider my request," Adio
said as he came to stand beside the chair he had occupied
earlier. Ryan stood close by his shoulder, his gaze narrowed
on my face. If the warlock was trying to read my thoughts,
he wasn't having much luck. After centuries of Jabari parad-
ing through my brain, and recently Nick, I had gotten better
about closing people out. Now the only one that could slip in
and out at will was Danaus.

"Yes, but have you considered my dilemma?" I countered. "Nick needs to be dealt with or the future you are hoping for with the arrival of the Great Awakening—which truly is just around the corner—will not happen as you hope."

Adio moved around to sit in the chair, but still remain turned so he could look at me. "It's that close?"

Danaus took a step closer to Adio, causing Ryan to shift, as if putting himself more between the hunter and Adio.

"Aurora means to destroy her sisters Nyx and Cynnia as soon as possible," I told Adio, "and she has no qualms about fighting that battle in front of humans. Nightwalkers and lycanthropes have been dragged into the battle in an attempt to control the damage and keep things secret. If we're lucky, we may succeed, but if we don't, the Great Awakening will be happening very soon in the worst possible fashion."

"This is . . . unexpected," Adio murmured. "I knew the Great Awakening was going to happen soon, but I didn't realize that the situation with the naturi had grown so dire."

"Jabari and Macaire haven't been keeping you informed?"

"I knew of the events at Machu Picchu, but I knew nothing of Aurora's newest plans. I assumed she would take some time to build her army and strike back at the nightwalkers here in Venice. I didn't know that a civil war was brewing."

"Cynnia seeks peace with the nightwalkers and simply wants to lead her people into a quiet existence away from humanity before they all fade into extinction. I've sworn to help her because my other choice is Aurora and her very public war against humanity."

"I see."

"Do you really?" I asked, finally coming off the bed to walk around so I was standing in front of him. "I'm torn on two fronts. The naturi need to finally be dealt with, and this alliance with Cynnia could afford us at least a temporary peace to get us through a few decades should the

Great Awakening occur. At the same time, I must deal with Nick and finally see that he is caged in some fashion so he can't cause us any additional problems. I fear that the Great Awakening would afford him too wonderful an opportunity to step forward into the power vacuum created by the chaos."

"I do not know what I can do to help you with your father, but I am sure you have a plan," Adio said with a smirk.

"I do."

"But for my help, you must first aid me in changing my friend here over to a nightwalker," he continued, motioning with his hand toward the warlock.

I stood and looked over Adio at Ryan, who was standing straight and stiff. He wore his usual charcoal suit with the light gray shirt that was open at the neck. His skin still held a nice tan, while his shoulder-length hair was a flawless white. He watched me with perceptive gold eyes, taking in my every movement.

When I first met the warlock at the Themis compound, I suspected he was going to be more trouble than he was worth. However, he had helped protect us when the naturi attacked, and came to our aid again on Crete when we were fighting the naturi once again. Unfortunately, he'd tried to exploit my weakness with glittering promises of walking around during the day. I hadn't considered the price when I agreed to the deal, only thinking I would be safe from an attack by Aurora. If we had continued, I believed he might have finally convinced me to change him without Adio's assistance, simply because I was already too strung out on his blood to know any better.

Now I knew that no one would survive if Ryan was trusted.

"So why are you so desperate to become a nightwalker?" I asked in a smooth voice as I stepped around Adio's chair to come face-to-face with the warlock.

"I've been Adio's friend for a long time and a close planner on the committee regarding the Great Awakening," Ryan replied with a nonchalant wave of his hand.

"As such, you must certainly know that those most likely to escape the 'witch hunts,' so to speak, will be the warlocks and witches. You won't be thrust into the limelight. You will be able to easily hide from the frightened and enraged humans."

"But there is no power in hiding," he countered.

"There is survival," Danaus interjected.

"I've spent more than three centuries surviving. I'm looking for a larger piece of the pie. The nightwalkers will be the real power players when the world changes following the Great Awakening, and I will be a part of it."

"But surely Adio has explained to you that when you are reborn a nightwalker, you will come back weak. Sure, you will have more abilities than a human, but you'll be little more than a plaything among your new brethren. You will have to acquire all new survival skills very quickly."

Ryan lifted his chin while clenching his jaw. "Adio has sworn to stay by my side and aid my growth. Besides, there is always a chance that I will retain some of my powers as a warlock. That knowledge won't slip away simply because I've become a nightwalker."

"What about the elixir?" Danaus asked from the opposite side of the room. The hunter had silently slipped away from where he had been standing near me, and was now leaning against the far wall with his arms folded across his chest.

Ryan's eyes flared for a moment while his lips pressed into a frown and he stared at the hunter. "You knew?" he bit out.

"Do you think I was going to willingly let you live under the same roof as those helpless Themis researchers if I didn't know some of your secrets? I knew you were a few centuries old, but I had to be sure you wouldn't use one of them to prolong your life."

"What elixir?" I demanded, my gaze jumping from Danaus to Ryan.

Both men fell stubbornly silent for nearly a minute, so that all that could be heard was the crackle of the fire and the fast heart rates of the two living creatures in the room.

"It's an elixir of life that my former master had created," Ryan finally said, grinding out each word between his clenched teeth. "It prolonged the life of the drinker. Unfortunately, potions have never been my strong suit. I've never been able to properly replicate it and my supply has finally run out. My real age will start to catch up to me within the next few weeks."

"So you're becoming a nightwalker because you want to live longer," I replied.

"Yes," Ryan hissed, glaring at me. He hadn't enjoyed revealing his own dirty little secret.

I leaned around to look at Adio. "You knew about this?"

"I did."

I stood upright again so I was facing Ryan. "Wanting to live is a much better reason for becoming a nightwalker than simply wanting power. It will get you through the transformation when Death comes for you."

The heat and anger left Ryan's eyes for the first time, and he blinked at me, looking a little confused. I smiled at him as I took a step closer. "You have to really want this. I have to drain you to nearly the point of death, and he will know that you are hovering on the brink. Death will come for you and he will grab onto your soul. Only the strong—only those that truly want to live and be a nightwalker—survive the process. You can be given all the nightwalker blood in the world, but if you don't have the will or the fight, you will not wake up again. Death wants you, but you have to want this more."

"I want this," Ryan said in a soft but firm voice.

I grinned. "I was hoping you'd say that."

In a flash I had a handful of his soft white hair and had twisted it around my fist as I brought his neck down to me. No one had time to react. It was only after I sank my fangs deep into the man's neck that I heard the strangled cries and shouts from both Adio and Danaus. Ryan grabbed my shoulders and instinctively tried to push away from me out of fear. The other times I had fed on him were slow and gentle, so he didn't feel threatened by me. Now the gloves were off and he finally knew he was at my mercy. I was going to drain him to the point of death, and he had to rely on the protection of his friend Adio to make sure I didn't let him cross over and die.

Wrapping my free arm around his waist, I dragged him away from the support of the back of Adio's chair to an open space in the room where I could easily lay him on the ground when he finally grew weak. Behind me, I could hear both Danaus and Adio moving around the room, their footsteps heavy and anxious as they watched me, but I didn't care. This was the first warm, full meal that I'd had in a long time.

Since taking up with Danaus, I had stretched out my feedings to less than once a week, and then they were quick little bites that could be grabbed in stolen moments when he was most unlikely to notice. He knew I was feeding, but I still did what I could to hide it from him. I didn't want to cause him any more strain than I already did. We were still trying to figure out this relationship thing, and me drinking blood was still a comfort issue for him. I was willing to give Danaus all the time he needed to get adjusted to the idea. He was worth a little sacrifice.

However, the thought of draining Ryan nearly dry was just too enticing. His blood was deliciously sweet and packed an amazing punch of power that rolled through my body in enticing waves. I could feel my half-starved cells and organs finally filling up to the brim and overflowing with his blood. I was bathed in an energy that tingled throughout my body.

"Mira, you can't do this! You can't change him!" Danaus growled, grabbing my shoulder to pull me off of the warlock. I didn't think. There was no thinking at that moment beyond that flood of blood. I reached back with my other hand and raked my long nails across his arm, causing him to suddenly jump back.

I know what I'm doing, I barely managed to send to Danaus above the red haze.

After another few minutes I heard Ryan's heart start to significantly slow and start to stutter in his chest as his body struggled under the last of his blood. With a gasp, I lifted my head and licked my lips and teeth before lowering him to the ground. He lay motionless then, his breathing shallow and his face paler than it had been. His eyes were closed and he was unconscious, which is what I had been aiming for.

I stepped away from Ryan and turned so I could look over my shoulder at Adio, who was closely watching Ryan with a look of concern on his face. "Well, are you going to finish the job?" I asked.

Adio looked up at me a little stunned. "What?"

"You asked for my help. I drained him. Now you give him your blood. Make him your pet. I don't need one."

"I—I—I can't," he stuttered, shaking his head.

"The god thing?"

"Yes, I can't risk it. I don't know what my blood would do to him. I can't risk . . ."

"Can't risk him coming back too powerful," I finished with a smirk. "And when you came to me, I seemed to be the right amount of power. A nightwalker that had a little something extra, but not like you. Unfortunately, until night, you didn't know that I am like you. It was too late to talk Ryan out of his little plan."

"Yes, but we can't leave him like this. He'll die."

"There are worse things," Danaus muttered, drawing Adio's glare.

"I have a backup plan, but it requires a little discretion on your part," I said to Adio. At that moment, I mentally reached out to an old friend who had been waiting in the wings for my signal. A second later Valerio appeared in the room, standing opposite me as we all looked down on Ryan's struggling body. "Adio, this is my close and trusted friend, Valerio."

Adio stiffly nodded, looking at the nightwalker for a moment, undoubtedly sizing him up. Valerio merely smiled under the scrutiny, unmoved by the other nightwalker or the body on the floor that was slowly dying. He simply looked at me and smiled as he extended his hand toward me. I grasped it and allowed him to brush a kiss across my knuckles that brought a low growl from Danaus. A little jealousy was always a good thing in a relationship.

"You said you were in desperate need if my assistance, my dear," Valerio said with his rich accent, which seemed to run fingers across my cheek.

"I am, my friend. This man here wants to be a night-walker, but neither Adio nor I, for very . . . distinct reasons, can use our own blood. I was hoping you would be willing to provide me with a bit of your own blood."

Valerio gave a little laugh before shaking his head. "I have no need for a new fledgling hanging on my coattails. No, thank you."

"He won't belong to you. He will never know you were ever here. He will belong exclusively to Adio."

Valerio's smile faded as he stared at me. "And what is wrong with your blood, my sweet Mira?"

"It's my heritage. Ryan is a powerful warlock, and I fear that my blood may give him some added abilities when we would all prefer him to be just a little bit of chum. Cage the possible monster that he may become." A seductive smile slipped across my lips and I stepped one foot over Ryan so I could lightly grasp one of Valerio's arms. "I know you made Knox, and you did a fabulous job with him. Such purity and strength. Give me a creature similar to Knox in strength and leave Adio here to the job of raising him."

Valerio gave me a fresh, knowing smile as he pressed a kiss to my forehead. "You shall have to try harder than that. I do not make nightwalkers on a whim. Will your blood create a monster?"

"No. It will give a potential monster the power to be a monster. Someone good at heart should not be affected so. Your blood will simply make him a weak nightwalker, which is what we all want."

"Except him."

"True."

"Entice me, Mira," he whispered in my ear. "Give me something that I truly want."

I looked up at Valerio to find that he had been staring at Danaus the whole time he'd spoken to me. He was trying very hard to make the hunter jealous, make him act, so he could pretend to be offended and disappear in a huff. But for now, Danaus was as still as stone and I was grateful.

I reached up and placed my hand against Valerio's cheek, turning his face so he was forced to look down at me. "One day you will come to me with a request. You will be desperate. It will be a request that I would under normal circumstances deny without thought. Make this nightwalker tonight, and I will be beholden to you for one request of your choosing."

"Anything?"

"Anything," I repeated, my gaze unwavering.

"Very well."

Releasing Valerio, I stepped back away from him and walked over toward Danaus, who was glaring at Ryan on the floor. Valerio knelt down, placing his hand over the man's chest. "He's nearly dead now."

"There's still a little blood left for you to take. I didn't drain him completely," I argued.

Valerio merely shook his head a moment before biting Ryan on the opposite side of the throat. He drank only a little before healing the wound so the deception would be preserved. He then slashed his wrist and allowed his own blood to pour past Ryan's parted lips. The warlock didn't respond, but I hadn't expected him to. He was deep in a coma and would remain there until the sun set the next night. If he was to become a nightwalker, we would only know it if he rose the next night. Valerio was forced to open the wound twice as it healed on its own before enough blood had been poured into Ryan's body. I had only witnessed the making of another nightwalker a couple other times, and always swore I would never complete the act myself. It was a responsibility I didn't want.

Valerio licked the remaining smear of blood from his wrist before rising to his feet and dusting off the knees of his slacks. He looked over at Adio for a moment and arched one dark brow. "Our Liege, I presume?"

"Correct," Adio said, sounding a little surprised. But then, I knew better. Valerio knew more than he would ever admit and was wilier than should have been allowed to live. Yet, I loved him too much to try to kill him, and he was too entertaining to allow him to slip out of my life.

"A pleasure," Valerio said with a slight bow from the waist. He then turned his attention to me and smiled. "An interesting flavor. One I've not run across with other warlocks."

"Yes." I smiled, resisting the urge to give him a hug of

thanks. Danaus had endured enough and I could feel his anger simmering beside me like a pot beginning to bubble over. "Just as a warning. If you don't feed again tonight, his blood will allow you to stay awake during the daylight hours, but you are still susceptible to the sun. Enjoy it for a day or two, then I would suggest some fresh blood."

"Interesting," he purred, then disappeared from sight.

With Valerio gone, I turned my attention back to Adio, who was now kneeling beside Ryan. I could hear now that his heartbeat was nearly nonexistent, and knew that in a few moments it would stop completely. It was all a matter of whether his soul remained hovering around the body. Otherwise it would never find its way back.

"I'm assuming you don't need me any longer."

"No, I will take care of matter from here," Adio said in a distracted manner.

"And there will be no mention of Valerio?"

"And reveal to Ryan that he's been double-crossed by us both? Of course not."

"Thank you."

"When will you need my help with Nick?" he asked without my need to prompt him, which was promising.

"Soon. I will be in contact. It shouldn't be a problem now that we've been introduced."

"True," Adio admitted with a certain curl to his upper lip. "I'm sure I can also find you in Savannah."

"Of course, but I will try to give you a couple nights with Ryan to get him adjusted before contacting you."

"I would appreciate that."

Ignoring Danaus's glare, I wrapped my arms around the hunter's waist and focused all my thoughts on my secret lair in the basement of my home. I had a feeling he was going to have a few loud words with me before the night was over.

Twenty-seven

A scream was ripped from me the second my feet touched the ground in the basement of my home. It felt as if my skull was being split into two while my soul was ripped from my chest. I hadn't thought of the time difference when I shot across the ocean to the United States. It hadn't been that late in Venice when we left, and the sun had yet to set in Savannah. The only thing keeping me awake at that moment was Ryan's blood. Unfortunately, it was too much of a shock to my system for my nightwalker body to suddenly go from night to day, and my body was being torn between the demand for death and the power of the blood to keep me awake.

I felt Danaus's hands grasp my shoulders as I crumpled to my knees on the concrete floor. The pain slowly ebbed and I felt as if I could think again. I blinked my eyes a couple of times and unclenched my fists in front of me.

"I'm okay," I murmured after a minute. "I forgot to check. The sun is still up here."

"I guess Ryan's blood proved to be a rare benefit this time," Danaus admitted.

I let the hunter help me back to my feet, but was disappointed when he suddenly released me and stepped away.

"Kind of. Otherwise, when we reappeared, I would have been immediately dead for the next few hours."

A tense silence filled the air as we watched each other. His expression was stern and he wasn't meeting my gaze as he stood on the opposite side of the room with his hands in his pockets. "You need to feed," he finally bit out.

"I'll call Gabriel, but I would rather wait until sunset. It's not far away and I don't want to drop dead the second I get a little blood into my system. I want to fall asleep on my own terms."

Danaus gave a little grunt as he opened the door and left the room. I could hear his footsteps trudging up the stairs as I pulled my cell phone out of my pocket. Gabriel, my trusted human bodyguard, was more than a little surprised to hear from me, but he was happy to lend his aid in my time of need. I closed the phone again and followed Danaus up the stairs to find him sitting in the growing darkness of the parlor.

"What part of the events that occurred tonight is bothering you?" I asked, taking the seat beside him.

"Most of it."

"And the biggest irritation is . . . ?"

"Valerio."

I bit back a smile as I wondered if jealousy was truly eating at him. "You know that Valerio was just flirting a bit to get under your skin. It was harmless."

"But your promise wasn't. I know you, Mira. You stick by your word. What if he asks you to kill me?"

"Then Valerio knows that I will kill myself in the same heartbeat that you drop dead. Valerio isn't stupid. He knows that I love you and would never harm you without causing equal harm to myself. And he has too much use for me alive."

"What if he asks for you to sleep with him?"

I couldn't hold the laugh back that time. "Valerio wouldn't waste a promise like that just to get me in his bed. He would prefer the challenge of seducing me if he truly wanted me to sleep with him. No, he will save that promise for a very special occasion. Please, don't mistake his carefree demeanor. Valerio is an extremely intelligent strategist and manipulator. He will save that promise for a moment when he is finally backed into a corner and has no escape."

Danaus didn't look placated by my explanation. In fact, he looked even more concerned than when I started. And in truth, I was a little worried myself. Whatever Valerio set before me, I knew it would be an ugly task that I would naturally refuse at first glance, but I would have no choice. I feared it might finally come between Danaus and me, but I didn't think it would be on a romantic level. No, I would have to sacrifice my honor and morals in order to fulfill this promise.

The only bright side I could think of was that I was likely to die trying to capture Nick, and would never be given the chance to live up to my promise to Valerio. My plan was dangerous and in many ways stupid. I feared telling Danaus because he would be determined to stop me. So I kept the thought buried deep within my brain, where neither Danaus nor Nick would be able to find it.

"How much danger are we in from Ryan now?" Danaus inquired, letting the previous subject drop.

"Actually, for the first time, he's little to no threat to us. He's going to take months to adjust to being a nightwalker. He will try to use his warlock powers, but it's going to be a strain because his body needs all the energy it can gather just to stay alive. Unless Adio actually gives him some of his blood, I wouldn't expect Ryan to be a problem for a century or two—assuming he lives that long."

"Adio's not going to do that."

"No, he knows that danger. That's why he didn't transform Ryan in the first place and why he balked when he discovered what I was. He didn't mind the idea of turning Ryan into a nightwalker, but he wanted to limit his powers. No nightwalker wants to risk creating something more powerful than themselves."

We sat in an uncomfortable silence for several minutes before we heard a car pull into the driveway and drive around to the back of the house. I rose and walked toward the kitchen to meet Gabriel, while Danaus remained sitting in the parlor. Something else was eating at the hunter, but I wasn't willing to go digging through his brain and invading his privacy just to find out the truth.

I stood toward the back of the kitchen as Gabriel used his keys to unlock the door and quickly punch in the code on the security keypad beside the door. Most of the shades were pulled in the house, blocking out the last of the sun's rays, but I was still trying to be cautious.

"You're awake," he announced with a lopsided grin. "I thought you had given up that dangerous lifestyle."

"It was for the last time, I promise," I said, holding my hand up to him. He crossed the distance between us and I gave him a quick hug before sliding out of his strong arms. Things had become somewhat awkward between us since I'd taken Danaus as a permanent lover. Gabriel and I had worked out an interesting relationship over the long years, which not only included his protection and blood, but also the occasional bout of sex. We had come to a silent understanding that the sex was at an end, and he showed no signs of remorse or disappointment with my choice, which was a relief.

I led my old friend down the hall to the entrance to my secret lair in the basement. "I'm sorry to drag you all the way out here, especially since I only need just a tiny bit to dilute

Ryan's blood so I can sleep again. I actually feel exhausted, but I couldn't sleep now no matter how hard I tried."

"I don't mind," he said. "Things have been quiet recently. With Danaus now here permanently, I was beginning to think you wouldn't have much use for me any longer. Well, at least not beyond that occasional donor."

I stopped when we reached the bottom of the steps and quickly spun around. I wrapped my arms around him in a tight embrace, rubbing my head against his hard jaw. "You are more than a source of blood for me. You are and always will be my personal guardian, my guardian angel. Yes, I have Danaus now, but I still need you to watch over me during the day. If you want to leave me and find another life, then I understand and wish you the best. I will support you in any way I can, but I am not trying to push you out of my life."

Gabriel wrapped his strong arms around me, one hand rubbing up and down my back for a moment. "I just didn't feel needed any longer."

I gazed up into his chocolate brown eyes and touched his soft brown hair, brushing it away from his forehead. "You protect me during the day. There is no greater task when it comes to a nightwalker."

"Thank you," he whispered, pressing a kiss to my temple. "Since Michael was killed and the deaths of Lily and Tristan, I thought you might try to push me away as a way of protecting me."

"I can't. You're one of the last few members of my family."

Gabriel nodded and released me as I dropped my hands. I led him to my private chamber and let him sit on the edge of the bed with me. We talked about the recent development with Matsui while we waited for the sun to finish its final descent beneath the horizon. Gabriel promised to begin his search for a new bodyguard to help him watch over me. I hated the first few months of trusting someone new to the job, but I trusted

Gabriel with my life and knew that he would not let anyone dangerous near me during the daylight hours. He would find someone trustworthy. In the end, Matsui had been my choice because I was curious about someone who already knew about nightwalkers. I had made the mistake, not Gabriel.

After the sun set, I leaned in and gently withdrew what amounted to only a few sips of his blood before I closed the wound. I was still full from gorging myself on Ryan's blood and only needed a bit to counteract his blood's ability to keep me awake during the day.

"That's it?" Gabriel asked when I stood again.

"Yeah, you should be careful. You could be a little woozy," I teased.

He gave a derisive snort as he pushed back to his feet with ease. "I've given more blood for a cholesterol test, Mira."

"I know. I'm sorry I wasted your time."

"It wasn't a waste. You needed me and that was enough," he said, squeezing my arm. "Besides, this will give me a chance to check over the outside security lights and other fixtures. I haven't looked them over in a couple of weeks. Get some sleep. I'll be around during the day."

I looked up to see Danaus enter the sparring room at the same time Gabriel left my private room. Gabriel nodded his greeting to the hunter, but Danaus didn't acknowledge him as he kept his focus on me. A frown pulled at the corner of his lips and his eyes were dark with anger.

"I told him about Matsui," I started when we were alone. "He's going to start looking for someone to replace him so I'll have two trustworthy guardians again."

"You mean blood donors," Danaus said in a sharp voice.

"No, Gabriel isn't just a blood donor for me. He is my bodyguard as well. He watches over me during the daylight hours," I said, feeling a strange sense of déjà vu.

"You have me for that."

"You need to sleep at some point. You would be awake guarding me during the day and staying up all night so we could be together. You can't live like that," I argued, flopping back down on the edge of the bed. "What is this all about? You've never had a problem with Gabriel before."

"Why isn't my blood good enough for you?" he finally demanded after a lengthy silence.

My mouth bobbed open and closed a couple times like a fish gasping for air. He couldn't have said anything that would have left me more speechless. "You don't want me to feed off you."

"You never asked."

"You give me a dirty look every time either one of us mentions that I need to feed. I've cut back on my feeding habits just to accommodate you."

"Maybe I'm not comfortable with the idea of you being in such an intimate position with all these men."

"Then I'll only feed from women."

"Are you still sleeping with Gabriel?"

"No! How can you ask that? You know that you're the only one in my life."

"Am I? Before me there was Michael and Gabriel and Valerio and God only knows how many other men."

"Yes, there have been other men in my life. I'm six hundred years old and I've refused to live the life of a hermit, but you're the only one in my life now, and I want it to stay that way for a very, very long time."

Danaus drew in a deep breath, a frown still lingering on his lips as he stared at me. "You still haven't answered my question. Why isn't my blood good enough for you?"

I stood, walked over to my lover and placed my hands on either side of his face, allowing my thumbs to caress his high, sharp cheekbones. "Is that what you want? Do you want me to bite you?"

"Would it bring us closer together?"

I closed my eyes and dropped my forehead against his chest, listening to his steady heartbeat.

"I've seen you when you drink from Gabriel," he continued in a softer voice. "It's different. You're not just feeding from him. There's a different kind of intimacy there. Something that we don't have."

"My love," I whispered before looking up at him. I dropped my hands down to grasp one of his. I led him over to the bed and pushed him down so he sat on the edge while I kneeled between his legs. "Danaus, I love you with everything that I am. If I were human, I would marry you and give you my children. I would grow old with you. I would give you my forever."

"But you won't feed off me."

"Yes, I won't feed off you, even if you ask me to. I have two very important reasons. One is your bori blood. I don't know what the impact of it would be on me. What if it's worse than what Ryan's blood does to me? What if I can't stop and I hurt you? What if I hurt others because of it? Neither one of us could live with that. I don't want to take the chance if I can find other ways of surviving."

"And the second reason?"

"You are my everything. I want to keep you above such things as being a source of food for me. I want to keep you spoiled and untouched by my kind. I want no one to touch you. You are so much more to me and this world than a source of blood. You are a great man and a great warrior. No one should ever touch you in such a way, particularly me."

"Why particularly you?"

"Because I am not a good person and never will be. I will not soil you. I've been blessed by the love that you've given me, and I will not ask for anything more. I need nothing more than that."

Danaus leaned down and took my mouth in a sweet kiss that brought tears to my eyes. Taking both of my hands, he gently helped me back to my feet as he stood as well. With infinite care, he slowly undressed me while I pulled off his clothes. My hands danced over his body, memorizing the texture, color, and scars I found. I wanted to remember everything about him so that when I closed my eyes each morning, I could see him clearly in my mind.

When we were both naked, he lifted me into bed and proceeded to slowly make love to me with a gentleness I had never felt before. It was as if it were both our first and last time together. When we kissed, I wanted to cry, and when he touched me, my heart sang out.

We spent the rest of the evening that way, locked in a lover's embrace, hardly speaking a word to each other because we had said enough. I loved him and I knew that he loved me. The rest of the world could fall away and we wouldn't care. I had everything I wanted when I touched him.

Just before the sun rose the next morning, Danaus rose and dressed. He tucked the covers around me and pressed one last lingering kiss on my lips. "Tomorrow night we're back to the way it usually is," he said, before nibbling on my lower lip.

"How's that?"

"Rough and frantic," he said with a smile. I smiled back at him, running my hand across his cheek before he stepped away from me.

"That'll be nice too," I said around a yawn.

"Sweet dreams, my love."

"Sweet dreams, dark hunter," I murmured as he closed the door and set the security lock. I was safe for another day, and I had Danaus waiting for me when the sun set in the sky again. Everything was right in the world for just one day.

Twenty-eight

Danaus's mental and vocal screams for me were almost deafening when I awoke the next night. I lay still in my bed in my house outside Savannah, trying to sort out the cacophonous noise, when I realized that both Knox and Gregor were mentally reaching out for me as well.

I'm here, I wearily replied to the group as I opened my eyes to the usual total darkness of the room. However, something was horribly different. There was the distinct acrid smell of burnt wood all around me. In addition, it seemed warmer than usual, as if the heater had been left on high all day.

Are you hurt? Danaus demanded.

Where are you? Knox quickly followed before I could answer.

I'm fine. I'm in my room in the basement. I'll be up in a minute, I said warily, unable to understand why they were acting so strange. I did a quick scan, extending my powers to their fullest extent, and sensed only those three in the immediate area. There were no naturi or humans that could cause problems. Just Danaus and a pair of anxious nightwalkers.

Stay where you are, Gregor directed. *We're coming to you.*

Closing out the other nightwalkers, I directly touched Danaus's mind so the others could not hear us as we privately spoke. *What is going on? Why is everyone here and in such an uproar?*

I could feel Danaus hesitate to answer me. His mind was a jumble of images and incoherent words. But the one thing I could pick out clearly was the image of bright, dancing flames. *I'm sorry, Mira. Your house was burned down during the day.*

"No!" I gasped both aloud and mentally. My hands flew to my mouth as if to stop the scream of pain that had risen to my throat. My home was gone? How could my house burn down? My mind just kept stumbling over those thoughts over and over again. This was the twenty-first century. I had a security system on the house that alerted the fire department at the first sign of smoke. Gabriel had once set it off while cooking in the house and had to shoo the fire department away. How could they have let the house burn down?

Danaus, how bad is the damage? I asked, though a part of me didn't want to know. I was sitting on the edge of my bed now, my eyes clenched shut as I tried to block out the smell of burned wood.

Just wait until we come and get you, Danaus firmly replied, causing my heart to sink in my chest. I pulled back from his mind as I struggled to get hold of the emotions rising within me. His avoidance of my question was enough of an answer.

After taking a slow steadying breath, I touched Danaus's mind again so I could see through his eyes. I could sense his heart pounding in his chest and sweat dripping down from his brow despite the fact that there was a chill in the evening air. His hands were black. After a moment the hunter finally paused to catch his breath and looked around. There was nothing left of the house but the random black timbers stretching up to where the second floor had been. Furniture was reduced to ash, books were mere cinders, and the second floor was now open to the starlit sky above me.

With shaking hands, I fell to my knees as I choked back a sob. My collection of nearly a lifetime was gone. So many memories that I had saved and protected were now turned to blackened ash. Tristan's room had been wiped from the earth along with the last of his scent. Lily's room was gone. I was left with only their ghosts haunting my memories.

Cracking wood nearby was quickly followed by the sound of pounding on the metal door that blocked entry into my secret room. I had made it of steel and concrete so it was fireproof, but a part of me had not expected such an eventuality.

"Mira, are you all right?" Gregor demanded, shouting from the other side of the door.

"Get me the hell out of here," I replied as I picked myself off the floor. I had been betrayed by someone. Gabriel would never turn his back on me, but he was the only person I could think of that should have been there and wasn't.

Metal screeched and groaned as it was pulled and bent, and then dim light finally penetrated the darkness. Danaus was the first one in the room, his arms sweeping around me in a tight embrace that threatened to crack my ribs. The pounding of his heart had nothing to do with exertion, but with fear. Despite being mostly human, he had developed the same sleeping habits as the nightwalkers. If the house had burned during the day, he would not have found out about it until the sun set. He hadn't known whether I was destroyed until that second when my mind finally touched his.

"I'm fine, Danaus," I said, snuggling my head against his neck and refusing to let go.

"When I saw the house . . ." He trailed off.

"I know. I'm fine," I replied, my voice a little firmer. I pushed away so he could look me in the eye. "I'm safe."

The hunter nodded and slowly released his tight hold on me. To my surprise, he took a step back and pulled off his light leather jacket before stripping off his shirt. He tossed the sweaty cloth to me and then donned his jacket again. It was only then that I remembered I was wearing only a pair of panties and a thin lace bra.

"Let's get out of here so I can survey the damage," I said, taking my first step toward the door. The other nightwalkers preceded me, while Danaus followed behind me. As soon as I stepped outside my private chamber, a sharp gasp escaped my throat. The room had been destroyed. The wooden timbers and drywall were gone, revealing blackened concrete. Part of the first floor had collapsed into the basement. I could see a broken shell of the desk in my study, along with a couple of blackened bits of furniture the parlor. Overall, it was a black mess that I was hardly able to discern, though I had spent more than a century picking out the special items that comprised my house.

Danaus stepped in front of me and hoisted me over his shoulder before making his way across the basement, which was covered in smoldering bits of wood, broken glass, and twisted nails. With a little help from Gregor and Knox, the hunter managed to get me unscathed to my yard, where I could look on the burnt remains of my house in shock. Words escaped me for several minutes—I had spent seemingly countless years there, accumulated all the knickknacks of a life well lived, and in the blink of an eye they were all gone. Just a distant, heart-wrenching memory.

"This was Nick," I whispered mostly to myself as I clenched my eyes shut to keep the tears from falling.

"This wasn't Nick, Mira." Danaus's slow voice sent a shiver up my spine. I didn't want to know the answer to the question I was about to ask, but it came tripping off my tongue before I could stop it.

"Who burned down my house?"

"Aurora," Knox said, causing my head to snap around to him. "She and other members of the naturi moved into the city during the day. They burned down more than a dozen homes in the historic district. The fire department was kept so busy trying to put out the fires that most of the homes burned straight to the ground, along with a few others that weren't intentionally set."

"How did she know which one was my house? I'm no-where near the historic district!" I shouted, waving one hand back at the burnt remains of my home.

Knox swallowed once and looked away from me, seeming unable to speak.

It was Gregor who finally answered. "Amanda told her."

"Are you sure?" I whispered, unable to believe I had been betrayed by the nightwalker. Amanda and I had our differences during the past several months, but she'd always been loyal to both me and the nightwalkers of Savannah.

"Her body was found half burned in the backyard, under a thick grove of trees," Danaus replied. "Aurora must have gotten hold of her before the sun rose and beat the information out of her before leaving her to the sun. Archie called to tell me he was incinerating the body before there could be an investigation." I nodded, grateful that Archie Deacon, the coroner for the county, was still covering my back.

A deep heavy sigh slipped past my lips as I shook my head. "Amanda gave up my private home to Aurora. Was the town house torched as well?"

"The town house is fine. No one approached it during the day," Danaus said, helping to ease some of the tension from my shoulders.

"Where is Gabriel?" I asked. "He would have been the first to be contacted and told the house was on fire along with the fire department. He should have been here to try to get me out if it was at all possible. Where is my bodyguard?"

Silence was my only answer as Danaus looked to Knox and Gregor, who only looked down at the ground. My stomach twisted in fear and the world seemed to spin around me. Gabriel. My sweet guardian angel. I couldn't lose him too. Not both him and Michael in less than a year. I needed my bodyguard. I needed his knowing smirk and dry humor. I needed his cautious nature to balance my reckless nature. I needed him guarding me when I slept and needed him waiting for me when I finally opened my eyes each night.

"Gabriel is in the hospital," Danaus said.

"Oh, thank God!" I cried, putting a steadying hand on his shoulder. "I thought he was dead."

"He's hanging on by a thread, and from what the doctor told me, things don't look good."

"What happened?" I choked out the words in my clogged throat, looking anywhere than at the men around me.

"From what I can guess, Gabriel was one of the first on the scene when the alarms went off at your house. The naturi attacked him and slashed his throat and then pinned him to a tree with several swords stuck through his body. The fire truck arrived with an ambulance, so they were able to get him to the hospital before he bled out, but he was in bad shape."

"I'm assuming you've been to the hospital. What's the doctor's prognosis?" I said in a low, even voice as I struggled to keep the last bit of my temper under control.

"Not good," Danaus replied. "If he survives the next couple of days, he might make it. One of his lungs collapsed and several of his other organs are in distress. The doctor also thinks that if he survives, he'll never speak again." His explanation put more fuel on the fire building within me. It was one thing to destroy my home and threaten my life, but Gabriel was mine and I would not tolerate any harm to him.

"Knox, Shelly will be with Cynnia. I want you to personally take her to Gabriel's side and make her to heal him," I bit out in slow, clearly enunciated words so there could be no mistake.

"Shelly is with Cynnia and the other naturi at Mira's town house," Danaus interjected, saving the nightwalker some unnecessary searching.

"What if she can't—" Knox started, but I quickly cut him off.

"She healed Barrett the night we were attacked in the tunnels by the naturi," I snarled, taking a quick step over to stare directly at him. "She can at least try to heal Gabriel. Don't let her leave that hospital room until she has given everything she can possibly give to heal him!" So far as I was concerned, Shelly had to heal Gabriel.

"I'll get her, Mira," Knox said, meeting my glowing gaze. "She'll find a way to help Gabriel." Then he paused. "But, if it's not enough . . . if it looks like we're going to lose him . . ." He paused, licking his lips. "Have you ever discussed changing him?"

This time I was the first to look away, lowering my eyes to the trampled grass. The earth was squishy and cold beneath my feet from where the hoses had been brought in to spray down the fire-engulfed house.

"We've discussed it and he's said that he would be proud to die in service to me. He said he wasn't interested in living forever and one lifetime was enough for him." I forced the words past the lump in my throat.

"If Shelly has any kind of problems, I will ask him a second time just to be sure," Knox reassured me, placing one of his hands on my shoulder and squeezing. "I would be honored to bring him over if he makes that decision."

"If you ask him, remove the pain first. I don't want his decision to be a pain-addled one," I murmured, still unable to raise my eyes to meet his. Equal parts anger and pain burned through me as I thought about my bodyguard dying slowly, alone in a hospital room. He deserved better than this after all his years of service to me.

My emotions were mixed. A part of me wanted Knox to bring him over, to make him a nightwalker so I couldn't lose him. But another part of me knew that Gabriel wouldn't take the offer. He was content with being human, and living a human's short, fragile life. I didn't expect him to take Knox's offer and I respected him for that bravery. He was willing to face whatever awaited us after death. It was something too few of us could claim.

"What do you want me to do?" Gregor demanded, surprising me. His black jacket and waistcoat were tossed over his arm, while his pristine white shirt was streaked with soot. His carefully coiffed hair was askew. The nightwalker perpetually trapped in the nineteenth century was starting to look as if he'd embraced the modern world. Gregor ran with a group of reckless nightwalkers consumed with only their own amusement, but his presence here tonight told me he was finally willing to step up. It was about fucking time.

"I want you to return to Savannah. Gather together all the nightwalkers you can find within the Savannah region. Find out who didn't make it through the night and send the survivors to my town house," I directed. "I will be there with Cynnia, making final plans on how we are going to deal with Aurora. We will have our vengeance against this attack. She didn't just attack me, she attacked our city, our home, and we will not stand for it."

"You will have your army at your doorstep before the moon reaches its peak tonight, coven Elder," Gregor said with a slight bow before he hurried across the yard toward a black car parked in the driveway.

"Do you need me for anything else?" Knox asked one last time.

"Just do what you can to save Gabriel," I said. "I will understand if he cannot be saved, but we must at least put forth all the effort we can muster. He deserves that."

"I will do everything within my power," Knox said. He pressed his right hand to his heart before bowing to me. He then ran across the yard and jumped into the passenger seat of the car Gregor was driving.

Danaus and I stood in silence, watching as they disappeared into the night, heading back toward the city. I managed to push aside my anger and hatred, but I knew that bottle would quickly come uncorked the moment I was finally faced with Aurora. She had struck first, but she'd failed. She should have killed me. She should have personally seen to it that I was destroyed by the fire, or at the very least cut off my head as I slept. But she didn't and now she was faced with my fury.

"What's our next step?" Danaus inquired.

"We meet with Cynnia. She better have a plan. If not, I will. Aurora struck first and struck hard. She is threatening to expose not only her own race, but also the nightwalkers. Such actions will not be tolerated by the nightwalkers, lycanthropes, or the magic users. It's time for her to be put down before we find ourselves faced with the Great Awakening."

And no matter how badly we wished it to be true, everyone knew that mankind was not ready for the Great Awakening. They had recently survived floods, earthquakes, and economic turmoil that left thousands homeless and helpless. Humanity wasn't ready to know that its nightmares were real as well. We needed to kill Aurora before the truth was finally released to the world.

Twenty-nine

Danaus was kind enough to keep Cynnia and her companions occupied while I slipped upstairs in the Savannah town house. I donned black leather pants, leather boots, and a thick leather top that provided an extra layer of protection against a blade. I was ready to step into war that night and I would take no prisoners. If they stood against us, they died. That was all.

When I finally entered the parlor, my gaze immediately fell on Rowe, as the naturi smoothly rose from the chair he had been sitting in on the opposite side of the room. Cynnia remained seated next to him, while her sister Nyx stood in the back of the room with a carefully blank expression. Rowe flashed me a mocking smile, but I ignored him. My main concern was Cynnia's all-too-silent sister. She and Rowe were the experienced warriors, not Cynnia.

"Thank you for your assistance with Daniel," I said, forcing my jaw to unclench. I never thought the night would come when I would not only invite Rowe into my home, but also thank him for his help. After centuries of torment and conflict, I nearly gagged on the words.

Rowe's smile grew as he stared at me, soaking up the hatred that filled my tense and tightly clipped words. "You know me," he said with a careless wave of one hand. "Always looking for a way to lend a hand to mankind."

I swallowed my next comment and turned my attention to Cynnia, who was looking more than a little uncomfortable. Most likely her discomfort came from the common knowledge that Rowe had performed more than one human organ harvest during his time here on Earth, separated from his own kind. Rowe didn't help humans. He slaughtered them every chance he got. How she expected me to believe he would actually help us was still beyond my comprehension.

"What can you tell me about the occurrences in Savannah during the daylight hours?" I demanded, turning away from Rowe before I lit his smug ass on fire. "Was Aurora actually in the city?"

"She was here," Nyx replied evenly.

Cynnia twisted around in her chair so she could look over her shoulder at her older sister. "Are you sure?"

"I spent more time around Aurora than you ever did. We're closer in age. I know when she's close. She's currently attempting to cloak herself so I can't pinpoint her exact location, but I can sense that she is just beyond the reach of the city. She is hovering close, waiting."

"Were you able to kill any of the naturi that were setting the fires around the city?" I demanded.

Nyx shook her head. "Rowe and I were outside the city during the day, meeting with the head of the animal clan. He and his people have just arrived, but are unwilling to actually enter the city until they meet with the Fire Starter. Kane is not exactly convinced this isn't a trap."

"I don't blame him," I muttered, crossing my arms over my chest. "Was there no one else available to stop the light clan from their attack?"

"The only naturi in the area are those acting as my personal bodyguards," Cynnia said. "The rest were outside of the city."

"And they didn't see fit to stop Aurora from entering the city?" I cried, raising my voice.

"They have been instructed not to directly engage Aurora," Nyx interjected, drawing my attention away from her younger sister, as if to protect her from my wrath. "We're not going to be the ones that start this war."

"Unless you haven't noticed, the war has been started," Danaus commented in a low growl. "Last night when she tried to burn the city down."

"How many were killed?" I inquired, turning to look at Danaus, who was standing near me at the entrance to the room.

"The news says the body count is still rising, but the last figure released was forty-three human lives have been lost."

The front door swung open then and Knox entered the town house, followed by a couple dozen nightwalkers. I directed the other nightwalkers to the upper floors so the naturi wouldn't feel more threatened than necessary—I still needed them to stay focused on the problem at hand. To my surprise, Knox was accompanied by Matsui and the four Soga nightwalkers.

Knox sidled into the room and stood in front of the fireplace, while Danaus and I also moved to the side of the room opposite Rowe and Cynnia. The Japanese nightwalkers remained in the entrance. It was getting more than a little crowded, but it gave me a feeling of security against Aurora.

Knox sighed heavily as he pushed one hand through his hair. His clothes were still stained with dirt and soot from digging me out of my basement. He was also starting to look a little weary as the weight of the world pressed on his broad shoulders. "Word is still spreading, but it appears that at least ten nightwalkers were killed, including Amanda."

"Gabriel?" I asked before I could stop myself. Now was not the time to worry about my broken bodyguard, but I knew my mind would not be at ease until I finally knew what was happening. I tried to take Shelly's absence as a positive sign.

"Hanging on," Knox replied. "Shelly is with him now, doing everything she can to speed along his healing, but she doesn't seem too hopeful that she will be of much help. Gregor and two other nightwalkers have been stationed at the hospital to watch over both of them."

"Thank you," I whispered. Knox always knew exactly the right course to take. He had just reassured both me and Cynnia that our friends were being watched over in the event that Aurora tried to strike again at those that meant the most to us.

Looking around the room, my gaze finally fell on the four Japanese nightwalkers. I had assumed they would immediately leave town, considering our disagreement regarding the naturi alliance and their attempt to kidnap me.

"Forgive me, but I'm surprised to find that you are still here," I said to my foreign companions. "You know the course of action I plan to take, and I am not changing that course, particularly now that Aurora has openly attacked the people of my city. I have also been in contact with Our Liege, who knows of my plans. There is nothing you can say that will sway me from my decision. I am also not willing to leave here to help you."

Tetsuya bowed his head to me before finally speaking. "In truth, we had thought to come to your aid after what happened during the daylight hours. We had assumed that the queen of the naturi would pursue a quiet war among the other races and not seek to expose us all. However, it seems she has chosen to show the humans that they are not alone in this world."

"'Had thought'?" I asked. "You've changed your mind already?"

"Your choice of who you have decided to work with does not sit well with us," said the one nightwalker I had yet to be introduced to. He was smaller than the others and looked considerably younger as well. However, I had no doubt that he was not only the oldest of the quartet, but was truly the leader of the group.

I opened my mouth to ask what he was talking about, but Rowe beat me to the punch by speaking up first. "Nomura happens to be talking about me," the naturi announced, meeting my gaze for a second. The one-eyed naturi then turned his narrowed stare on the Japanese nightwalkers and forced a thin-lipped smile to his face. "It's been a long time. I didn't expect to ever see you again, let alone in Mira's home."

"We are very surprised to see you as well," Nomura replied as he shoved his hands into his pockets. "We never expected you to survive as long as you have." By the slump of his shoulders and the frown teasing at the corners of his mouth, I could tell there was a great deal of animosity between these two creatures, and I was afraid it would explode all over my living room. Unfortunately, curiosity was winning out over common sense.

"How do you know each other?"

"I've been on this earth for several centuries, Mira," Rowe drawled, hatred glinting in his one good eye. "I've traveled far and wide in search of ways to free my people. It stands to reason that I slipped far beyond the reach of the West. It was then that I ran across the nightwalkers inhabiting the islands of Japan. I thought we could come to some sort of arrangement. The naturi had been no threat to them in the past, and I assumed our futures would remain on separate courses. As a result, I sought an exchange of knowledge with them."

"I am afraid to ask what happened."

"Take a good look at me, Mira, and you will easily see

the result of my so-called alliance with the Soga clan," Rowe bit out.

I stared at the naturi for nearly a minute, trying to see what he was talking about before it suddenly dawned on me. The Soga clan was responsible for his changed appearance, which resulted in him being banished from his people by Aurora. I had met Rowe when I was human, when he was a golden-skinned creature with pale blond hair and sparkling green eyes.

Now, scars stretched across one side of Rowe's face, half hidden behind an eye patch that covered his right eye. His hair was black as night and the color of his one remaining eye seemed to match it. His skin had taken on a swarthy complexion and was streaked with more scars. Like night-walkers, naturi healed from nearly everything. And yet it appeared that the members of the Soga clan had found a way to mark him permanently.

"It is not as if you walked away empty-handed from our time together," Nomura stated.

"Oh, you're correct. I gained more than my fair share of blood magic—"

"You taught him how to use blood magic?" I demanded, raising my voice for the first time. "Do you know what trouble that has caused for all nightwalkers during the past year? Do you know that knowledge enabled him to open the doorway between the worlds in the first place? You are the reason Aurora is here now."

"Don't lay too much blame at their doorstep, Mira," Rowe noted, earning a growl from me as I looked over at him. "They tried very hard to kill me over a five-year period. I'm sure while they were teaching me the magic, they never expected me to survive the lessons."

"I don't understand," Danaus spoke up. The hunter laid a hand on my shoulder and squeezed, subtly hinting that I needed to calm down. There was no need to start a fight with four very powerful nightwalkers when I still had a fight with Aurora ahead of me. "Why bother teaching him in the first place if you only planned to kill him?"

"It was a form of torture," Nomura replied in a nonchalant voice. "The learning process was extremely painful for the naturi since the style of magic went against his very essence. We were curious if it could even be done. Unfortunately, Rowe escaped us before we were able to complete our process."

"You mean, the process of slowly trying to destroy him," I said in a cold voice. "Leave."

"I beg your pardon," Nomura said softly, cocking his head to the side. "I don't believe I understood you correctly."

"No, I'm sure you did," I snapped, glaring at the quartet of nightwalkers. "Leave. Leave Savannah and the New World. Return to Japan, and if I have my wish, never leave your home again. You are not welcome in this world."

"You're turning your back on our superior strength and abilities because you would rather side with the naturi?" Nomura demanded.

"I'm turning my back on you because of what you did to him! Because of what you tried to do to me!" I snarled. "I'm turning my back on you because of the fact that you brought this on us all in the end. If you had not been so cocky in your decision to give him knowledge of blood magic, Aurora might not be here. Leave here and take Matsui with you, now."

"As you wish," Nomura replied in clipped tones. He turned on his right heel and quickly exited the town house, his companions following close behind him. Matsui paused in the hallway outside the parlor and bowed deeply to me before he left the house as well. There was a look of genuine regret on his face. I preferred to think that he actually liked serving as my bodyguard. It had to at least be less formal than following behind the Japanese nightwalkers.

"I'm confused," Rowe announced when the door slammed shut. "Are you angry at them for torturing me or for failing to kill me?"

"I'm angry they used you as a science experiment that could have triggered the end of humanity as we know it if we don't stop Aurora," I replied, glaring at the naturi. The story was all too familiar, as Jabari had been content to experiment on me. Both Rowe and I had merely been puppets, playthings for powerful creatures. And in the end, if the Soga clan had succeeded to get me to Japan to help them with their naturi problem, I would have been forced to stay so I would become their next pet project.

Rowe pushed out of his chair, standing so he was looking me directly in the eye. "It didn't have to be the Soga clan. I would have begged for the knowledge of blood magic from anyone willing to teach me, regardless of the cost. My job was to free Aurora and the others."

I took a couple steps closer to him. "And you don't regret it, do you?"

Rowe smirked at me. "Nope."

"Considering all the lives that have been lost over the years, do you regret anything at all?"

"Just not killing you when I had the chance."

I matched his smirk with one of my own. "Which time?" Rowe had more than one shot at me over the long years, and here I still stood, alive and smiling at him.

"All of them, from our first meeting till this very second," he replied.

Shaking my head, I turned my back on the naturi and started to return to the other side of the room. To my shock, Danaus brushed by me in a quick sweeping motion. I twisted around in time to see his meaty fist land squarely on Rowe's nose, throwing the naturi back into his chair. I placed my hand on Danaus's chest to keep him from taking another step toward Rowe. However, my eyes were locked squarely on Nyx, who had come away from the far corner like a dark shadow. Her face remained expressionless, but there was a new burning in her gray eyes that hadn't been there before. This seemed to be more than just protectiveness of her own kind—there was something between her and Rowe.

"She spared your life in Budapest," Danaus growled. "She gave you a second chance at life and still you persist in hunting her."

"I'm not as easily tamed as some," Rowe said in a low voice as he rubbed his nose, checking to make sure it wasn't broken. Danaus tried to lunge at the naturi again, but I held him back, my eyes remaining on Nyx. There was no weapon in her hand, but I had a feeling she was only waiting for Danaus to make another move toward Rowe.

"Enough!" I shouted, shoving against Danaus so he was forced to take a couple steps back away from Rowe. Summoning up the energy swirling in the air around me, I turned off the lamps in the room, plunging the room into complete darkness for a breath before lighting all the candles as well as igniting a fire in the fireplace. Everyone grew still, seeming to hold their breath as they waited to see if my temper had reached its breaking point.

"We're not getting anywhere with these talks!" I complained, returning to the other side of the room with Danaus. It was better if there was physical space between Rowe and us. I still wanted to set the bastard on fire after his little dig at Danaus, but I knew we would need him healthy for the battle ahead. "Aurora is out there somewhere waiting to attack. She is not only looking for the heads of you three, but I'm willing to bet she would like to add mine to her collection as well."

"It's more than that," Cynnia said, letting her voice fill the silence for the first time in a while. "Aurora launched an open attack on the city. I think she's picked the place where she wants to have her final battle with you and her sisters."

"You mean Savannah?" I asked. "She wants to fight out in the open?"

Nyx fell back into the shadows, but her voice crept forward to replace Cynnia's soft soothing words. "What better way to strike fear in the hearts of men than for them to witness a battle of the magical arts they can't hope to understand or win. She will intimidate them, subjugate them, and then finally destroy them all."

"We need to give her a reason to draw away from the city," I argued. "We need to give her a reason to pull back her forces to some of the open, uninhabited areas that surround Savannah. Get her out of the city."

"How will we do that?" Knox asked.

I smiled at him for a second before turning my attention to Cynnia. "With bait. We make her come after Cynnia outside the city."

"I'm not leaving my sister unguarded and vulnerable," Nyx countered.

"Who said unguarded?" I shook my head at her, still smiling. "Didn't you say the animal clan was waiting outside the city at a safe location? Stick Cynnia in the middle of the clan for a time. They'll keep her safe, correct?"

"They would protect her," Nyx reluctantly conceded.

"Hell, you and Rowe can go with her as added protection if that's what you want."

"And what if you're her target?" Rowe inquired.

"Then we're fucked," I snapped. "I'm not leaving my city without some kind of protection. If it looks like Aurora is going to come after Cynnia outside the city, then Danaus, the nightwalkers, the lycans, and I will come riding to the rescue, attacking her from behind. But until I know that she has turned her sights elsewhere, I'm not budging from Savannah. She's done enough damage here and destroyed enough lives."

Rowe stared at me with a strange expression as he scratched his chin with his right hand. "You're willing to take a lot of risk for a group of people that are going to come at you with a cross and wooden stake once they discover you exist."

"This is my home and I will protect it," I said. "I'll worry about what they think about me later."

Rowe gave a soft snort and shook his head. "I wish you luck."

I remained silent, holding onto the luck bequeathed to me by my enemy. I knew I was going to need it. Aurora's shocking daylight raid on the city proved to me that she was willing to take chances we weren't willing to take, in an effort to not only protect the humans, but also protect our secret from the humans. I had a dark feeling this war was going to take a turn that I couldn't protect my people from, and result in more deaths. And possibly even the truth.

Thirty

The wind threaded its fingers through the black feathers of my wings as I soared overhead toward a distant thicket of trees. The sun had just broken over the horizon and was glazing the earth in its golden glow. I could feel myself growing weaker the brighter the sky became. We had spent most of the night arguing tactics before we were all evicted from Mira's town house in Savannah a couple hours before sunrise. The Fire Starter declared that she needed to have a private meeting with the other gathered nightwalkers before they sought a safe place to spend the daylight hours.

Cynnia, Rowe, and I retreated to the house Shelly was renting in another part of the city. The witch tripped into the house minutes after our arrival, looking exhausted and pale, but also relieved. The human called Gabriel would not only survive, but might also regain his ability to speak due to her diligent ministrations. I had a feeling the news would go a long way toward calming the Fire Starter's frazzled nerves, but her temper would not be under tight rein again until we finally took care of Aurora.

With protective spells in place, we all settled into our respective sleeping spots an hour before dawn, but sleep would not come. I lay with Rowe's arm possessively thrown across my stomach, his soft snoring rumbling in my ear. However, my own rush of thoughts kept me awake. I knew what we were planning would never be enough if we hoped to defeat Aurora. Something else needed to be done if Cynnia, Rowe, and so many others were going to survive the coming days and nights.

Using a spell to deepen Rowe's sleep, I slipped away from him and out of the house without disturbing the protective spells or alerting anyone to my exodus. With a sigh on my lips, I took to the sky with my wings spread wide on the breeze I had conjured up. The feeling of flying free above the earth, even as the sun rose behind me, was exhilarating. For just a brief moment in time I felt free of the burdens that had been weighing on my shoulders during the past several months. There was only me and the soft caress of the wind blessed by the Great Mother.

Yet, as I drew closer to Aurora, I knew it all was an illusion. The weight was still there and growing heavier by the second as I approached her camp. I didn't know her exact location, but then I only needed to step into the perimeter of her camp and her guards would pick me up and take me to the demented queen. I hated not telling Cynnia or Rowe about my plans, but I knew that neither would have let me out of the house if I'd revealed my intentions.

I circled the clearing once before bringing in my wings enough to glide down to the earth. My feet had barely sunk into the soft soil when a harsh voice ordered me to halt. I raised both of my hands, palms out, to show that I was unarmed. I extended my wings as far as they would reach on either side of me, keeping myself vulnerable. I was surrounded by six naturi, all of whom had weapons trained on me.

"I've come to speak with Aurora," I announced in a loud voice, so it carried to the other guards, who were waiting in the shadows of the forest. A low murmur of conversation drifted through the trees like a breeze whispering through the leaves.

"Her Majesty has nothing to say to you, traitor," barked one of the naturi. "She simply wants you dead along with your traitorous sister."

"She'll meet with me. Just ask her," I said, my voice full of confidence.

The murmur of conversation resumed as they weighed my words. I'd been banking on their hesitance to kill the one person who had led them through the centuries. Once Rowe had been trapped outside the cage, I became the captain and commander of Aurora's armed forces. They were accustomed to following my orders.

"Besides, wouldn't she rather see me killed in person than hear about it later?" I asked. This new incentive was enough to get one naturi ordered back to Aurora's camp for orders. I was a dangerous creature in my own right, and they were more than a little wary of bringing me within their safe haven.

Slowly lowering my hands while wrapping my wings around my shoulders, I sat on the ground and crossed my legs as we all waited to hear what Aurora wanted. The five naturi that stepped out of the woods upon my landing edged closer. Wrist crossbows, short swords, and bows and arrows were trained on me, ready to be loosed if I so much as breathed too deeply.

While I didn't come to Aurora's camp unarmed, I was careful to keep my weapons limited to a couple small daggers concealed on my person. I was secretly hoping they would forget to search me—I might need to fight my way out of Aurora's camp before this meeting was over.

After several minutes, two naturi returned to the clearing, including one I'd rather not have seen.

Greenwood was tall and lanky, his long brown hair flecked with gray. His face was slashed with wrinkles, as if worn by exposure to the elements. The earth clan did not age gracefully, but remained long-lived and spry despite their appearance. Greenwood had always been upset that Rowe was chosen to be Aurora's consort over him. He had both age and experience over the wind clan member. However, Rowe's ruthless grace had appealed to Aurora at the time. Now it seemed that Greenwood was finally getting his shot.

"I'm surprised you came," he said, opening with a soft chuckle. "You were always a careful strategist, taking only calculated risks that were in your favor to win. Surely you realize you're not leaving this camp alive, even if you are permitted an audience with Aurora."

"I did not come to speak with you, Greenwood. The earth clan and your play at politics are of no interest to me. Take me to Aurora. She will want to hear what I have to say."

Greenwood took a wary step backward as I rose, eyeing me with a new caution. I showed no fear despite the fact that my heart was pounding like a thing gone mad in my chest, and my stomach was twisting into knots. Six naturi surrounded me in the immediate vicinity, but I could sense another dozen waiting in the shadows of the trees. I didn't have much of a chance against these odds. Even if I took straight to the sky, there was a good chance they would shoot me down before I got far. But given my reputation, the naturi watching me now were afraid to be the first to strike. I had to use that fear to my advantage.

After a long silence, Greenwood let out a low chuckle that sounded strained and forced to my ears. "Lose the wings and let us bind your hands, then I will have you escorted to Aurora so she can see you killed in person. I'm sure that would bring her some pleasure. Wouldn't it be a great triumph to carry your head on a pike into battle so it is the first thing Cynnia sees as she faces us?"

I said nothing, focusing on causing my wings to dissolve into black sand that poured like a waterfall down my back to the ground. Putting my hands together in front of me, I kept my face perfectly blank as one pale naturi stepped forward and roughly bound my wrists behind my back with a thick piece of rope. At the same time, a second naturi stepped forward and patted me down, removing my two knives.

The naturi that bound my hands gave me a hard kick that sent me stumbling forward. "Get moving," he ordered with a laugh.

The walk to Aurora's camp was one of the longest in my entire memory. It seemed as if all the naturi that rallied around her banner had come out to see me, jeering, spitting, and stabbing me. While most of the wounds were relatively superficial in nature, I was bruised, bloody, and covered in dirt when I was finally brought to Aurora's pristine white tent. Beside it, there was a somewhat less grand green tent, most likely Greenwood's. It was somewhat reassuring that they were maintaining separate residences for now. If I knew Aurora as well as I thought I did, I suspected she was waiting for him to deliver both Cynnia and me to her feet dead before finally taking him as her consort.

As I came within a dozen feet of the tent, the two sides were parted and Aurora stepped out. It seemed as if a shaft of golden light shot through the trees to shine on her beautiful blond hair and pale skin. She shone before me like a fallen star or a ray of perfect sunlight on a cloudy day. She wore her usual white robes, but now with a breastplate made of polished, gleaming gold. I knew, however, it was merely a ceremonial piece in an effort to more closely align herself with the army that she would soon order to their death.

My older sister looked down on me and smiled smugly. She didn't care that she would never have been able to accomplish this if I hadn't willingly turned myself over to her. Her only care was that she had me bound and battered, striking a blow against the traitors rising up against her.

"The first of the traitors has come to meet their fate!" she exclaimed to the crowd that had gathered before her. A loud cheer went up, causing the tree limbs to tremble. A shiver ran through me as I listened to those bloodthirsty voices. It sounded as if she had acquired a greater army than I initially thought she would. I knew all the naturi would not flock to her side. Some had rallied around Cynnia's banner, while another group remained as far from the two sides as they could, hoping to remain unnoticed until the fighting finally blew over.

"I've come to talk," I sharply said as the cheering died down.

"You lost the opportunity to talk your way out of your execution a long time ago," Aurora smirked at me.

"You never gave me that opportunity. You proclaimed me to be a traitor and then ordered my execution before I could plead my case to you," I growled, taking a step forward. As I did, a pair of swords points dug were pointed at my throat, keeping me from moving any closer. "But I've not come to plead for mercy from you. I've come to offer you a chance at preserving your own life. It will be your one and only chance. I wouldn't turn my back on it."

"My life?" Aurora laughed, tossing her blond locks away from her face. "If you've not figured it out by now, we are the ones that are going to destroy Cynnia and her little army. We are the ones that are going to restore order to the planet and save the Great Mother."

"That would be hard to accomplish without the Great Mother on your side. Is she listening to you now?" Aurora's face twisted with rage. I was questioning her connection to the earth, something that should have been absolute, since she was the queen of the naturi. But I knew better. During her time in the cage, she had lost her connection with the earth, and I had a feeling it was the reason for the madness that now claimed her fragile mind and spirit.

"How dare you question me?" she screamed, pointing one quivering finger at me.

"In all the years that you have known me, have I ever lied to you?" I demanded. She knew that I had never told her a falsehood in the all the time I'd served her. She would know if I were lying to her. "Just a quick meeting to discuss the future of the naturi people. Isn't that what's best for both sides? What's best for the earth?"

Aurora stared at me for more than a minute in silence, her arms stubbornly crossed over her chest as if to protect herself from my words. She wasn't happy, but she was turning over my words in the back of her mind. I was willing to bet that she was hoping to get some valuable information out of me regarding Cynnia's forces before she killed me, but then I had hoped to gather the same. I just needed to think of a way to escape again so I could get the information back to Cynnia.

"Bring her into the tent," Aurora snapped before turning in a swirl of robes and reentering it. The swords at my throat were lowered and I was shoved forward. My escort took me to the center of the tent, where I was pushed down to my knees on a bearskin rug in front of Aurora, who was now seated in a golden throne with plush pillows of deep green.

"Leave us alone," Aurora ordered. The guards hesitated, glancing at each other and then back at Greenwood, who had entered the tent behind me. "Leave us, I said! Do you think I cannot handle my own sister, who has already been bound and beaten?"

"Me as well?" Greenwood inquired.

"Leave us alone!" Aurora screamed, tightly gripping both arms of the chair so she nearly came out of her seat again. No one hesitated. They all quickly scrambled to leave her sight and close the tent door behind them.

I watched as Aurora sank back in the chair and took a deep breath, as if to calm her frazzled nerves. In the shadows of the tent, I could see the lines of worry starting to extend from her eyes, and long, deep furrows at the corners of her mouth, which was perpetually pulled into a frown. Returning to earth should have rejuvenated my older sister, but it seems the healing powers of the earth were not reaching her. For some reason I had yet to understand, she had truly lost her connection with the earth. A part of me wondered if I could restore it the same way I had for Rowe, but I knew she would not see it as the gift that it was, but a power that I had over her, which would only get me killed faster.

"I see that Greenwood is still trying to insinuate himself at your side," I observed in a low voice. Slowly, I moved off my knees and sat so my legs were crossed before me. Not only was that position more comfortable and less formal, but I could also rise with more stability and speed than if I'd been kneeling.

Aurora gave a low snort and slumped in her chair. "He cares nothing about me or the naturi people. He's still only determined to see an earth clan member wearing the crown. It's been eons since they last sat on the throne, and it's eating away at him still that I did not choose him when we were all younger."

"But you're dangling the carrot in front of him now," I said as one corner of my mouth quirked in a half smile. "Very wise. You've won the allegiance of the earth clan under any circumstances so long as Greenwood thinks he may one day become your consort."

Aurora matched my smile with a devilish one of her own. "He thinks I'm a fool. If I were to make him consort, I would be found the next morning dead in my bed and him on the throne."

"As long as Greenwood is leading them," I said, "I would not trust the earth clan. They follow him blindly and will turn on you at a moment's notice. They have not been what I would call a trustworthy group for centuries."

"Trustworthy?" Aurora exclaimed, sitting straight up in her chair again and gripping the arms for support. "What do you know of trustworthy?"

For just a second she had forgotten that I was no longer her devoted sister, but her enemy.

"I never turned my back on you, Aurora," I calmly said, hoping my soothing voice would help to ease her temper. "Not even when you ordered the death of our staunchest friends and allies. I followed your orders to find Cynnia and bring her back home to you. I knew nothing of her plans. I just wanted us to be a family again and enjoy the power that flowed from the earth now that we were home."

"You never should have been permitted to live," she sneered, easing back into her chair again. "Father was wrong to protect you. You should have been killed at birth, and now you're a blight on our people. I wouldn't be surprised if it was your influence that corrupted our Cynnia in the end."

"I'm not what's killing our people," I firmly said, trying to brush aside the same venom I had put up with for most of my existence. I had to remain focused on the reason I'd taken this risk in the first place. "I know you saw it while we were caged. There was no hiding from it. Our women were no longer producing children, and those few babies that were born died at a young age. And then there were the hunts. Hundreds of our people were slaughtered in the name of treason."

"And what is your point?"

"Our people are dying!" I cried, outraged by her bland attitude. "We can't afford another war. Not a civil war amongst ourselves or a war with the humans, who have grown infinitely more dangerous with time. A war will destroy any hope we have of seeing the continuation of our race."

"Oh, do not act as if you care about our people!" Aurora snapped. "You are the Dark One. The one who should never have been born. You don't care about a race that never wanted you."

"Regardless of their feelings for me, I am still a naturi, and I don't want to see the slaughter of our people to continue. You have to know that we can't survive much longer as we are. This division of the clans is weakening us."

Aurora remained silent for a long time, staring just past me, lost in some dark thought. I could only hope I was finally reaching her; that the madness that had claimed her was only temporary and she was coming back to reason now that she was out of the grasp of our gilded cage.

"What do you propose?"

I sucked in a deep breath through my nose and released it through my clenched teeth. "We have to end the wars. All of them. I propose that you leave Cynnia and me alone. Leave us to pursue a quiet life and let us simply return to the earth. I also propose that you abandon this need to destroy the human race. Pursuing a war with the humans will not only lead to exposure after centuries of being little more than a myth, but they will actively hunt down those of our people that remain. We will eventually be wiped from existence."

Aurora's reply was a low laugh that grew both in volume and intensity until she was nearly rocking in her chair. And then the laughter stopped almost as quickly as it started. She stared at me with cold, merciless eyes that held no memory of the fact that I was her own flesh and blood.

"You want me to abandon the earth?" she whispered.

"No, that's not what I said."

"But that's exactly what you want if I am to leave the humans untouched. You're proposing that I abandon the earth to those monsters."

"Attacking the humans will destroy our people."

"You must be willing to make sacrifices for the Great Mother!" she cried, shaking her fist in the air. She slammed it down on the arm of the chair before leaning forward to glare at me. "The humans are destroying the earth. You cannot be blind to that even if you have lost all contact with the earth."

"I am aware of their actions," I admitted.

"Then you must know that they cannot continue to go unpunished. That is why we were created. We must protect the earth at all costs, preserve and nurture her strength. If we protect the earth, then she will in turn give us strength in battle."

I shook my head sadly at her. She wasn't listening to me at all. At one time she had closely listened and considered my counsel, but now she was deaf to my words. "If we continue on this course, there will be no one left to protect the earth. You are leading our people to extinction."

"No, I am leading us to salvation," she proclaimed with a beatific smile. "However, I am happy to see to your extinction before I turn my attention to our other traitorous sister and her band of misfits."

"Aurora! This is a mistake!"

"Guards!" she shouted in a loud, angry voice. In the blink of an eye two guards pushed into the tent and stood on either side of me. Aurora sat back in her chair again and absently waved one hand in my direction. "Take her outside and kill her."

"Aurora! You're not just killing me! You're killing our people!" I shouted as the two guards hooked their arms through mine and lifted me up off the ground. They proceeded to drag me out of the tent while I continued shouting at my sister. "You can't save the earth if Cynnia kills you first! Call off this war now!"

The last thing I saw before I exited the tent was Aurora's smiling face. Triumph filled her features. She was going to have me dead at long last. She had tolerated my existence for centuries, used me to do her dirty work, and now that I had reached the end of my usefulness, she was happily putting me down.

Thirty-one

As the two guards dragged me down the hill from Aurora's enormous white tent, I pushed my feet against the slanted earth and flipped over the two naturi, pulling free of their grasp. I quickly backed away from them, remaining wary of the other naturi soldiers closing on me from other directions. I had to think of a way to safely get out of Aurora's camp, but then I had always known that my chances of escape were extremely thin and highly unlikely.

Tapping into the energy flowing up from the earth, my enormous black wings sprung from my back while at the same time I summoned up a massive burst of wind. I curled my body into a tight ball while extending my wings to their fullest extent. The wind carried me higher into the trees while arrows soared toward me straight and true. Their tips buried deep in my arms and around my body, forcing a scream of pain to rise up in my throat, but I swallowed it back. I had bigger problems. My hands were still tied, and the trees I was attempting to fly through were beginning to reach for me. The earth clan was using its powers to control the trees so their brittle limbs clawed at my wings, plucking black feathers.

The wind gusted again and again, hammering at the trees

as they struggled to reach for me while being pushed about by the wind. I was pulled back but found a thick branch with my feet. I shoved off and stretched my wings again, struggling to gain altitude. This was my only hope of escape. If I didn't get away through the air, they would hunt me down too easily on the ground.

Beneath me the shouting of the naturi increased as I flew higher. Above the din, I could hear Greenwood's deep voice directing his people to go after me. There was desperation in his tone as his voice rose to a shriek. And then silence fell over the camp. My stomach twisted with a new fear even though I managed to clear the last of the treetops. With the wind blowing fiercely, I flapped my wings once as I turned around in time to see Aurora standing outside her tent, staring up at me. I knew the look of rage that twisted her features, sweeping her beauty aside.

You will not escape me!

You'll have your shot at me another time, I replied, but I knew she wasn't going to let me go so easily. Fire surrounded her in a crackling rush before it shot from the ground in a massive swirling vortex toward me. Pulling my wings in against my body, I dive-bombed, plunging back through the trees. A rush of heat surged up one side of me as I narrowly dodged the funnel of flames, but it was still close enough that several of my feathers were singed and burned. Tree limbs scratched at my face and pulled at the arrows and darts that protruded from my body. I dodged the fire in time but was back on the ground again.

Keeping my wings tucked close to my body in case I got a second chance to use them, I ran as fast as I could through the woods. I darted between trees and leapt over fallen logs while sliding through piles of dead leaves left from the previous fall. My arms, tied behind my back, screamed in pain. On my heels I could hear the light footfalls of naturi closing in. I had put enough distance between Aurora and myself that she wouldn't have another shot, but that didn't mean I was safe. The rest of her army was hot on my trail. To make matters worse, I was stuck on the ground, while being chased by the earth clan. It was only a matter of time before they halted my progress. I had to get back to the clearing where I had initially landed so I could regain flight.

As I ran, more arrows thunked into tree trunks and whizzed by my head. Laughter followed my progress as they tracked me. My heart pounded in my chest and my lungs struggled to pull in enough air as I plunged through the woods. My legs were starting to ache, causing me to misstep here and there. I slid down a small grade, nearly losing my balance before pushing on like a rabbit being chased by a fox.

This couldn't continue much longer. I needed to stop and free my hands. I needed to get back into the air. I had spent a lifetime in battle against those that would kill me, but the odds had never been so great in their favor. And in truth, I didn't want to kill them. I had spilled enough blood of my people and I'd grown sick of it. They followed Aurora because she was the only queen they knew and they had always trusted in her judgment. They didn't realize they had a choice.

With a grunt of exhaustion, I pushed forward while in the back of my mind focusing on the powers coming up from the earth. I turned the energy toward the skies above me. Dark clouds rolled in overhead, blotting out the sun. For a moment I could feel another force in the area pushing against the coming storm, leaving the sun to break through in sparkling patches. Aurora was fighting me. Gritting my teeth, I summoned up more energy and pushed harder against the spell she was attempting to weave to block my own. We pushed and pulled for several seconds before I could hear her scream in the back of my mind in either pain or frustration.

Clouds poured forth like a black wave, blotting out the sun so that night reclaimed the earth. The wind gusted, throwing my hair in front of my face, nearly blocking my vision as I dodged between one set of trees after another. Occasionally, limbs would reach for me, but I pushed on, moving just out of their grasp. My shirt ripped in several locations and the weight of my wings seemed to grow on my back. They needed to be stretched, lifting me into the sky instead of pulling me down.

As I leapt over another fallen log, the heel of my right foot landed in a sinkhole covered by leaves. I slammed to the ground hard, knocking the wind out of me and nearly breaking my nose as I was unable to catch myself with my arms. Twisting onto my side, I tried to get my feet under me again, but the ground was shifting beneath me from all the leaves.

"Stay down!" ordered a familiar voice. I jerked around so I was lying on my back, looking up at Rowe as he stood over me with swords drawn. The one-eyed naturi charged forward and in a few swift motions killed six of the naturi that had been chasing me. Sliding one sword into its sheath again, he spun around and walked back over to me. His face was a blank mask, but I could sense the rage boiling inside him. He pulled me up to my feet with one arm, then used the sword he was still holding to cut the rope that bound my wrists together. Then, wordlessly, he shoved me forward.

We never spoke as we ran through the woods. He simply handed me one of the swords and remained one step back to protect me from behind, while it was my job to take out anything that got in our way from the front. For several minutes we plunged through the dark woods, killing anything that crossed our path before we finally reached the clearing.

Standing in the center of the clearing, both Rowe and I threw out our wings while a group of naturi surrounded us on all sides. Plunging the tip of the sword I was carrying into the ground, I held my arms out to my sides, letting the power of the growing storm consume me. Lightning jumped from cloud to cloud, only to be followed by a hammer of thunder. When the naturi had closed in far enough and I could feel the earth beneath my feet starting to grow soft, I called down the storm. The clouds broke open in a tidal wave of rain while lightning pounded the earth in a brilliant blast of white light. My enemies were charred in an instant, leaving me standing alone in the rain with Rowe.

Calling up one last large gust of air, I threw out my wounded wings and caught the wind, allowing it to lift me high into the dark sky. Rowe was behind me, keeping a close watch to make sure we weren't being followed. I wasn't willing to take the chance of leading them back to Cynnia in the heart of Savannah while the nightwalkers were sleeping. Kane's forces remained just outside the city, like Aurora's, leaving Cynnia's only immediate defense a handful of naturi and an exhausted witch.

We flew silently for nearly twenty minutes before I decided to land in pasture below that appeared halfway between Aurora's camp and the camp of the animal clan. I didn't need to deal with Kane and his people looking as I did. Besides, I had a feeling Rowe might have a few choice words for me that I didn't want anyone else to hear.

My legs were wobbly when I hit the ground, but they held me up. I slowly pulled in my sore wings, not wanting to look at the burned and broken feathers. I was lucky I'd been able to take flight at all. Rowe's wings disintegrated almost as soon as his feet touched the earth, while I was slower to remove mine. He stood before me and roughly turned me to the left and then to the right, pulling out small crossbow darts still embedded in my body.

"Does Cynnia know?" I asked, finally breaking the silence that had grown so thick I could hardly breathe.

"No."

"How did you—"

"Because I'm not the fucking novice you take me for," Rowe snapped at me. "I taught you that spell. Did you honestly think I would ever teach you something you could use against me?"

"How long were you following me?"

"Almost from the moment you took to the skies." He paced away from me before spinning back around. "Do you have any idea what it was like watching you march into that camp and know that I couldn't follow you? Do you know what it's like waiting to see if you could actually make it back to a place where I might be of some help to you?" He grabbed both of my shoulders in his strong hands and gave me a hard shake. "I couldn't follow you into the camp because they would have sensed me. I had to hope that you had enough smarts to get yourself out again."

I jerked out of his grasp and took a step back. "I was managing fine on my own."

"At first maybe, but when I last saw you, you were laying facedown on the ground waiting for those bastards to shove a knife in your back!"

And he was right. I had been managing on my own until I fell. Then Rowe bought me the crucial seconds I needed to escape the naturi chasing us. By some slim chance I might have been able to make it to the clearing on my own, where I could easily strike down my opponents, but Rowe ensured that I made it out of the woods alive, and I owed him.

"I'm sorry," I said, bowing my head to him. "You're right. I would never have made it out of there without your assistance."

Rowe cupped my face with both of his rough hands and kissed me deeply. His tongue thrust into my mouth, claiming possession, reassuring him that I was safe and alive. I kissed him back, sighing deeply as I put both of my hands on his chest. Beneath the palm of one hand, I could feel his heart beating like a frightened hare. Anger gilded his words for now, but behind those words was a looming fear that I had nearly been killed.

Slowly, he broke off the kiss and leaned his forehead against mine. His breathing was heavy, sounding more labored now than when we were on the run. "If you ever do something stupid like that again, I'm going to kill you myself. What the hell were you thinking?"

"I needed to know something," I murmured, closing my eyes as I took a deep breath. He smelled of summer rain and freshly dug earth. Heat radiated off him, chasing away the chill left by the spring rainstorm.

"What?" he demanded, finally releasing me so he could step away and clearly look me in the face. "What did you have to know so badly that you had to risk your life and mine?"

I was about to argue that I had never intended to risk his life, but I swallowed the sentence before it could leave my throat. If he caught me sneaking out of the house, then there was no question that he was going to follow me wherever I went.

"I wanted to talk to Aurora one last time. I wanted to try to reason with her," I said. "I thought that maybe now that she had been on the earth for a while, the sickness in her brain could have passed. I thought she might have healed and was thinking more clearly."

"She's insane, Nyx! There's no changing that," Rowe snapped. "Nerian spent his entire existence on earth and it didn't stop him from losing his grasp of reality, particularly when it came to Mira. Our only choice is to stop Aurora."

"I had to know."

"Why? Why was this more important than your own life?"

"I had to know before we went into battle. She's my sister, Rowe."

"Aurora never cared about you," he snarled, beginning to pace again. "You said it yourself—that she used you. In the few years we were together, I saw how she despised and abused you. Everyone saw it."

"She's still my sister," I repeated, my voice starting to waver. "And there was something else that I had to know."

"What?"

I hesitated, staring down at the ground as I struggled to organize my fragmented thoughts. As I stood before Rowe, I realized what kind of a liability I was becoming.

"I had a shot at her and I didn't take it," I admitted in a soft voice.

"Are you sure?"

"Yes. It probably would have resulted in both our deaths, but I didn't do it and I should have. Killing Aurora today in her own camp would have stopped the war. It would have spared you, Cynnia, and countless other naturi. If I had just killed Aurora today, I could have given our people a second chance. But I didn't. I couldn't."

"Nyx, it doesn't mean—"

"But it does. I don't think I can kill her," I admitted, hating to even utter the words aloud.

"She's hated you since the moment you were born," Rowe argued, shoving one hand through his hair in frustration. "I have no doubt that she can sense you are more powerful than her. She's paranoid and jealous when it comes to you. And as you saw tonight, Aurora will not hesitate to kill you."

I shook my head at him, knowing I would never be able to get him to understand my feelings. "You're not telling me anything that I don't already know. But in the end, she is my sister and she is my queen, despite all the promises I have made to Cynnia. I will defend and protect Cynnia with every breath in my body, but I also can't kill Aurora."

Rowe heaved a heavy sigh as he reached up and placed one hand against the back of my head. He pulled me forward and pressed a gentle kiss against my forehead. "Then I guess you will have to leave me to the task of killing her."

"Do you honestly think you can?" I asked when he pulled back and I could look him directly in the eye.

"She's tried to kill both me and you. I think that's enough to sign her death warrant. I can't leave someone that wants me dead walking around."

"What about the Fire Starter?"

Rowe gave a sharp bark of laughter before pressing another quick kiss to my lips, leaving me feeling more than a little confused. "Mira's the only real challenge left in this world, and it seems that we're allies instead of enemies for now. I guess the Great Mother had a plan for the Fire Starter after all. Otherwise, I'm quite sure I would have succeeded in killing her already."

With a shake of my head, we started walking across the field, back toward Savannah. We wouldn't enter the city again until the sun was preparing to set. I didn't want to be anywhere near Cynnia's hidden location until I knew there was another layer of protection in place. Exhaustion weighed on my shoulders. I was both physically tired and emotionally sick. When the final battle came and went, at least one of my sisters was going to be dead. In the end, I could only hope that the Great Mother had a plan for us all.

Thirty-two

The first sound to greet me the next evening was the soft warble of Danaus's cell phone. A smile lifted the corners of my mouth as I rolled over, shifting my legs in the smooth cotton sheets. The fabric felt good against my naked body, and a deep feeling of security swept through me as I thought of Danaus guarding me throughout the day. Opening my eyes, I found the hunter sitting in a comfortable chair at the foot of the bed, facing me. He had just closed his cell phone and was shoving it into his pocket again. There was no smile to greet me after the soothing evening we had shared. Just his usual stone-faced looks that warned of more trouble.

Pushing out of the chair, he walked over to stand beside my shoulder. "Get dressed. Barrett is on his way over."

A soft sigh escaped me, but I knew that the lycanthrope would be visiting soon, considering the destruction that had consumed the city. We had yet to talk in person since Daniel's arrival back in Savannah. I was curious to know if his people managed to get anything off the computer towers they had stolen. We needed to know what the Daylight Coalition knew.

"Go get something to eat. I'll be down in a few minutes," I said, throwing back the covers.

Danaus nodded and headed toward the bedroom door. "I'd keep the shower a quick one. Barrett was already in the car when he called. He should be here any minute."

Frowning, I stumbled toward the bathroom. The night was not going how I had hoped it would start. I'd hoped Danaus would crawl back into bed with me for a while.

I jumped in the shower and back out again with hardly enough time to get wet. Barrett was knocking on the front door as I pulled on a pair of jeans and threw on a T-shirt. Jogging down the stairs, I met him in the doorway to the parlor. His expression was twisted with grief and anger, causing my stomach to sink. What could the naturi have done this time?

I found myself shaking my head as I paused on the stairs. A part of my mind screamed to run back up the stairs and away from the news that he was about to deliver. Instead, I steeled myself. "What happened?"

"Daniel is dead," Barrett announced in a rough voice, balling his hands into helpless fists at his side. "Daniel and his whole family were slaughtered in their home."

"How?" I whispered in shock, and then violently shook my head. "You said you would have people guarding them. How could this have possibly happened?"

"I lost four of my own people in the fight!"

"Why would the naturi have attacked Daniel and his family?"

"It wasn't the naturi. The Daylight Coalition is back in town, and in greater numbers than before. We may have taken out one of their headquarters, but apparently they were able to get out a message to the other branches as to who the culprits were. They sent more people to Savannah. The four shifters guarding Daniel and his family were torn apart with gunfire and knives, while the Crowleys were—"

"Enough!" I shouted, holding my hands near my ears. I didn't need to know the gruesome details of their deaths.

Daniel had done everything he could to protect the lycans and nightwalkers of Savannah. He didn't deserve this death after his sacrifice. And neither did his wife Anne or their five sweet daughters. I sank to the steps, sitting on the edge of one as I pulled my knees against my chest. Daniel had shown me their picture once. Five girls with blond hair and bright, loving smiles for their father.

Lily had been carelessly slaughtered because of her association with Danaus and me. Now another family with children had been killed because they were associated with nightwalkers and shifters. I couldn't stand it any longer.

Shoving back to my feet, I stomped down the last of the stairs to the ground floor. "What are we going to do next? Do you have any idea where they are hiding?"

"No. The police of Savannah are in an uproar—they're out for blood and I've noticed more patrols in the area. Tell your people to keep a low profile and stick to the shadows. These cops have itchy trigger fingers."

"And Archie?"

"He's doing what he can with the lycans currently in his care. He's getting a lot of pressure to get some positive IDs on them and he's stalling as long as he possibly can. My own people have been informed of the deaths and are out for blood as well. I'm trying to hold them together and keep them from hunting on their own, but that's not going to last very long."

Pacing into the parlor, I shoved one hand through my wet hair to push it back from where it was crowding around my eyes. The war that was brewing had opened up to include a new set of players we hadn't been counting on. Our numbers were already stretched thin when it came to Aurora. We couldn't take a chance of fighting a two-sided war with the Daylight Coalition as well.

"Have your people gotten anything off the computers you

took?" Danaus asked as my own thoughts seemed to swirl in useless circles.

"Nothing of great use yet. Just a bunch of names and locations of other branches of the Daylight Coalition."

"That's not much help," I muttered.

"Unfortunately, they did find one thing." Barrett paused, causing me to turn to look over my shoulder at him. "They ran across one instance of your name and a picture. They are still trying to hack that particular file. Either way, they've identified you as either a sympathizer or as one of the *other* races. You're out of time, Mira."

"Not yet," I said, holding up one finger to halt him. "They can't possibly know where I live. I've kept both locations hidden under false names over the years. I come and go under a cloak, so no one has seen me."

"But eventually they will," Danaus warned. "They won't attack right away. They're going to watch for you, see who you associate with and make a list of who else they need to kill when they go after you."

I stared at Barrett for more than a minute, knowing the words I needed to utter, but they seemed stuck in my throat. My heart was breaking on the inside and a lump had grown in my throat. A part of me had never thought this day would come, but it had, and far too soon in my opinion.

"Once we take care of Aurora, I'll leave Savannah," I said in a soft voice that seemed to creep through the room like a thin phantom. This was my home. The only place that had felt like home during my seemingly endless existence. I had hoped it would never come to this, but if the Daylight Coalition knew my name and my face, it was time to go somewhere far away and create a new identity so I could live in peace.

"Are you ready for such a thing?" Barrett asked.

I sighed and nodded. I had been preparing for a couple

months now. I'd survived too many years on my instincts, and they were telling me that my time in Savannah was growing short.

"The Starlight Foundation has nearly been dissolved," I said, referring to the investment corporation I headed with the help of my assistant Charlotte. "My money has been moved into offshore accounts under a variety of names and dummy corporations. My home outside the city has been destroyed so I have nothing to pack. After we're done, I'll go to Gabriel and see if he wants to go with me. I'm not sure he has been identified, but I'll at least warn him that the coalition could come after him next. I've already set up a trust fund for him in Switzerland, so he is set for the rest of his life."

"If he decides to stay, I'll assign some people to keep an eye on him while he's in the hospital," Barrett offered.

"I appreciate that, especially after all you have lost with your pack," I replied as my frown deepened.

Barrett shifted from foot to foot for a second, staring at the floor. "My pack is down to less than a dozen members. My sister Erica and my mother have already been moved from the area with an escort. With a detail of guards put on Gabriel, we won't be able to offer much help when it comes time to face Aurora."

"You've helped and sacrificed enough already," Danaus said, placing a hand on Barrett's shoulder. "Get the remainder of your people out of Savannah and to a safe location. Come back after everything has calmed down."

Barrett shook his head before raising it to look both me and Danaus squarely in the eye. "I vowed that the Savannah pack would assist Cynnia in her fight against Aurora, and that is what I intend to do. The Daylight Coalition is not the only group that could make our lives a living nightmare if they succeed. Aurora will see to the subjugation and destruction of the rest of my pack if she has her way. If the Savannah pack is to be destroyed, they will go down in battle with their comrades."

"Thank you, Barrett. I know that both Cynnia and I appreciate your sacrifice in all of this. I suggest you pull the remaining members of your pack that are prepared to go to battle and bring them back to my town house at midnight. I will be having another planning session with Cynnia, Rowe, and Nyx tonight—by then we must have a plan of attack."

Barrett nodded and turned to leave. I wished I could throw some words of encouragement after him, but in the end silence filled the house as the door slammed shut. There was nothing I could say that would make the situation any better. On one side, we were being hunted and killed by the naturi, on the other, by the Daylight Coalition. The lycanthropes of Savannah had nearly been wiped out despite the position of power they once held in the city. And my nightwalkers were slowly being picked off one by one each night.

Looking over at Danaus, I saw the hunter watching me, waiting for me to decide what the next move was. I was no longer sure. When I was chasing after Rowe and the other naturi, I knew where my next stop would be. But now the battle was closing in on my own backyard, and I was unwilling to risk the lives of the nightwalkers that had followed my leadership for so many years. And yet, I was keeper of this domain. It was my duty to call them forward to deal with this threat.

"Have you heard the news for the day? Were more killed?" I demanded.

"No, there were no further attacks on the humans during the day. I've not heard from Knox yet regarding the nightwalkers."

"What was the final body count from the fires?"

"Over two hundred."

"What? How is that possible?"

"One of the dorms over at SCAD was torched, and some of the students were trapped in the building."

I dropped my face into both of my hands and stumbled blindly away from him for a second. The college students of the Savannah College of Art and Design had been instrumental in reconstructing the city to its former glory. Now Aurora was striking at the innocent youth of my city, the protectors of her history. I'd had enough.

We'll get her. Danaus's words softly slipped across my brain in a soothing caress. *We'll end this war forever.*

Leaving us to face the Daylight Coalition, I grimly reminded him as I dropped my hands. *And my father.*

"Barrett's people will keep working on the computers. They will tell us if anyone else has been identified. In the meantime, we'll leave Savannah and set up a home somewhere else. Maybe it's time for us both to go back to Europe," he suggested, surprising me.

"You're going to come with me?" I asked.

Danaus shook his head and gave a little smirk. "You're an idiot sometimes. After everything that we've been through, do you honestly think that I would leave you now? Just when things are starting to get interesting?"

"I'm so glad I can keep you entertained," I growled, but there was no real venom in my tone. I was just relieved to find that Danaus would be staying at my side, even if it meant that I and possibly he would need to take on new identities as we started a new life wherever we landed next. "Aren't you concerned about the coven if we go to Europe?"

"For the most part, you are the coven now, and it appears that Our Liege has his hands full with Ryan," Danaus replied, brushing off my concerns.

I opened my mouth to voice another concern about Europe, but the words never left my tongue as the front door to the house burst open and slammed against the back wall. I didn't have time to move from the spot where I was standing when Shelly ran into the house. Her face was red and sweat had collected at her temples, dampening her pretty blond hair. She gasped for air, desperately trying to catch her breath. It appeared as if she had run the entire distance from Cynnia's secret lair to my house.

"What's wrong?" I demanded, impatient for her to finally catch her breath.

"Aurora! She's here!" Shelly exclaimed between gulps of air.

"What do you mean she's here? There's no way she would be insane enough to launch an attack at night when the nightwalkers are available for battle," Danaus said.

"No, she's here. In Savannah."

"Where?" I asked in a low, cold voice. This creature had set fire to my home, killed hundreds of humans, nightwalkers, and lycanthropes, and was now threatening to expose our world to the humans. She had to be stopped at last.

Shelly leaned against the doorway with her arms wrapped around her waist. "She's headed toward Forsyth Park. Cynnia and Rowe have gone to meet her, while Nyx is bringing in Kane and the rest of the animal clan."

With a stiff nod, I turned my attention to Danaus. "Call Barrett and tell him to bring his people to Forsyth Park. The war ends now."

Thirty-three

Danaus and I left my car on a quiet, shadow-covered street and walked the last few blocks to Forsyth Park. The massive green area stretched several city blocks, but I knew where Aurora would be: in the center of the empty green expanse, waiting with her army. I had mentally contacted Knox and all the other nightwalkers in the city, ordering them to converge on the park and wait for my signal to attack. All around me, I could sense nightwalkers slowly approaching the park, falling into step behind me as I drew closer. They remained cloaked, little more than soundless shadows in the deepening night. My army was small, numbering less than two dozen after all the deaths that had plagued my city during the past several months. However, we were strong and ready to call an end to the war with the naturi as Cynnia had promised.

As we reached the green space, I noticed two distinct sides lined up against each other with a wide swath of ground separating them. Rowe stood beside Cynnia in the center, and Nyx was next to a pair of large naturi along the far left flank. I could only assume that this was the illustrious animal clan I'd been hearing about. I guesstimated there were more than a hundred of them, adding to the rest of Cynnia's army lined behind her.

Meanwhile, Aurora had taken up a position on a hill so she could look down on her little sister. By sheer numbers, the two sides looked evenly matched. I knew that I wasn't looking at the entire naturi race, only those that had answered the call to war by either Aurora or Cynnia. The rest were most likely waiting for a winner to be officially declared.

Pausing before crossing the street to enter the park, I watched as a man walking his dog slowed down and stared into the park. His brow furrowed and he shook his head before hurrying on his way. My eyes followed the direction of his gaze.

"Fuck," I hissed, now hesitant to enter the park.

"What's wrong?" Danaus demanded, standing directly beside me.

Aurora and her army aren't cloaking themselves. They want to fight this battle in the open, in plain view of the humans, I mentally said, blasting the information out to Danaus and all the nightwalkers in the region.

What do we do? Knox inquired, briefly touching my mind. *Engaging them will nullify our own cloaking and people will be able to see us. What about the secret?*

We made a promise to assist Cynnia, I replied. *It's the only way that we will finally be free of Aurora. Remain cloaked as long as possible, but do not hide from the battle. Aurora's army must be exterminated.*

Danaus touched my arm, bringing my gaze up to his face. *What about the coalition?* he asked me privately.

I guess they'll finally get their proof positive that we exist. The only problem is whether they will survive long enough to show the world.

Steeling myself for the fight that loomed ahead, I marched across the street and entered the park and felt the other nightwalkers moving as well, bravely entering. They had to know that many of them weren't going to survive the fight ahead of them. It was going to be a bloody night, and I was ready for it.

Danaus and I slipped through the crowd of naturi and came to stand behind Cynnia and Rowe. Aurora smirked down at me when I appeared at her sister's side. My cloak was only effective against those who didn't use magic, which was a shame. I would have been more than happy to climb the hill unseen and knife the bitch in the back, ending this contest all too quickly.

"I see that you've not only chosen to side with your fellow traitors, but also useless mongrels such as these nightwalkers," Aurora declared disdainfully.

I opened my mouth to throw my own barbs at the naturi queen, but Cynnia spoke up before I could. "I have surrounded myself with those that have the same vision as me. We are looking to pursue a peaceful existence on the earth, coexistence with all the other races rather than running blindly into one war after another. You're killing off our people when we are at our weakest."

"The naturi are not weak!" she shouted, shaking both of her fists at us. "We have returned to the earth and are back to our former strength. Our numbers will grow instead of diminish. We will sweep away the waste and protect the Great Mother."

"You've lost the support of the Great Mother," Nyx called out from another part of the field. The declaration caused a rumble of concerned conversation among the ranks before she could continue. "I've seen it in your aura. I've seen it when I look and speak to you. You've grown weak as your connection with the earth has nearly been severed. The Great Mother has turned her back on you. You have no right to lead the naturi now. Step down."

"Enough!" Aurora screamed. "This is your last chance. Throw down your arms and hand over your lives to me and I will spare all those that have chosen to side with you."

Out of the corner of my eye I saw Cynnia look up at Rowe one last time, as if for confirmation. The one-eyed naturi merely smiled at his former wife. "Go fuck yourself, Aurora. We're coming for your head."

I couldn't stop the smile that rose on my lips.

Aurora floated into the air, a wreath of fire surrounding her, making her a beacon in the night. It was the signal her armies had been waiting for, and with it her people charged into battle. In response, Rowe sprouted a pair of black leathery wings and launched himself into the air, sending the naturi armies forward to meet the attack in a clash of short swords and arrows. My people hung back, waiting to catch up those that slipped through the ranks. Everyone was armed in some fashion, though I had warned that no one was to bring a gun without a silencer. I'd thought we would be able to keep this battle a secret from the humans, but now we were completely exposed to the world.

Danaus remained tight at my side, and Knox soon joined our group. My main concern was to act as a defense against Aurora so Rowe or Nyx could launch their attack against the queen. In fact, I knew I was the only defense Cynnia's people had against Aurora's light clan. Cynnia had a handful of the light clan members on her side, but they were already engaged in one-on-one battles with their clan members.

Fireballs were launched through the air in quick succession, but I quickly captured them, stopping them from crashing into our own forces. This quickly captured the attention of the light clan, which turned its attention toward me. I smiled, welcoming the battle with them. I'd shove that fire back down their throats.

"Back off a little, boys," I said to Danaus and Knox as I widened my stance. I tapped the powers swirling like a wild dervish around me. With all the naturi, nightwalkers, and lycanthropes in the region, it felt as if I were growing drunk on the power at my disposal. Summoning up a ring of fireballs around myself and my companions, I fired one after another at the light clan members. They caught the fire, but I could feel their struggle to control it and dissipate the energy before they were torched. I needed to put only a little more power behind it.

Overhead, thunder rumbled like two cars slamming into each other, then the skies opened in a massive downpour. The fire I'd created flickered and popped as it strained to remaining burning through the sheets of falling rain. My clothes were instantly plastered against my skin and I struggled to blink back the water dripping into my eyes. The wind clan was making its move to bring down the lightning and eliminate a chunk of Aurora's army. I paused in the fight with the light clan to notice that Rowe had returned to the ground and was hacking through one enemy after another with a smooth grace that spoke of years of bloody practice. I smiled as I glanced over to see Danaus performing the same elegant dance of blood and death.

Turning my attention back to the light clan, which had closed the distance between us, I summoned up more fire. This time I simply encircled them with a ring of flames that sprang up from the ground and stretched more than seven feet into the air despite the pounding rain. Pulling free both my sword and knife, I stepped away from Danaus and Knox's protection and walked through the ring of fire, where they could not follow. The naturi seemed stunned within the flames as they struggled to put out the fire and continue on their march toward the other fighters.

"You picked the wrong side," I mocked as I leveled my sword on one of the light clan members, removing her head in a flash of steel. Others in the light clan quickly drew their weapons, but they looked awkward with the pieces of metal in their hands. They were heavy magic users, not used to getting their hands dirty in a battle. Despite being outnumbered by six to one, I made quick work of them, cutting them down in a bath of blood. I was sprayed as I sliced through arteries and removed limbs, but the continuous downpour washed me clean again.

When I lowered the flames again, seven naturi light clan members lay in pieces in the mud. However, my victory proved short-lived as I looked over to find that two of Cynnia's guards had been killed. The young princess was standing against trained naturi fighters with a sword trembling in both hands while the guards at her back were slowly being overwhelmed. This fight was nothing if Cynnia was killed. I knew that these naturi wouldn't follow Rowe or Nyx. They needed Cynnia. With a violent wave of my hand, a swirl of fire whipped through the crowd and engulfed the fighters surrounding Cynnia and her guards. Their screams tore through the night as they fell thrashing to the ground in an effort to put out the fire.

"Get your naturi ass in the air," I growled at Cynnia when I finally reached her side.

"I belong at the side of my people," she stubbornly replied, though her hands were still trembling.

"And if you get killed, all your people would have died for nothing. Get your wind clan ass in the air so we don't have to worry about protecting you. Rain down some lightning."

Cynnia glared at me, but at the same time a set of pristine white wings sprouted from her back. She wordlessly took to the sky with her arms stretched over her head. What's more, I noticed an increase in lighting striking the ground with pinpoint accuracy. The young princess was finally working to her strengths. It was a small lesson she would need to learn if she had any hope of succeeding as the next queen of the naturi. I only prayed that Nyx survived this as well. Cynnia would need her experienced and level-headed guidance over the next several years.

With sword and knife clutched tightly in my hands, I started to turn my attention back to the fight being waged around me when fresh screams erupted. I twisted around to find the nightwalkers were quickly sinking into the ground. At the same time, the wind clan had taken to the air. Even the animal clan had abandoned their enemies and changed to winged creatures so they could take to the air. The earth clan siding with Aurora was finally getting into the fight. They were causing the ground to change to quicksand, pulling my people down into the earth so they could no longer move, let alone fight.

Twisting around, I found Danaus and Knox up to their knees in the muck but still fighting one naturi after another with their weapons. A part of me wished I had let Danaus bring his guns, but he had favored his old-fashioned blades after so many centuries. He would have been able to cut through so many of these bastards that much faster, turning the war in our favor.

I summoned up another wave of fire to wash through members of the earth clan I could spot weaving their spells, but the fire was just as quickly extinguished. I frowned when I heard Aurora's laughter above the fighting. I might have decimated the members of her light clan, but she could still stop me from using fire against her forces. I needed another form of attack.

Pulling together the energy again, I wrapped it around

my fists and balled it deep in the dark pit of my chest. This was going to take everything I had, leaving me extremely vulnerable.

"Danaus, when I give the word, you need to wipe out the earth clan."

"I don't know if I can," he replied as he dodged a blow, then slammed his own blade through the throat of his opponent. "I can't be that exacting with such a broad stroke. I might kill some of our own forces."

"Concentrate, damn it!"

Sucking in a deep breath, I reached out with my powers and encircled each of the nightwalkers I could sense. I pulled them out of the earth while struggling to lift myself out as well. Straining, I plucked Danaus's energy out of the mess and lifted him so he hovered just an inch above the soggy ground. At the same time, I felt a set of roots spring from the ground and try to pull everyone back down.

"Do it," I said in a ragged voice, praying that Aurora didn't notice my preoccupation. I couldn't defend myself or anyone else from a fireball as I struggled to keep all of my people out of the mud.

A wave of warm energy swept past me and into the fight as Danaus reached out and started boiling members of the earth clan from the inside. Their screams rang out through the night, echoing across the vast expanse of the park to bounce off nearby homes. I knew without a doubt that we were running out of time. Soon, the Savannah police would be arriving to respond to the multiple calls of death and destruction in their precious Forsyth Park.

I held my people steady above the earth as long as I possibly could before the strain finally got to me. With a groan, I released them, allowing everyone to fall that one inch back down to the ground. Danaus instantly collapsed to his knees in exhaustion, but the ground held him. He had managed to kill at least enough of the earth clan that they could no longer pull us into the ground.

Pausing long enough to get the trembling in my arms to stop, I looked around the battlefield to find it littered with bodies from both sides. However, a quick count revealed that Cynnia's army was holding up better than Aurora's.

Apparently, Rowe had come to the same conclusion. "We're going after Aurora," he announced in a low voice after he and Nyx approached me. Despite the pounding rain, he was still covered in blood from the battle. "We need you to keep her fire attack at bay."

I started to agree that I would cover their backs when I heard gunshots. I twisted around to see at least twenty men ringing the park with semiautomatic weapons trained on us all. They weren't the cops. The Daylight Coalition had finally arrived.

"I can't," I growled with frustration. I wanted nothing more in this world than to climb that hilltop with Rowe and Nyx and aid in removing Aurora's head once and for all. But I couldn't. "The coalition is here, and I need to lead the nightwalkers against these fucking zealots."

"Mira!" Rowe snapped.

"No, it's okay," Nyx said quickly, laying a hand on his shoulder. "I can handle Aurora. I just need your help taking her down. Leave Mira to cover our backs. You know the Daylight Coalition won't stop with just killing the nightwalkers. We will be next."

"Thank you. I'll leave Danaus to watch over Cynnia," I offered. It was the best I could do. The hunter wasn't going to be pleased with my decision, but he was better skilled to deal with the naturi than some of the other fighters, and the remaining nightwalkers could join me in taking out the Daylight Coalition members that had slaughtered Daniel and his family as well as four lycans.

"Don't play too long," Rowe admonished.

"Good luck," I replied, giving him a small smile. "You know I envy you."

Rowe smirked at me, his one good eye dancing with laughter. "Eat your heart out."

A low chuckle escaped me as I turned my back on my unexpected comrades and focused on the Daylight Coalition. It was time for a little payback. I would teach them what it meant to mess with a nightwalker, particularly one called the Fire Starter.

Thirty-four

Rowe turned his stern gaze on me as Mira led her group of nightwalkers in the opposite direction to take on the Daylight Coalition. We were left to finish up with Aurora's army. My sister-queen, underestimating the number of naturi willing to side with Cynnia, had not brought a large enough army. It was only a matter of time before she realized as much and beat a hasty retreat that we couldn't allow or afford.

"Can you do this?" Rowe demanded. I had fought in this battle and killed dozens of my own people that were trying to kill me. The queen of the naturi was out for blood, and she was going to give her two sisters and her former consort no quarter. I should have had the same mind-set, and yet I was hesitating.

"I will try," I admitted.

"'Try' is going to get me killed," he snapped. "You get an open shot at her, you take it. Otherwise you, Cynnia, and I are all dead."

I nodded and squared my shoulders as I stood facing him. He was right, and deep down I knew it. This was no time for an emotional attachment to someone who had never cared for me or the people she was chosen to protect. It was time for Aurora to be destroyed.

Unfortunately, she was already one step ahead of us. Cynnia's terrified scream shattered the night, sending a chill down my spine. Aurora was using her ability of telekinesis to pull Cynnia toward her through the air. Rowe and I turned at the same time to see Shelly desperately holding onto Cynnia's hands, trying to pull her back down to the earth. Rowe and I sprang forward, reaching for Cynnia, but the naturi slipped through Shelly's hands, sending the witch sprawling forward in the deep mud.

A scream of rage rose in my throat as I watched Cynnia fly straight and true through the air toward our sister. Aurora returned to the earth herself and tightly grasped a hunk of Cynnia's hair, pushing her down on her knees while laughing manically. She knew that she finally had the upper hand.

With sword drawn, I climbed the hill, rushing through the crowd of naturi that surrounded Aurora. My feet slipped in the wet grass and mud, but my legs continued to churn, forcing me forward. I chopped through one naturi after another in a blind fury, no longer aware of what I was doing. It wasn't about the death and destruction that seemed to eat at my soul. It was about saving Cynnia.

At the same time, Rowe took to the air, flying over the horde that stood between me and Aurora, hoping to engage the queen before I could reach her. I not only needed to save Cynnia, but had to help Rowe counter Aurora, who was capable of anything, and might well knife Rowe in the back while he tried to save the sister of his former wife-queen.

"Release her, Aurora!" he shouted just before touching down on the hill she was claiming as her own territory.

"Not until she takes her last breath," Aurora said with a wild laugh.

As I cleared my final combatant, I saw Aurora raise her free hand toward Rowe. He flapped his wings once, trying to pull back and away from the blast about to hit him. I dropped my sword and raised both my hands to summon all the powers of the earth I could feel just beneath my feet. As the flames poured from Aurora's fingertips, a protective sphere surrounded Rowe, blocking the flames before they could touch him.

Aurora screamed in frustration and tried again, but he remained untouched. Through the flames that lit up the night sky, I could hear Rowe's deep laughter, which only enraged Aurora more. She jerked on Cynnia's hair, tightening her grip as she flung out her free hand, sending a barrage of fireballs through the night, just hoping to hit something, but they dissipated almost as quickly as they formed.

"It's over, Aurora," I called to her, my hands still raised as I awaited the next attack. I knew my sister and what she was capable of better than anyone else. Her powers were limited to only the use of fire and telekinesis, which gave her the illusion of flight without wings. Light clan queens of the past were able to summon up the sun, but Aurora had spent too many centuries relying on me as her muscle, and I had spent many years studying the magical arts of our people. But I'd never imagined I would be using my skills against my sister.

"Traitor!" she screamed in a wavering voice. "I am *your* queen! You must obey me!"

"You abandoned me when I was born. You're nothing to me," I replied. "Cynnia and Rowe are the only ones who believe in me now."

"Then I'll take them both from you!" she snarled. From her waistband, Aurora pulled a long jagged blade and held it over Cynnia.

"No!" I screamed, charging the remaining distance up the hill. My heart felt like it had stopped in my chest, and time seemed to slow down to a crawl as I watched Aurora lower the blade toward Cynnia's chest. The knife would rip through her and tear apart her heart. There would be no chance of healing her, no possibility of survival after such a wound.

Then Rowe pulled his wings tight against his body in order to crash into Aurora. Cynnia went flying free as Aurora lost her grip on her hair. She rolled away, pale and shaking. But I saw no fresh blood on her. She had escaped harm for now.

Rowe, however, was wobbly as he returned to his feet, backpedaling away from Aurora with one hand pressed to his throat. And yet, he still managed to pull his sword from his sheath and stand ready to engage her. I reached him in time to see blood running between his fingers from a wound in his throat. He was struggling to breathe as his eye narrowed on Aurora. Clearly, he intended to finally end this war, even if it meant dying in the process.

"Get Cynnia to safety," he said in a low, gurgling voice.

"I'm not leaving you behind. We're going to finish this."

"Leave," he whispered before lunging forward with his sword. At the same time, two more naturi that had mounted the hill from the other side tried to attack Rowe as he engaged the knife-wielding Aurora. I jumped to his defense, pushing them back and eventually removing their heads.

When I turned back, Rowe and Aurora were locked together, bodies inches apart as their blades pressed together. One slip and someone was going to lose a head. There wasn't time to try to get between them or to slip around Aurora to aid Rowe, who was weak from his loss of blood. A lump grew in my throat, and I mentally promised myself that I would fix everything once it was all over. That thin promise was the only thing that made my feet take those final steps toward Rowe and Aurora.

Pulling back my blade, I plunged it through Rowe's back and through Aurora's chest. Both of them gasped in unison and went stiff as a board. I grasped the hilt with both hands and jerked it out of their bodies. Aurora fell forward, but I put my shoulder into Rowe's back to keep him from falling backward.

"Take her!" I shouted, holding him up as blood gushed out of his back and front from the massive wound I had made. With shaking arms, I watched as Rowe raised his sword and brought it down, removing Aurora's head in a long fluid motion. She fell dead, her white robes stained red from her blood and black from the mud.

There was no time to mourn the death of my older sister, which I would have done no matter how much she hated me. I needed to do what I could to save Rowe's life while his body still had the strength to hold onto his soul. Carefully, I laid him down on the ground. His eye was closed and his breathing labored.

"Cynnia, come over here and help me!" I screamed as I knelt in the sinking mud.

My sister instantly crawled over to Rowe's limp body and stared down at him in horror.

"I told you to go for an *open* shot," Rowe mocked as bubbles of blood passed over his lips.

"I got tired of waiting for you to move," I said, grabbing Cynnia's hands and pressing them to the large cut along his neck. "Keep your hands there and hold tight to slow the bleeding," I told her. "I need you to do what I do to save him."

"What are you going to do?" Cynnia asked.

"Ask for the Great Mother's help."

"I think she gave up on me a long time ago," Rowe murmured, his voice growing weaker. My heart thudded in my chest and I could feel tears gathering in my eyes, but I refused to let them fall. I was not going to let him die.

Closing my eyes, I touched Cynnia's mind so she could both hear and feel exactly what I was doing. I reached deep into the powerful flows of the earth and let my soul sink down into the very essence of the earth until I felt a larger consciousness. The Great Mother was watching everything, listening to the battle that was taking place on her soul. She was aware of the abuses of power. She was aware of everything at once.

Pressing my hands on the wound in Rowe's chest, I pushed his soul down into the earth as well, so it brushed against this deeper consciousness. I waited, holding my breath, praying this would work. I had healed my own deeper, life-threatening wounds this way, but then I'd always had a deep connection to the Great Mother. She spoke to me when my mind was quiet and warned me of many things. I only prayed now that she would see the same goodness that I felt in Rowe and heal him.

After a couple of seconds, deep within the earth, I felt Cynnia's confused and awe-filled presence. A plea for Rowe's life had formed in her brain as she begged the Great Mother to be merciful to this poor creature after all his centuries of service.

Blood continued to pour forth and I felt my grasp on Rowe's soul starting to slip. I was losing him. Gritting my teeth, I tightened my grip and called forth even more energy. The tree burned on my back and down my arms. I could feel it growing, stretching down my arms and up my throat to the point where I thought it would soon strangle me. The energy of the earth was flowing into me, and finally into Rowe. The wounds slowly closed beneath Cynnia's and my hands, and I could feel wounded organs mending with amazing speed and precision.

Rowe coughed and groaned, drawing in a ragged breath and then another before placing one of his hands over mine. I opened my eyes and looked down to find him smirking up at me. He was covered in his own blood and looking extremely pale, but I knew he would live.

"I'm impressed," he said in a low rough voice. "You commanded the earth to give me a second chance."

"You never give commands to the Great Mother," I said, squeezing his hand in mine.

"No, Nyx," Cynnia countered. I looked up to find a look of horror written across her mud- and blood-smeared face. "I heard you. You weren't asking for help. You were demanding it, and she listened to you. I have no right to claim to be queen of our people. You're the one chosen by the Great Mother to be the true source of our power."

"And I decline," I simply said with a soft smile.

Cynnia shook her head and backed away a few inches. "But I didn't even know you could do such a thing. I've never touched the Great Mother in such a way."

"I guess you'll have to prove to be smarter than Aurora and listen to your sister when she offers you advice," Rowe said. The one-eyed naturi took a deep breath before pushing into an upright position. I placed a hand and knee gently at his back to help hold him upright as he seemed to waver. "The naturi that fought against Aurora were following you, not me or Nyx. They were following you and your vision. Now is not the time to question it. It's time to lead."

"I can't do this alone. Aurora—" Cynnia began, but I held up my hand and halted her words.

"Aurora chose to be alone. You never will be."

With a nod, Cynnia pushed to her feet and walked over to the edge of the hill to look at the naturi gathered below, who were still fighting. She bent down, picked up Aurora's severed head by the hair and held it high in the air. The fighting instantly stopped and an eerie silence fell over the park as everyone waited for her to speak.

"Aurora is dead. I, Cynnia, am your new queen. The war is over."

I looked over at Rowe, to find him watching me with an odd look on his face.

"You stabbed me in the back," he whispered.

"If you were in the same position, you would have done the same thing," I said, rubbing my thumb across his scarred cheek.

"But I wouldn't have been able to save you."

"You would have tried, and that would have been enough."

"I can feel a part of your soul attached to my own now."

A half smile tweaked one corner of my mouth. "It looks like you're stuck with me then."

Rowe matched my smile and leaned in closer, letting his lips brush against mine. "I've heard worse news today." My laugh was smothered by his lips as he kissed me in the mud and rain and blood.

Thirty-five

The Daylight Coalition was waiting for us as the night-walkers turned their attention from the warring naturi to the scattering of humans positioned behind a grove of trees with guns. It was too late to try to cloak ourselves from view, as they had already seen us. However, we still had a few other tricks up our sleeves. On a silent count of three, we all ran at the coalition members in a blur of movement in the darkness. Gunfire exploded in the night as they desperately tried to hit us, but we easily dodged the bullets and fell onto our targets. Each man in the coalition force was paired up, in the hope that they would be better protected.

Sliding around one particularly massive live oak tree, I swung my blade so it sliced through the throat of one man before ripping a gun out of the hands of his partner. I tossed the weapon aside like a broken toy and sank my fangs into the jugular of my enemy. He squirmed beneath me, desperate to be free as I drained him of his life. I drank deeply, not bothering to push away his conscious thought. He wanted to fight nightwalkers. Well, then I was going to give him a good taste of what it meant to go up against a nightwalker and lose.

In the middle of my feast, I didn't notice that he had

palmed a large knife, but I felt it the moment he shoved it into the middle of my back. I released him, pushing him violently away as I reached around to pull the knife free. Quivering, he backed against the tree he'd been hiding behind and searched himself with trembling hands for another weapon. Blood continued to pour from his neck where I had bitten him. I sighed with relief when the weapon was finally free of my back. With a glow in my eyes, I surged forward, plunged his knife into his stomach and pulled upward, gutting him. He screamed once before passing out from the pain. It would be only seconds before he finally bled to death.

Standing with my hands on my hips, I turned to see my companions finishing up the last of the Daylight Coalition as if they were taking out a bit of trash to the waste bin. It had been a minor scrap compared to the fight with the naturi, which now appeared to be over. The sounds of battle no longer reached me, and on the hill I could see Cynnia standing with her sister's head dangling from one bloody hand. A new reign had started.

For a breath, relief crept through my frame. Danaus stood at the edge of the woods with weapons drawn, waiting for me to join him. A number of nightwalkers were killed during the night, but many of my companions had survived. I could even sense a few lycanthropes out there among the naturi. We had done the impossible by taking on Aurora's army, and not only survived the encounter, but triumphed.

My relief instantly disappeared when floodlights snapped on, blanketing the park with harsh white light from both sides. I stepped to the edge of the woods, shielding my eyes as best as I could to take a closer look at what surrounded us. My stomach twisted and a trembling started in my fingers as I saw not only signs of the Savannah police, but the National Guard as well. While we were engrossed in the battle with the naturi and the Daylight Coalition, the police had moved in to keep us trapped within the park.

To make matters worse, they were accompanied by the local TV channels as well as the press. Cameras were rolling, flashbulbs popping, and commentators were out, trying to make some sense of the carnage before them. No one had tried to stop us, because for the first few minutes no one understood what they were seeing. Humanlike creatures were flying through the air, balls of fire were spontaneously appearing and disappearing, and people were changing into animal form. Our world had been spread out for display at its worst possible moment, and now there was no taking it back. The Great Awakening was here.

I knew that everything as we knew it would be different from that moment on. Hiding would be more than a natural way of life to make feeding and sleeping easier, it would be an absolute necessity as humans who had never taken up arms before suddenly hunted creatures they didn't understand and feared. Governments would quickly step in to calm the masses as they attempted to reestablish some type of order, which would mean, so far as they saw it, finding a way to rule over creatures that defied so many of their rules. They would demand blood samples and possible tagging so they knew where all the nightwalkers, lycanthropes, and other creatures were hiding each day. They would do it all in the name of protecting not only humans but also the supernatural world, but in the end, I knew if we were not extremely careful, the supernatural world was going to become the monster under the bed that had to be hunted.

We would have to proceed slowly, find ways to contact world leaders and reassure them—if not blackmail them—into believing that our peoples were not a threat to the human race. With the presence of the Daylight Coalition, no transi-

tion would be easy. Nightwalkers and lycanthropes were undoubtedly exposed, though the naturi might be able to sneak
off into hiding for a while. I wondered if the witches and
warlocks would stand with us and accept exposure, or wait
in hiding for the worst of the chaos to blow over.

As the rain started to abate, I noticed a dark figure flying
across the night sky toward me. I barely restrained the urge
to pull a knife when I realized it was Rowe. The naturi
landed lightly a few feet in front of me. His clothes were
soaked in what appeared to be his own blood, and his neck
had a fresh cut that had just crusted over with dried blood.
Apparently, the battle against Aurora had been tough.

"The humans are here," he needlessly announced. They
were a little hard to miss on either side of us, with their
bright lights and weapons. "Do we fight?"

"And make the situation even worse?" I cried, looking at
him as if he had lost his mind. But that was Rowe, always
out for a little—or a lot—of human blood. I could only hope
that Nyx could change that.

"It's too late. We're exposed to the world."

Rowe shrugged one shoulder, wincing at the motion as
wounds still tried to mend. "I guess it was only a matter of
time before they found out."

"I would have preferred to handle it in a more civilized
manner."

"Why hide the truth?" he asked.

"Self-preservation," I snapped. "They are going to be
hunting us now to rein in the danger we present to them."

As if on cue, a human barked out over a blow horn, "Everyone step out into the open with your hands behind your
head! You are all under arrest."

Rowe gave a snort as his hand fell on the hilt of the sword
at his side. He was more than ready to jump into battle with
a bunch of humans. To him, they were nothing more than

vermin that needed to be exterminated. I gently laid a hand over his, stopping him from drawing the weapon.

"We can't fight them," I firmly said. "This is the Great Awakening. We have to face this mess and not make a bigger one."

"Then what do you propose?"

I frowned, hating to utter the words. It was not something I was accustomed to. Like Rowe, I was a fighter, ready to face any situation head on, but now was not the time. "We run," I said.

Rowe stared out at the gathering of humans around us, a dark look on his face. I think he was beginning to realize the futility of trying to fight this many humans at once. It would only bring more, and the humans outnumbered us, after all. It would be an endless battle that we couldn't win. As Cynnia had suggested, we had to find a way to coexist, which wasn't going to be easy or pretty.

"Okay," he finally conceded.

"Can you get your people out of here and somewhere safe outside the city?" Danaus asked him. "Somewhere hidden?"

"Yes, we can get out of here. What about you?"

"What about us?" Knox demanded, coming up behind me. I thought that I'd sensed him alive earlier, but it was a relief to see him in person.

"I'll provide a distraction for the nightwalkers and the lycanthropes," I said, fighting back a relieved grin. "Spread the word. The distraction won't last long, so they have to move fast. Tell everyone they need to lay low for the next few weeks. Find new hiding places outside the city if necessary. Wait for direction from me."

Knox nodded once and then disappeared back into the shadows thrown by the massive trees, to spread the word to the rest of the nightwalkers in the area. I turned to Rowe, who gave me a little salute before launching back into the air. I held my breath as he streaked across the sky on massive black wings. Spotlights followed him as he moved, but not a single shot was fired. From the crowd of humans, I could hear exclamations of terror and shock. For now, however, they were too stunned and afraid to fire. I hoped that mind-set would last a little while longer.

Alone with Danaus, I found the hunter staring at me, waiting for my next move. I had one shot at this, and only one way of getting him out of there alive. I just prayed that I had enough strength left to pull off this little stunt. I was shaking with exhaustion, but still had to carry on, for both his protection and the protection of my people.

"I'm hoping you've got an escape plan for the both of us," he said with a smirk. "I would really prefer not to spend the rest of the night and the next few centuries locked in a human prison while they try to figure out exactly what I am."

"I've got a trick or two left up my sleeve. However, you're just going to have to trust me on this one." I extended my right hand toward him, with the palm open. Without hesitation, he threaded his fingers through mine as we slowly walked out into the opening that was littered with the dead bodies of both naturi and nightwalkers.

"Put your hands behind your heads!" ordered the same gruff human voice.

With a smile, I raised our entwined hands and pressed a kiss to the back of Danaus's hand before I released it and placed both of my hands behind my head.

"Drama queen," Danaus muttered under his breath as he did the same with his hands.

"You only wish you would have thought of it first," I teased, squinting against the bright light.

Danaus gave a snort but said nothing more as I mentally contacted the other nightwalkers, warning them to be ready. Closing my eyes, I tapped into the powers that had been with me since birth, the power that had caught the attention of nightwalkers, naturi, bori, and even a god. All around the park a wall of fire sprang up, separating us from the humans. At different intervals I created breaks in the fire, allowing the lycanthropes, naturi, and nightwalkers to slip through while the humans focused on the unexpected fire.

To my surprise, Danaus's hands were on either side of my face and he turned me to face him. I opened my eyes in time to see him lean down, and then my eyes fell shut again as he deeply kissed me. I tasted both his strength and his fear for what was to come. I tasted his dry sense of humor and his protectiveness in that kiss. But most of all, I tasted his love for me.

I dropped my hands so they rested on his shoulders and leaned my forehead against his. "Are you ready for this?"

"I'll follow you anywhere," he whispered, brushing a kiss against my cheek so that he caught a falling tear.

Extinguishing the flames in a sudden flash, I tapped into some of the powers Nick had blessed me with and we disappeared from the park in the blink of an eye, without a trace, leaving the humans with only the image of two creatures in a loving embrace.

Thirty-six

Holding Danaus close, I buried my face in his chest, not wanting to look around at the all-too-familiar pale white-gray stone that rose up around us to make the ruins of Machu Picchu. In August we had marched up this mountain to stop Rowe and the other naturi from setting Aurora and the rest of the naturi horde free. It had taken us a few months, the sacrifice of several good friends, and the loss of our secrecy, but Aurora had finally been dispatched. And oddly enough, I now counted Rowe as one of my allies, though I didn't expect that particular development to last long.

Now we had returned for an equally dark and dangerous task I was once again hesitant to face. If it were at all possible, the stakes were higher, but then I had more to lose this time around. I was relying on Danaus to follow my direction, though I knew it would clash with everything he believed. It was too much to ask, so I was meeting my accomplice.

At a small metallic click behind me, I turned around. Adio stood on a ledge just a few feet above where Danaus and I stood in an open field with a single tree. In his hand, he held a gold pocket watch, which he shoved into his pant pocket. He stepped down to the grassy area with a vampire's grace and slowly walked over to where I clung to Danaus.

The hunter had yet to speak, but then, I feared he was beginning to guess at my grand plan to stop Nick.

"You look as if you've had a rough evening already," Adio stated, his eyes skimming over me from my mud-caked boots, to my blood- and mud-splattered clothes, to my wet hair and face. Where the rain had just abated in Savannah as the various forces retreated, the air in mountains surrounding Machu Picchu, Peru, was clear and cool. Overhead, millions of stars twinkled in a cloudless sky, enveloping us as if we were the only three creatures left on the planet.

"You've gotten your wish," I said, reluctantly dropping one hand from around Danaus's waist so I could better turn to face Our Liege. "The Great Awakening has started. The humans witnessed the battle with the naturi, and then a second fight with the Daylight Coalition. By now the war has been broadcast all across the world. Nightwalkers will awaken to discover that the world is now hunting for them."

"We will make this right, Mira," Adio tried to smoothly reassure me, but I wasn't buying it. "I have nightwalkers picked to step forward and act as spokespeople for our race. We will do some damage control. The Daylight Coalition will not be the only force out there making their message heard. Our people will survive."

"But what kind of a world will they face?"

"A different one," Danaus said, squeezing the arm that was still wrapped around his waist. "But one that they will find a way to survive and thrive in. It just might take a little time."

I nodded, closing my eyes for a moment, then raising my gaze back to Adio. It was nearing time. "I sent a packet of information to my closest assistant and friend. His name is Knox, child of Valerio. He has been given money and directions on how to reach my second domain of Budapest if things become too difficult in Savannah. He has also been given instructions to seek out Valerio in Vienna if necessary.

I would like your word that you will keep a protective eye over them."

"I will,"

"Knox may also be traveling with a human named Gabriel. He is to be protected as well."

"I understand."

"There is nothing I can do for the remains of the Savannah pack," I murmured mostly to myself with a shake of my head. Barrett had suffered so much, mostly because of me. So many lives had been lost, and yet he'd stuck by me through so much death and destruction.

"You have done what you can," Danaus said, stopping my train of thought. "Barrett will see to his people. He will protect his family and James."

"Valerio and Knox have been among my closest companions and trusted allies. See to their safety. Also, as much as Stefan and I don't see eye-to-eye, I believe he will be a good leader of the coven if it remains intact. Find others with a similar strength and vision to save our people."

"I will see to it, taking a more active role now that the Great Awakening has occurred," Adio promised.

I stared at the nightwalker that could still look into the beauty of the sunlight each morning and smile. I wanted to tell Adio to watch over Danaus as well. I wanted to tell him to protect Danaus from the nightwalkers that would tear him apart if I were not there at his side, but I didn't dare utter the words out loud. I could only look at Adio with pleading eyes, praying that he understood what I so desperately wanted to say. To my surprise, he placed his right hand lightly over his heart and bowed to me.

"Are you sure you have the strength for this?" Adio asked after a moment of silence. "You've already been in quite a tussle this evening, and you need to be at your peak if you're to have any hope of succeeding."

I started walking across the ground to the main ceremonial clearing, which was up at another level. "The energy flowing through this sacred place is mind blowing. It will be enough to carry me through the tasks at hand."

"Are you sure he will come?" Danaus asked.

"He will the moment he realizes what I have done, I'm counting on it."

I paused at the massive clearing, my vision blurring for a moment to another time. Some of the walls of Machu Picchu were now lit with a handful of lamps, throwing broad swaths of yellow lights against the white stones, but the night I was remembering had been filled with torchlight and a bonfire. In the middle of the open area thirteen humans had been tied together in a circle. The naturi had in one smooth stroke cut out their hearts and offered them up as a sacrifice to whatever gods that might be listening, opening the door I had closed centuries earlier.

Tonight I would not need a flood of human blood to paint the grass, or the cries of the innocent to float into the air moments before their death. I could open the door on my own because I had made this door and I was its key.

"What's the plan?" Danaus asked.

"I open the door. We go in. You and Adio will kill any naturi that attempts to escape through the opening. I doubt they will be paying much attention to me when they face potential freedom. I will go in looking for the goddess. When I find her, Danaus, you will take her out and get her somewhere safe."

"And Nick?"

"He will follow me in."

"And you've got some brilliant plan for trapping him and you getting out again?" he asked, his tone growing more brusque.

"I do."

"Once I get the goddess settled—"

"You will stay by her side no matter what. You will not reenter the cage. Once I engage Nick in the cage, Adio is going to come out and help you guard her. She must be protected."

"Mira!"

"No, Danaus!" I snapped, turning on my right heel to face him. "We follow my plan or I take you back to Savannah now and I will leave you there." We glared at each other for several seconds. I could hear his heart pounding in his chest, and for a moment I could feel a pressure in my brain as he tried to enter my thoughts and read my full intentions, but I kept him blocked out. The only feelings I wanted him to sense from me at that moment were love and determination. I would not be swayed from this course. Nick had to be stopped, and he had to be stopped now, when the world was so precariously balanced on the cusp of a major transition. He could not be permitted to step in as the next major power.

Danaus said nothing as I turned to Adio. Pulling the sword from my side, I handed it to him. He tested the weight and the balance before giving it a few good swipes through the air. I was vastly relieved that it seemed he at least knew how to use a sword. I hadn't been sure, but it was hard to live a long existence in this world without picking up a few skills in self-defense.

Stepping away from my companions, I approached the center of the field where I had last seen the rip in the sky through which the naturi escaped from their prison. I sucked in a deep breath and held it in my chest as I pulled all the earth energy swirling about me to my fingertips. It was so much easier now than it had been in the summer. Then, it had been like trying to swim upstream in a rushing torrent of water. Now, it was just another part of who I was. The power came to me fast and strong and hot, as if heated by the bowels of the earth before finally reaching my body.

With my eyes closed, I reached out with my fingers toward the open sky and easily felt where the scar was, marking the entrance into the naturi cage. A faint groan escaped me as I grasped the two jagged edges and pulled them apart. A bright light blinded me for only a moment before my eyes focused on a world that looked all too similar to my own.

There were green fields edged with dark trees sparsely decorated with shining green leaves. However, the sky above was a leaden gray instead of a deep blue. As I stepped through the opening, I also noticed that the ground was hard and unyielding, with patches of dried dirt showing through the thinning grass. The air was completely still and there were no sounds of singing birds or the scurry of wildlife. This world was dying.

Behind me, I heard the crunch of earth under heavy feet as Danaus quickly joined me, followed by the lighter step of Adio. I glanced over my shoulder to see that both men had their swords drawn and at the ready. And I felt guilty. Any naturi still trapped in this world were already sick and dying. If they ran, they faced death at the hands of Adio and Danaus, and if they stayed, they faced an even slower death of this world. Were they to escape to the real Earth, they had a chance at life again, this time under Cynnia's enlightened rule. They had a chance to live.

"I've changed my mind," I said in a low voice. "Don't attack anyone unless you are attacked first."

"Are you sure?" Adio inquired.

"You want to give them the chance to escape?" Danaus said.

"They are already dying here and are doomed to death if they stay, even if we most likely succeed today. Cynnia will give them a second chance."

"As you wish," Adio said softly, to my surprise. I hadn't expected Our Liege to so quickly follow my direction, but then I believed that his larger focus was on his own survival and the eventual survival of our people. Now that Aurora was dead, the naturi were a smaller concern for the nightwalkers.

"Do you know where you are going?" Danaus asked as we started across the field and into the surrounding woods. Off in the distance I could see the crumbling remnants of stone and thatch houses built among the trees. I could feel a faint swirling earth energy surrounding us as we preceded, marking the presence of the naturi, but they didn't approach us. For now they were content to watch from a distance and edge closer to the opening that I was maintaining in the back of my mind. The pull of power to keep the door open was minimal, like a slowly growing headache in my temple. Nothing more than an annoyance.

"I can feel a great source of energy ahead of us. It has to be her," I said as I continued to trudge forward. I placed the knife I had been carrying in my right hand back in its sheath. I wouldn't need it for the time being.

"I can feel it as well," Adio added.

Unfortunately, a second source of great energy was hovering around what felt to be the entrance to the naturi world. Nick was starting to grow suspicious of my absence from this world and he didn't trust me. We were running out of time. Danaus and Adio needed to have the goddess in hand by the time Nick appeared or this was all for nothing.

Grabbing the arms of Danaus and Adio on either my side, I clenched my eyes shut and caused us all to disappear and then suddenly reappear closer to the source of the energy. I couldn't pinpoint her exact location with the first jump, but we were significantly closer. It felt as if she was in the center of the world, and yet I didn't know how vast this world was.

I would have to rely on Adio to do the same thing with Danaus—to get him out again with the goddess.

I kept a tight hold on their arms as I jumped us forward a second time, getting significantly closer to the power this time. We jogged the rest of the way to what appeared to be a large tree in the center of a barren field. Here the grass was at its greenest and a castle rose up in the distance. I was willing to bet that Aurora had set up her home as close as she could to the source of the power for her new realm, in hopes that it would strengthen her own powers, regardless of what kind of drain it proved to be on the goddess.

As we drew closer to the tree, we discovered that it wasn't a tree at all, but large, thick vines that had grown up from the ground, wrapping around something. The power I had sensed at the doorway was now starting to slowly grow closer to our position. We were running out of time. Stepping back, I raised my hands above my head and let my eyelids drop shut. I dug deep into the energy I sensed from the earth, which was leaking through the doorway, and used it to touch the vines. They proved to be more than a little resistant at first, but after some loud creaking and snapping, the vines started to part and recede back into the ground to reveal a crystal chamber hovering just a few inches above the ground.

Encased in the diamondlike structure was a woman with thick brown hair and dark skin. She appeared thin and frail, with her head leaning against the side of the crystal as if she were trapped in a deep sleep. I stared at her a moment, her appearance reminding me too much of the dark-haired Inca women who had been sacrificed for the amusement of the naturi so many centuries ago at the ruins of Machu Picchu. But she wasn't an Inca woman. She was *the* goddess; the creator goddess of all things great and small. And she was dying.

"Give me your sword," I commanded, holding out my right hand, not caring who gave up their weapon. As soon as I felt the heavy weight against my palm, I wrapped my fingers around it and raised it above my head as I stepped forward. I was prepared to pound against the crystal until the end of the world wrapped around us, but to my surprise, a chunk of the crystal broke off with the first hit. In her weakness, her own cage had become fragile. Her last bit of protection had been the vines. A second blow to the crystal created an opening large enough for her limp body to slide through. Danaus immediately stepped forward and caught her before she could hit the ground.

I slid the sword he had handed me back into the sheath strapped to his back. When I looked at his face, I saw a tear roll down his cheek as he stared down at the woman cradled gently like a child in his strong arms. She was exquisitely beautiful and immensely frail. Her chest barely rose and fell with each breath, and I could barely make out her heartbeat.

"Adio, can you get Danaus to the doorway the same way I got us here?" I asked, slowly dragging my gaze from my lover's heartbroken expression.

"Yes, it shouldn't be a problem," the nightwalker said, taking a step closer to Danaus so he could lay a hand on his shoulder.

"Danaus, get her to the clearing with the tree and lay her flat on the ground," I said. "The connection with earth should help rejuvenate her." He merely nodded, unable to break his gaze from the woman's face. "You are to stay at her side no matter what. Protect her with your life. Promise me."

"I promise," he whispered.

A dark, ominous voice rumbled across the plains. "Mira!" Nick was nearly upon us.

The sound of Nick's voice was enough to suddenly snap Danaus out of his trancelike state. He looked up at me with narrowed eyes as he realized what kind of corner I had backed him into. He had promised to watch over the goddess and so would not be able to help me in my fight against Nick. He was trapped.

"Go now!" I screamed, backing away from my two companions. Danaus gripped me with one last desperate look, and then he and Adio were gone from my sight. I could feel Nick approaching with lightning speed, but I turned my back and approached the crystal chamber that had held the dying goddess.

"Stop!" Nick commanded as soon as I laid my left hand on the edge of the opening to the crystal. "What lunacy do you have cooked up now, my little daughter?" There was a desperation to his voice I had never heard before, causing his usual calm to splinter. I glanced over my shoulder to find him standing just a few feet away. He was back to the appearance I had briefly seen upon our first meeting, with his wild red hair and lavender eyes. It was as close to human that this god of chaos could come, and it only succeeded in solidifying my link to this creature in my mind.

"The goddess that inhabited this world is dying because of her lack of contact with the earth and her mate. If this world falls, then so will the cage that hold the bori," I argued. "The world has been shaken enough by the presence of the naturi. They cannot survive the arrival of the bori as well."

The bori were the natural enemy of the naturi. Creatures that drew their powers from the souls of living creatures, they had no bodies of their own, but succeeded in tricking humans into becoming hosts for them. They shapeshifted into various creatures, tempting the weak and the vulnerable with promises and desperate pleas. Where the naturi wanted to destroy mankind and save the world, the bori were determined to enslave mankind and destroy the Earth.

"What could you possibly hope to accomplish by entering this world and taking out the goddess?" Nick demanded, smoothing out his voice in an attempt to sound reasonable.

"She was dying. Someone needs to replace her," I said, grasping the other side of the crystal case before placing my foot on one of the vines closest to the entrance.

"Mira, my dear, you're not a goddess. You can't replace her. You're simply not strong enough."

"I can try."

"I don't think so," Nick hissed. A heavy blast of energy slammed into my chest, ripping the crystal out of my grasp as I was thrown several yards across the field. I hit the ground with my back and rolled several feet before finally hitting the side of a tree. Gritting my teeth, I pushed off the tree and regained my feet so I was once again facing my father. He immediately wrapped his energy around me again, and I had a feeling he intended to drag us both out of the naturi world, but I wouldn't allow it. Summoning up my own powers, which he had taught me to use, I pushed off his grasp, shoving the energy back at him with enough force that he stumbled a step backward.

"I'm not allowing this place to falter any further," I bit out as I wrapped more energy around my hands.

"The naturi and the bori are no longer your concern. Your only thought should be pleasing me," Nick said with an evil grin.

"You've been accommodated enough, I believe." With the energy spiraling around me, I commanded one of the vines to wrap around Nick, but the bastard suddenly disappeared from sight. I shifted my focus to grab him back, but he reappeared before I could grasp him. His fist slammed into my jaw, snapping my head around as I slammed into the ground again. His punishment didn't stop there. He kicked me several times in the ribs, breaking more than one before he reached down to wrap his fist in a length of my hair.

"You're coming home, child," he snarled, his foul breath dancing under my nose.

"I think the lady prefers to stay," announced an unexpected voice seconds before Nick was pulled away from me. I twisted around to see the god of chaos hurtling through the air until he slammed into the side of the vines still wrapped around the crystal chamber. Adio knelt beside me, gingerly helping me back to my feet.

"You shouldn't be here," I grumbled as I pulled my arm free of his assistance.

"I can help."

"Where's Danaus?"

"Where he promised to be."

A weak smile lifted one corner of my lips. "I can't keep the door open much longer. I have to focus on Nick."

"We understand. Danaus told me to tell you that 'he will be your Rowe,' whatever that means."

Tears welled up in my eyes as I quickly looked away from Our Liege and turned my attention back to my father. I knew what it meant. Danaus intended to spend the rest of his life fighting to find a way to open the doors to the naturi world again to set me free, just as Rowe had in an effort to free his queen, Aurora. I could ask for no greater gift.

"Son of the dawn?" Nick said as he stood, brushing himself off. "I don't know what you think you're doing here, but this is a family affair."

"As head of the nightwalkers, this is now a nightwalker affair. If Mira wishes to enter the chamber and hold this world together, there is nothing I can do but help her," Adio said in an easygoing manner that was more than a little frightening to hear. For a moment I was convinced that Adio would have been content to have either or both of us trapped in this world, he only lacked the ability to close the doors again.

To prove his point, Adio waved one of his hands toward me and I floated off my feet toward the crystal chamber. My stomach twisted into a knot as I approached the tiny prison, but I didn't hesitate to grab the sides and try to pull myself in. At the same moment, Nick screamed in frustration and used his own powers to pull me away, once again slamming me to the ground. However, this time Adio was there to soften the blow.

Rolling to my feet, I grabbed as much energy as my body would hold and threw it at Nick. I could only guess that Adio felt what I was doing because he mimicked my move, succeeding in shoving the god back until he was pinned against the vines. With my left hand, I tore a limb off a nearby tree and bashed Nick in the face with it, hoping to disorient him.

The god crumpled to his knees, shaking his bleeding head. I seized the opportunity and ran for the crystal chamber once again. "Get ready to close it!" I screamed at Adio.

Getting my hands on the edges of the chamber, I pulled myself in and was immediately encased in the feeling of something draining away my energy like a great suction pump. My eyelids flickered for a moment as I tried to focus over the disorienting feeling. Nick bellowed and lunged at me, his foot stepping onto the edge of the chamber at the same time his hand grabbed my arm to pull me out.

Clenching my teeth against my growing lethargy, I grabbed both of Nick's arms and pulled him into the chamber while I slid around to the opening. He screamed, but the sound was cut off as I released one of his arms long enough to smash my fist into his nose. Nick released me to cover his broken nose, allowing me the chance to fall out of the opening. My legs scraped against large chunks of crystal as they rushed back into place to cover the opening. If I had hesitated a second longer, Adio would have closed us both in the chamber together.

I lay on my back for a second, trying to get my head to stop spinning while energy seeped back into my frame. I could feel the door to this world starting to close as I weakened. We needed to get out of there.

"Mira, help me!" Adio cried, drawing my attention back to him and the crystal chamber. I looked up to find Nick pounding against the crystal with both of his fists, screaming at me, while Adio used his own powers to mend the broken bits. I added my own energy, sealing my father away.

After a couple seconds I noticed that the chamber seemed to grow stronger and thicker as it absorbed his powers. I looked around the world to find that the leaves on trees were quickly growing black and falling off, while the ground split open and spouts of fire shot up. While the great creator goddess had created a second earth with her powers, the god of chaos was creating a world much more akin to the human idea of Hell.

"I think it would be a good time to beat a hasty retreat," Adio said, grabbing my elbow. While I gathered up all the energy I had to focus on keeping the door open, Adio teleported us from the crystal chamber to the doorway, which was quickly closing. I pushed Adio through the opening and then dove through myself, landing in a heap on top of him. I summoned up enough energy to roll over Our Liege and lie on my back in the grass, letting the energy from the earth seep back into the frame as I closed my eyes.

"You seemed a little eager to close up that chamber," I criticized, opening my eyes to find him sitting next to me, staring down at my scratched and bloody face. A smirk twisted his full lips.

"While the thought of locking you both away and out of my hair was tempting, I feared that if you were locked away, I would not be able to escape that world myself," he admitted.

"Oh, yeah, I would have definitely kept you trapped if I was to be locked for eternity in a crystal chamber with Nick," I said with a soft chuckle.

Adio smiled down at me. "The great trickster god tricked by his own daughter. It seems fitting."

"I just hope it holds for a few millennia," I grumbled. With muscles protesting, I pushed into a seated position and looked around the empty plaza. The stars still twinkled above and a steady wind swept across the silent ruins. The world seemed untouched by the feat we had accomplished, which was exactly as I hoped it would be.

Adio pushed to his feet and offered me his hand. "Come on. There is someone who is waiting for you."

We walked across the plaza and down to the small clearing that held the only tree that grew in the ruins of Machu Picchu. Danaus knelt beside the figure that lay in the grass beneath the tree, but I noticed that his eyes were not on her, but staring in our direction, anxious and fearful. His shoulders slumped as we came into view and his head bowed as I heard a heavy sigh slip past his parted lips.

Standing over the goddess, I noticed that her heartbeat seemed a little stronger than before, and her breathing was deeper and more even. To my surprise, her eyelids fluttered and opened, pinning me with an intense stare. I fell into those brown eyes, losing all sense of time and place. Machu Picchu slipped away along with the rest of the world. There was just the swirl of energy that had taken on a variety of colors and shades as they danced around me and the goddess. Not only was she alive, but she was growing stronger with each passing second.

Fear trembled through me, but I didn't question the choice I had made. The great creator goddess had to be a more benevolent force for the earth than the god of chaos.

My only concern was that I might have separated her even farther from her mate, who was still trapped with the bori.

And then she smiled at me. The world came back into focus, and I watched as she sank into the earth as if returning back to the womb of her own birth. The earth closed in around her so that there was no mark left of her ever being present. There was nothing left but a new layer of energy dancing in the air, caressing my flesh, taking the place of Nick's cold touch.

"She's gone," Danaus murmured, rising to his feet.

I extended my hand to him and he tightly clasped it in his large one. "She's home."

"I think it's time we did that as well," Danaus said as he pulled me closer.

Wincing, I raised my hand to shield my eyes. "We can't." The sky around us was quickly turning from dark blue to slate gray as the sun rose in the east. By now the sun would already be up in Savannah, and I could not even begin to guess at what might be a suitable hiding place in the city at the moment.

"Allow me," Adio said, placing a hand on both our shoulders. In the blink of an eye we were enveloped in darkness, only to reappear less than a second later. The ground shifted beneath my feet and the air was considerably warmer than the mountains of Peru. "Consider this a belated honeymoon," Adio added, and then quickly disappeared again.

Danaus stood close beside me, one arm wrapped around my waist as we gazed over at our new surroundings. We stood on a white beach just at the shoreline. The air was silent except for the sound of the waves lapping against the shore, while lights lit tall buildings in the distance. At the edge of the beach was a well-lit road lined with swaying palm trees. The thick scent of flowers filled the air.

"Where are we? He had to have taken us west," Danaus murmured.

It took only another second for it to dawn on me, as I thought about what Adio had said just before he disappeared. He had taken us to one of the honeymoon capitals of the world. "We're in Hawaii," I said, laughing as I leaned into Danaus. I wrapped both my arms around his waist and held him tightly. He was alive and safe. We both were. Aurora was dead and Nick was in permanent exile. For once, we were both safe and free. The world had become a vastly different place overnight, but it was a world we could attempt to live in, not a world under the shadow of Aurora and my father.

With a low chuckle, Danaus swept one arm under my legs and carried me out into the surf before dropping down to dunk us both underwater. We came up together, sputtering and laughing in the warm water.

"What was that for?" I cried.

"That was for your stupid promise! I could have helped—"

I placed my hand against his cheek as my feet searched for a bottom in the ocean. "And you could have been trapped in there with Nick and me. I didn't want that for you. Never. I wanted you to go on living."

Danaus reached up and moved some wet hair away from my eyes. "I would have never stopped searching for a way to get to you."

"And I would have waited for you to come," I whispered, my lips brushing against his.

Danaus closed the last few centimeters between us and kissed me as we bobbed weightless in the surf. His arms wrapped around my body and I could taste his love for me as it washed away the last memories of the past few nights. Together we had faced impossible odds again and again, and each time we came out alive and in each other's arms. With Danaus, the world held no horrors for me now.

Slowly breaking off the kiss, Danaus rubbed the tip of his nose against mine before loosening one arm so he could slowly paddle back toward the shore. "I say we find a quiet hotel where we can forget about the naturi and the Great Awakening for a few weeks."

"That sounds like the best idea I've heard in months."

"You think you can stand to be alone with me for a while with no impending danger?"

Wrapping my arms around his neck, I let him carry me out of the water and back onto dry land. A deep sense of peace seeped into the marrow of my bones as he pressed a kiss to my forehead. "Together, as God intended."